The Ness Deception

Tormod Cockburn

A "Mysterious Scotland" novel.

Set along Loch Ness

Mys.Scot

First published by Mys.Scot Media in 2022

Copyright © Tormod Cockburn, 2022

The moral right of the author has been asserted

Print ISBN: 978-1-915612-03-8

E-Book ISBN: 978-1-915612-02-1

Cover photo credit: Ezra Winston, licensed by Unsplash

This is a work of fiction. Names, characters, places, and incidents are the products of the author's imagination or are used fictitiously. Any resemblance to actual events, locales, or persons, living or dead, is entirely coincidental.

For updates and free books we invite you to join our Readers Syndicate. Either click the logo above in a digital copy or see details at the back of the book.

Mys.Scot

Dedication

Dedicated to Frederick Roberts, MBE.
A major in the 7th Armoured Division, the
'Desert Rats' during WWII.
A gentleman and a friend.

Thanks, Freddie. Your life was an inspiration.
Until we meet again.

Also by Tormod Cockburn

The Bone Trap
The Ness Deception
The Stone Cypher
This Jagged Way
The Ice Covenant
This Emerald Veil
Dark Sayings
The Crystal Armour
The Torn Isle

Chapter 1

East bank of Loch Ness - four weeks ago

A solitary wave travelled across the loch. On this windless morning, its gentle progress was the only disturbance on a thousand acres of tranquil water. Every square foot of the oily surface undulated gently under the low sun until the moment came for the ripple to pass. Then the surface rose, a few inches at first, gliding upwards, then falling again as the wave swept past.

Ernie Lehman had been on his observation deck since before dawn. The unblemished water allowed him to spot the wave as it emerged from the opposite bank several minutes before. As he stood watching its progress, the camera shutter on his digital SLR fired in three short bursts before he paused, realigning the tripod. Only then did he lift his head to study the approaching wave, dissecting it, applying years of experience to assess its speed, height and point of origin. As the ripple passed him, he observed the wave was crossing the loch on a diagonal trajectory. His binoculars zoomed in on the wave, studying it, sweeping slowly back and forward over the lead section. His hands were steady. Professional hands always are.

'Come on, old girl, come on,' he muttered under his breath. He watched as the wave met the bank on his side of the loch, its definition lost among little gravel beds and hazel thickets. It had run its course. It was gone.

Lehman sighed. Then he laid down his bins and picked up his reading glasses and iPad. For a few moments, he typed furiously. With practised efficiency, he reviewed the forty or so images. Selecting one, he dropped it into his iPad and entered it on his blog. A quick review of his paragraphs and the posting was ready. He popped the device back into its waterproof case and refocused the camera on a castle on the opposite bank. Tomorrow he'd be back in the city, working his day job. But today, he'd stay on the estate continuing his life's calling. He picked up his binoculars again and began another slow sweep of the surface of Loch Ness.

<u>Pittenweem, Fife – two weeks ago</u>

The brass ship's bell in the outside porch rang for the third time. Ackerson ignored it. A friend would have walked in by now as the door was permanently unlocked. And if this caller wasn't a friend, he needn't bother himself.

The bell rang again. This visitor was persistent.

The front door's rusty hinge creaked. 'Mr Ackerson? Hello?'

The distance from the galley kitchen to the porch wasn't far. Ackerson stood up and covered the distance in three deliberate strides, rounding the corner to confront the intruder.

The man blinked with surprise. 'Sorry to disturb you. I've got a personal message for Steven Ackerson.' Smartly dressed, in his early thirties, the man's smile was a little too willing.

Ackerson didn't care if his own expression was impenetrable and uninviting. His raised eyebrows were substitutes for words. The young man was of average height, but even at the age of seventy-five, Ackerson was several inches taller.

The man frowned. 'Are you, Mr Ackerson? It's really very important.'

Ackerson nodded past the visitor, using his eyebrows to gesticulate back out to the open stone courtyard. 'We'll talk in my office.'

The visitor retreated out of the porch, looking uncomfortable. He was silent, waiting for further instructions. Ackerson leaned up against a stack of lobster traps. Then he stood again and pulled one off the top of the heap, upending it in front of his visitor. 'I'm sorry. Rude of me. Have a seat.'

The smell of decaying shellfish enveloped the crowded yard. 'Thanks,' said the visitor. 'I'll stand.' His gaze followed the row of fishermen's cottages tumbling downhill towards the sea. 'Nice spot. Have you lived here long?'

'Are you an estate agent?'

'Just being friendly,' said the visitor. He delved into the breast pocket of his suit, searching for his identification. 'They told me you'd be difficult.' He didn't relinquish his credentials but held them close to Ackerson's face until he could have read them twice over.

Ackerson allowed his mouth to show just a flicker of a smile. 'And what can I do for you, Sub-Lieutenant?'

The young man produced a slim white envelope. 'Are you keeping up with the news from your former office?'

'No need. I'm a fisherman these days.'

The young man threw him an exasperated glance. 'You're being reactivated, Mr Ackerson,' he said, offering the envelope. 'Here are the details.'

'Am I now?' Ackerson let his expression harden again.

'Just two months to begin with. We have data we need you to review.'

Ackerson ignored the proffered hand and the envelope it held.

'You're not curious?'

'It was just work,' Ackerson snapped back.

'Your life's work.'

'Not the one I'd choose if I got my time again.'

'You're the only one left who worked on this from the beginning,' said the young man, dropping the letter onto the upturned creel. He turned and walked up five stone steps towards the gate. Then he paused, his back to Ackerson. 'Knowing what you know? Honestly, I thought you'd be intrigued.' After a last backward glance, the metal gate clicked shut, and he was gone.

Ackerson shook his head and walked back inside. Some minutes passed before he returned, a mug of tea in hand. He picked up the letter and turned to lean against the stacked creels. Seeing the small letters in old-fashioned type was bittersweet. *'Commander Steven Ackerson (retired). Project Leviathan,'* he read.

Caithness – present day

'There's not a lot of space at the bottom. We'll need to send you down in small groups.' The officer had kept them all at bay since early on Tuesday afternoon until a telephone call from a prestigious Edinburgh office finally persuaded his superior. Might further delay be interpreted as an infringement of press freedom? Finally, the officer could relent.

'Please make sure that your press badges are visible at all times and follow the instructions of the police officers at the bottom of the steps.' Glancing around at the assortment of reporters, camera crews and photographers, his attention lingered for a few seconds on one overweight man encumbered with several cameras. 'I'll remind you there are three hundred and sixty-five stairs between here and the shore. Please take your time on the steps. And it's warm for the time of year, so I suggest you carry some water with you for the return trip.'

Anticipating further delay, the small crowd edged forward. Ignoring the subliminal pressure, the officer pulled out a wad of business cards and began calling out the names of the dozen reporters who first arrived on the scene. Then he stood aside and indicated the group could begin their descent of the Whaligoe Steps. With the cordon closing behind them, the group could hear the officer speaking into his radio to relay information to a colleague.

The troop started to string out as they followed the rough path down towards the sea, easing wary feet over rough cobbles and a never-ending succession of stone steps. The going was too uneven for anyone to gain a significant time advantage, so they bunched up again after ten minutes and arrived at the bottom together. They were now one hundred metres below the sparse grazing lands of Caithness, standing at the base of the high cliffs, forming the backbone of a rugged coastline. They halted at a ribbon of police tape and looked left and right for further guidance. Ten metres away, another group of men stood in a cluster. Two were casually dressed, while a third wore ill-fitting disposable protective clothing. They were in earnest conversation with another police officer, although the cries of hundreds of guillemots and razorbills wheeling overhead made it impossible to overhear what was being said. It was late March, and it appeared the seabirds resented a human invasion at the moment when the breeding season was getting underway.

Still unobserved, the men behind the police tape glanced at each other. They could smell it now. Pungent and oily. Like a lorry load of smoked fish left to rot in the sun. They knew they were close, and it was only a matter of time before someone broke ranks. The first one to press down the tape and step over was a lanky photographer from the Daily Record. This movement disrupted the ongoing conversation, and the man in the white boilersuit suit moved toward the new arrivals. Sweating in the bulky garment and looking ill slept, the man raised a hand to gather their attention.

'Thanks for your patience, guys. Could I ask you to stick together? Lots of nasty wee drops in here. The last thing we need is for someone to break a leg so far from the road.'

The photographer reluctantly retreated and stood with the group.

'I'm Arthur Deveron from the Scottish Marine Laboratory in St Andrews. I'll direct you to a vantage point where you can take photographs in a few moments. Then I'm going to hand you over to our team leader. She'll answer any questions you might have.'

The police officer strolled over and lifted the tape, allowing the reporters to move out onto a grassy knoll. Verdant and dotted with emerging sea pinks, it would have made a perfect spot for a picnic on any ordinary day. 'Careful. It's a sheer drop after this.' Arthur's appearance was less than athletic, and his approach to health and safety seemed a little condescending. Like children, he bid them move down almost to their hands and knees as they edged out onto the tip of the rocky promontory. But no one objected. No one wanted to miss what Arthur had to show them.

The view opened up as they moved away from the base of the steps. To the left of their position ran a high wall of rock, towering above a narrow channel of deep green water leading to the open sea. Far to the right, almost behind where they crouched, the fissure narrowed. It ended on a tiny shingle beach with a shallow cave at its apex. Whaligoe had been a natural harbour in the 19th century from where small boats would have plied the rich seas south of Wick for whitefish and herring. Even now, a stack of derelict lobster pots stood at the edge of a thicket of ferns, hinting at a recent industry. From where the men crouched, it was fifty metres to the beach, while in the opposite direction, the high cliffs suggested it was another fifty metres or so to the open sea.

Arthur slid onto his stomach as he approached the drop-off and indicated the others should do likewise. He drew himself to the edge of the grass and pointed towards a low island straddling the middle section of the rocky inlet. The camera shutters started to fire as soon as the men drew alongside him. Below them, a small wooden rowing boat was making its way back from the island. Apart from the rower, the only other person was a figure dressed in protective clothing, their face shrouded by a hood and mask. But all this detail was incidental compared to the body lying sprawled across the island. It wasn't clear what type of creature it was. Its shape was snake-like, the body draped over the rock like a great coil of flexible pipe that might have broken from an oil rig. That it had once been a living creature was obvious enough. A yellow-white belly faced the sky, darkening to black on the side pressed against the rock. A pectoral fin jutted from the creature's side, even though its head and tail hung obscured in the deep water of the inlet.

'Man, it stinks,' said the reporter from The Record. 'Is it some kind of whale?'

'You'll be ready to ask a few questions,' said Arthur to no one in particular. 'I'll take you down now to meet Dr Ahmed.'

The group reversed back from the edge and joined a narrow path weaving through ferns that took them down to the beach. The rowing boat had drawn up on the shingle, and the oarsman looked bemused as he held out a steadying hand to his passenger clad in PPE. Once on the beach, the figure raised a hand in thanks, gesticulating to Arthur to approach. After a muffled exchange, Arthur flashed an embarrassed glance at the bemused onlookers. 'It appears the zipper is stuck. Too much Caithness air, I think.' He struggled with a catch and stood back as the hood section finally sprang free to reveal a woman's face. She had a wide and generous smile that did more than cover her embarrassment. The men glanced at each other as she quickly discarded the rest of her protective clothing.

'Sorry for the delay. I thought I was going to pass out in that suit. I'm Salina Ahmed,' she said, stepping over and shaking the nearest man's hand. A murmur of hasty introductions followed her as she greeted those standing closest to her. Having regained her poise, Dr Ahmed leaned back against the rusting remains of an old winch and took a second to shake out a mane of long black hair from her hoodie. She gazed around the group, her dark brown eyes darting between the men's faces and name badges. 'Do you gentlemen have any questions for me?'

The Daily Record man was first off the mark. 'Just what is that thing?'

'It's a large eel,' said Dr Ahmed, smoothing out a wrinkle from her clothing.

'It's a bit big for an eel? It looks like it's about ten metres long.'

'Nearer to fourteen metres. And a metre plus change around its girth. And before you ask, it's not something we've seen before. Entirely possible it's a new species.'

'Do you know what killed it?'

'I'm not seeing injuries from a ship strike or predation. Given its size, it's a working assumption that it died from natural causes. It may simply have reached the end of its life.'

'Decomposition doesn't seem advanced. Where did it come from?'

'At this stage, I'd only be speculating.'

'The first reports last night called this thing a sea monster. Can you show us its head?'

'A trawler is coming down from Wick at high tide. We will recover the carcase and have it towed to Helmsdale. We'll be able to examine it more closely, and yes, we'll arrange a further photo opportunity at that time.'

'You've been close to it,' said a man with a short beard and a sweep of copper-coloured hair. 'Aside from its extreme size, did anything about the animal strike you as particularly odd?'

Dr Ahmed turned to face the man, pursing her lips as if smothering some amusement. 'Sorry, I didn't catch your name.'

'No worries,' said the man, stepping forward to grip her hand and give it a single firm shake. 'Gill McArdle, *Mysterious Scotland*.' Almost as an afterthought, he plunged his right hand into the pocket of his old tweed waistcoat and presented her with a crumpled business card.

Dr Ahmed searched the man's pale blue eyes for a few moments, then seemed to suppress a smile. 'Well, we are honoured. But I suspect you've had a wasted trip, Mr McArdle. If you're looking for mythical creatures, you'll not find any around here.'

'No,' said Gill, accepting the return of his card. 'Just an abnormally large eel.' He glanced around at the other journalists before adding, 'What could possibly be mysterious about that?'

More questions exploded from the group. Technicalities about moving the dead animal and next steps towards possible identification. It wasn't long before the police officer appeared at their back, with the second batch of wide-eyed journalists in tow.

Ushered back towards the steps, the first group talked amongst themselves. Only Gill walked alone, lingering behind the others. As the hill steepened on the last stretch of the return trip, he looked for a place to sit. Diverting off the main path onto a sheep track, he found a warm spot at the edge of last season's bracken and settled down. All afternoon, he watched small parties pass by, making their way up and down the path and catching snatches of conversation. 'Get these shots over to the news desk ...,' 'talk this through with the editor before the 10 pm bulletin …,' 'That Dr Ahmed's a bit of a looker ...'

As the shadows started to lengthen over the east coast cliff, he heard the deep throaty roar of a large diesel engine. He craned over to see the black bulk of a trawler reversing carefully into the inlet. After a few moments, it moved too close to the cliff for him to keep it in view, but over the next half-hour, he could hear the tone of the engine rising and falling as the boat manoeuvred. It idled for a little while, and then the pitch intensified again as the vessel slowly made its way back out to sea.

Traffic on the path thinned as the last stragglers made the return trip. At the back of the final party came the weary figures of Arthur Deveron and Dr Ahmed. Gill nodded and smiled as they made guarded eye contact.

'You know, a creature isn't mythical if you find its bones,' he said from his resting place.

The figures paused, but Dr Ahmed gently pushed Deveron's arm to urge him to continue before she turned to face Gill. 'You're still here?' Her forehead tilted towards him a little, and her bare arms, freed from the black hoodie, rested on her hips.

Was her posture friendly or aggressive? Just at that moment, Gill wasn't sure. 'Yep. Dogged reporter in search of a story.'

'Helmsdale, tomorrow at 4 pm. We'll do a news conference and give you our preliminary findings. I'll have more for you then.' She turned to walk away, but Gill jumped up and jogged up the track until he stood beside her in the late evening sunshine.

'Buy you a beer?' He smiled. 'I'll show you the bright lights of Wick if you'll tell me what you really think that thing is.'

'Tempting,' she said slowly. 'But luckily for me, I don't drink.' She gave him a tired half-smile. 'And if I'm honest, I'm not a big fan of Wick either.'

'Fair enough,' he said to her back as she bent forward into the final flight of steps and slowly walked away.

Chapter 2

Gill was up and about early the next morning. On trips away from the office, he'd nurtured a habit of taking a run before breakfast to get a feel for the locality. To those who knew him, this presented a newer, healthier lifestyle. But his real motivation was something he only admitted to himself. Simply that running in the morning had become the leverage he exerted on himself to drink less in the evenings. Running was bad enough. Running on a hangover was appalling.

Unlike Dr Ahmed, Gill liked Wick. Starting with a turn around the harbour, he found much that was familiar to him from his days in Aberdeenshire. Fishing vessels of various sizes mingled with oil industry service vessels. Everywhere had the same tired feeling of two great industries in steady decline. Like wrinkles on the face of a canny old man, they showed his age but lent him character.

Leaving the town centre behind, he followed the coast road south for a mile as it hugged a rocky shoreline. Then he struck inland again, using two church spires to navigate his way back to his hotel.

Showered and ready for breakfast, he had the pleasant sensation of a day begun well. By 9 am, he was ready to check out of his room. Before he did so, he put in a call to Cassy.

Acting as his editorial assistant, and Office Manager for *Mysterious Scotland*, Cassy was his eyes and ears when he wasn't at his desk in Dundee.

'Morning, stranger. How's the monster hunting?' He could hear the gentle crackle of a newspaper page being turned.

'I'll guess you've seen the pictures,' said Gill.

'Yeah, but you can't see much. It looks big, alright, but more like an industrial accident than a dead animal. Do they know what it is?'

'Not yet. The people from St Andrews Uni are studying it today.'

'Your old hunting ground,' breathed Cassy, taking a noisy sip of coffee. 'Will that give you an inside track?'

'I doubt it. The Marine Laboratory folk were always on overseas trips, so I never really knew anyone from that department. Anyway, what's happening in our world?'

Cassy paused as if taking a moment to check who was in earshot. 'Tony was by earlier. He said he wants to debate the size of the next print run at the Publisher's Meeting on Friday.'

Gill sighed. These meetings had diminishing appeal in the nine months since the first issue of *Mysterious Scotland*. 'Tell him I trust his judgement. He'll make the call at the end of the day. And he'll probably still end up printing too many. Which reminds me, has the distributor given us a sales estimate for issue seven?'

He could hear Cassy tapping her keyboard a few times. 'First estimate is sixty-seven per cent sales efficiency, but it might go lower once the final returns are in.'

Gill made a quick mental calculation. 'So, we've sold less than thirty-five thousand copies. He won't be pleased.' Between print sales and online paywall, the first issue of the magazine had been a stellar success selling almost two hundred thousand copies. It had been falling steadily ever since.

'You'll let me know if I need to start looking for another job,' said Cassy.

'No panic yet,' he responded. 'Tony knows that even if he has a mag selling thirty K on a forty K print run, he'll still have a profitable business.' He paused. 'If it goes south of that, we should start polishing our LinkedIn profiles.'

'Tony says you shouldn't spend too much time on the *Caithness Kraken*. Our next issue won't be in the shops for three weeks, so it'll be old news by then.'

'*Caithness Kraken*! Who on earth is calling it that?'

He heard the sound of the tabloid being abruptly folded. 'Oh, all the papers are calling it that. Don't they have newspapers in Wick?'

'This job has anesthetised me to the printed word, so no, I haven't read the newspapers. That's why I need you to read them for me.' He paused before adding, 'Which you do very well, by the way.'

'Awesome,' she muttered. 'At this rate, I'm never gonna be famous.'

Gill paused for a few moments to let her vent her boredom. Maybe it was the poor quality coffee, but Cassy could be distracted first thing in the morning. 'Is anything of significance happening in the world outside our office?'

'Yeah, sorry. Wednesday's papers, then. Let's have a look.'

As Publishing Director, Tony had seen the danger early on that the magazine and its web pages could easily spiral down into little more than a history lecture. Its readership base could narrow, forcing it to close. So, he'd established a rule, with Gill's agreement, that at least half of editorial space would cover contemporary stories. That meant Cassy had to keep track of Scottish news items that might be of interest to their own paper. On top of that, Gill's editorial stance actively encouraged readers to send in all manner of their own experiences. Strange sightings, mysteries, observations of the supernatural and anything unexplained. The file she prepared each morning went to Gill and the rest of their small team and formed the germs of ideas they'd work up into future features.

'There's still no word on the creel boat that's gone missing out of Loch Melfort,' she began.

'That's a pity. I heard about that on the radio coming up yesterday. Father and son, weren't they? Do you know where they were fishing?'

'They were full-timers, so they had gear all over the place. That's what's hampering the search. They could be anywhere from Craignish to Jura or Kintyre.'

'Okay, that's a sad one, but in all likelihood, it's routine. Anything else?'

Cassy rattled off a few other minor news stories before concluding. 'And this morning, we've received a "For Editor's Eyes Only."'

'Have you opened it?'

'Duh!'

'Thanks, Cassy. I respect your integrity. But we both know it'll be a letter from a kid telling us all about how they think their granny is an alien. Remind me. What's the other one ...?'

'Panther-like creature lurking the moors with a lamb in its mouth,' Cassy whispered theatrically. 'Followed by sightings of miscellaneous monsters in just about every loch in Scotland.' She sighed sadly. 'More proof, if any were needed, the Scots drink too much.'

Gill flinched. 'Open the envelope, Cassy, and tell me what it says, or if that is too much for your conscience to bear, don't read it. Just scan it and send it to my phone.'

'No can do. This isn't a letter; it's a full package, close to four kilos. Someone must have sent you their full log of alien encounters.'

He was briefly intrigued. 'What's the return address?'

'That's actually quite strange. It came from a rented mailbox. No street address, just a postcode. Do you want me to look it up for you?'

'Aye, do that. But hold onto the package until Friday. Then send it on to my dad's place in Stonehaven. I'll be up there this weekend.'

'You're not coming back for the Publisher's Meeting?'

'Give Tony my apologies. I want to linger around this Caithness thing for a couple of days and see what comes up. Then I need to spend time at the Montrose dig. I still need to nail what angle we're taking on that.'

Cassy wished him "good hunting" and hung up. Gill turned his attention back to the hotel bedroom and started tossing his belongings back into a bag. Distracted, he stood and looked out over the harbour for a few more minutes, trying to analyse the feeling that had come over him since his visit to Whaligoe the previous day. His senses were tingling. Perhaps the absence of a hangover? He'd no other tangible reason to explain the way he felt. He tried to think of the last time he'd experienced this sensation. He'd been in the Outer Hebrides, standing in an open field below an ancient stone circle. A haunted space unexplored by the archaeologist's spade.

That had been another day. Today, with many hours to kill before the Helmsdale press conference, he dived into his work. He was one of the first customers at the local library. In fact, he was the only customer for most of the hour he was there. He ignored the convenience of the internet and browsed the shelves looking for inspiration. Gradually the need for caffeine asserted itself, and he moved off to the nearest café. Finding decent Wi-Fi, he started to augment his thoughts. Grabbing a sandwich for later, he set out towards the north coast, driving west of Thurso. He found a layby overlooking the Dounreay Nuclear research facility. He paused for a while, taking a few distant pictures and allowing his mind to wander.

Chapter 3

Dr Ahmed looked quite different the next time Gill saw her. Her eyes looked red and tired from a night and a day spent studying the dead animal. But her clean hair was glossy, and her posture and expression made her look strong. The protective suit was gone, swapped for a business skirt and tailored white blouse, emphasising her figure. And although she stood several inches taller than most women, an improvised podium had been built for her. Standing on a platform of up-turned fish boxes, topped off with a piece of hardboard, she was ready to start. She glanced at Arthur, waiting for the noise to diminish so that she could launch into her presentation. Behind her, the white sides of a large marquee flapped gently in the breeze on the Helmsdale harbour side. Taking the hint, Arthur Deveron called out for quiet.

'Thank you all for coming,' she began.

After introducing herself and her team, she related the circumstances around the discovery of the carcase and its transportation to Helmsdale. Her delivery was confident but a little long on detail for the impatient crowd. Copy deadlines were getting close and they all had reports to file.

'Do you know what the creature is yet?' asked a large man at the front.

Dr Ahmed nodded. 'We haven't got a conclusive identification yet, but we're almost certain it's a conger eel.'

'Can't be,' retorted the man. 'I've done a bit of fishing, and I'm pretty sure they only grow to three metres max. How long is this one?'

'It measures just over fourteen,' she replied. 'But we're still confident it is a conger.'

'How so?'

'A scale analysis for starters. We're running the DNA to confirm that.'

'But how can it be a conger if it's that big?' the man pressed.

'We got clues from the autopsy. We think the creature's abnormal size is because it was sterile.'

'What difference would that make?'

'Like most eels, congers have a defined life cycle. They grow, they reproduce just once, and then they die. For this creature, with its reproductive switch in the "off" position, the creature just continued to grow.'

'So, do you know how old it is?'

'Again, we have indicative data from the scale samples. Early estimates put the animal at about two hundred and thirty years old, which is obviously exceptional.'

A murmur ran through the crowd until someone called out from the back, 'Do you know where it came from?'

Dr Ahmed shrugged. 'We can only guess. Despite its size, it would have followed normal conger behaviour and kept to a rocky habitat to give it cover. Tissue samples from the animal's swim bladder suggested it has some decompression damage. That would imply it lived in deep water in the North Sea like the Norwegian Trench or the Devil's Hole.

Most of those areas are coated in thick silt, so they don't present a decent hiding place for a rock-dwelling animal of this size. So, we really can't be sure.'

A flurry of questions gave Dr Ahmed an opportunity to explain some of her methodologies. While she was doing that, Arthur Deveron started moving through the crowd, passing out face masks.

'I'm going to invite you now to view the remains. I do need to warn you that the smell is quite strong. This is your only opportunity to take photographs as the carcase will be towed out to sea before it becomes a health hazard.'

Gill accepted a face mask and a brief nod of recognition from Arthur before deliberately joining the back of the crowd as they filed into the marquee. In contrast to Dr Ahmed, Arthur looked unkempt. Underneath his lab coat, his shirt was stained, and he was in dire need of a shower.

'Long night?' asked Gill.

Arthur smiled weakly. 'Someone had to courier the samples down to St Andrews. Given the importance of this, I decided it should be me.'

'Did you have to hang around all night waiting for the results?'

'No. I dropped them in capable hands and came straight back up. The autopsy had just reached an interesting stage, so I got stuck back in.'

'How so?'

'The discovery that the animal had reabsorbed its reproductive organs got us thinking. We had to dig pretty deep to make sure we hadn't just overlooked them. That wasn't fun.'

'Dr Ahmed got freshened up,' said Gill changing tack. 'I suppose it helps to be the one in charge.'

Arthur suppressed a smile. 'Well, she has the benefit of her relative youth. But she worked all night like the rest of us. And as the public face of our team, we agreed she'd need a change of clothes before the press conference.'

The doors of the marquee moved a little in the light wind, revealing the great eel stretched out along the harbour side. Almost as long as an articulated lorry, the bulk and presence of the animal hushed the reporters. For a few moments, it seemed like anything more than their terse whispers might risk waking the beast. But the eyes were misted, and the immense mouth hung open, reinforcing the absence of life.

'We will be severing the skull and preserving it before the rest of the body is disposed of,' said Dr Ahmed into the silence. 'As you can see, the mouth is immense.' She glanced around at the faces, 'it could have swallowed a human child in just one gulp.'

'Do you know what it lived on?' asked a reporter.

'We have no idea,' replied Dr Ahmed. 'As no one has ever encountered an eel this size, we have to assume that it hunted at great depth. It might have preyed on large squid. We just can't be sure.'

The reporters were loosening up again, and one or two posed for photos beside the eel's head. One or two laughs broke out, and Dr Ahmed fell into conversation with some younger women who wanted more detail. But eventually, the smell became too strong for most, and the group started to melt away.

'Arthur, Dr Ahmed, could I ask you to pose with the animal's head?' said Gill, levelling his camera while the scientists squatted on either side of the carcase. 'Thanks, folks. That's great.'

'Do you have everything you need?' asked Dr Ahmed over her shoulder as she reached for a set of white overalls.

'Not really,' said Gill matter-of-factly. 'I mean, it's a stunning specimen, but we know so little about it.'

'Sorry,' said Dr Ahmed, stepping into the protective garment. 'It wasn't carrying a passport.'

Gill thought he was detecting weary humour rather than blunt sarcasm. 'I'm guessing that you believe it starved to death,' he asked.

'We didn't say that.'

'No, but if you don't know what the animal ate, then it implies its stomach was empty. Did you see any evidence of muscle wastage?'

Arthur nodded. 'Aye, we did. The digestive system was so shrunken it was all but dormant.'

'This wasn't something that you shared with the reporters?'

Dr Ahmed shrugged, her dark eyes fixing him in a steady gaze. 'To be honest, Mr McArdle, we didn't think they'd be all that interested. But it will be in our final report.'

'Please, call me Gill. And I'm not suggesting you're hiding anything. I'm just deeply curious about what motivates a creature as long-lived as this to suddenly decide to abandon whatever safe haven it had found for itself. What made it launch off into the deep and expire?'

'Animals sometimes do strange things just before they die,' said Arthur. 'Maybe it somehow knew its time was up.'

Gill nodded and stepped away from them, walking slowly down the length of the animal on one side and taking his time on the walk back up the other side. By the time he reached the head again, a team of fitters was starting to dismantle the marquee. A little way off, a group of men readied a mobile crane.

'Makes you think,' said Arthur, tipping his head as the last of the news crews packed away their equipment. 'What kind of story it would take to keep those guys interested.'

'As a journalist, I do know what you mean,' said Gill, reaching out to shake Arthur's hand as he made preparations to leave.

Arthur nodded back at the body of the eel. 'If our specimen had turned up in London or Glasgow, it would be an altogether different story, wouldn't it?'

Gill grinned and nodded once.

With a last farewell, Arthur walked off towards a cluster of white vans.

'You're almost finished here?' Gill said to Dr Ahmed as they watched him go.

'Yes. Arthur is taking the last batch of samples down to St Andrews before he takes a couple of days off.'

'And you?'

'I'm going to hang around for another 24 hours. Supervise the removal of the head and the disposal of the rest of the animal out at sea sometime tomorrow.'

'Back on your trawler?'

'Nothing so crude. The local council is funding one of the service vessels from the rigs to come and take it out. They are going to ballast the body, so it doesn't come ashore again a few weeks from now in an even worse state.'

'So, you'll be staying in town one more night at least.'

'Yep. I'm in a hotel in Dornoch.'

Gill mustered his warmest smile. 'Now that you are almost separated from your enormous eel, can I up my offer of a drink? Perhaps we could grab some food?'

She glanced at him through strands of her long black hair. 'And why would I want to do that?'

Gill shrugged. 'I used to work in St Andrews. I was hoping you'd update me on my old alma mater.'

'I'm away a lot, so I'm probably not the person to ask.'

'Come on. All I'm asking for is an hour of like-minded company. After that, I'll be out of your hair, and you'll probably never see me again.'

She sighed and took a few seconds to add a face mask to her attire. 'Then it's a deal,' she said, turning away.

The bar in the Dornoch Hotel that evening had the happy hush of couples enjoying a drink in pleasant surroundings. Gill could see Dr Ahmed sitting at the bar, the remains of a dark red drink in front of her.

'Hi, Dr Ahmed. Sorry, I thought I was early,' he said, giving her hand a gentle shake.

'It's Salina, please. And you're not late; I think I'm losing track of time. We've been on the go for forty-eight hours, and I'm shattered.' Her smile was weary but better than any other smile he'd seen that day. 'Look, thanks for the offer of a meal, but I'll have one more of these then beat it for an early night.'

'Bloody Mary?' he said, catching the barman's eye.

'Almost. Just a tomato juice and a dash of Worcester sauce,' she replied.

He paid for the drinks and pulled up a stool to join her at the bar. 'So, you've had an interesting couple of days.'

'Fascinating. Totally out of the blue. A genuine monster of the sea,' she looked down at the bar and avoided his gaze. 'Then all the press attention.'

'Persistent parasites like me.'

'You have a job to do. But you are persistent.'

He smiled. 'As sea monsters go, the *Caithness Kraken* is a beauty, but she's not the first you know.'

She pulled a face. 'Really? Let me down gently, why don't you. Go on then, what was first?'

'Well, I'm thinking about the *Stronsay Beast* for a start.'

'Nineteenth-century Orkney. I'll think you'll find that was a very decayed animal. Probably a basking shark.'

'You do know your cryptozoology,' said Gill, happy to show her he was impressed.

Salina stared into the blood-red drink and nodded. 'Basking sharks are a speciality of mine. They have a cartilage body and three sets of claspers. They can look quite eerie in a partially decomposed state.'

'Basking sharks top out at what? About ten, maybe twelve metres. The Stronsay Beast was almost eighteen metres, and the drawings suggest it wasn't even complete.'

'So, it was twenty-five to thirty metres, but only if they measured it right,' she said, sipping her drink. 'The problem is the data came from a single source, so it doesn't have any veracity.'

'But my point is the same. Occasionally large or mysterious animals turn up, and as scientists, it is our happy work to research them and classify what we find.'

She drew her drink to her mouth and surveyed him for a few seconds. 'The best discoveries most of us get to make are a decent example of known species, like my humble conger eel. My previous best was the classification of a new type of mollusc. I can't compete with the man who uncovered the remains of *Equus pictus*.'

He shrugged. 'I had a lot of help with that. Fortunately, I was in the right place at the right time.'

'Well, as a fellow scientist, I salute you. You made the rest of us very jealous.'

Gill dropped his gaze and gave a slow nod. 'Thank you. It means my work here is done.'

Salina's smile was brief but genuine. Her dark, tired eyes flicked away from him to the drink in front of her. 'Tell me, have you heard of the Dianthus encounter?'

He thought for a moment, then shook his head.

'Second World War,' said Salina. 'A British warship called HMS Dianthus was dropping depth charges against a suspected target fifty miles off St Kilda. You're sure you never heard of it?'

When he again shook his head, Salina did her best to look astonished. 'A creature similar to our mysterious eel surfaced near the warship and swam alongside it. Based on the boat's length, an eyewitness reckoned it was over thirty-five metres long. It seemed dazed by all the mines, but after a minute, it seemed to recover and submerged again.'

'Did anyone take photos?'

'It was in the middle of the night, in the midst of a battle,' said Salina, spreading her arms in a theatrical protest. 'No one was updating their Instagram account, unfortunately.'

Gill smiled. 'There you go. No hard evidence, and poor visibility during a stressful situation. I can see why it didn't make the history books.'

She pulled a face at him of mock horror. 'You surprise me. I thought rumours like that would be meat and drink to your little magazine.'

'Common misunderstanding,' he said. 'Despite the rather superficial credentials of my newspaper, we try to stay anchored in hard science.' He bobbed his head from side to side. 'Well, kinda where hard science meets thinnish myth.' He reached out and gently touched her nearest elbow. 'And I assure you, when it comes to writing up the story, the hard science always wins.'

Salina didn't flinch, but her gaze flashed to where his hand was touching her skin. Gill withdrew immediately.

'Back at Helmsdale, you seemed to think our evaluation was incomplete. What was bothering you?' she asked.

He shifted in his chair and thought for a second. 'A couple of things. Firstly, I don't understand the rush to dispose of the carcase. I mean, there must be some institution in this country with a deep freeze big enough to store the body.'

Salina spread her hands. 'Sheer practicality combined with local politics, I guess. The county council insisted the remains should be dumped as soon as possible. We did reach out to a couple of other labs, but aside from requests for the head and some tissue samples, no one wanted the full eel.'

'Secondly, I wondered about the lacerations on the creature's back.'

'Yes, we saw those. Our super-sized eel must have found the deep sea caves a tight squeeze.'

'I agree,' said Gill. 'But why were most of the scars quite fresh?'

'It would have tumbled about on the rocks as it came ashore at Whaligoe.'

'Yes. And the resulting scratches are scattered around its body. But they are random and post-mortem. You can see that because they didn't heal. But the lacerations I'm talking about are along the top of the body, and they did start to heal.'

Salina looked down again at her drink. 'I didn't think about that. So, you're thinking something disturbed the animal from its hiding place? Maybe it had outgrown its home?'

He shrugged. 'Or maybe the cave collapsed, injuring it as it escaped. In which case, the damage the animal sustained might have been enough to cause its death.'

Salina nodded. 'In any case, you have to agree that it was still death by natural causes.'

'I do agree, unfortunately,' said Gill, swirling the beer in his glass. 'A great big eel decides to leave home and die,' he said. 'Not much of a headline.'

The conversation fell into a natural lull. 'What's next for you?' he asked.

Salina drew long fingers through her hair. 'A quiet week next week. Then I'm up on Orkney on a coral survey.'

He smiled. 'Sounds great. I've never been to the northern isles.'

'You surprise me. I thought all Scottish archaeologists cut their teeth in Orkney?'

He glanced away. 'I'm more of a west coast guy. Harris and Lewis are the only credentials I like to advertise.'

Salina nodded. 'I love the west coast. Argyll is my favourite place on the whole planet.'

'Beautiful,' said Gill. 'Still, you can't beat the east for big smelly eels.'

Salina laughed, then stood up. 'Thanks for the drink, Gill. It's been nice to meet you.'

Chapter 4

Self-awareness breaks upon Salina. She feels herself in motion, and her head jerks on her shoulders in a painful reflex to the sense of movement. The hotel bedroom is gone, and instead, she finds herself in a small, triangular space draped with meagre hunting tapestries. Beneath her, timbers creak and groan, the signature tune of an old sailing ship at sea. The alarm rising within her diminishes almost immediately. Sighing, she pushes herself back against rough wooden panelling, screwing her eyes shut in the poor light and rocks herself gently. These dreams are getting worse. All she wants to do is waken up.

After a minute or so, she becomes so uncomfortable she gives up the fight and surrenders to the choreography of her dream. The source of her cramp is the prone body of a small child. A girl aged about six or seven with lank brown hair, lies sprawled across Salina's midriff, pinning her against the headboard of a makeshift bed. Overcome by the need to move, she rearranges the girl's limbs and discovers the child has been sick. She decides she can overlook this, reasoning that it has no consequence in a dream. The girl is so pale Salina feels for her pulse. Finding it fast but weak, she eases herself from the child's clasp, wincing as she puts weight on her own stiff limbs.

As she stands, more smells assert themselves. The heavy velvet dress she wears is anything but fresh, even before its smear of vomit. She grabs an edge of the bed as the gown's weight conspires with a cacophony of unpleasant odours to rock her on her feet. Pungent oils, the sweat of men, and undertones of rotten food. She has to fight an urge to throw up. And then, her senses detect something far better. Slicing through the nightmare is the thing she loves most, the fresh sweet smell of the sea.

The child groans and stirs a little. Salina bends her legs painfully and kneels beside the girl. 'Hello, little one. Peace now. We'll be home soon.' She understands herself, even though she speaks the words in an unfamiliar language.

The child's eyes open for a second, and the glimmer of a smile washes over her face. Moments later and she has fallen back into her uncomfortable sleep. After checking the girl cannot roll out of the cot, Salina strokes her hair a few times to check she is settled. Satisfied, she looks around to find a door. Grasping a heavy wooden latch with both hands, she leans back against its weight, pauses for a few moments, and then steps out on deck.

The ship is not large, perhaps twenty-five metres of hewn timbers. Its style is older than anything she has experienced in real life, like an overgrown Viking galley. Looking up, she can see a single rectangular sail held to the wind by a yardarm and a simple system of ropes. The boat pitches steadily on a long diagonal tack across a gentle sea. The room she emerged from is formed from the high bow of the vessel, crudely partitioned and covered with boards. At the stern, another elevated platform carries the steering gear. Around her, sailors tug on ropes to push the sail's luff out into the wind. She forces one man to make eye contact with her, holding his gaze for a few moments until he lowers his eyes and gives her the slightest nod. Like all the others, he does not seem surprised to see a young British Pakistani woman in the velvet layers of a period dress. But then, in a dream, nothing seems unreasonable at first. Determined to force the pace of whatever narrative her mind is subjecting her to, she looks around for whoever is in charge. Seeing movement on the steering platform, she gathers her skirts and starts to navigate the hazards on the deck. Sailors notice her and step back, creating a respectful path. Stepping over the butts of two dozen shipped oars, she finally reaches the high stern of the boat.

Mounting a steep staircase, she finds more men intent on their tasks, but one stands out from the rest.

He fixes her with a wary stare. 'What news, nurse?'

'The child's not well,' she replies.

His response is sharp. 'That much is obvious, woman. But will Maid Margaret live?'

Salina shrugs and peers towards the horizon. 'Ask a doctor, my friend. Marine Biology just doesn't cut it at moments like this.'

She doesn't see his movement but suddenly finds her chin grasped in his right hand and wrenched towards his gaze. 'Enough of your mockery. If the child dies, it will play badly for both of us.' Of his many odours, his breath is the most repellent. She gasps as he flings her face free. 'If she dies, it plays badly for all of Scotland.'

She stands her ground, taking the opportunity for a deep breath of clean air, before turning to face the man again. 'Seasickness plays havoc with my memory,' she says, rubbing her forehead for effect. 'For clarity, can you remind me who the girl is?'

The blow that spins from the back of his hand fells her instantly. She is on all fours, blood streaming from a split lip. She crouches for a full minute, fighting to regain her breath. Nothing she does ever seems to stop these dreams from getting worse. But now she is up again, facing her tormentor.

She braces as he steps toward her again. 'When we next make land, your service to our queen is at an end.'

'That's a pity,' said Salina. 'I think she likes me.'

He leans towards her, and against her will, she can't help but recoil. 'Go back to her then.'

He pulls back his hand again, but before he can strike, a call rings out from above them. 'Land to starboard!'

Distracted, the man lowers his arm. He steps away from her, leaning out over the high gunnel, straining to see the land for himself. 'Away from me. Share this good news with your queen.'

Salina backs away from him and eases herself down the stairs. Her passage back to the bow becomes crowded with menace. What the sailors haven't seen, they've all heard, and now she finds the deck strewn with obstruction and abuse.

'I'll wager that one's a witch.'

'See her dark skin. She's the devil's own.'

'She wants to kill the Queen of Scotland.'

'Aye, we'll make her pay.'

Stepping around a burly, olive-skinned seaman, she's surprised to see compassion in his eyes. She smiles at him because something about him is familiar, but now someone behind her deftly catches her heel, and she falls heavily to a chorus of coarse laughing. She glances back as one lad approaches her, drawing back his foot to kick her backside. But before he can deliver his blow, the man she had tried to step around inserts himself between her and her attacker and takes the full force of the impact. Then with a grunt, the larger man picks up the boy and tosses him bodily across the deck in a single swift movement. Another explosion of laughter follows a stream of cursing from the bruised youth. 'To hell with you, Raphael! Witch lover.'

Salina's rescuer flicks his chin at her, an encouragement to get back to the room. Behind him, she can see the youth has picked himself up again and is starting to charge. Others are limbering up, preparing for the fight that is about to break out. But she uses the distraction to clamber back onto her feet and into the little room.

When Salina makes it back inside, she heels the door closed and leans against it. A sob rises within her, and she draws her left hand across her mouth to stop her cry from reaching her tormentors. Standing like this for a long minute, she fights to reclaim her composure, begging for this worst of dreams to end. When that doesn't happen, she steps back to the girl's cot, takes the limp wrist in her hands and feels again for a pulse.

She sighs. 'Guess I should have seen this coming.' Her head drops onto her chest as she wonders what to do. 'Come on, Salina. Wake up!' she yells.

The door bursts open, and the ship's captain stands glaring at her. She lets the lifeless hand drop and turns to face him. 'Thing is, I don't understand why my subconscious creates you this way,' she says. 'I mean, you're not my father. And most of the men in my life have been quite reasonable people. Maybe I've got a "thing" with authority figures.'

'The child?' bellows the man.

Salina looks up. 'Quite dead,' she says matter of factly. 'Can I go now?'

Ashen-faced, the captain rocks back against the door frame, grasping for an upright to steady himself. For a moment, he retreats from the cramped room, turning slowly on the deck until he completes a full round of the compass. Then anger rises in his face, and she knows he is coming for her.

The man reaches, and although she flinches from him, he catches her wrists and pulls her to her feet. He glares at her as if she is a disobedient child. 'Aye, lass,' he says. 'You can go.'

In the face of his superior physical strength, she cannot stop herself from being dragged from the room and out onto the deck. A roar goes up among the sailors. It echoes across the ship as the captain forces her away from him and towards the gunnel. She fights to steady herself, but no sooner does she regain her balance than he pushes her again. The backs of her thighs are against the rail, and she panics as she realises she cannot recover from another blow. As his punch hits her in the middle of her chest, the air is forced out of her lungs, even as she spins through a heavy circle into the sea.

The water is a relief, catching and cushioning, closing around her until she is beyond the reach of his anger. But the velvet dress soaks quickly, and her limbs feel heavy. She summons her strength and forces her legs to kick towards the surface so she can take a fierce gasp of air. She holds the water surface for a few seconds but finds the weight of the dress is sucking her under again. She needs to shake it off. Her fingers work around her body, trying to find a way to release the dress, even as her face submerges. Within moments a few centimetres of water become a metre, and she gives up the search and kicks for the surface. As her sore chest gulps for air, her limbs ache badly, and she knows it will be the last time she will be able to reach the surface.

The birlinn had passed her now, working its course towards the land. She sees the olive-skinned man appear at the stern of the ship, stand for a second to fix Salina's position, and then leap into the water. But her strength is gone, and her limbs fall faint around her. She wonders why he would leave the boat to rescue her? Not that it matters. They are a long way from shore. It would be good to have company, though. Truly it would be a sad thing to die alone. Her screaming lungs interrupt her thoughts, and she battles to keep the depleted air inside her body.

Desperately.

Frantically.

With a deep and painful intake of breath, she awakes in her hotel bedroom. Her grip on the sheets is so tight, her fingertips throb with pain. The dream is over. Rolling over onto her back, she sucks in air. Searching her body for any injury she might have done to herself, the pain in her chest begins to ease. In a slow, deliberate movement, she sits up and swings her legs over the side of the bed. She sits looking at her feet; the big toes turned in to touch each other like she used to do when she was a child. She catches her face in her hands and angrily releases her pent-up sob.

Chapter 5

Passing through the edge of Montrose on Thursday morning, Gill glanced across at the sandy expanse of the tidal basin. It was low tide, and the many hundreds of acres of mudflats seemed bare, despite the presence of thousands of seabirds picking out a living on the sands. Passing through the western side of town, he turned inland and, after a few miles, left the Montrose Basin behind. He followed the Brechin road for ten minutes, then turned down a country lane. Soon he was close enough to the South Esk to give him a glimpse of the river through the trees. Slowing, he found what he was looking for, coming to a new gate set in an old fence. The gate was open, and Gill swung his car into the field and parked alongside a pair of old Land Rovers and a minibus that had seen better days. He changed into his walking boots and made his way down the field towards the river. The path became an improvised boardwalk of wooden pallets nailed to shallow posts. Walking with care across the rough timbers, it was another five minutes before he arrived at the dig site.

To his satisfaction, the scene was one of quiet industry. A dozen, mainly young people, scraped in trenches or pushed barrows of excavated soil for either further analysis or disposal. He nodded a greeting to one or two before spotting Fiona working one of the nearby ledges. Immediately recognisable in her grubby grey fleece, Fiona always kept her straw blonde hair pulled back in a hasty bunch that bobbed on her head as she worked. He'd known Fiona a long time in one form or another, and when this opportunity came up, she was his first choice as site supervisor.

'So, this is where the real work happens,' he muttered, peering over her shoulder.

'Oh. Hi, Stranger.' Fiona glanced up at his clean jeans, white shirt and tweed waistcoat. 'Fancy getting your hands dirty?' She stood up and leaned towards him to kiss his cheek. He reciprocated, leaning over her, so their physical contact was fleeting.

'You know me, Fi. Always keen to get down to where the action is. But perhaps today, you could just give me a catch-up? Hot date in Stonehaven tonight, so I need to keep my glad rags clean.'

'Lemme guess. Farmer's daughter. Late-twenties, big-bosomed with childbearing hips, maybe a little short-sighted.'

Gill fought back an embarrassed smile. Subconsciously, Fiona had neatly described herself. 'Fi! You know I've only got eyes for you. And if you must know, his name is Gordon, mid-sixties and well past child-rearing in any capacity you care to mention.'

'Aye,' said Fiona, flexing her wrists and straightening her back. 'Say "Hi" to your dad for me.'

'I'll put on my grubbies and give you a full day tomorrow, I promise.' He flicked his chin towards the ever-expanding trench. 'What's happening?'

'Well, this particular trench isn't as promising as I first hoped, but the good news is, we've upgraded the log boat from a six to a seven.'

Gill smiled with genuine pleasure. 'Cool. Show me.' The "Waterhorse Scale" was something the St Andrews students casually applied to their fieldwork. A score of ten was the highest and almost impossible score representing the discovery of a tusked mammal unknown to science. A score of one was an insignificant find, like an aluminium ring pull from the 1970s. Achieving a seven was good.

Fiona clambered out of the trench and led the way, weaving through sticks marked with orange tape that operated as signposts across the excavations. Gill glanced around him as they walked. Due east, the church spire on Montrose high street was just visible in the distance, while the South Esk meandered across farmland a little to the south. As editor of *Mysterious Scotland*, he enjoyed this foray into his old world of archaeology. A local farmer had turned up some Neolithic stone tools while laying field drainage. Initial excavations by the Scottish Foundation for Archaeology in St Andrews had suggested the site was promising, and his magazine had recruited a local trust to sponsor the dig.

After a few minutes, they came to an area where the team had painstakingly dug a waist-deep pit over twelve square metres. Fiona greeted the three young women kneeling in the trench, carefully peeling back pale-coloured sediment from half a dozen log timbers.

'My goodness, you've got more organics,' Gill exclaimed. 'How is that possible?'

Fiona moved around to the northern edge of the trench and pointed to a thick layer of sandy grey sediment. 'This is the tsunami layer, pretty much the same stuff we see all over Eastern Scotland. Beneath it is a layer of clay and gravel, about a metre deep. But it's localised, running approximately north-south and four metres wide. Our working theory is that in Neolithic times, this was the junction with an old stream bed joining a larger river. We picked up the feature using the magnetometer and did a trial dig to take a look. The log boat I mentioned to you yesterday? Turns out, there's a bunch of them.'

Gill took a careful step forward and squatted to look at the remains. They consisted of rough wooden beams lying in parallel rows and still deeply embedded in the clay. He followed the lie of the timbers until they disappeared into the wall of the trench. 'So, the remains are sitting on the fine sediment, and the deluge material is lying on top. I still don't get how it's all so well preserved.'

'Ah,' said Fiona. 'It's all down to the site.' She stood up and fished in her pockets for a booklet of pH paper. She tore off a strip and leaned down to dip it in a puddle. 'I haven't looked, but I'm pretty sure the high ground to the north and west is peaty. There's enough acidity here to drive out the oxygen and slow down the rate of decomposition.'

'Of course,' broke in Gill. 'The buried stream bed remained a watercourse, keeping the log boats saturated for all these years. If that explains the preservation, the next obvious question is why so many boats are in the same place?'

Fiona shrugged. 'We'll need to do more digging before we find that out. In Neolithic times, this area would have been deciduous forest, so I'll take a wild guess that boats were being manufactured here.'

Gill stood up and scratched his head. 'Fi, that would be amazing. I'll need to check, but we could be looking at the best-preserved Neolithic site ever uncovered in Eastern Scotland.'

Fiona beamed back a smile. 'Let's not get ahead of ourselves. I've got a bit more digging before we can prove that.'

'Granted. But if this is half as good as it looks, we will need to hand this back to St Andrews pretty soon.'

'Aye. Ed Johnson has already been up and sniffing around.'

'He'll get his turn. This is still your dig for now. How much gas do we have left in the tank?'

'Your seed money gives me another week to ten days. We'd have to rotate some of the team by then, and a job like this might need a tonne more labour.'

Gill lifted a hand and gave her a gentle high five. 'Agreed. In the meantime, let's see how far we can get.'

The two spent the remains of the morning hunched over a site plan in Fiona's makeshift HQ. They walked out to particular features from time to time, evaluating the remaining excavations the team could attempt. In his mind, Gill started to storyboard the article that would appear in the magazine. This discovery wasn't going to set the world on fire, but it was a solid piece of science that would generate plenty of academic interest. Best of all, it would be the magazine's biggest coup since the Callanish dig nine months before. The progress encouraged him to put in a call to his boss, Tony Farquharson.

'Hey, Gill. Cassy tells me you're not coming to the Publisher's Meeting tomorrow. You leaving me to fight it out with the others?'

Gill sighed. 'I've fallen behind on issue ten, and I need to finish some of the Montrose copy tomorrow while it's still fresh. Besides, I know the drill. The advertising people will want us to print more copies, and the distributor will want less. I'm not sure what my presence would contribute.'

'You're the editor, Gill. You should have an opinion and be here to express it.'

'I think it's better if I'm out here giving everyone a better product to sell, don't you?'

'Just don't be a stranger in the office, Gill. You know what I'm saying.'

Gill wasn't sure what Tony was saying, but he let it pass. 'Anyway, the Montrose dig looks like it will produce the goods. I need another week, but I'm hopeful we can devote half the next issue to the preliminary findings.'

'That's a relief. What have you come up with?'

Gill talked Tony through the findings to date and speculated on the possible conclusions. Tony seemed to grasp the scientific significance but didn't exactly bubble with enthusiasm.

'Okay, so how are you going to present the story?'

'I'm going to suggest historians have completely underestimated the amount of human activity in Scotland after the end of the last ice age. Given the size and collaborative nature of the activities here, it's fair to say that some textbooks will be re-written.'

'Aye, aye. But what about a more human angle? What about "Ancient Scottish civilisation obliterated by tsunami apocalypse?" That kind of thing.'

Gill took a moment before responding. 'We might be looking at a small boatyard and a cluster of dwellings,' he said eventually. 'It's significant but hardly qualifies as a civilisation.'

'But you take my point. I think you need to ease back on the heavy science and create a more compelling narrative.'

'How so?'

'Well, for example, you could imagine the inhabitants of these dwellings. Give them names and put them at the forefront of human endeavour in post-glacial Scotland's brave new world. Then walk the reader through the last minutes of their lives as the inundation arrived from the east. Perhaps you could finish with an editor's comment about how far back the earliest inhabitants of our isle got knocked by that disaster. Think of our readers and play to the Scots' sense of themselves as the underdog.'

Gill nodded and did his best to sound appreciative. 'Thanks, Tony. Still got a lot to learn from you about this editorial lark.'

'Like I always say. You uncover the facts, and let me help you find the story.'

Gill rang off, promising to spend at least part of the following week at his desk. It didn't enthuse him. No. It didn't enthuse him in the slightest.

Chapter 6

Gill switched off the engine and allowed his body to slump back against the headrest. He stretched his limbs and closed his eyes, weary at the end of a long Thursday. Summoning his energy, he was glad of a little fresh air while he prepared himself to greet his father. The parking space he had chanced upon was some way back from his father's place. But this was Stonehaven on a bonny spring evening, so he'd anticipated a bit of a walk. Wandering down a street dense with cars and high stone buildings, he emerged at the narrow harbour that gave the town its name. As was his custom, he took a moment to cross the road and stand on the wall overlooking the sandy beach at the harbour head. He stood for a moment recognising boats he had known for many years and spotting a few that were new. Behind him, the Harbour Inn spilt its evening load out onto the street while the hearty voices of men in kilts celebrated the tail end of some couple's wedding day.

He nodded to one or two faces he half recognised and made his way along to the harbour before diverting into one of the little vennels that faced the sea. For a moment, his burdens lightened a little. He'd not been raised in Stonehaven, but following his mother's death eight years before, his father had moved south and made a fresh start in a place he loved. With each passing year, Gill applauded this decision. The dark days of his mother's illness were left behind in Aberdeen city as his dad adapted to life on his own. When it came his time to retire, he was already settled in his bothy by the sea. It would be good for as long as it lasted.

Abrasive and opinionated, his father had dominated him as a child. Sparing with his praise and always ready to see the downside in any of Gill's new endeavours, his father had been a hard man to love. With hindsight, Gill could see how his father's dementia had been creeping up on him for years. And grief had accelerated the disease. Gill's mother had succumbed after a long battle with cancer, and soon after, Gordon lost his youngest son in a helicopter accident. To Gill's shame, the only bright side to this sadness was that it made the old man more dependent on his remaining son. In turn, this made him easier company. And so, after several years of not talking, they had reconciled. Then, a bad fall led to a hospital stay, which heralded Gordon's diagnosis. The strangeness about this new situation was that Gill was getting to know his father, all over again. The old man's stern gaze had softened, and now his pale blue eyes pleaded to understand and be understood. His face, once loaded with scorn, now begged for human connection. Gordon seemed to grasp that his life was staggering towards an untidy end and, in this fragile state, gifted back to Gill his dad.

He found Gordon, as he often did, bustling around the postage stamp garden nestling at the gable end of his house.

The door to the shed lay open, and Gill observed that planks now rose to cover half the ribs of the 'Icthus'.

'You're honestly not going to fish creels from that thing,' he observed quietly to his father's stooped back.

'Gill!' said Gordon McArdle, half turning to greet his son, his face cracking into a warm smile. 'Where have you been? I was expecting you hours ago.'

Gill glanced at his watch. It was just past 6 pm. He wasn't late, although it benefited nobody if he argued about it. 'Sorry, Dad. Accident on the A92,' he lied. 'I should have phoned.'

Gordon's back loosened enough for him to stand fully upright. 'Well, I'm glad you're here safely. Cuppa?'

'Aye,' said Gill.

'Or a beer?'

'Let's start with tea.'

He followed his father inside and nipped to the bathroom while Gordon filled the kettle. While Gill watched, his father meticulously gathered up sheets of numbers laid across the kitchen work surface. It looked like meteorological data from a distance, which wasn't a surprise. In better times, he would have asked Gordon about what he was working on, but today he was careful not to talk while Gordon paused, checked, and then rechecked the order of the documents. Only when he bundled them into an old manila folder did Gill speak again.

'So, how are things?'

'Oh, you know. Not bad. Good mostly.' Gordon gave his son a cagey glance. 'Things are fine.'

Gill smiled and nodded once. In response, Gordon got up out of his chair and walked back to the kettle. He returned with two mugs of tea, and a small note lifted from its usual resting place beside the kettle. 'I have lots of these scattered around the house.'

Gill read the list and nodded more convincingly. 'It was one of the tips your doctor gave us. Glad to see you using it.' Gordon had presented him with the list before, but Gill saw no value in mentioning that. 'Does it help with the anxiety?'

'Definitely. I even have my list of lists. So, when I go to bed at night, I make sure I've finished my outside list, my kitchen list and so on.' He paused, waiting for Gill to respond. When the pause became too much for him, he added, 'I'm fine, son. Good as gold.'

Gill forced a smile. 'And you're playing plenty of chess?'

'Every time I can get a game. We can set the board up later if you like.'

The two sat sharing stories for twenty minutes and tried their best to catch up with their news. By filtering out the pieces he'd heard before, Gill became more reassured that his father was coping.

'Now,' said Gordon tapping the table with his knuckles. 'Come and have a proper look at this boat.' They made their way outside and around to the open shed. Again, Gill marvelled at how trusting his father was, leaving his tools in full view of any opportunistic thief. And this wasn't a symptom of his illness; it had always been like that around here. 'Close neighbours,' his dad always said, nodding at the cheek-by-jowl houses. 'Nothing happens in Stonehaven that someone else doesn't see.'

The boat now looked the full six metres she would be when complete. She was a St Ayles class rowing boat; her sleek lines, sculpted from marine plywood, denoted her racing pedigree. Bought in kit form from a boat builder in Fife, she would be ready for the water by the summer and by early autumn, she would be racing against her kin all over Scotland. That she would ever be a lobster boat was a simmering jest between them.

'Is this the club's second or third boat?' asked Gill.

'Icthus will be our fourth.' Gordon ran his hand down the partly completed hull. 'We've got seventy folk rowing regularly now. The club is grateful for the extra capacity.'

'And no one has raised any concerns about this being your first build?'

Gordon smiled. 'It's basically a big Lego kit. Besides, if I hit a tricky bit, there are plenty of folk in town who can come and lend a hand.' He stroked part of the boat's underside. 'Of course, she'll have sea trials and all that.'

Gill completed his slow circle of the craft, savouring the smell of dark unvarnished wood. 'Well, I think she's beautiful. Mum would have been proud of you.'

Gordon turned his back, waving his hand as he moved towards the door. 'Now, I'll get some supper on the go.'

They drank more tea in the living room with the door open, the last strength of the sun warming the small room while Gill caught up on any paperwork where Gordon needed help. He navigated the various bills, official correspondence and junk mail, distilling the things needing action and filing the rest. He tried not to notice his brother's wedding photograph on the wall but ended up looking at it anyway. He couldn't help but observe the family's most cherished photo of his mother was starting to fade, a metaphor for much of Gordon's life.

'Just these two, Dad,' said Gill, tapping a small pile of paper. 'I'll help you complete the online payments in the morning.'

'You're sure I can ignore the rest?'

'I've put the important bits in your file. I'll just bin the rest if that's okay.'

'Thank you, Gill. I really appreciate it. Now, let me buy you a beer.'

The evening passed restfully, sitting together in a booth just inside the door of the pub. Then home for the slow-cooked casserole that was Gordon's regular fare, followed by the opening volleys of a chess game that would likely stumble on for a week or so. Later, when they bid each other goodnight, Gill reached the welcome conclusion his father was in better form. He did his best to make himself comfortable in the box room that served as the guest suite. That meant moving aside the clutter that inevitably accumulated between his visits. After he lay down, his mind wouldn't rest, and he thought sleep would never come. Eventually, fatigue overtook him, and he drifted off.

He wasn't sure what disturbed him. At 3 am, he found himself awake, trying to decode tiny sounds from around the house. Unsettled, he dragged himself out of bed and slipped downstairs. Through the partially open kitchen door, he saw his father bent over the sheets of numbers he'd been tidying away when Gill arrived. Methodically scanning down the data, he stopped and shook his head every few moments. Seeing his father's increasing agitation, a wave of pessimism swept over him. Needing to bring calm, Gill eased himself into the kitchen.

His father's face was almost distraught. He picked up a sheet of numbers and vigorously shook it at Gill.

'Something's wrong. Something's wrong, and I don't understand.'

When Gordon finally settled back to sleep, Gill was too awake to go back to bed. Instead, he pulled on warm clothes and set out for a walk in the dawn twilight. A lobster fisherman was loading boxes of bait for the morning creel run. Gill nodded a curt 'hello' then struck out over the rock armour surrounding the harbour and onto the esplanade rimming Stonehaven beach. Despite the promise of a lovely spring day, he struggled to chase away his melancholy. Sunlight already framed the edge of the raised beach above the village, washing the fields an almost surreal green. Seaward of this high ground, tumbles of pretty stone houses waited to feel the sunlight of the new day.

When he had walked the short mile to the end of the beach, he turned around and found himself in a more practical frame of mind. His challenge would be to get his father to accept whatever help Gill could bring to bear. In the meantime, he'd try to manage the difficulties one at a time. The first logical step was to address what had been bothering his dad last night. That meant trying to work out what was wrong with Gordon's weather station.

In his years in the oil industry, Gordon had been many things. Trained as a geologist, he had worked through the years when multi-directional drilling had been in its infancy.

Gill remembered his father talking for hours about the application of seismic data to map the oil-bearing rocks. Around the time his wife died, Gordon's management job became a burden. With clarity of thinking that had once been his hallmark, he stepped sideways into other things. By his retirement, he headed up a compact department in a cross-industry body, providing weather forecast services to North Sea rigs. He'd taken a particular interest in climate change modelling and contingency planning for a major oil spill. All this had influenced him to take an intensive interest in the weather forecast that bordered on the obsessive.

To access the weather station, Gill walked down the pontoon to a gated section of the harbour. He flashed his father's key fob at the electronic lock and walked past half a dozen of the larger commercial boats. Gordon's cluster of devices lodged in a nook in the pontoon too small for a boat. Gill ducked around a pole under the whirring of the wind monitor, checking the moving parts were free and the wires to the main controls were secure. He glanced at the aerial that provided the GPS link to the main instrument set. Then he dropped to his knees to check the sea-level calibration tube, slung like a proboscis out into the water. This was the device that was bothering Gordon with its erroneous data. And then he stood up and gently leaned his weight against the housing, letting the device sway slightly. Finally, he opened the instrument compartment holding the atmospheric pressure barometer and a simple digital device for recording the various readings. He kept this final inspection brief as he honestly couldn't tell if these devices were in working order or not. Satisfied that he had done what he could, he closed up and strolled back to the house.

His father had dressed and was making a pot of tea when Gill kicked his shoes off in the porch that doubled as a tiny sunroom.

'Grand morning. If I'd known you were going out, I'd have come along.'

'Och, I've been up for a bit. Took a dander to the end of the beach.'

'You working today?'

Gill sensed his father's question was a sincere one. 'Aye. I'll grab some breakfast, then I've got a full day at our dig in Montrose.'

His father gave a half nod to acknowledge the remark. He poured Gill a mug and started to gather breakfast things in silence.

'I looked at your weather station,' said Gill eventually, swinging the pontoon keys back up on the kitchen hook. 'I think I see what your problem is.'

The papers from the night before were hidden again, along with Gordon's memory of the episode. 'Oh, right. What's the matter then?'

'I think the barometric unit may have thrown off a couple of the screws that pin it to the deck. I know it's pretty solid, but it could rock back and forth a bit in a big sea. That would give you unusual readings.'

Gordon thought for a moment, then shook his head. 'No, that would increase the variances in my recording. I'd expect to see the highs and lows look a bit erratic. But I wouldn't expect to see a counter-intuitive trend.'

'What about the pontoon itself?' asked Gill. 'The whole thing rises and falls with the tide. Might your kit work better if we could mount it directly onto the land?'

'I agree that would be better. It would remove some of the variables. But in reality, the pontoon should work fine. The GPS adjusts for the height of the tides, and the barometer tells me what adjustments I need to make for atmospheric pressure. I've got synopsis data to help me predict any knock-on effect of storm surge ...' He stopped, a ripple of uncertainty sweeping his face, glancing down at his drink, then back at Gill. 'I'm sorry, what was I saying?'

Gill cleared his throat before mustering an encouraging smile. 'You were telling me you can't think of any reason why the weather station would be malfunctioning.'

Gordon set his mug in the sink with deliberate precision. 'So, our conclusion ...' he said, trailing off. 'Either I really am recording a period of falling sea levels, and wouldn't that be a relief.' His eyes gave a fleeting smile across at Gill. 'Or, I'm becoming a mad old man.'

Gill stared out at the bow of the *Icthus*, protruding from her shed and thought for a moment. 'I can give the installers a call if you like. See if they can find the problem. How old is the kit? Just three or four years?'

'Aye, son. Thank you. I might struggle to explain. I'll find you the number.' He scrabbled around the work surface for one of his lists and recorded what he needed to find and for whom.

'I'll give them a ring when I get back from Montrose,' Gill added.

Gordon laid down the note, tapping it twice as if to remind himself. Then he nodded at the boat. 'This coming weekend, would you give me a hand? Bending the top two boards and getting them glued in place will be a bugger on my own.'

Chapter 7

Gill was back on the road early on Monday morning and arrived at the Montrose dig site by 9 am.
Sitting in his car, he waved to a couple of familiar faces while he began his week with a phone call to his office.

'How was your weekend?' asked Cassy with a little more sobriety than usual. 'Your dad doing any better?'

Gill sighed. 'What can I tell you? Highs and lows. On the one hand, he's building a beautiful rowing boat. But then, at night, he's up wandering around looking agitated. His memory is going down the tubes, despite all the lists he leaves for himself.'

'Sorry to hear that. My gran was the same. Just make sure he gets the support he needs. They become a danger to themselves.'

Gill sighed. 'Yeah, I guess.'

She threw in a slight pause into the conversation before turning to business. 'Did you get your package?'

'Nope. Thought you'd forgotten it.'

Cassy clicked impatiently at the other end of the line. 'Sorry. It's in the system somewhere. It was pretty bulky.'

Gill groaned. 'If there's one thing that amazes me about this job, it's people's capacity to mail in great amounts of rubbish. I wonder how long it is before someone sends us a box of grouse turds as proof they've seen flying sheep.'

'Och, Gill. Five more days, and then you can take the whole weekend off.'

'Some hope,' said Gill. 'Anything happening that I should be aware of?'

'Nothing serious. Just cookie stuff. I've got one lady in Dumfries who believes she is the reincarnation of Mary Queen of Scots. The local rag is running a story claiming she plans to raise an army to invade England. So far, her finest hour is a fistfight at the motorway services near Carnforth.'

'Beautiful. Makes you proud to be a Scot. Anything else?'

'A lady in Fort Augustus. Apparently, she's been praying for some nearby mountain to pick itself up and throw itself into the sea for the last thirty years.'

'What?'

'I dunno. It's in the Bible or something.'

'Okay. And the angle is ...?'

'Well, someone measured the mountain recently, and it's not as high as last year. The local walking fraternity is up in arms because if it gets any smaller, it will no longer qualify as a munro.'

Gill felt his face break into a smile. 'I like that one. Definitely worth *Mys.Scot* taking a look. Can I borrow a tape measure from the office?'

'I'll find it for you. How's Montrose? Tony was telling me you have some pretty good stuff.'

'Yes, excellent. I was here all day Friday, and just arrived for another session. I'm with Fiona this morning, working on camera angles and tidying up the last few days of the primary dig. I'll have that story worked up by mid-week so Craig can get going on the next layout.'

'You're planning to lead issue ten with Montrose?'

'Aye. Followed by an in-depth on the *Caithness Kraken* and other historical sea creatures. I'm speaking to a potential expert contributor later in the week.'

'Cool. Don't forget to ask him if he's seen any flying sheep.'

'No problem. And if I find any poop, I'll mail it to you.'

Gill heard the news alert go off on Cassy's phone.

'Oh, man,' she said. 'Something else for you to think about.'

'Sure, what you got?' In the background, he could hear Cassy's furious tapping on her keyboard.

'The missing creel boat has just been found. The one from the west coast. It's quite a mess.'

Gill thought for a moment. 'Are you sure that's a story for us? I mean, it's tragic and all, but it doesn't scream "Mystery."'

Cassy's enthusiasm was bursting down the line at him. 'I'm not so sure. Do you have enough reception to receive a photo that just went up on Facebook?'

Gill glanced at his phone. 'Yep. Send me a link.'

The conversation paused for a few moments while Gill waited for the image to download. 'Good grief,' he said as the image appeared on his screen. Stripped of all its fittings, the boat was only just recognisable as a man-made craft. The hull was lacerated with deep scratches.

'I see what you mean. Any sign of the crew?'

'No, unfortunately.'

'Any clue what happened? '

'Let's see,' said Cassy scanning the page in front of her. 'No one is saying for certain what happened, but the circumstances look unusual.' She paused. 'But it makes you think, doesn't it?'

Gill looked at the image again and thought for a moment. 'In what way?'

'This could be another Kraken!' Cassy hissed. 'Except this time, it's attacked humans.'

Gill didn't respond straight away. He wasn't sure if Cassy was being serious. She had a brutal sense of humour and was brighter than most graduates he'd ever worked with. 'I'm struggling to see that,' he said at last.

'All that damage! Come on, Gill. Jokes aside, this isn't a regular everyday sinking.'

Gill stroked his chin with his phone. 'Yes, okay. Sunken boats aren't always found. You say this one washed up?'

'It drifted belly-up into a bay near Lochgilphead.'

Gill glanced at his watch and thought for a moment. 'Okay, I'll spend the morning here. Then if I can make the time, I'll head out west. In the meantime, see if you can find out where they recovered the boat.'

As he drove by the Crinan boatyard in the early evening sunlight, Gill caught sight of small groups of sombre-faced people. He parked his car at the nearby hotel, and after checking in, he walked the two hundred metres back to the yard. A police officer saw him approach and moved to intercept him.

'Sorry, sir. The yard is closed tonight for a salvage operation.'

'Thanks, Officer. I heard about the incident.' Gill flashed his press credentials. 'Gill McArdle. I'm a reporter investigating the fishing boat accident.'

'We held a short news conference earlier, sir. The local newsboys came in then, so it's off-limits now. I expect we'll make another announcement tomorrow.'

'Sorry, I'm with one of the nationals. I was in Montrose this morning so I couldn't get over until now.

The officer straightened his hat. 'Well, I'm sorry. Can you try again tomorrow?'

Gill allowed his shoulders to sag a little. It had been a long drive if it was for nothing. 'I'm doing an investigative piece. I've been busy on a couple of stories on the east coast.'

The officer paused, then waved a finger at Gill's chest. 'I thought I recognised your face. You're that unicorn guy.'

Gill shrugged modestly. 'That's me. Sorry, you are …?'

'PC Jeffries. I read about your unicorn stuff. Amazing that was.'

Gill nodded and pressed the advantage his brief fame allowed him. 'The fishing boat. Any idea what happened?'

The officer shrugged. 'It's a mess. The RNLI guys who recovered it have never seen anything like it.'

'Any chance of a look?'

The officer shook his head. 'Accident investigators are coming in tomorrow. Until then, the wreck is off-limits.'

'I assure you, I won't touch anything.'

'I dunno …'

'Officer Jeffries, this might be important.' Gill paused and juggled a thought that hung somewhere between a half-truth and an outright lie. 'Look, can I tell you something in confidence?'

The policeman nodded, so Gill continued. 'You've heard about the giant eel found in the east?'

The officer nodded, his eyes widening.

'Well, I am investigating the possibility of a similar creature, alive and active, here in the west.'

PC Jeffries looked incredulous for a second. 'You're not telling me one of these things could take down a fishing boat?'

'At this stage, it's only a remote possibility. But having been at Helmsdale last week, I'm looking for any links between the two cases.'

He was nodding now. 'Okay, I see.' He glanced at his watch. 'Some of the relatives are in attendance. Once they go, you can take a quick peek. Just a few minutes, though. I'll be locking up shortly.'

'Thank you,' said Gill.

'Make sure you mention anything you find to the investigators,' called Jeffries to his back.

Gill followed his directions down to a partially covered area where a trawler was mid-way through a refurbishment. He stood at a respectful distance in the fading light while a group dressed in dark clothes made their way slowly away from the wreck lying further down the slipway. When they left, Gill waited for a few minutes, then moved closer to see for himself. The craft was heavily damaged. But even at this distance, he could see the death of the fishing boat had been by a thousand cuts rather than a single killer blow. Moving in more closely, he could see no individual impacts that could have doomed the boat. Everywhere the hull was chipped and scratched. Those deck fittings that remained were twisted and broken. Applying his archaeological skills, he examined the boat for any damage an animal might have inflicted.

Gill was grabbing a few photos when PC Jeffries came over.

'How does it look?'

'It's very unusual. I can't explain the damage.'

'Oh,' said the officer, a little disappointed.

'It's weird,' said Gill. 'It's like the boat was tumble dried with a lorry load of steel girders. Was it found on rocks?'

'Free floating, I gather. However, it has had a bash or two. Plenty of sharp rocks around here.'

'Great, well, thanks for the look.' He reached and shook the officer's hand. I'll get along to the press conference tomorrow. Be interested to hear what the investigators make of it.'

Hands in pockets, deep in thought, he strolled back to his accommodation. The hotel had a glorious view of the bay, and he paused to absorb the sights, sounds and smells of the scene. As the sunset ran to molten gold, he stood by the side of the road and watched for a few minutes. A creel boat, not unlike the wreck, sat on its mooring, framed against a perfect backdrop of low hills and blood orange sky. Feeling compelled to share the moment with someone, he snapped a photo. On an impulse, hung as it was on just a snatch of conversation, he messaged it to Salina Ahmed.

'Thanks for your help last week. Out west today – saw this and thought of you. Gill,' he wrote.

The response came back in moments. 'Crinan Bay! One of my all-time favourites. Tell me you are not alone! S'

'Work I'm afraid.'

'Still searching for sea monsters?'

He hesitated. It was almost 8 pm, and he was uncertain if he should encroach on her personal time. While he recognised he was scrounging more of her professional expertise, he sensed something else was happening to muddy his emotional waters. He loaded up an image of the damaged fishing boat without resolving this personal debate and mailed it to her. 'I'm investigating this.'

No response came for several minutes, and he rebuked himself for being too quick to talk about work. He was walking into the hotel when he heard his phone. Her text arrested his attention. 'I think I know what did this.'

The conversation fell into a forced silence while he climbed the stairs, searching for his room down a dimly lit corridor smelling of old carpet. Pressing against the levered door into his bedroom, he stepped into a flood of golden sunset that left him dazzled.

'You say the boat came ashore locally?' Salina didn't seem to resent his phone call and had rushed past the usual pleasantries.

'Aye. Just outside the bay.' He hesitated, still uncertain whether he should be bothering her. 'You said you have some idea what happened to it?'

'I saw something similar a couple of years ago at Saltstraumen in Norway. They have a beast of a whirlpool near there. I was in the area leading a study on pelagic fish migration when one of our survey vessels got into difficulty.

It was missing for several days, and when it finally came ashore, it looked just like the one in your photo.'

'That must have been distressing.'

'Yeah. I lost a friend that day.'

The conversation paused while Gill gave Salina a moment to process her sadness.

'I saw advertising for a whirlpool around here,' he said, rummaging through a folder of local tourist attractions until he found what he was looking for. 'Corryvreckan.' He thumbed the small brochure for a moment. 'Seems innocent enough. But do you think it might be powerful enough to sink a creel boat?'

'Corryvreckan isn't the biggest whirlpool in the world, but it's not far off. If a boat got into trouble, say it sank or became submerged somehow, it might get sucked in. I take it there was no sign of the crew?'

'None. Their bodies will be miles away by now.'

'Maybe not,' said Salina. 'In that Norwegian incident, the bodies were eventually recovered from the whirlpool. They were in pretty bad shape and still suspended in the water column just above the base of the vortex.'

'Freaky,' said Gill, imagining the eerie dance of the dead fisherman and his son, spinning round and round in the deep waters off the Isle of Jura. 'Thanks for the tip. I'll alert the authorities in the morning.'

'I hope they don't hang around. It's so important the families get their loved ones back,' said Salina.

'Yeah. But even if the bodies are still in the area, I don't know what they can do about it,' said Gill.

'Surely they'll call in the right teams?'

'I guess.'

'Listen. If you think they're missing any expertise, let me know. I might be able to help you.'

'Really?'

'There aren't many boats like ours in Scotland. We've done rescue work before.'

'Thanks. I'll mention that.' Gill shuddered. 'It would be horrible to think the bodies might be out there when we could do something about it.'

'Let me make a couple of calls in the morning. That way, if you need us, we'll be good to go.'

'You sure?'

'Ach, it's the right thing to do. I'll need to find a business angle. Maybe shoot a nature video? Let me talk to my boss before I promise anything.'

'Thanks. Appreciate it,' said Gill, reticent to hang up. He set his phone down slowly and walked to the window. For the fifteen minutes it took for the sun to drop behind the hills of Jura, he stood and wondered what it was about Salina Ahmed that made his pulse race.

Chapter 8

By the time Gill sat down to breakfast the following morning, he was already halfway through his day. Bright sunlight had streamed into the room in the early hours, and finding himself awake, he had opened his laptop and drafted a lengthy article on the Montrose dig. Satisfied with that, he took a morning run down the Crinan Canal towards Lochgilphead, then back along a single-track road that wound through a forest of small oaks. He was almost back at the hotel when a convoy of three official-looking Land Rovers overtook him. Changing course, he arrived at the boatyard a few minutes behind the cars. A team made up of accident investigators, coastguard reps and witnesses from the RNLI were starting to plan their day. A sweat-stained tracksuit was never going to make it easy for Gill to muscle in on the meeting, but he was fortunate to catch the eye of PC Jeffries, who could confirm his credentials.

'You've no role or jurisdiction here,' said George Henderson, a short, barrel-chested man in his late fifties. An I.D. tag hung neatly from a tightly drawn black jacket, while a firmly knotted black tie emphasised his sobriety.

'Granted,' said Gill. 'But I can put you in touch with some expert help.'

'How so?' said Henderson with a flicker of impatience. 'What can an archaeologist bring to a marine investigation?'

'I know an expert who might be able to explain what caused this.'

'Well, I'm happy to listen to his point of view. Perhaps he could write to my office.'

Gill glanced around the half dozen faces who were not warming to his interruption. To get any further, he would have to take a risk. 'The missing fishermen. My contact thinks, she, can help you find the bodies.'

One of the dark-suited men cleared his throat and introduced himself as the solicitor representing the bereaved family. His opinion counted more than any other in the conversation that ensued. After a short, energetic discussion, the committee gave Gill the nod to proceed. It was time to call Salina.

'Sorry to call you so early. You won't even have got to your office yet,' said Gill.

'I'm an early riser, especially if it earns me a few hours on the sea.'

'I wanted to ask if I could take you up on your offer last night. I've spoken to the salvage committee here. The lead guy isn't exactly a ball of energy. Looks like they could use your help.'

'Well, we're in luck. I checked this morning. Our deep-submergence vehicle goes to Orkney next week on the coral survey I mentioned. That means the DSV is primed and ready to go. Given the circumstances, my director says that as long as we don't book more than twenty hours flight-time, we're happy to assist.'

'That's amazing.'

'Not so fast! I've just got the issue of finding a pilot. Two of my three regular guys are busy, so that leaves Arthur. I haven't been able to reach him yet.'

'The poor guy is probably still knackered after last week,' said Gill.

'Yeah. A couple of late nights in Helmsdale, then a couple more since he returned to St Andrews.'

'He deserves it. A few beers and a night out with his mates to tell them the story.'

'Arthur?' said Salina. 'No, I suspect he's got other fish to fry. Look, let me try him again in an hour. The DSV is on a purpose-built trailer, but I'll need to hire a towing vehicle. I'll be back to you.'

Gill relayed a précised version of the conversation to the men in black before asking to spend a few minutes getting a closer view of the wreck. While Henderson hesitated, the family solicitor stepped in to give permission.

Bathed in sunlight, the Oban registered *Bounty* had been a solid craft. Eight metres of robust fibreglass ringed around with steel strips to protect her from the constant scoring of creels or stern gear dragged aboard day after day. The wheelhouse was slung deep into the boat's bow to keep her profile low to the wind, while at the stern, a cage of marine-grade steel encompassed the working area. Gill had seen many like her in his time, at sea in all weathers and virtually unsinkable.

But it was the total absence of glass in the wheelhouse windows that made the boat look so dead. Thousands of scars criss-crossed the hull like knife slashes delivered post-mortem. While the boat wasn't damaged beyond repair, he imagined the shadow of whatever cataclysm had overwhelmed the *Bounty* meant she would never fish again.

When his phone rang half an hour later, he was still staring at the boat.

'Gill, it's Salina. I've got Arthur. We'll be on the road by mid-morning.'

'Fantastic. I'll tell the people here. We can get a plan together as the day goes on.'

After a shower and an hour-long call with Cassy, Gill was on the road before 11 am. He knew some naval architects had arrived to pick over the remains of the *Bounty*, and she would be out of bounds for the rest of the day. So, he decided to leave Crinan behind for a few hours to pursue another possible story. It wasn't a headline-grabber, but it was an intriguing little idea that had drifted around his head these past two days, pricking his curiosity.

He drove up to Oban and along the banks of Loch Linnhe towards Fort William, stopping for fuel before heading north to the small town of Spean Bridge. He paused in a layby to check directions, then drove north again on the A82 until he reached a tiny hamlet called Bencraig.

The *Loch View Guest House* was immediately signposted down a short track lined with Larch trees. He parked carefully beside a modest farmhouse and rang the bell. After a minute's delay, a buxom lady in her early seventies sprang to the door with a welcoming smile. She wore tight grey curls pulled close to rosy-red cheeks by a navy-blue scarf that matched her bulky coat.

'I'm sorry, my dear. Have you been ringing? I was just in with the dogs when I heard the bell.' Right on cue, a springer spaniel appeared beneath her skirts and bolted past them into the garden. A few moments later, an aged retriever followed at a more regal pace. Gill watched as the retriever worked across the lawn, following some scent, while the spaniel ran around it in an ever-tightening circle. The old lady laughed happily as the circle imploded in a flurry of legs, tails and contented barking.

'Gill McArdle,' he said, passing her a business card. 'And no, I haven't been waiting long. Are you Mrs McLean?'

Taking the card, a shadow of concern flitted across her face. 'Oh dear, are you a reporter? Have you come about my mountain?'

Gill nodded.

The old lady sighed. 'I didn't mean anyone any harm. I never meant to cause all this upset.'

'I'm sure you didn't,' said Gill. 'But I'm intrigued by what I've heard.' He threw her his most endearing smile. 'Would you mind if I asked you a few questions about it?'

Mrs McLean drooped a little as she turned back into the porch. 'Not a problem. Please come in.'

She led the way into a busy parlour set with small tables, waving a hand behind her. 'Just leave the door for the dogs. Would you like a cup of tea or coffee?'

'Please don't let me bother you, Mrs McLean.'

'Margo, please. And it's no problem. What would you like?'

Gill followed her through a kitchen stacked with the morning's dishes and out into a small metal-framed conservatory, smothered in a gentle clutter that suggested it was beyond the realm of her paying guests. They chatted for a few minutes about the fine spring weather and the consequential benefits to the tourist season. Eventually, Gill nodded out the window at a peak on the horizon. 'Is that your mountain?'

'Meall na Teanga,' said Margo. 'It's hard to see much of it from here, but it sits on the far side of Loch Lochy.'

What Gill could see of the mountain looked dark, steep and forbidding. 'I looked it up,' he said. 'A munro of 3012 feet.' He took a deliberate sip of his coffee. 'At least it was until recently.'

Margo smiled and gave a little shrug before turning to stare at the faraway summit.

'I've read that you've been praying for that mountain since 1992. Is that right?' said Gill.

'Aye. Every day.'

'May I ask you what you prayed?'

'That God would throw it into the sea, of course.' She turned and blinked at him, her eyes adjusting from the long distance. She measured his smile before continuing. 'Maybe I'm being too literal, but it says in the Bible that you can do that. The book of Mark, chapter 11, verse 23. 'Truly I tell you, if anyone says to this mountain, "Go, throw yourself into the sea," and does not doubt in their heart but believes that what they say will happen, it will be done for them.'

He nodded and stared again at the mountain. 'But why would you do that? I'm no Bible scholar, but surely that verse intends to illustrate the magnitude of what might be possible if one has enough faith?'

'I pray about lots of things, Gill. Expecting answers to my petitions requires a measure of faith. Adding a mountain to my daily list didn't seem like a big deal at the time.'

'Take me back to 1992. Can you tell me what motivated you to start praying for the mountain?'

'It seems a bit silly now. I had a neighbour, a farmer, who fell ill with some unusual cancer. I called on him one day to encourage him. I said I would pray every day for his healing.'

'That was kind of you. How did your neighbour respond?'

Margo gave a sad sigh. 'He said his cancer was inoperable, and he saw no possibility of healing. Then I quoted him that same verse I told you, because I believe nothing is impossible with our Creator.'

'And how did he respond?'

Margo took off her glasses again to stare at the horizon. She wiped the side of her left eye and said, 'He told me in no uncertain terms he wasn't a believer. Then in words I won't repeat, he told me I could clear off and pray for the damn mountain instead.' Her hands clasped together in her lap, and she pulled an apologetic face. 'I was so indignant! In a moment of anger, I promised him I would.'

'I'm sorry. That was a harsh response to your kindness. How did he fare?'

'He died within the year. But not before he'd tried to make a fool of me. There wasn't a soul in this glen who didn't get to know about my rash little pledge.' She jabbed a thumb over her right shoulder towards the mountain. 'But I kept it.'

Gill gave her an affirming smile. 'Well done.' He pulled open a pad and started to jot down a few facts. 'Do you feel any regret?'

'I keep on forgiving him. I never regretted offering to help.'

'And you never stopped praying.'

Margo sighed. 'Never. Not even when the burden of it seemed like a punishment for my anger.'

'What burden?'

'Praying and not getting an answer. I'm used to getting answers. For thirty-two years, I have prayed about it every day. Most days, just for a moment or two. But the memory of it …' She trailed off and laughed. 'Listen, it was the last rash promise I ever made anyone.'

'When did you realise that the mountain was beginning to change?' said Gill.

'Earlier this year. The mountain is pretty remote, so the only people climbing it are the most dedicated walkers. They all carry devices to tell them what height they are at, and a few had noticed the mountain was forty centimetres lower this January compared to last. Then someone was up in April and found it was more than a metre lower. That's when it made the local paper. One of the climbing clubs said that at this rate, the mountain would no longer be a munro in a year or two. Well, someone read the story and remembered my promise to the farmer.'

'And the rest is history,' said Gill.

'Indeed.' Her bosom heaved while she suppressed another laugh. 'Now someone is running a petition to stop me praying! *Save Teanga* dot something or other. I think it's their idea of a joke.'

'And will you?'

'Stand up a second,' said Margo, springing to her feet and taking him lightly by the hands. 'From here, do you think the mountain is getting any smaller?'

Gill squinted at the distant object. 'Well, I don't have a historical reference point, but I guess, at this distance, if it lost a few metres, you'd hardly notice.'

'And that Gill is a great lesson about prayer. It's often hard to know if you are having an effect, but once you do, your faith increases,' she said, moving towards the kitchen.

Gill followed her to the door. 'Can I ask one last question?'

'Of course.'

'And my apologies. I can't speak as a believer.'

'Not a problem. Go on.'

'I can imagine why God might listen to a prayer to heal a person with cancer, but why would he bother about moving a mountain?'

'Do you take exercise, Gill?'

'I run. Most mornings.'

'And you run with no particular destination in mind. You're just strengthening your body?'

'I guess.'

'Well, that's why I'm praying for my mountain. I'm strengthened by knowing my Creator is answering me.'

The interview ended as the two dogs bounced into the kitchen, demanding her attention. She waved warmly at him as he drove off, and he responded in kind. Perplexed, he wondered what to make of her story.

Chapter 9

As he arrived back at Crinan, a darkening sky was laying down a carpet of soft rain. He called first at the boatyard, but the gates were locked, and all the lights were off. Through the fence, the outline of the Bounty was just visible on the slipway. Alongside her stood two large multi-terrain vehicles with trailers. An industrial rib, in excess of eight metres, dwarfed a much smaller vessel on the adjacent trailer. Bright yellow and shaped like a fat torpedo, it bristled with instruments. Gill did little more than glance into the yard before jumping back in the car and driving down to the hotel.

He found George Henderson's makeshift HQ in the public bar attached to the hotel. The man stooped over three large marine maps while Salina Ahmed stood on his right-hand side, circling her finger over a particular feature. In the background, Arthur Deveron nursed a pint glass while PC Jeffries and another uniformed officer pecked at cups of tea.

Salina noticed him and smiled briefly before dropping her gaze back to the maps. Henderson swept a finger across a series of rocky bays.

'Your wee submarine is no use to us in here,' he said. 'It's all nooks and crannies, and the whole lot is covered in kelp as tall as a house.'

'I agree,' said Salina. 'The DSV is mostly for deeper water. If the bodies are still in the area, that's where they'll be.'

'More likely they'll be off Rathlin by now,' said Jeffries. 'Have you any idea what the currents are like around here?'

'She does,' said Arthur, smiling through a long sip.

Salina glanced across at him, then back at the map. 'Corryvreckan,' she announced. 'That's our best bet. That's where we should search first.'

Henderson shook his head slowly. 'I keep telling you; there just isn't the power in that thing to pull down a decent sea boat. This sinking was either a collision or human error.'

'The evidence on the boat doesn't suggest either of those scenarios,' said another man at the bar. 'Besides, Dan was a bloody good skipper.'

Henderson searched the room for a familiar face. 'Pete, you fish around Jura. Any sign of the whirlpool being stronger than usual?'

Pete was sitting at the bar, his back to the proceedings. Grey and slightly stooping, he did not respond right away. 'Might be,' he said at last without turning round.

'What's that supposed to mean?' snapped Henderson. 'Either it's bigger or it isn't.'

'It ain't a piece of clockwork, Mr Henderson. The power in that pool depends on a lot of things. The speed of the current for a start. And the state and size of the tide. Course, the weather conditions play a role.'

'But speaking generally, do you think the pool might be strong enough to take down Dan's boat?'

Pete took a long slow pull on his pint before speaking over his shoulder. 'Best if you take a look for yourself.'

'What's the plan for tomorrow?' asked Gill, trying to defuse the confrontation.

'I've got a support vessel coming up from Campbeltown tonight,' said Henderson. 'We'll get the DSV kindly provided by the Marine Laboratory loaded up first thing in the morning, then head over to Scarba.'

'May I tag along?' Gill asked.

Henderson turned to face him. 'I'm grateful to you for connecting us to the St Andrews team, but you've no official justification for being on the boat.'

'Actually, he has,' said Salina.

'How so?'

'We rely on a mixture of corporate and public sponsors to maintain our services,' she said. 'To keep the money coming in, we need a certain amount of publicity. Mr McArdle is featuring us in *Mysterious Scotland*, so if we're going to help you tomorrow, I'll need him on the support vessel.'

Henderson said nothing while he buttoned up his jacket and prepared to leave. 'Very well. I'll see you all first thing in the morning,' he said at last.

A ripple of "good nights" went around the bar as all the officials went out to their cars. Arthur bought himself another pint and fell into conversation with Pete, leaving Gill and Salina to sit beside the maps.

'Thanks for that,' he said.

'I was serious about the feature,' said Salina. 'And I'd like you to do some voice commentary for a short film I plan to shoot tomorrow.'

'Ewan McGregor not available then?'

'Bit out of my price range. Your voice will do.'

Gill raised an eyebrow in her direction.

'You know, authentically Scottish and a little bookish.'

'Well, I'm flattered, I think,' said Gill. 'Right. It's a deal. Let me buy you a tomato juice, and then I really must go and work on some copy.'

The service vessel gunned its engines as it reversed against the sea gates at the entrance to the Crinan Canal. Gill watched as the skipper expertly manoeuvred his boat, the size of a large trawler, in the confined space, then jumped ashore to make fast. He glanced at the boat's name and then at the captain's name badge. 'Your ship?' he asked.

Captain Quinn jerked his thumb towards his first mate. '10% his, 40% mine. The rest belongs to a bank.'

It was just before dawn, and Gill was still trying to muster his enthusiasm for the trip. It had been a short night, and he wasn't feeling conversational. He watched, his hands deep in his pockets, as Arthur and the skipper of the MV Harlequinn fussed over the loading of the DSV. It was past high tide, and the crew were itching to leave the shallowing berth. With the mini-submarine safely stowed, they soon made their way out to sea, heading west towards Jura before tacking north towards Scarba. The short journey allowed the team enough time to fine-tune the plan for the day.

'We know the *Bounty* came ashore on the west side of Jura,' said Henderson. 'The data we recovered from her GPS recorder confirms that her course took her south from Oban then westwards through the Gulf of Corryvreckan.' Henderson stopped to tap at the digital map that dominated the wheelhouse. 'At the mid-point in the channel, her movements became erratic. Then the device stopped recording.'

'Any of her gear show up?' asked Quinn.

Henderson shook his head. 'No sign of debris, nor the crew. We presume that anything not fixed on the boat will have drifted south and westwards.'

'And you still want to risk putting a submersible down in these waters?' said Quinn.

'She's a tough wee boat,' said Salina. 'And we need to know what caused the accident.'

The captain nodded, then tapped the map. 'Okay. I suggest I drop you here, just below Barnhill at the entrance to the channel. Sailing in that direction, you'll have the force of the tide behind you.'

'Is that safe?' asked Gill.

'It's the only practical way to do it,' Salina replied. 'The speed of the tide won't be too bad at depth, maybe eight knots. The DSV can manage twelve knots in any direction, so if we need to slow down, we'll keep the thrusters ticking over in reverse.'

'I will pass through the channel ahead of you and hold station in Pig Bay,' said the captain. 'I'm assuming the rib will stay above your location at all times?'

'We stay connected to the rib via a radio beacon,' said Arthur. 'You'll be patched in. We can all chat football or whatever.'

'Science and exploration please, Arthur,' said Salina giving him a mock frown. 'Right, we need to get suited up.'

'Hang on,' said Gill. 'You're going with him?'

'I'm second pilot on the DSV,' said Salina. I'd offer you a shot, but it's tight enough with two of us.'

Gill raised his hands. 'I'll follow your progress from the Harlequinn.'

The next hour progressed slowly while Salina and Arthur went through instrument checks. When the extending crane on the deck of the Harlequinn finally deployed the DSV to the water, Arthur spent another thirty minutes testing the propulsion system and the data link. During the wait, Gill observed a long low farmhouse on the brow of a low hill on the northern tip of Jura. He remarked on the building's remoteness to the captain when he returned to the vessel's control room.

'That's Barnhill,' said the captain. 'George Orwell lived there for a spell in the 1930s when he was writing *Nineteen Eighty-four*.'

'When he wasn't out swimming,' added Jack, the first mate.

Captain Quinn smiled. 'The story goes that old George was taking a trip to the mainland with his son. On the way back, his engine broke down, and the current pushed them through the Corryvreckan channel. They had to abandon their boat and swim to a skerry to avoid being swept out to sea.'

'That's nice to know,' Gill remarked. With its engines idling, he could see the Harlequinn was already drifting sideways away from the rib.

Quinn lifted the radio mic. 'DSV, this is Harlequinn. Radio check.'

'Harlequinn, DSV. Loud and clear.'

'DSV. We're entering the channel now. Shout if you need us.'

Salina's voice came back across the data link. 'Harlequinn, this is DSV. We've started our descent. Water visibility is excellent. Water speed as predicted. See you on the other side.'

Gill listened to the communications back and forth as the DSV managed its descent to the sea floor. As he understood it, the plan was to sweep through this section of the seabed and search the flooded canyon to its maximum depth of two hundred and twenty metres. Later in the dive, the DSV would approach a pinnacle of rock. Rising from the seabed to within thirty metres of the surface, this natural obstruction in the rapidly flowing water was the source the whirlpool.

From his vantage point high above the water, Gill could see the surface water begin to boil and race. He imagined the massive volume of water, driven by the changing tide, constrained by the narrowing gap between the islands.

'Think of the whirlpool as a giant eddy,' said Jack to no one in particular. 'The pinnacle is like a dirty great rock planted in the middle of a fast-flowing river. Everything downstream of the stone gets tossed about as the water cascades around it.'

'Enough to take down a fishing boat?' asked Gill.

Quinn smiled. 'It's spectacular to see, but it didn't have enough power to sink Orwell's punt.'

'What do you think happened to the *Bounty*?' said Henderson, cradling a cup of coffee.

'My money would be on a collision,' said Jack. 'Something to knock her off balance. It would account for the erratic GPS signal before she submerged.'

'Or maybe one of Mr McArdle's eels,' said Quinn, looking straight ahead.

'Naw. It'll have been a sub. Russian. British. Who knows? But it's happened before.'

The chatter in the background became calm and business-like. Salina was operating lights and cameras, constantly confirming course corrections with Arthur. Fish, corals, crabs, rock formations were her audio backdrop to the slow journey down the channel.

After twenty minutes, the fast-moving water had propelled the Harlequinn several hundred metres ahead of the rib. Quinn periodically grunted and swore as he worked to keep his boat aiming at the open sea at the end of the channel.

'You can see it now, Gill,' he said. Two hundred metres just off the starboard bow. He pointed ahead to a stretch of water where great boils tore at the surface and eddies crisscrossed each other before disappearing into the eye of the whirlpool. Henderson stood close to the window, his binoculars scanning for anything capable of sinking a fishing boat. Quinn throttled back. The force of the water moving through the channel was enough to keep the ship moving at a steady pace.

An alarm like the ringing of an old-fashioned telephone sounded in the wheelhouse. 'Depth alarm,' shouted Jack from the navigation counter. 'Kill our speed, Quinn.'

Quinn swiftly threw the twin engines into reverse. 'Give me numbers, Jack,' he called as the boat's momentum slowed dramatically.

'Got fifteen metres of water dead ahead,' shouted Jack.

'Bollocks,' muttered Quinn. 'The charts say twenty-two metres minimum at the pinnacle. Swap places.'

Jack swiftly moved over to the steering controls while Quinn moved around and hunched over the sounder display. 'Ten points to port, Jack. Ahead slow,' said Quinn, lifting his head to get visual confirmation of the instrument's readings.

'Trouble, Mr Quinn?' said Henderson.

Quinn shook his head. 'We've got plenty of water. It's just that the damn rock isn't where it's supposed to be.' He snatched up the mic and spoke to the submersible. 'DSV, this is Harlequinn.'

Salina's voice came back. 'Go ahead, Harlequinn.'

'DSV, be advised that we're seeing differences between our topography readings and our mapping software. Specifically, we read the pinnacle ten metres higher than the maps.'

Arthur's voice could be heard, muffled in the background before Salina came back. 'Harlequinn, we also have strange readings. What did you say is the maximum depth of the trench?'

'DSV, at your position charts say two-one-nine metres.'

'Harlequinn, we are at two-thirty, and we have lost sight of the seabed.'

'Hold station, DSV. We are coming around.'

Jack moved back to the instrument panel while Quinn assessed where to make his turn. Easing into reverse with his left hand down, he coaxed the boat to a gradual standstill. When she was broadside to the fast-flowing channel, he gunned the engines and powered Harlequinn round and back up in the direction she had come. At full power, it took several minutes against the flowing tide to get back to the rib. He held station above the DSV long enough to get a fix on the depth. Then he powered up again, away from the smaller craft. Once he was at a safe distance, he executed another turn.

'DSV, we have you thirty metres clear of the bottom. Depth is two-six-zero metres at your position.'

Arthur's voice crackled over the radio. He sounded calm but puzzled. 'Harlequinn, we find background water speed has increased to ten knots. We're losing some ground.'

Henderson saw the danger first. 'Quinn. Deeper than expected water here and narrower at the top. The water speed is only going to increase.'

In the background, Jack had been punching numbers on a laptop. 'DSV, be advised that the gradient on the approach to the pinnacle is revised from eight degrees to fourteen degrees.

Arthur's voice in the DSV was clearly audible this time. 'We'll have to go around it. You okay with that, Salina?'

Salina took a few seconds to respond. 'Too much uncertainty. Hold course for now but take us up.'

Salina's voice on the radio again, calmly. 'Harlequinn, this is DSV. We are aborting the dive. Standby for recovery.'

'DSV, we'll go ahead of you. We'll confirm what's in your path.'

Harlequinn moved down the channel again, slightly south of its track on the first pass. Henderson, meanwhile, had unfurled his marine maps. 'I've never known one of these things to be wrong. I don't understand.'

'Harlequinn, this is DSV.' Tension had crept into Salina's voice for the first time. 'Speed now twelve knots and increasing. We can't risk recovery. We're going to run the rapids.'

Jack glanced at Gill and tapped the sounder screen in front of him. The torpedo body of the DSV was rising as it bore down on the slopes of the submerged mountain.

'Do they have enough space?' whispered Gill.

No one answered him. Everyone glanced at the torrent of water around the boat, then at the on-screen drama in digital technicolour, then back to the water. Moments later, the DSV crested the rock with three metres to spare.

'DSV, we are proceeding with recovery,' said Quinn, as if nothing had happened.

'Hold fire, Harlequinn. We've got tranquil water in the immediate shelter of the pinnacle.' The mic sounded muffled while Salina and Arthur talked offline. 'We're going to catch our breath here. Will update you shortly.'

Quinn nodded. 'Proceed with caution, DSV.'

He moved away from the comms equipment before tapping Henderson on the arm. 'You're the safety guy. Are you still okay with this?'

Beads of sweat had formed on Henderson's brow. 'They seem to know what they're doing,' he said.

Quinn nodded curtly. 'Maybe this channel did for the *Bounty* after all.'

'I'm beginning to see that it might,' said Henderson.

Things settled for a few moments. Then Salina came back on comms. 'Harlequinn. DSV is now skirting the pinnacle on its south side.' She went quiet for a few more moments. 'The whirlpool is an amazing sight from below. The vortex is visible, like a long silver funnel reaching down to mid-water.'

Muffled voices again, conversation in broken snatches. '... Beautiful shot ... Camera angle ... water speed down to three knots ... lift the lights a little.'

'Harlequinn, we're seeing a deep eddy below the whirlpool. It's mainly seaweed, but we can see some debris. We're going to take a closer look.'

A few more moments of broken conversation as the DSV kept the line open. Then Salina's voice again. 'It's a pocket of trapped water. The water speed is negligible.'

Arthur spoke. 'Yeah, it's mainly natural stuff, but I can see flotsam that's probably come off a fishing boat.'

They all heard a muffled bump. Gill heard Salina gasp just before Arthur unleashed a volley of swearing.

Quinn pulled the mic sharply towards him. 'DSV, what is your status?'

Salina's voice rose in pitch. 'There's a body in the debris cloud. It just bounced off our forward window.'

Two hours later, the recovery of the DSV was nearly complete. Gill watched first Salina, then Arthur, ease themselves out of their vessel. They stood on the deck of the Harlequinn, rubbing blood back into cramped limbs. Salina was drenched with sweat, so he fetched a blanket from the wheelhouse and offered it to her. Quinn and his crew made fast the DSV, then turned their attention to the rib that patiently bobbed beside the larger boat. A single body bag hung tethered to its side, partially submerged in the water.

Gill sat in the hotel bar, shaken by the day's events. He'd taken a short run around the Crinan peninsula to get time to think. He was lingering over his first beer and was on the verge of ordering a second when Salina appeared.

'How are you doing?' he asked as she settled across the table from him.

She flashed him a wide smile meeting his gaze before dropping her face a little. 'Better, now I've had a long soak. Still a bit embarrassed about today, though.'

'No need. You got quite a shock.'

Her hair fell across her face, and she sat back, sweeping it over her shoulder. 'It was just so sudden. I mean, it's not the first time I've found a body.'

'Regular thing in your line of work?'

'Not regular. But my career is all about exploring interesting bits of the sea. And "interesting" often means dangerous. I've come across a few dead anglers.'

Gill winced. In sympathy, he said, 'Dead bodies are a daily hazard in my profession too.'

'You're an archaeologist. Yours have been dead for centuries,' said Salina.

'I'll grant you that.' He got up and organised a drink for her, plus some menus. When he came back, she was deep in thought, twisting a ring round and round the fourth finger of her left hand. A slim band of white gold, mounted with a single large diamond.

'Thanks,' she said, flicking the ring back in place.

'I've not seen that before,' he said. 'It's a beauty.'

She looked down at the ring as if seeing it for the first time. 'It's quite new. I don't like wearing it when I'm working.'

Gill watched her face for a few seconds. 'He must have been quite worried about you today.'

Salina's dark eyes met his for a few seconds, then dropped again. 'What about you?' she asked. 'Do you have a significant other?'

'Not at the moment,' said Gill, pausing. 'Actually, not for quite a few moments.'

'Not met the right girl?'

He shrugged. 'The last year has been about other things. Getting the magazine going for one thing. Not much time for personal stuff.'

Salina nodded. 'Yeah. You get times like that.'

'I'm virtually a workaholic. Serves me right if I don't make time to socialise.'

She pushed back her hair again. 'I'm the same. It takes you so many years to get this far in your career. Once you are in the sweet spot, you just want to do as much as you can.' She was looking straight at him again. Something in her eyes made her look a little sad.

Changing the subject, he asked, 'Is Arthur joining us?'

Salina shook her head. 'No. He's going to get beer and chips next door and have an early night.'

'Are you guys okay for the next couple of days?' said Gill.

'Fine,' said Salina. 'We still have a chance to find the second body. And from a scientific point of view, we want to study the change in the seabed.'

'That looked weird,' said Gill. 'I can't think I've ever heard of that before, not around Britain anyway.'

Salina was nodding vigorously. 'Exactly. Scotland is geologically pretty static. It's not like Iceland, where you get a new island pop up every other year.'

'Take care out there,' said Gill.

'You're not joining us?'

'Not tomorrow. I've got a dig going on at Montrose, which finishes in a few days. I need to wrap up a few things. Then I'll overnight with my dad. He lives in the area.'

Salina nodded but said nothing.

'I'll come back over here on Friday morning if that's okay. Join you and the merry crew of the Harlequinn for the final day.'

'Great. We should have a rough edit of our video by then. Can I mail you the draft narrative for your voice-over?'

'Please do,' he said.

Chapter 10

Salina wakes with her head throbbing, lying on her side, staring at a wall of mottled silver. As her sight clears, she watches ripples form in the metal, the globules tripping over each other, sliding down the wall in vibrant molten streams. Startled by its purity, she decides the freshly melted silver is the most beautiful thing she has ever seen in her life.

But then the rest of her senses crowd in. She's trapped in another dream. In a different boat.

'Are ye aw'richt, lass?' A heavy hand grips her shoulder. She turns from the stream of silver to face a man with gentle eyes and a wild, whiskery beard. 'Ye tak quite a fall.'

She remembers her sore head and runs a hand over her left temple and up over her skull. Her hand comes back sticky. She expects to see blood, but instead, her fingers are daubed in golden caviar. She glances at the man leaning over her. His face, hair and waxed oilskin are smeared with fish scales. He holds his hands towards her and gently eases her into a sitting position. 'Look intae my eyes, girl.' He grips her firmly by her jaw, staring intently at her for a few moments, then nods, dropping his hands. 'Easy now. These decks are gey slippy when you're tired.'

A younger man appears at his shoulder and glares down at her. 'Told you it's bad luck to have women on the boat.'

The older man turns and scowls at him. 'Ye ken what I think. While we dinnae hae enough sons in this family, I'll gae tae sea with any dochter that cares tae fish.'

The younger man turns away. 'Herrin' boat's no place for a girl, that's all.'

'When you're ready, gentlemen.' A voice, loud and authoritative, booms from the stern of the boat. Salina can hear the grunt of men's effort and the creak of ropes tightening against wood.

The old man touches her arm and points to an open hatch on the boat's deck. 'As soon as ye can, lass. Back tae the baskets.' Salina looks about her for the first time. She is sitting on the black deck of a large fishing boat, the first rays of dawn casting their light on a busy harbour scene. Around her, six men and two boys work to haul baskets of fish up the high wall of the harbour. The molten silver she has seen is, in fact, a river of herring scales trickling down the wall from boxes on the quayside.

Nowhere can she see any form of machine or automation, and she recognises that fishing hasn't looked like this for over a century. At the stern of the boat, the two biggest men tug on ropes attached to a pulley, their raw power propelling a heavy basket up the wall. Hands reach out from the quayside above to grasp the basket, and the haulers pause to wipe their brows. One in a stained leather smock calls out in the booming voice.

'Get moving now. We've less than an hour to get back out on this tide.'

A head pops up from the hatch, a blond girl in her late teens; her hair pulled back tightly from her face to reveal appealing features smeared with dirt. 'Come on, Sals. I'm dying down here.'

'Coming,' Salina hears herself say. She starts to move but finds her limbs sore and heavy under her greasy smock. It takes great effort to swing her legs over the hatch and ease herself down the slippery stairs. She finds herself in a dark cavern illuminated by three oil lanterns. Below decks, the boat is partitioned into square sections, faced with boards held in place by metal slots. Behind the boards, innumerable dead herring lie in coils. In one of the sections, a lad of about fifteen stands amongst the fish, raking them into baskets using a crude metal scoop. The blond girl taps Salina on her arm and points to a half-filled section. 'Do starboard five just now, or Jim will be yelling at us tae trim the boat.

Salina looks at the section, which is about two metres square. She estimates that it contains almost a tonne of fish. She clambers in and starts to scoop.

'Mare baskets, Annie,' calls the lad in the adjoining section. Annie duly delivers a small stack of filthy wicker baskets before dragging a full one down a greasy gangway towards the stern, where another hatch spills welcome sunlight into the centre of the boat. Two ropes are dangling with a rough metal hook on each. Annie deftly clips the hooks onto the loaded basket and stands back as it disappears in a flash, a few herring falling in its wake.

Salina pushes her aching body to work. Mechanically, relentlessly, basket after basket. Slowly the level of fish around her goes down. Eddie, the lad beside her, finishes his section and starts on another.

'What's left?' Jim's head peers down from the hatch.

'Ten cran,' says Annie, dragging another basket to the hatch.

'Nearer fourteen,' Eddie contradicts.

'That'll do,' says Jim. 'We've eighty-five on the quayside. Build up the boards. We're going back to sea.' His head disappears, and they hear him calling out orders on the deck. Salina sees Annie glance at her. Eddie has already stepped out of his section and swoops up behind them, grabbing them both by the waist. 'Hell of a payday.'

Annie's weary eyes fall towards the deck. 'I dunno, Eddie. I'm dead beat already.' She looks up at him. 'I'm not sure I can do all this again today.'

Salina feels his grip tighten. 'Course you can. It's Friday. Remember? We get tomorrow off.'

Annie doesn't seem convinced. 'How much you reckon is still in the water?'

Eddie looks up at one of the lanterns swinging from the roof. 'We've got in two-thirds of the nets. Mind you, the first two were blank, so we might catch the same again.'

Annie sinks wearily to her knees, looking close to tears.

'You go on,' Salina hears herself say to Eddie. 'We'll finish up down here.'

She kneels for a minute, holding Annie's hand until the girl's silent sobbing burns itself out. Then she gives it a gentle tug. 'Hey, don't let them see you like this. I've let the side down once already. I need you to score one for the girls.'

Annie looks up and smiles, her fish-stained cheeks streaked with clean pink skin. 'Aye, aye, skipper,' she says meekly.

They work together, lifting the heavy boards and rebuilding the fish pens until they are just above waist high. Feeling better, Annie chatters about how she had never seen the pens so full as the last haul. As the fish had flowed from the nets above, down the wooden chutes, they had built up the pens board by board until they could hold no more. They feel a sudden lurch and hear a barrage of swearing from the deck above. Eddie's head drops into sight. 'The Cap'n just bounced *Gentle Bow* to make it through the cut-mouth. Come and see.'

Annie is first to scramble up the ladder, and as Salina follows her, she is dazzled as she emerges into full daylight. It takes a few seconds for her eyes to adjust and comprehend the incredible industry around her. The stern of the boat is shaded under a partially raised sail. The men use oars to propel their vessel across the shallowing harbour in the way a gondolier would use a pole to guide his craft. Behind them, another herring boat is not so fortunate. The skipper of *Gentle Bow* has miscalculated trying to outrun Salina's much larger craft, and she is stuck fast by the retreating sea in the mouth of the inner harbour. No amount of pushing by her crew will move her until the tide returns.

Meanwhile, Salina's boat is clear and making its way through the outer harbour towards the sea. All around her, boats are making ready to sail or are washing down. She tries to count them but loses track once she gets past fifty. She can't see the inner harbour from here, but a forest of masts is evidence of a further large fleet. The quaysides in every direction, liberally stained with silver, are laden with boxes.

Horses and carts stand in long queues, working relentlessly to ferry herring up to gutting sheds.

'Scuse us, ladies.' Two fresh-faced young men squeeze past them and into the hold below.

'Off for a lie down?' chides Annie as they pass.

'Only if you're comin' with me,' says one. The other lad slaps his friend's arm and gives a sharp nod toward Jim.

'Archie, John! Bread and tea. And be quick about it,' Jim barks from the high tiller at the stern of the boat.

'The men cook?' Salina asks.

'If you call it cooking,' Annie mutters. 'Mind you put on plenty of butter,' she calls to the heels of the disappearing men. Then she lies down on the deck, covers her eyes with an arm and goes straight to sleep.

Salina scans the deck. It is entirely open, and the perilous gunnel rises just a few centimetres higher than the deck boards. Below lies the cavernous hold she toiled in with Annie and Eddie. He sits with another lad at Jim's feet. They look dazed, beyond exhausted, and after a few minutes, Jim chases them away to get some rest. Five older men relax on the deck, working the sail with gentle efficiency. If they want for sleep, they don't show it. Instead, they quietly talk, adjust their ropes, and smoke strong cigarettes, one after another.

The boat is leaving the shore behind, pushed along by the gentlest of winds across a smooth sea. The coastline at their back is matched by a parallel one ten miles away. She knows this place. The Bass Rock, the Isle of May, and other familiar landmarks in the Firth of Forth. Glancing back at the harbour, she pictures the East Neuk villages. Pittenweem perhaps? Or St Monans? No, a more prominent place, probably Anstruther. The town is smaller than she remembers it, tightly gathered around a church spire she doesn't recognise.

Salina has rarely seen the Forth so still. Dotted around them, a few herring boats are still working on their catch, nets hanging over the sides like silver cables, boats shrouded in gulls. Occasionally they pass a bobbing float marked with a name or number, and eventually, she deduces that Jim is looking for his own mark. Piecing it together, she realises her vessel abandoned half its nets last night when it could hold no more fish. They had landed what they could before slipping out in the retreating tide to haul the rest. Her stomach lurches when she realises how much physical effort will soon be required of her.

A cry from the bow alerts the crew to their marker. Carefully the men tack the boat to reach it. To keep the nets taut in the water, they must haul from the east, pulling the boat against the ebbing tide. When Jim barks, the weary crew assemble again. All have eaten, and some have slept. Their disposition is like survivors on a battlefield, getting ready to face another onslaught. And when it comes, it is like a battle. The men spread out across the deck, working together to drag the heavy boat, inch by inch, towards some far away anchor stone, gathering the net taut between them, shaking and flicking until the air seems full of fish springing free from the gill nets. Annie and Salina work like devils, using brooms to sweep the fish towards the chutes. Below them, Eddie is either singing or swearing as he wages war with the torrent of fish. And the gulls! They appear from nowhere but fight like a swarm, grabbing fish that fall back in the water, grabbing fish that fly through the air, swooping among their legs to lift fish from the deck. The younger man who had propositioned Annie grabs one of the birds by its feet and flings it down the hatch. They hear Eddie explode in a fury, the bird emerging moments later, its wings beating hard as a herring disappears down its gullet, even as it lifts away from the boat.

A little to the north of them, another boat is waging a similar war against a tide of fish. Gradually, the path of the two boats converges.

'Don't recognise her,' says Archie, nodding in the direction of the black hulk beside them, gradually settling lower in the water.

'Look at her number. An Arbroath boat,' says Jim, grunting against the weight of the line.

'They've got a "dark one" too,' says John.

Jim reaches forward and claps the back of the boy's head so hard, he turns and scowls with pain. 'Mind your mouth, boy.'

Salina isn't sure if she is flattered or offended. Instead, she distracts herself by studying the nearby vessel. It takes a few seconds to spot him through the veil of fish and darting gulls. Standing in the other boat's stern, she sees a large olive-skinned man working with all his might.

'Thought they'd shot over us,' says Jim. 'Looks like we'll be okay.'

On and on they work, until finally, the tail of the last net drops into the boat. Everyone lies gasping on the deck. From below, Eddie reports they have eighty cran on board. A total of one hundred and sixty-five for the night.

Salina sits numb with tiredness, a single fish lying across the palm of her hand. Most of the fish are already dead, drowned during the long night as the net held them in a silent stranglehold. But this one lays gulping in her hand, its eyeballs flicking left and right, the creamy golden spew of its eggs smearing across her hands. Salina does a calculation. 165 cran, 1200 fish to a cran, and this is just one boat from hundreds. The whole fleet working half the nights of the year. No wonder the herring would one day die out.

A shout from the skipper brings her back into focus. 'All hands.' The anchor stone is stuck, locked tight against a skerry while they towed the boat back towards it. Exhausted, the crew line up on the rope, with Salina at the back. Then they begin to haul. The work is methodical, retrieving the remaining slack on the rope until the boat stands above the anchor stone. The trick is to pull the cord fast enough against the tide so that when the boat reaches the point where she is above the stone, the momentum will carry her past the obstacle, allowing the anchor to spring free. If that doesn't work, they'll have to cut the rope, go to the beach and find another suitable stone.

'She's coming, lads,' Jim encourages them. He doesn't want to spend his day off looking for a replacement.

'Hang on.' He's peering over the stern now. On either side of the boat, a pipe of molten silver rises out of the water. 'It's the Arbroath man's nets,' he calls. 'Let it go. We're gonna have to wait while he hauls past us.'

Salina isn't ready for what happens next. The rest of the crew stand back from the rope, dropping it to the deck so that it barrels back into the water. If she'd known what was going to happen, she'd not have stood among the coils, feeling them tighten to her ankles, throwing her on her back and dragging her towards the low gunnel. Only Annie sees what is happening and reaches out urgent fingers as she screams for help. The blow to Salina's head as she passes over the gunnel is painful, and at first, the cold water is a relief. She doesn't feel panic. Not straight away. But then she looks up and sees the boat's silhouette against the sky.

Diminishing.

Growing fainter.

The stone hits the seabed, and she halts in mid-water. Other than the dimly lit silver bodies of a few dozen dead herring flowing past her in the tide, everything is still.

A gulp of air leaves her lungs, and as she watches it dash to the surface, she realises she is going to die. A moment of panic brings with it a mouthful of seawater. She chokes, and the rest of her precious air escapes. Above her, a shape looms. A semi-familiar figure, bulky and dark-skinned, is swimming down towards her with powerful strokes as her consciousness slips away.

Salina wakes with a gasp in the hotel bedroom. Even though the dream is over, her chest is compressed and empty of air. She rolls out of bed and drops to the floor to fight for a breath. Then her lungs burn as they fill.

She lies, gasping. Her hands are clean, and her clothes are dry, but at the back of her mouth, she's sure she can taste seawater.

Chapter 11

Gill was up and away from Crinan early on Thursday morning. His first stop was Montrose, where Fiona's team had almost finished the excavation of the Neolithic log boats. A small team from the National Museum were taking photos of the boats in situ, while other academics Gill knew from the university circuit were shown around by Gill's old colleague, Ed Johnson. Ed had spent the previous day working with Fiona. Together, they confirmed that two of the five boats were unfinished when the tsunami struck, adding significant credence to the boatyard theory. Satisfied he now had an important story to write, Gill knew he needed to follow Tony's advice and breathe life into the narrative. Slipping away from the survey area, he looked for a place to think.

Walking to the river and following it upstream for a few hundred metres, he eventually settled on a heathery knoll that overlooked the surrounding land. He studied the geography and tried to imagine how the terrain must have appeared eight thousand years ago, devoid of roads and towns. Scotland had been warmer back then; the ice ages were a distant memory. The basic shape of the Montrose basin would have looked like it did today, although its boundary would have been marshes rather than farmland.

The basin would have represented a safe harbour to the Neolithic hunter-gathers with its single navigable river leading to the sea. On the landward side of the bay, stands of oak and birch must have stretched for miles beyond the marshland. One of the many creeks leading into the marsh must have run a little deeper than the others, providing access to the forest. And it was in a place like this where one small community started to build crude boats.

In the near future, Fiona's samples would guide Ed Johnson to estimate when the Neolithic community had become established. Right now, the only date they knew for certain was that all industry had abruptly stopped on the day of the tsunami. While this ancient tribe had laboured to build its boats, a far-away submerged landscape was about to change. Sixty miles off the Norwegian coast and running almost two hundred miles lay a tenuous coastal shelf. This enormous ledge of sediment had accumulated from silt carried by hundreds of rivers as meltwater signalled the end of the last ice age. Building incrementally over thousands of years, the ledge of soft clay must have looked like submerged cliffs.

Whether it was an earthquake or some other geological event that triggered the disaster, the Storegga shelf collapsed in a series of massive landslides. As millions of cubic metres of sediment tumbled into deeper water, it set off a wave that would ripple across the Atlantic. On the Shetland Islands, a wave twenty metres high left a line of debris along its eastern shores. In Orkney and the mainland, the surge was smaller but devastating for human communities in its path.

Gill looked over the basin and imagined the surging waters spreading up from the coast, crushing everything. As with the Japan tsunami some years before, it had been a massive body of slow-moving water that inflicted damage rather than a fast-moving wave. The Storegga event wasn't just a ripple or a splash. It was a bulldozer tearing into the east coast of Scotland.

The ancient boat builders of Montrose would have been defenceless against the sea. Taking their chances among the trees and the tumbling debris, every man, woman and child must have died. Their possessions scattered, and their industry buried under a layer of sediment that had travelled hundreds of miles to smother them.

Gill was grateful for the sediment. Pale in colour, it was the fingerprint of the tsunami, and all across Scotland, people like him could find it today. But how could he bring this ancient tragedy to life? He set to work, casting the day of the disaster into the lives of an imaginary family. A father and his sons are in the woods, looking for timber. A mother and her girls patiently hollow out a boat using pieces of flint. All were caught in the act of simply living, just as the wave struck. The words come easily for him, spilling out into a notebook. Sketches too. Maps and drawings that would illustrate the events. In two hours, he had the whole magazine planned out. He finished by listing the various specialist sub-articles he would need. Some of those he would write himself, with others written by experts he could call on. One or two would need a contact from Tony Farquharson's little black book. While he thought of it, he texted Cassy, asking her to contact The Scottish Geological Society.

Later that afternoon, Gill was sitting in his father's kitchen typing up his notes, adding flesh to the bones of his story. Gordon had seemed surprised to see him, the telephone conversation of the previous evening apparently forgotten. Gordon was hard at work on the *Icthus*, sanding the boards of the new boat in preparation for painting. With his father content in his labours, Gill was relieved to have some time in front of his laptop. He was finishing up when Gordon came in and put the kettle on.

'She's looking good, Dad. Going to be a great little sea boat.'

'Aye, son. That she is.' Gordon stooped over the sink to wash the fine wood dust off his hands while glancing at one of his lists on the window sill. 'I don't suppose you had time to phone the weather station people?'

'Spoke to them this morning,' said Gill. 'The guy was quite apologetic. He said he'd had complaints from two other installations in the past couple of weeks. He reckons there must be a software fault in the GPS.'

'Can they fix it?'

'The other faulty machines are in Aberdeen and Inverness, so they are sending an engineer next week. They'll be in touch to make arrangements.'

Gordon nodded. 'I'll add that to my list for next week.' He bent to scribble on his notepad. When he turned back to Gill, his face suddenly fell. 'I'm so sorry, Gill, but a package came for you the other day. I don't recall exactly when. I forgot to give it to you.'

'Thanks,' said Gill. 'It's from the office. Nothing urgent. Where is it?'

'I put it in your room. I'm really sorry I forgot.'

'Dad, no problem.'

When Gordon settled, the two men fell into an easy conversation for over an hour. The west coast creel boat and recovery of a man's body had been on the news, giving Gill plenty to say. Meanwhile, a text exchange with Cassy confirmed his appointment with the Scottish Geological Society for Monday morning. Another discussion with Salina confirmed that he would be on the Harlequinn the following day. Because of the tides, he needed to arrive in Crinan by 10 am. That would mean another early start, so he and Gordon ate, then stretched their legs around Stonehaven Harbour before catching an early night.

Cassy's package lay on his bed, and without much enthusiasm, he slit it open and spilt the contents onto the bed. He immediately regretted this decision as the smell of old paper filled the tiny room. The package held half a dozen manila folders. He briefly opened each one and scanned the contents. Each contained several large pieces of paper, neatly folded and bound together by thin blue ribbons. He pulled out one set and observed the single word 'Secret' had been stamped on the top right-hand corner on every sheet in red ink. Beneath it, the word 'Admiralty' in faded blue ink. A quick inspection showed that all the contents had the same stamps. None had any covering letter or explanation of any kind. Gill thought for a moment, reluctant to expose himself to any wrongdoing. A secret from whom and for how long? He wouldn't know that until he looked at the material, so he randomly picked one and spread the contents on the bed.

A series of detailed but incomprehensible hand-drawn diagrams confronted him. One had survey terms he recognised, so he deduced it was some kind of map. Their vintage was anything from eighty to one hundred years old. It took a minute of head-scratching to decode that the hills on the map were, in fact, depressions, and the numbers scattered across the drawing were depths rather than heights. So, this was a map of the sea bed. A glance at the upper margin revealed some numbers he recognised as longitude and latitude. He tapped these coordinates into his phone and found they pointed to a patch of open sea two hundred kilometres east of Dundee. Casting this sheet aside, he scanned the others in the pack. In each, he found technical drawings that were beyond his comprehension. With gathering frustration, he realised he didn't understand any of the material.

He glanced at this watch. He needed sleep. The person sending the material had given no clue as to their intention or of their identity. He concluded that nothing here required his immediate attention. It would have to wait until the next issue was out and his in-tray less pressing. Bundling the sheets back into their respective folders, he caught sight of tiny indented letters on one folder. Holding it up to his bedside light, he angled the card until the light cast a shadow into the faded lettering. Someone had used an eraser to rub out the pencilled folder subject. It took a few minutes, but gradually he discerned, *Project Leviathan – cancelled June 1974*.

Early the following evening, Gill was tired after a long day spent in the control room of the Harlequinn. The ship was sailing past the southern coast of Mull, which meant that in half an hour, they would berth at Oban. He could see

Arthur leaning over the bow on the deck below, taking deep breaths of fresh air after another long stint in the DSV. Needing a diversion, Gill decided to join him.

Arthur's eyes were closed, and for a moment, Gill was uncertain if he should bother him.

'Hey, Gill.' Arthur swayed a little as the boat rose and fell in a gentle swell. Gill caught the odour of his sweat and wondered how Salina had coped in the confines of the small metal cabin.

'Good work again today,' said Gill, studiously avoiding the body bag lying in the shadow of the boat's high wheelhouse.

Arthur gave a deft little shrug. 'Two bodies, a nature video and plenty of boat-time. Been a busy three days.'

'Are you heading north after this?' On Saturday, Gill knew that the DSV was being transferred onto the Oban docks before collection by an ocean-going service vessel.

'No. There's another team coming up to join Salina for the Orkney leg. I've got some time off.'

Gill nodded. 'You'll be glad of some R&R.'

Arthur turned his face a little to glance at Gill sideways. 'Actually, I'll be working. Nothing for the Uni. It's a personal project.'

'Oh aye?' said Gill.

'It's an area where you might be able to help me. I'm writing a book, you see.'

'What about?'

Arthur surveyed him for a second. 'Exotic forms of sea life. Been working on it for a year or two.'

'Awesome,' said Gill. 'The Caithness eel must've been a real gift to you. Will that be your centrepiece?'

Arthur kept looking sideways at Gill. 'Aye, it'll get a page or two. I've got a few other ideas, but I'm not sure I should be telling you about those.' He forced his face into a smile. 'We are competitors, up to a point.'

'Fair enough,' said Gill. 'But if you need any reference material, I've built up quite a library on cryptozoology over the past nine months.'

'Thanks,' said Arthur, bobbing his head. 'Appreciate it.'

'Are you already published, or is this your first book?' asked Gill.

Arthur shrugged. 'I've published plenty, but all in academic fields.' He dropped into a friendlier posture. 'This is my first commercial book.'

Gill nodded vigorously. 'You'll never get rich on a researcher's salary. Any chance of professorship?'

Arthur shifted his stance and faced forward again. 'Not at my age. I applied for Salina's position, but I won't get it. They'll bring in some other bright young thing. So, I'll need to plough my own furrow.'

Gill couldn't suppress his surprise. 'Salina's leaving?'

'Taken a teaching job at Southampton Uni. It's marine biology but not quite her usual fieldwork and DSVs.'

Gill nodded slowly, joining pieces of information together. 'I saw her ring on Wednesday evening. I didn't realise she's giving this up.'

'It's a sudden thing,' said Arthur. 'I think her parents have pushed her into it. Apparently, they think she needs to get on with her life.'

'Now you mention it, she wasn't exactly bursting with excitement,' said Gill recalling the dinner conversation from two nights ago.

'I wouldn't go talking to her about it,' Arthur said, leaning forward to spit into the sea. 'A career-minded, British-born Pakistani woman? Parents with a traditional attitude to arranged marriage? A veritable cauldron of competing traditions. Total car crash.'

'Do you think she'll enjoy teaching?'

'I dunno. It's less risky than diving a DSV for a living. Anyway, her prospective hubby owns a chain of care homes down south, so I doubt she'll want for much.' Arthur sensed movement and glanced behind him. 'Watch out. All hands,' he muttered as Salina appeared on deck and walked towards them. She had changed into tan-coloured slacks and a white top. She seemed to realise the garment was too thin for the exposed deck and quickly folded her arms across her chest.

'You two look like a scene from Titanic,' she said as soon as she was in earshot.

'Thanks,' said Gill. 'I was just about to give Arthur a hug.'

Salina shuddered a little, perhaps her mental image or maybe the sudden crispness in the air. 'Gill, are you staying in town tonight? I've got a couple of hours tomorrow morning, so if you're up for it, I'd like to try and sync the draft voice-over to our video edit.'

'Happy to. I wasn't sure what time we'd be in, so I made a provisional booking at the Harbour Hotel.'

Salina turned to Arthur. 'What about you? Heading home tonight?'

Arthur shook his head. 'No, I'm heading up to Fort William tomorrow.'

'Research for your book?'

'Aye.'

Salina gave a slight bow. 'Thanks for piloting the DSV this week. Enjoy the change of pace.' She excused herself and returned to the wheelhouse.

'Right,' said Arthur. 'Better make sure the sub is safely stowed. I wouldn't trust these Harlequinn boys to tie my shoelace.'

Gill gave him a fleeting wave, then turned forward to watch Oban gradually loom up on the starboard bow. In the distance, he could just see the peak of Mrs McLean's shrinking mountain. And behind him lay the Corryvreckan sea stack, dramatically enlarged. Dare he phone the old lady and query where she thought her mountain might be going? Perhaps one person's answer to prayer was another person's coincidence? On reflection, he decided the kind old lady should be left in peace.

Chapter 12

Above the stands of towering kelp, eddies dance across the churning water. Soaring over this bizarre and changing landscape, the greatest vortex of them all reaches down to where the great sea stack lurks. If this maelstrom had a voice, its siren song would be, "Beware all you who dare traverse these waters."

So, we leave it behind now, to brood beneath the waves, until the next time we risk our lives in the Gulf of Corryvreckan.'

Gill and Salina sat hunched over Salina's PC while the video closed on the tip of the sea stack, as seen from below. Gradually the screen flared in the sunlight, and the whole picture faded to white.

'Excellent,' said Salina. 'You've got a great voice for this kind of thing. Gravelly and Scottish, but still really clear.'

'Thanks. The narrative is still a little cheesy, but we've made progress.'

'You're okay to work on the redraft?'

'Sure. Now that I've seen your video rough, I know what meter I'm working to. I'll mail you my revisions next week.'

'Cool.' Salina's smile was generous and open.

They packed up and walked through to reception. Gill ordered some coffees while Salina went to her room to fetch her bags. They sat sipping their drinks in silence while they waited for confirmation that the Harlequinn was ready to offload the DSV.

'I hope you don't mind me asking,' said Gill. 'When I was chatting to Arthur yesterday, he mentioned you're moving on.'

Salina pushed back into her chair and took a slow, deliberate sip of coffee.

Gill raised a hand. 'Sorry. Arthur said I shouldn't ask you about it. None of my business.'

Salina shook her head quickly. 'No, it's okay. It's just complicated.'

'Well, I hope you find happiness. And again, sorry for mentioning it.'

She didn't look at him but reached out suddenly across the space between the two chairs and stretched four fingers of her left hand across his wrist. A few moments passed before she spoke. 'You're a good person, Gill. If I'm honest, a little bit of me is envious of you.'

'How so?'

She turned to look at him. 'Your freedom. These past two weeks since I met you, you've done nothing but dash around Scotland doing a job you love.'

'But you have that too, don't you?'

She turned away and withdrew her hand. After another sip of coffee, she said. 'I've got other responsibilities,' she paused, looking for words. 'Duties.'

Her phone rang, and a brief exchange confirmed that the DSV was ready to go.

He stood and gathered up her laptop bag while she picked up her case. He wanted to speak but was suddenly awash in schoolboy uncertainty. She stood and waited for him. Her continuing attention was the permission he needed.

'Salina, you are a beautiful and intelligent woman. You've got your career at your feet. I don't understand why you need to compromise?'

Salina accepted the laptop onto her shoulder. 'I'm going to a good job. The National Oceanographic Centre is a world leader. I'll be proud to be associated with it. And maybe it's time I stopped messing around in boats.'

He stared at her but said nothing.

With her free right hand, she patted him gently in the middle of his chest. After the most fleeting of smiles she said, 'See you around, Gill McArdle.'

Twenty minutes later, Gill had tossed his bags in the back of his car when Arthur came over to say "Goodbye." They'd parked their cars next to each other, Arthur's solid, black 4x4 making Gill's road-weary Passat Estate look rather tired.

'I was thinking,' said Arthur, shaking his hand. 'I might take you up on your offer of a few books.'

'Sure. I'll get my office to email you a list of what we have.'

Arthur smiled. 'Great. Maybe we can meet up. Or I can come to Dundee if you like?'

The two men said their farewells, and Gill sat in his car, watching Arthur drive off first. The parting exchange with Salina left him feeling heavy. It was a Saturday, and if he was fair to his dad, he should start the long drive back to Stonehaven. Mindful the *Bounty* had distracted him from preparing the next magazine, he had one work-related task that would usefully break his journey. He pulled out his phone and tapped a number Cassy had emailed him yesterday.

The phone rang three times before a cheerful voice answered. 'Lochy Rectory. Padre Duncan Campbell speaking.'

'Padre, it's Gill McArdle here. I wonder if I could have a few minutes of your time.'

An hour later, Gill pulled up outside a pleasant, detached house in the centre of Fort Augustus. He took a second to absorb the surroundings. A row of pretty houses ran parallel to the River Lochy, and a little downstream in a westerly direction, he could see the turrets of a ruined castle and the distinctive outline of a distillery. To the east lay the Great Glen and Loch Ness. He turned to face the rectory and found the front door was already open. Padre Campbell was a slightly built but athletic-looking man with pale blue eyes and tidy grey hair. He gripped Gill's hand before waving a finger at him.

'I thought I recognised your name. Fantastic to meet you.'

Gill followed his host into a substantial front room, obsessively neat and lined with books. Duncan briefly waved a copy of *Mysterious Scotland* in the air before carefully laying it back onto a pile of magazines. He directed Gill to a comfortable armchair and left the room, returning moments later with a cafetiere of coffee. Conversation tumbled along, and Gill quickly found himself at ease.

'So, Gill, do all *Mys.Scot* journalists work on Saturdays?' Duncan leaned back in his chair; his short straight back pushed into a good posture.

Gill suppressed a smile. He'd only heard this slang for his magazine used around the office. He realised he was in the safe company of a fellow geek.

'Seven days a week, Duncan. In the happy service of all our readers.'

'Glad to hear it. How can I help you?'

'As I mentioned on the phone, it's an opportunistic call. I'm in the west working on a story while at the same time trying to get some context material for the *Caithness Kraken*.'

Duncan nodded as Gill continued. 'I've read your book on Celtic Cryptids; I thoroughly enjoyed that, by the way. You're as close as I'm going to get to an expert, and I wanted to ask what you made of the Caithness specimen?'

Duncan's shoulders rose and fell in a shallow shrug. 'That's a very open question. Help me answer you by telling me what you made of it?'

Gill glanced around the room. It was tidy and well-ordered, meticulous but with something missing. He turned and faced Duncan again. 'The whole thing sits in the twilight zone between myth and reality. An old tale everyone sneers at until hard evidence washes up on a beach one day. Suddenly the old stories seem more believable.'

'You sound like you're describing my vocation,' said Duncan, peeling himself out of his chair and reaching to touch a Bible that was the centrepiece on the coffee table. He turned and slid back the glass panel that covered a floor-to-ceiling bookcase behind his chair. He took a few seconds to find what he was looking for and heaved a leatherbound volume off the shelf. Carrying it with two hands, he laid it on a low table that rested between them. A twitch of a smile excused his embarrassment at donning a pair of white gloves so he could turn the pages. 'This is a first edition from 1883 by a chap called Oudeman,' he explained. 'It covers many topics, but one section is, in essence, a compendium of the known types of sea monsters encountered by Her Majesty's navy.'

Gill watched for a few minutes while Duncan turned pages of the old book and explained the family groups of monsters encountered at sea. 'As you can appreciate,' Duncan continued, 'Oudeman wrote this when palaeontology was in its infancy. People were digging up bones, recording them in museums and jumping to all sorts of conclusions about what these creatures might be. The seas were still full of whales, so it was natural for experienced sea captains to have a healthy fear of all sorts of mythical creatures that might lurk in the depths.'

'Then scientific rigour brought order to chaos as we sorted out the animal phyla,' said Gill.

'Exactly. Richard Owen - you'll have heard of him, was writing at the time, and he was a proponent of establishing fact by observation. If we didn't have a specimen or the bones of an animal, then he classified it as myth rather than fact. I think by about 1895, they had it all buttoned down.' He tapped the pages of the old book fondly. 'And by then, books like this suddenly looked ridiculous.'

'Where do you think the Caithness specimen fits in?'

Duncan had closed the book and sat, his gloved fingers arched into a human steeple. 'By turning up a specimen like this, it moves the goalposts. What was once a myth becomes a proven fact. You demonstrated this yourself with your discoveries on Lewis last year. We might need to re-evaluate whole families of so-called mythical creatures and consider if they might have some basis in reality.'

Gill was nodding vigorously. 'Yes, I like that.' He gulped a mouthful of coffee and surveyed the lean, intelligent man in front of him. 'That's a worthwhile line of investigation.' He paused. 'Duncan, would you consider becoming an occasional writer for *Mysterious Scotland*?'

Duncan's eyes lit up. 'Are you serious?'

Gill nodded. 'I've got a long list of topics that could do with the rational thinking you've just demonstrated. Here, let me explain where I'm going with this.'

The two men talked for an hour before Duncan had to excuse himself to finish his sermon for the following day. They'd agreed on no formalities, but a handshake promised they would be working together soon.

'Thanks for your time, Duncan. And I appreciate that other people might approach you for your knowledge, so I'm not asking for exclusivity here.'

Duncan stood at the door and shook his head. 'I had a couple of calls from news outlets this week; people researching Caithness who'd picked up my name off the web. Apart from you, I've only had one other visitor.'

'Interesting. Do you mind me asking who it was?'

'Hang on. I might still have his card.' Duncan slipped back into the house and reappeared with a small business card he passed to Gill. 'Keep it.'

'You weren't able to help him?'

'No. This guy is a Nessie hunter. He seemed a clever enough chap but a little too much on the fringe for my liking.'

Gill scanned the card. "Ernie Lehman", an email address and a registered address in Edinburgh. 'Not local then.'

'I think he said he has a wee house in the area. Spends a lot of time up here, I imagine.'

Gill flicked the card between his fingers for a moment. 'I'm curious why he came to see you about the Kraken?'

'He told me he saw your eel in Helmsdale when it was on display to the public,' said Duncan. 'Species migration was his big thing, so while he wasn't specific, my guess is he was sizing up the eel as a contender for being the Loch Ness Monster.'

'He'll be disappointed to hear it was just an overgrown conger,' said Gill.

Duncan shrugged. 'He still seemed to think it was significant. Anyway, he kept his cards close to his chest, so it was hard to help him. Have you heard of him?'

Gill glanced at the card again. 'Nope, can't say I have.'

Chapter 13

Gill sat in the reception area of the Scottish Geological Society and suppressed a yawn. It had just gone 11 am on Monday, and his appointment had been for an hour ago. That was partly his fault as he'd left Gordon's early to ensure he wasn't delayed on the Queensferry Crossing, arriving on the university campus west of Edinburgh in plenty of time. To ease his boredom, he cracked open his laptop and checked his emails. That drew him into a flurry of exchanges with Cassy, even though he was due back in the office that afternoon. Then on impulse, he opened Google and searched for *Project Leviathan*. The search produced a couple of pages of results, but nothing reminiscent of the maps and drawings now relegated to a plastic bag in the back of his car. He was just closing his browser when a tall thin man in his late fifties burst into reception. He spotted Gill and stepped over to shake his hand while at the same time pushing metal-rimmed glasses back onto his nose.

'I'm sorry to keep you waiting, Mr McArdle. It's been all go this morning. My name is John Houston.' He waited while Gill gathered his things. 'I'm afraid our head of department isn't able to see you today, so she asked me to step in.'

'No problem,' said Gill. 'I'm grateful for your time.'

John led the way into a modern if undistinguished set of offices made up of panelled glass rooms. Most had three or four people sitting at PCs around a cluster of desks, while several spaces had large data servers humming alongside air conditioning units. He directed Gill into a conference room before swiftly sitting down.

'We had a three-point eight in Comrie last night, which is the reason for all the excitement,' he explained.

Gill blinked at him. 'I take it you mean the Richter scale?'

'Yes. Very exciting. We've been developing some new predictive software, and it's been our first chance to do a live test.'

'I didn't hear about it on the news,' Gill confessed. 'I hope no one was hurt.'

John sat back sharply and clasped his hands together. 'No, no. A three-point eight is tiny. It might rattle some windows, nothing more. But we only get a quake of that magnitude in the UK every couple of years, so it's a great opportunity to run our project through its paces.'

'I have to confess a journalistic interest in this,' said Gill. 'Can you tell me anything more?'

John pursed his lips and gripped his hands more tightly together. 'We're working with the oil exploration industry. It's been obvious for a while we could use some of the techniques used in multi-directional drilling to improve our interpretation of seismic data. But I can't tell you anymore, because of the commercial angle.'

'Well, thank you anyway.'

'What did you want to ask us about, Mr McArdle?'

Gill opened his laptop while he talked. 'I'm working on two upcoming features that would benefit from an SGS comment.' John nodded, so Gill continued. 'Firstly, Montrose. Have you caught that one on the news?'

John thought for a second. 'I saw the briefest of clips on the BBC over the weekend. Something about a Neolithic boatyard dating from the time of the Storegga Slide?'

'That's right. Sounds like you're up to speed. My magazine organised the preliminary dig.'

John nodded again as Gill pressed on. 'The event we are talking about happened eight thousand years ago, resulting in Scotland's east coast being devastated by a tsunami. So, the question I have for you is, if it happened again today, would we get any warning, and if so, how much?'

John leaned back for a few moments and seemed to stare at a spot a few centimetres from the end of his nose. 'The Storegga event was pretty large. If it happened today, we would quickly get some indication from Scandinavia. But it's not straightforward.'

'How so?'

'The Storegga was a one-time event. It represented the slippage of ice age silts accumulated in the North Sea. Those silts aren't being replenished, so a slide of that magnitude couldn't happen again. The other point is that a subsea mudslide is not a seismic event. The trigger might be an earthquake we could detect. But the movement of vast quantities of mud and silts could happen for many reasons and not be discovered until a wave started to show itself.'

'Don't we have tsunami warning systems?' asked Gill.

'Not in the North Atlantic. I've heard talk about installing one, but the risk has never warranted the expense.'

'You don't see any danger?'

'I doubt if there is a story here, Mr McArdle. The oil industry has surveyed and quantified possible silt falls in the North Sea.' John stopped and gave a theatrical shrug. 'We might one day see a one-metre wave triggered off the Norwegian coastline. But that might translate into a surge of just a few centimetres by the time it reached Scotland.'

They were interrupted by a tap on the glass door, and the two men turned to face a neatly dressed woman in her late forties who gave a brief nod to Gill. 'Agnes Fairbank. Sorry I couldn't meet you this morning, Gill.' Without pausing, she turned to face John. 'Can you get me the analysis of the Comrie aftershocks? I want to see if the model predicted magnitude and spread.' John nodded, and she raised a hand in farewell.

'Sorry,' said John. 'We're going to have to make this quick. What was the other thing you wanted to ask?'

'I was up in the west last week working on something else,' Gill explained. 'While I was there, I picked up anecdotal evidence of certain geological changes. I was wondering if your systems had detected any unusual activity?'

'What kind of changes?'

'A mountain on the banks of Loch Lochy is a metre lower than it was a year ago. Then a sea stack in the Gulf of Corryvreckan is ten metres higher than recorded on the marine charts.'

John thrust his hands towards Gill in a sudden open gesture. 'The first one is simple. Scottish mountains get smaller; they erode, pieces fall off them. A metre sounds like a lot in a year, but it's possible. It depends on how accurately it is measured. We've got better GPS data with every passing year, so for example, the height of Ben Nevis was recently revised up a little.' He tapped the table a few times before continuing. 'I've seen an email on the Corryvreckan thing. A local maritime inspector proposes the Corryvreckan Strait be closed to all craft.' He shook his head. 'Ten metres sounds like a lot. I'll bet that one will be an instrument error.'

'I was on the bridge of the boat taking the readings. Everything seemed in order.'

John shrugged. 'Until the data is verified, I'm not sure I can comment.'

'But you've not detected an increase in seismic activity in Argyll or the Loch Linnhe end of the Great Glen?'

John slowly shook his head. 'No, it's all quiet as usual. The Great Glen Fault, which runs northeast up through Loch Ness, is geologically dormant. We get the odd little rumble up there. But it's the Highland Boundary fault that runs up the Clyde, across Loch Lomond, then up through Comrie and Crieff; that's the interesting one. We get lots of bumps and bangs along that one. As you can see this morning.'

'Nothing at all in the northwest?'

John was standing now, bringing the meeting to a close. 'Come over here for a second.' He moved to stand by a large wall map of Scotland marked in a grid pattern. 'These red spots are our seismic stations. They're evenly spaced, more or less, depending on where we need the coverage.' He swept a hand over the northwest highlands. 'None of these stations are picking up anything other than the creaks and groans of the planet. You have to go back in time to understand how such a dramatic fault line can be rendered benign. The Highland region used to form part of a landmass now more associated with North America. When the Pangean supercontinent formed, and by that, I'm talking eons ago, several far older continents collided. What is now Scotland's highland area got locked into the landmass from which the rest of the British Isles originated. The Great Glen is the boundary between the two old continents. But it's geologically dead. Far distant from where the real action is these days.'

'Doesn't look geologically dead when you drive through it,' countered Gill.

John smiled. 'Don't be fooled by the high mountains; they would have looked like the Swiss Alps when they were really active. And the lochs are pretty recent. The ice age glaciers tended to slice through areas with the weakest rock. That's why they gouged out the old Highland Boundary fault for a hundred thousand years. But that's the work of water and ice, not plate tectonics, I'm afraid.'

Gill nodded. 'Okay, thanks for your time. Can I get in touch if I have any more questions?'

'Certainly. I'll get you my contact details on the way out.'

'Welcome back, stranger.' Cassy greeted him by thumping a load of mail down on his desk.

'Hello, yourself,' he replied, turning to smile at the petite woman lingering by his desk. Just shy of her thirties, Cassy's face was only lightly made-up, with dark, intelligent eyes and neat features. Her hair was long and brown, usually pinned into a tight round plait behind her head. She was a pretty woman, but one who hid her figure beneath her signature dress code of oversized men's formal shirts, shortened, so they didn't hang around her knees. Larry, a writer and webmaster on the *Mys.Scot* team, memorably described her "like a tent, wie a pretty wee heid sticking oot o it."

'Tony wants to see you. Right away.'

'Doesn't sound good.'

'He's fretting about the cover design for the next issue.'

Gill sighed. 'I'll just open my post.'

Cassy shook her head. 'Your absence last week didn't do you any favours. Better to get this over with.'

'Come with me then.'

Cassy screwed up her face. 'Like, I'm your ma?'

'Come on. He likes you more than me. You can be my human shield.'

Dropping her shoulders like a petulant teenager, Cassy trailed after Gill as he knocked on the publisher's door.

Tony didn't bother with a greeting. 'A couple of old log boats lying in the mud just isn't going to cut it,' he said, waving a printout of an early draft. 'It's got no shelf standout. We need to grab people as they browse the fixture.'

'Boss. It's a fair representation of what we found at Montrose.'

'But where's the call to action? Where's the, "Oh shit! What if that ever happened again?" '

Gill found his hands were already on his hips as he tried again to explain his point of view. 'The suggestion that a tsunami could happen again next week just doesn't stand up to scientific reasoning.'

'Maybe. But you need something to bring it to life,' said Tony, tossing the printout onto the table.

'Or death,' chipped in Cassy from the margins of the conversation.

'What do you mean?' asked Tony.

'Your cover could be a drawing or even a staged photo of the mangled bodies of the tsunami victims,' said Cassy.

'Newsagents wouldn't stock it,' grunted Tony.

'The people wouldn't be torn up and gory.' She shrugged. 'Just a bit jumbled and tumbled.'

Tony glanced at his watch, then back at Gill. 'I've got to make the 5 pm to London City. Look, at the end of the day, you're the editor. It's your decision. But as your publisher, I'm telling you your sales slide needs to stop. So, whatever you do, be brave.'

The meeting broke up as Tony shooed them out of his office and slammed the door.

'That went well,' Cassy whispered as she slipped away to answer a ringing phone.

Gill slumped down at his desk, chastened by Tony's manner. Once he'd taken out his anger on his mail pile, he cast his mind back to the Montrose excavations and tried to imagine a river bank strewn with bodies. A little reluctantly, he began to see the idea might work.

The phone rang again. Cassy caught Gill's attention, indicating the call was for him. He lifted his phone and immediately put the call on hold. 'I'm going to go with your idea, Cass. Can you get onto some model agencies and find a crew to stage this? We'll need a local outfit, with actors who look at least vaguely Pictish. A mixture of big guys, redheaded girls and some kids. We might as well shoot some shots of life before and after the disaster.'

Cassy gave him a thumbs-up, and he reconnected the call. '*Mysterious Scotland*, Gill McArdle speaking.'

'Gill, it's Salina.'

'Hey, Salina.' Gill was immediately aware how pleased he was to hear from her. 'How's it going?'

'I'm okay,' she said. 'A little slow up here. The weather is too rough to deploy the DSV, so I'm catching up on some business before we get down to it tomorrow.'

'Did you want to run through the voice-over again?'

'Not particularly. That's in hand.' She paused, and he could hear her breathe a few times. 'I was phoning to apologise about last week. When we parted company on Saturday, you were being kind. I was a bit nippy with you. I wanted to say sorry.'

'No worries. It's none of my business anyway.' Gill immediately regretted sounding so cool.

'But you could tell I was struggling with giving up my St Andrews job, and I just wanted to thank you for caring.'

Gill hesitated, forming his words. 'You're a good person, Salina. And talented. You deserve to thrive in your marriage and your profession.'

'Thanks, Gill. Anyway, I just wanted to say that I appreciated it.' Her voice changed, forced to carry a little more sparkle. 'So, what's happening with you?'

Gill glanced around the *Mys.Scot* section of the office where his small team were busy with various tasks. 'We're closing the next issue. It's all dashing and deadlines. Then next month, we get to do the same thing all over again.'

'The Montrose dig sounds fascinating. I haven't seen many newsagents up here, but I'll look out for it.'

'Aye,' said Gill, winking at Cassy as she passed. 'The front cover will be stunning.'

'Are you okay? You sound a bit agitated.'

'Oh, just office blues after a week on the road.' He knew he was lying. He could sense he was on the edge of something. It was as if someone had mailed him parts of a puzzle, but so far he hadn't seen enough pieces to guess the outline of the picture. That reminded him. 'You're an expert on all things marine. Can I ask you a work question?'

'Shoot.'

'Have you ever heard of something called *Project Leviathan*?'

After a short silence, Salina came back. 'Doesn't ring any bells. Can you give me any context?'

Gill thought about the complex drawings accompanying the marine maps. 'Maybe industrial, or even military. Going back to the 1970s or before.'

'Arthur Deveron is your man for that. I know he's been gathering historical data about the seas around the British Isles for his book. And he used to be a navy bod. He might have come across it.'

'Thanks, I'll give him a shout.'

The conversation fell to a natural lull. Gill wanted to suggest they meet sometime but sensed he shouldn't intrude. In the end, it was Salina who spoke.

'I'll catch up with you on the voice-over when I get back. Take care, Gill,' she said before terminating the call.

Chapter 14

Gill crouched silently in the heather, looking down at the carnage on the river bank below him.

Amidst a jumble of branches, tree trunks, and piles of sand lay the bruised and twisted bodies of eight human beings. A powerful man lay with a shattered leg unnaturally forced behind his head, his dead eyes wide in shock. Nearby lay a woman's body, the lifeless legs of an infant just visible beneath her simple shawl. Another woman, younger with red hair, lay sprawled on her side, her slim, white thighs stark against the mud. Here and there, amidst the debris, limbs protruded from the sandy river bank. Gill let the tragedy of the scene wash over him until finally, a tear rolled down his face, and he had to turn away.

'Thanks, everybody, that's a wrap,' said the photographer standing down the drone he'd been hovering over the scene.

The riverbank exploded into life as the living dolls erupted from their static positions. 'Aye, man. Finally!' shouted the biggest. 'Anither ten minutes and you could hae buried me where I lay' He dragged his legs from their hiding place under the sand and staggered to his feet. He stretched, stooping to pull a prosthetic leg from the dirt. The young redheaded woman dusted herself down, took one of the children by the hand and walked off swinging a large doll by its ankles.

The photographer recovered his drone and excitedly flicked some images past Gill. 'It's when we got above them that it becomes compelling.'

'You are certain that they are not too disturbing?' Gill was still concerned about how shop managers might react to the magazine cover.

'We've stuck to the guidelines,' said the photographer. 'No gore or gratuitous violence. We're not going to have any trouble with these.'

Gill bit his lip and nodded. The chosen photo would run under the banner headline, "Wave of Death." At least Tony would love it.

He didn't linger long at the Montrose site as he only had one person he really needed to see. He found Fiona checking through the dig catalogue before she passed responsibility for the site to a collaboration of trusts and universities who would see the project through to conclusion. She would stay on for a few days, although today was her last day working for *Mysterious Scotland*.

'Great work, Fi. Hopefully not long before I'll have something else for you.'

He leant in and gave her a hug which she reciprocated. 'Been a pleasure, Gill. Gimme a shout next time you are passing.'

'Remember what I said about getting a book out of this? You've made a name for yourself these past few weeks.'

'Naw, I cannae write,' said Fiona.

'It's not a romance novel, Fi. Just get the facts down on paper. I'll help you pull it together. Once it starts to shape up, we might find a suitable academic to sponsor it.'

Fiona threw him a shallow shrug. 'If you think it's worth a punt.'

'Definitely.' He glanced down at his watch. 'Right, I need to move. Got two days to finish a magazine.'

They hugged again, at her insistence, and then he was back on the road.

The following two days passed in a blur. Gill had finished most of the writing, but some of the commissioned work needed checking and revising. He had several technical illustrations showing the origin and impact of the wave, some of which needed redrafting. The photos from Wednesday's shoot came back early on Thursday. Mercifully, the front cover picked itself. They still needed to select other images to illustrate the story, so the team worked hard to get the right balance between allowing the reader to develop empathy with the Pictish family but without laying it on too thick. Once they chose their photos, they scrutinised them for anachronisms like power lines and telephone masts.

They closed the issue on Thursday evening, meaning the magazine could go to press on schedule at 2 am. Pulling together around the final task in the monthly cycle, the team sat around the office at 7 pm reviewing the colour proofs.

'We're getting later each month,' muttered Cassy as she initialled the footer on another A3 spread.

'You can't hurry art,' responded Gill in the flattest monotone he could muster.

'Aw'right for you, boss,' said Larry. 'I'm missin' mae darts night.'

'No problem, Larry,' said Cassy without lifting her head. 'Gill says we can get pizza and beer after we've put the magazine to bed.'

'I did?' said Gill.

'Well, it's either that or sign off on the overtime,' said Cassy.

'The company doesn't operate an overtime policy,' droned Gill.

'Okay,' said Cassy brightly. 'Beer and pizza it is.'

Later, after a few drinks, Gill found himself with a sense of satisfaction he hadn't experienced before. The team had ridden out a tough couple of issues and still found the energy to give the Montrose dig the coverage it deserved. As editor, he'd tried to strike a balance between leading from the front and keeping an eye on the team's morale back at base. The unspoken consensus around the table said it would be their best issue yet. Gill knew they'd worked hard. At this moment in time, they weren't capable of better. Off the presses tonight, the magazine would be delivered to the eighty UK magazine wholesalers responsible for breaking the bulk of the print run across twenty-five thousand news outlets. This process ran so swiftly that the magazine would start going on the shelves by dawn on Monday morning. In the meantime, tomorrow would be a quiet day for the rest of the team, enlivened by copies of the new magazine arriving in the office around lunchtime. For Gill, Friday meant the 2 pm Publisher's Meeting. This time, it was a meeting he couldn't dodge. Sales targets, advertising bookings, projected print runs. It would all be gone over with a fine comb. And all in the knowledge, they wouldn't know what the current issue had sold for another three weeks. Gill couldn't wait to put Friday behind him and get back in the field. He felt increasingly anxious because the provisional lead stories for issue eleven all looked weak. Once the presses ran on issue ten, the spotlight was back on him.

'Move a mountain,' said Gill, citing a potential tag line at the Publisher's Meeting the following day.

Tony's eyebrows tilted towards him. 'Honestly?' He paused long enough to blink twice. 'You're going to follow up a potential award-winning issue with a story about an old lady who prays for a mountain?'

'That's just part of the story. We've got a tonne of material on the Corryvreckan thing.'

'Not sure how it fits together,' said Carl, editor of a military part work.

Tony waved away his point and firmly made one of his own. 'I think it's all too subjective. If I understand correctly, experts dispute the geological data, so this could be a story about nothing.'

Gill pushed his hands flat on the desk in front of him. Being honest with himself, the facts he had to hand were less than compelling. 'My instinct tells me something bigger is going on here. I'm just not sure what.'

Tony sat back in his chair, looking troubled. 'We're on a production line here, Gill. What you're talking about might mature into a decent story, but I think that's six or seven issues out. What else have you got for me?'

Gill knew that Tony was right. But his lack of enthusiasm for the other potential storylines made the west coast goings-on more interesting. He sat and rattled off several partially researched ideas. Most were historical. Angles on events long past on which he might eventually shed new light. He left one idea to the end, hoping that Tony wouldn't get a sniff of it. In the end, Tony nodded through the historical pieces like he was sorting through a bag of rotten potatoes.

'Finally,' said Gill. 'We have Loch Ness.'

'What about it?' Tony's glasses had slid so far forward; they looked like they might drop off the end of his nose.

'Because of what *Mys.Scot* represents, lots of people contact us to tell us about things they've seen. Cassy keeps a register, but basically ... in a nutshell ... monster sightings are up.'

'Up?' Tony barked.

'Off the scale,' said Gill. 'Bits and pieces in the general media, but we are getting over a dozen sightings a week straight into our office.'

'Bloody hell,' said Tony, taking off his glasses to rub his eyes. 'For a moment there, I thought we were in trouble.' Gill sat blinking, uncertain what Tony was saying. 'There you are wringing your hands about the next issue, and you're already sitting on gold dust,' Tony continued. 'Look, I'm not going to tell you your job, but in your shoes, I'd focus on one thing.'

Gill nodded. For ten months, he'd been avoiding this moment. Now, with all exits closed, it descended softly around him like a net.

After the meeting, he sat at his desk, waiting for an opportune moment to excuse himself and leave the office. He had promised to go to Stonehaven for the weekend. The roadworks on the A90 were going to be a bitch.

'Order of business for next week?' asked Cassy, wandering over to his desk.

Gill sank forward in his chair, letting his head slip lower until his face touched the surface of the desk. 'Loch Ness Monster,' he said, his lips so close to the polished Formica they brushed against it as he spoke. He lifted his head slightly, then let his forehead drop onto the desk with a dull thud. After a few seconds, he turned to see if she was still looking at him.

Cassy's dark eyes ignored him, as if every Friday afternoon in the office finished this way. She pursed her lips and rolled her tongue as she uttered, 'I think you'll want to refer to her as "Lucy."'

'Pardon?'

'I looked it up. It's what expert Nessie hunters call their quarry. It's shorthand for "Our Elusive Friend." Makes them sound less weird.' She sniffed. 'Apparently.'

Gill slowly released pent-up air from his chest. 'Well, whatever they call it, can you do me a list of all the recent sightings? I need to know who, and where, and whether any other media picked them up.'

'Sure,' said Cassy, unperturbed. 'I'll do you a map with all the locations and look for any similarities.'

She sighed, and her long shirt bunched at the sides as she raised her hands to her hips, watching as his forehead hovered over the closed lid of his laptop. Eventually, she flicked her wrists in a shooing motion. 'Go away, Gill. Take the weekend off and recharge, for goodness sake.'

Monday morning, and for the first time in this job, Gill felt stressed about his work. He returned from Stonehaven the night before, ready to start early in his Dundee office. He planned to go in with a clear head and brainstorm the Loch Ness thing with Cassy, so they were on top of it before the rest of the team staggered in, looking for direction. Instead, Tony nabbed him just before 8 am and he had to endure a motivational speech about the progression of a good editor through the industry. He left Tony's office just before 9 am, concluding the only point Tony was trying to make was that Gill needed to plan much further ahead. He returned to his desk to find a cluster of expectant faces. A couple of the Sunday papers had picked up the cover of the current magazine and given it glowing reviews. Their tails were up, and they were ready to go.

The burden of the next issue had already robbed Gill of any sense of satisfaction. The last place he wanted to go was Loch Ness.

'Right, you lot. Cassy. You and me, Starbucks, asap to do some planning. The rest of you, background reading. I want to know every theory anyone has ever had on "Lucy." I want case studies on the various "personalities" who have hunted for her over the years. And I need the names of a few legitimate experts. If they exist, that is. Divvy up the tasks, and let's get to it.'

He grabbed his rain jacket and notepad, pausing at Cassy's desk while she gathered some folders. Larry watched them closely. As soon as they moved, he followed them to the door and blocked Gill's path. 'Ye got tae be the jammie wee bastard wi' the Waterhorses, Gill. If yer gang aefter the Loch Ness Manester, dae ye think lightin' will strike twice?'

Gill stopped and cleared his throat. '*Mys.Scot* is a serious magazine, Larry. We'll approach the topic in a thorough and professional manner.'

'Aye, so it's pure garbage,' said Larry with a satisfied nod. 'As lang as we're no gettin' misty eyed aboot it.'

Gill turned to join Cassy, who was holding the door open. 'No, Larry. Absolutely no chance of that.'

Coffee with Cassy always brought clarity. And today, she was exasperated by him. She didn't wait for his professional opinion or a nod from him as her team leader. Instead, she leapt in with an instant rebuke. 'Look, Gill. Just because you don't have the heart for this one, don't let it undermine all you have achieved in the past year.'

'I know, Cass. But it's more than that. If we go after this, I feel we're taking the whole magazine down a notch. Next thing you know, we'll be chasing ghosts and fairies.'

'Some of my best mates are fairies. Don't knock 'em.' She nudged Gill, trying to coax a smile. 'Come on, Gill. Let's make a plan.'

'I once spent a hot six weeks in Utah,' said Gill.

'Relevance?' said Cassy, raising her eyebrows.

'We dug for over a month and didn't find a thing.'

'Looking in the wrong place, weren't you?'

'Aye, Cass, I was.' Gill paused to unfurl a detailed Ordnance Survey map of the Loch Ness area. 'Look at this. Twenty-three miles long, nearly twenty-two square miles of water. Easy to look in the wrong place. In fact, where the hell do we even start?'

Cassy pulled a list from one of her folders, plus a simple A4 map. 'I've marked up the sightings. They cluster around Urquhart castle.'

'Where the loch is widest,' Gill observed.

'And the castle is a place where people tend to relax and look out over the water,' said Cassy. 'Larry and I will phone the people who sent in reports, starting this afternoon. Hopefully, that will identify a few people for you to go and see.'

Gill wrote a couple of notes on his pad. 'Okay. And does this help us?'

Cassy smiled. 'The dates and times of their reported sightings cluster into four distinct groups.'

Gill blinked. For a moment, he wasn't sure what to say. 'You're kidding me?'

Cassy was already shaking her head.

Gill sat up straight and thought for a second. 'For the love of everything mysterious,' he said quietly.

'I'll track down anyone who can be considered an expert,' said Cassy. 'I should have a couple of names for you by the end of the day. Do you know anyone else you can speak to in the meantime to get you going?'

'My new pal, Duncan Campbell, is an enthusiast. Then there's a guy I met last week, Arthur Deveron. He owes me a favour, although he's more of a saltwater man.'

'Does he know anything about the loch monster myths?'

Gill shook his head. 'I doubt it. But he's a writer so he might give me some useful contacts. I'll talk to him this afternoon.'

'And have you thought about the angle you're going to take on the whole subject?'

'Tony and I talked this morning. At the moment, our tagline will be "Enduring myth of Loch Ness." We can change it if we develop a stronger storyline.'

'Did you two talk about anything else? You had the world on your shoulders when you left his office.'

Gill sank deeper into his chair again. 'He is anxious we're living too much hand to mouth. He wants us prepping the outline of the next three issues. Kind of a rolling plan that we'd refine as we go along.'

'Sounds like good discipline.'

Gill swilled the last of his coffee in the bottom of his cup. 'Not if you're used to digging one hole at a time, it's not.'

Cassy smiled and picked up her bag to leave. 'We've got plenty of ideas in the drawer. I'll throw it into some kind of order for you to cast your eyes over.'

'You, my tiny and most precious colleague, are a star.'

The rest of the morning passed quickly for Gill as he prepared for another lengthy spell out of the office. Satisfied the significant tasks were in hand, he picked up the phone and made a few appointments for the rest of the week. On impulse, he called Arthur Deveron.

'Arthur. I'm leaving the office for the Loch Ness area and was thinking about your book. Can I bring you any materials?'

The phone line sounded muffled for a few moments, and as it cleared, Gill got the impression that Arthur was walking. Even so, he spoke in a voice so low, Gill could barely hear him. 'Thanks, Gill. Appreciate it.' Arthur stopped walking and listed a few volumes on Cryptozoology that were out of print.

'I have those. Anything else?'

Arthur didn't respond straight away. 'I don't suppose you have any contemporary stuff on the Loch Ness Monster, do you? By contemporary, I mean bang up to date.'

Gill felt his grip on the phone tighten a little. 'Bits and pieces. Sounds like we should meet up.' He paused. 'Where are you this week?'

Arthur cleared his throat. 'Up north. I'd rather not say exactly.'

'Well, name a place, and we'll meet,' said Gill.

'If you're up this way, how about Fort William?'

'Okay. Say, tomorrow evening for a bite? I'll text you once I'm in town.'

After Arthur hung up, Gill sat tapping his chin with his phone. Cassy was walking back to her desk with a mug of tea. 'Sorry. I would have got you one if I'd known you were still here.' She peered at him curiously. 'You look better, all of a sudden.'

Gill swung his laptop bag over his shoulder. 'I've decided I quite like mysteries.' He brushed against her arm as he headed for the door. 'Talk to you tomorrow.'

Chapter 15

If Gill had ever been to Drumnadrochit, he didn't remember. As one of the few settlements along the long west bank of Loch Ness, it was a sparsely built village whose entire enterprise culture revolved around a traditional interpretation of the Loch Ness Monster. Built away from the loch to avoid the marshy outfalls of two rivers entering Urquhart Bay, it had the look of a place that was perpetually wet. Its crowning glory, however, were the ruins of Urquhart Castle, nestling on a rocky outcrop where it had a clear view out over the widest part of the loch, and historically, the best place to see Nessie.

Gill stood in the car park of the *Ness Explorer Visitor Centre* and took a second to gather his thoughts. His reluctance to work on this particular story surged again. He'd had a chance to reflect on what it was about the Loch Ness myth that was so distasteful to him. Firstly, he disliked the half-baked ideas of people more ruled by their hearts than their heads. Though, to be fair, a few folk had accused him of that over the past ten months. Secondly, he hated dogma wherever he encountered it. Religion, politics, football, science. Any situation where people held a strong sense of personal worldview and an urgent need to burden this on others. He dearly hoped he wouldn't encounter both vices during this next appointment.

Cassy had researched possible experts and suggested Dr Alexandra Brightman as the best place to start. At least Gill could enjoy the exhibition if the interview didn't go well. Entering through the gift shop, he did his best to ignore the plastic kitsch and tourist tat. He introduced himself at the counter and, discreetly, stood watching a video reel of old movies set on the loch and prayed he wouldn't be recognised.

Dr Brightman was an agile-looking woman in her early sixties with a long streak of silver hair looped around her neck and onto her chest. Keen blue eyes fixed Gill as he offered her a tentative handshake.

'Dr Brightman. I'm very grateful you could meet me at such short notice.'

The eyes twinkled above a small, neat smile. 'Please, call me Sandy.' Gill felt his handshake firmly returned. 'Actually, I've been hoping our paths would cross.' She turned and gesticulated at a small magazine rack in the visitor shop behind him. Copies of *Mysterious Scotland* were neatly presented alongside fishing and walking magazines. 'You've quite a healthy readership in here.' Gill pushed back a ripple of pride while Brightman turned to him again. 'And it's right and proper that Loch Ness finally comes to the attention of your publication.'

Gill was confident that he wouldn't have to speak. He would stand and nod occasionally, look interested under a tirade of monster facts and figures while she got carried away with her expertise. So, he was surprised when Brightman steered them through the building to a café, set in the old dining room of a once-grand hotel, and ordered coffees.

After a few pleasantries, she asked, 'How can I help you, Gill?'

Gill hauled his laptop bag onto his knees and rummaged for a sheet of paper. 'We get lots of people contacting our website. As a consequence, we track a number of things. Predation of domestic animals, missing people.' He winced. 'Bizarrely, we even have a weekly ghost count.' He laid the sheet on the table facing Brightman. 'Sightings of unidentified creatures get split into land, loch and sea. This chart is for lochs.'

Brightman produced glasses from the trouser pocket and studied the steeply rising curve. She glanced up at Gill. 'How many of these sightings are from Loch Ness?'

'Most of them.'

Brightman slowly shook her head. 'Goodness. A lean few years and now this.'

Gill arched his eyebrows and gave her a puzzled expression.

'We had no sightings at all in 2020 for obvious reasons. The next couple of years weren't much better. This year has produced lots more reports, but we put it down to the good weather. The tour buses have been out even earlier this year.' She looked at the chart again before arresting him with a stern expression over the rim of her glasses. 'Have you corroborated all these?'

'My office is in the process. I've spoken to a few folks personally during my drive up. They all seem quite plausible.'

Brightman pushed back her glasses. 'This data is in weekly increments. I don't suppose you have it day-by-day?'

'We do. And to answer your question before you ask it, we've pinpointed four significant events in the last thirty days.'

Brightman pushed the sheet back to Gill, allowing the fingers of her left hand to run down her ponytail in long gentle strokes. 'You do realise there's probably a perfectly plausible explanation?'

Gill was briefly surprised. 'I'm sure.'

Her eyes fixed him again. 'You didn't honestly think I'd get all cock-a-hoop about this?'

Gill lifted his palms. 'I'm a scientist. You're a scientist. It sounds like we can have a sensible conversation about what might be causing this spike in sightings.'

'Absolutely. Finish your coffee, and then let me show you something.'

Some small part of Gill yearned for Sandy to lead him down a narrow stairway to a hidden lab, where the remains of a great beast unknown to science would lie preserved in a sumptuous bath of formaldehyde. Instead, he was introduced to an extended display board categorising the types of sightings that occur on the loch.

'When people think of "Lucy", they often think of the long neck. That is based on the now-classic hoax of 1934 when a London gynaecologist called Robert Wilson took the most famous photo of our erstwhile monster. But people still see the same basic sighting today!' Her voice rose in volume and pitch as she rushed to explain the phenomenon. 'It's a big loch, you see. Big enough to discern the curvature of the earth. In a heat haze, and you can get that in just about any clear weather, the effect is a distortion that elongates any object close to the waterline. People look across the loch over a long distance, and what do they see? The long neck and partially submerged body of a strange beast.'

'But it's just an optical illusion,' said Gill.

'Yes. Perhaps a swimming deer or a cormorant preparing to dive.' She smiled happily. 'It can look quite strange.'

'What about the sightings of humps?' said Gill. 'What are people seeing?'

Brightman shrugged. 'Waves. Usually, it's just the dispersed ripple from a boat wake. But it can be caused by less common phenomena. In these really deep lochs, the water volume lies in layers of starkly different temperatures. They're caused by snowmelt running into the loch. The physics are quite tricky, but depending on the heights of these layers, you can have a kind of resonance set up where some waves on the surface become amplified.'

'Awesome. Can you show me how that works?'

Gill and Brightman retired back to the café with a pad of paper. At one point, a staff member came over to ask Gill to sign an old copy of the magazine, but other than that, the two talked solidly for over an hour.

'My apologies, Gill, but I need to go shortly. I'm taking a party out on the loch.'

Gill held up his hands in acknowledgement. 'No problem. I'm very grateful for the time you've spent with me.'

He paused briefly, considering if his new friendship could withstand an awkward question. 'Sandy, can I ask you why you go along with this whole monster-tourist thing when it seems to me that you don't believe any such creature exists?'

Sandy smiled. If she was embarrassed, she didn't show it. 'No one has spent more time than me looking for evidence to prove the existence of "Lucy." Just because I haven't found her doesn't mean I don't believe.'

'And you're never tempted to lower the burden of proof?'

Brightman waved a hand in front of her face. 'You mean, see a shadow on a sonar scan and decide that's it? That I've got the proof I need?'

'I guess,' said Gill.

'A million times,' Brightman laughed. 'But I've still got to sleep at night, so "no", I never lower the burden of proof. Besides, I've had too much fun just doing the science. We've developed techniques on this loch that have become international standards for deep water exploration.'

'You'll have met a few interesting people too,' said Gill.

'Aye. And many a nut case.'

On the spur of the moment, Gill threw in another question. 'Ever heard of a bloke called Lehman?'

Brightman leaned back in her chair and gathered herself to stand. 'Ernie Lehman. Bit of a dark horse. I doubt he's a team player.'

'You've met him then?'

'Two or three months back. He came to the centre and pumped me for the latest "Lucy" theories. I've not seen him since. But I know a few who have.'

'Okay. What impression do you get?'

Brightman stood and pushed her chair back against the table. 'The monster hunting fraternity is a community. They sit and drink pints together, share stories, and laugh at their mistakes. Most of them are here a few months, then get bored and move on.' She shook her head. 'But none of that for Ernie. I've heard it said he has a house on the east shore. A big old hunting lodge.'

'Do you know his address?'

Brightman shook her head. 'The east shore is a mile by boat, thirty miles by car. It's a world apart. If someone isn't sociable, you might never bump into them.'

'Can't be many houses like that?'

'Oh, half a dozen at most. They have gated drives and security if you're thinking of going calling.'

'What did you make of him?'

Sandy lifted her eyes to the ceiling. 'Quite upper crust. Good scientific vocabulary. A clever man but not personable. When I asked for his personal opinion on the origins of the "Lucy" myth, he wasn't very forthcoming.'

'Maybe he's on to something? A working theory he wants to keep to himself.'

Brightman reached out and took Gill by the hand. 'And isn't that the beauty of it? It's an awfully big loch. It could hold a truly unique species, and as much as it pains me to admit it, we might never know for sure.'

Gill ploughed on with his day. After the energising meeting with Sandy Brightman, he made three house calls on folk who had seen something on the loch. But the despondency he'd experienced over the weekend started to reassert itself. None of the people claiming to have sighted "Lucy" had anything substantial to report, other than unexplained disturbances in the water surface. None had any photographs that were worth publishing. All the witnesses seemed reliable, and none ever claimed to have seen anything on the loch before. That their stories were all so similar gave his curiosity a tiny nudge. A low ripple traversing the loch, nothing visible in the water, but evidence perhaps of something moving quickly just below the surface? It was intriguing. And it was insubstantial.

He took his thoughts into a rundown pub on the edge of Fort William town centre. Arthur had chosen the venue as it was close to his B&B.

'Buy you a pint?' Arthur was there ahead of him, and looked like he was already a couple to the good.

'Aye, thanks. I'll just have the one. Have you ordered any food?' Gill glanced around the bar, looking for a menu.

'Chicken in a basket,' said Arthur matter of factly. 'Or scampi, or a burger, but that's it, and it all comes in a basket, apparently.'

'Okay,' said Gill. 'No real ale either, by the looks of things.'

'We can go somewhere else.'

'No, it's fine.' Gill smiled. 'Working in Dundee turns me into a gastro snob.'

Arthur raised his glass. 'Back in the real world now, my friend.'

They ordered food, and for several minutes, Gill listened to Arthur moaning about the levels of tourist traffic in the Highlands. 'And it's only bloody April.'

'How's the book?' said Gill, keen to get down to business.

Arthur nodded modestly. 'Going pretty well, actually. That guy I went to see after we berthed in Oban provided some good stuff.'

'Cool. Tell me about him.'

Arthur's eyes fixed on his glass for a few moments until he looked back at Gill. 'Can't do that, I'm afraid.'

Gill was puzzled. 'Why not?'

'Well, I don't know what you ever did to piss this guy off, but you're "persona non grata" in his books.'

'Okay. What's his name? Maybe I can clear this up.'

'Can't tell you that either. When I said I knew you, he specifically asked me not to mention his name.'

'But he knows we're meeting.'

Arthur lifted both hands and waved them defensively. 'Yeah. He thinks we're just having a few beers while I sound you out on what you're working on.'

Gill lifted his glass and took a swift sip. 'Arthur. Exactly what are we doing?'

'Everyone's protecting their corner, Gill. You've got your mag to publish. I've got my book. We're all simply doing our science.'

'Science!' Gill suppressed a surge of sarcasm. He took another sip, slower this time and steadied his glass. 'This week, I'm working Loch Ness. So far, the science is pretty thin.'

'You know what I mean. Discovering something. Confirming something. Lifting the lid.'

Gill thought for a second. 'This guy, I take it he's Ernie Lehman?'

Arthur's glass paused midway to his mouth. 'You know him?'

'Only by reputation. And that's pretty scant. He's a "Lucy" enthusiast, isn't he?' Gill observed Arthur. He was already shrugging and appeared reluctant to defend someone else's secret.

'I guess,' he said.

'What's he got against me?'

Arthur sat fingering his glass, letting the base slide back and forth through a little pool of spilt beer. 'My impression is he feels he has put a lot of work into his research. He doesn't want some celebrity sweeping in and grabbing the glory.'

Gill laughed. 'Is that how he sees me?'

Arthur waved a finger in the air. 'In the narrow world of cryptozoology, you are a goliath.'

'Jeepers, man. I never realised.' Gill gave himself a little shake. 'Anyway, Lehman and I should get together. See if we can put this behind us.'

'Not sure it'll happen,' muttered Arthur. 'This guy is pretty tight.'

Gill sighed. 'Well, whether he likes it or not, I'm up here doing a feature on Loch Ness. Talk to him, Arthur. See if you can set up a meeting.'

Arthur's eyes swerved to watch their meals being plonked onto the bar in front of them. 'Pistols at dawn more like.' He held a hand up to stop Gill from protesting. 'But I'll ask.'

The conversation paused for a minute as they started to eat. 'Do you still want to lend me those books?' asked Arthur.

'Sure. They're outside in the car. Can you tell me what it is you're looking for?' Gill munched on a piece of overcooked chicken for a few seconds. 'Or is that also a secret?'

Arthur sat and slowly dismembered a chicken thigh. 'I have a chapter on Loch Ness in my book, which is why I talked with Lehman. If Lehman can prove the thing exists, my angle is to explain where it came from and where it goes when it's not in the loch.' Arthur glanced up to see the puzzled expression on Gill's face. 'Lehman believes the creatures migrate. I won't say any more than that.'

'Gotta meet this guy,' said Gill through a mouthful.

Arthur bit into a piece of chicken and didn't respond. With the conversation in a lull, Gill remembered something else. 'On another topic.' He waited until he had Arthur's attention again. 'Have you ever encountered something called *Project Leviathan*?'

Arthur glanced up at the bottles lined along the top of the bar. He slowly shook his head, then stopped and asked, 'Where did you hear about that?'

'Someone mentioned it in a letter the other day but gave no explanation,' said Gill. 'I don't even know if it's civilian or military?'

'Write back and ask them.'

'Just to add to the mystery, the letter was anonymous. You haven't heard of it then?'

Arthur rocked his upper body a few times before answering. 'Don't think I've ever come across it.' He picked up his drink and drained the rest of his beer. 'Another? He asked, tilting his glass.

'No thanks,' said Gill. 'I'm gonna need to drive.'

Gill found a simple B&B in the north end of Fort William and slept well. The following morning, he was up for a run, showered and breakfasted before a scheduled call with Cassy at 8.30.

'How was yesterday?' she asked after filling him in on office comings and goings.

'Good, I think,' said Gill.

'You don't sound so sure. Did you meet Brightman?'

'Yes. Great old girl. Very grounded.' Gill paused. 'But although she didn't come out and say it, she isn't convinced anything unusual lives in the loch.'

'But, that's what you think too, right?'

Gill grimaced. 'Yes. But it doesn't take us any closer to a storyline.'

'Bloody hell. You're starting to sound like Tony.'

'Anyway, have you had a chance to follow up on the reported sightings?' said Gill

Cassy rattled a sheet of paper at the other end of the phone. 'Spoke to a couple of people yesterday. Most of it pretty mundane.' Gill could hear the anticipation in her voice. 'But I think I've got you one decent lead.'

'Okay, shoot.'

'I spoke to a lady farmer in Invermoriston. That's on the west bank, but towards the southerly end of the loch.'

'I passed through yesterday. Go on.'

'She reported a sighting about ten days ago. When I asked her for a few details, she got all stressed and said she didn't know why she bothered saying anything. She said nothing would come of it because nothing did in the past.'

Gill drummed his fingers on the back of the phone. 'Uh huh.'

'When I asked her what she meant by that, she mentioned an amateur archaeologist she'd permitted on her land three years ago. He dug a series of trenches and, after a week or so, got quite excited by something he had found.'

'Which was?'

'She didn't know. She returned from a day trip to Inverness and found the archaeologist had filled his excavations and left. She never heard another peep from him.'

'That was rude,' observed Gill.

'Kinda strange too, don't you think?'

'At *Mys.Scot*, we do strange,' said Gill. 'I'll go see her later. Can you text me her details?'

'Will do. You got much else on?'

'I'm popping in with Duncan. He's finished the background piece I commissioned from him on the *Caithness Kraken*. If he can write the way I hope he can write, he might take some of the pressure off us for a couple of months.'

'We'll be fine, Gill. And as promised, I've taken our in-tray and roughed out half a dozen issues. Promise it will get your juices flowing and get Tony off your back.'

'Thanks, Cassy. I really appreciate it. Listen, can you do one thing for me? This guy Ernie Lehman is turning into something of an enigma. I checked out an email address I had for him, but it redirects to a black hole. From what I can glean, he's got a big ego, so he's bound to have a website somewhere, even if he's not using his real name.'

'Google, here I come,' said Cassy. 'Speak later.'

Chapter 16

Duncan fixed a light lunch while Gill sat at a pine kitchen table and read the articles he'd commissioned. The table was set for two, although big enough for eight, which allowed Gill to spread the documents out in front of him. With almost a year in the job, Tony had coached him in the editorial craft, so he moved deftly through Duncan's draft documents, marking them up as he went. Duncan had plenty of writing experience, but despite his confident posture, an uneasy silence filled the room until Gill finished the last piece.

'How do they look?' asked Duncan as Gill laid down his pen and reached for a glass of water.

'Good,' said Gill. 'I think you strike a perfect balance between the rational explanations for creatures people have seen at sea, but without killing the sense that we can't explain everything.'

Duncan's smile was fleeting, betraying his relief. 'I tried to match your house style. Shine the light of science without dismissing all the mystery.' Duncan laid down the food and said a few brief words of grace before encouraging Gill to start. 'Big old place this,' said Gill, glancing around the kitchen. 'I guess there can't be many of these traditional rectories left.'

Duncan nodded. 'Aye. Many a family would love a place this size.'

'What do you do with all these rooms?'

Duncan was concentrating on his food and took a moment to respond. 'In addition to my local duties, I used to run this building as a respite hostel. Somewhere safe for city kids to get away from it all.'

'But you don't anymore?' asked Gill, reaching for a slice of bread.

Duncan shook his head while he finished a mouthful. 'No. It's difficult to get funding.'

'I'm sorry,' said Gill. 'And there must be so many young people in need of that kind of help.'

Duncan shook his head. 'It's a great sadness to me. I miss having all that youthful energy around.'

Gill nodded slowly, uncertain what to say. Suddenly the big house felt even more empty.

The two men sat in uncomfortable silence for a few seconds while Duncan refreshed their water glasses. 'When we first met, you started asking about Loch Ness,' he said, sounding brighter.

Gill nodded and laid down his fork. 'Yeah. I've got to find a viewpoint for an upcoming article.

'And how's that going?'

Gill gave a shallow shrug while he ate. 'I'm trying to keep it rational, which is why it's helpful talking to you.'

'And what rational questions are you asking?'

'I suppose it's a matter of potential. Ignoring for a second what the creature might be or where it came from, I have one unanswered question; could the loch support a large creature?'

'The crucial issue is food supply,' said Duncan. 'Every big animal, be it a fish, a reptile, or a mammal, has to eat. For all its size, Loch Ness doesn't hold a lot of food. The plankton bloom in the loch must be brief and sparse compared to what you get at sea. The sides of the loch are very steep, and the winters are long, so a vegetarian diet isn't really an option either. Besides, any weed growth is in the top two metres of water, so we would easily see any animal harvesting it.'

'What about fish?' Gill interrupted.

'I know a guy who is a gamekeeper on one of the big estates. He says you are unlikely to have more than a tonne of fish per square kilometre, even on these deep lochs.'

Gill did a quick mental calculation. 'So, fifty-six square kilometres of water would translate into less than sixty tonnes of fish. And that's spread across the whole loch.'

'Our hungry monster would have to work pretty hard for his daily bread,' said Duncan, biting down on a slice of cheese.

'Can we rule out big ferox trout as a contender?' asked Gill.

'Now you are asking me to guess,' said Duncan, waving the cheese at Gill. 'But your biggest ferox would be about thirty pounds. They're deep water fish, and I gather they only live for about fifteen years. I doubt they would be an adequate explanation for any of the sightings.'

Gill grunted. 'Met an eel once that was over two hundred years old.'

Duncan smiled and reached for another piece of bread.

'So, that leaves the migration theory, favoured by Ernie Lehman,' said Gill.

Duncan glanced up from his food. 'Sounds bonkers, but it might be genius. That said, I've never read any plausible explanation of how Nessie could make its way in and out of the loch.'

'Well, if I ever meet Lehman, I'll ask him for you.' Gill thought for a second. 'Just a long shot, but have you ever heard of something called *Project Leviathan*?'

Duncan looked thoughtful while he finished making a sandwich. 'I've heard the name. Not that I know much. But I do recall something from a conversation in a bookshop years ago.'

Gill nodded, so Duncan continued. 'During the first world war, the rumour was the navy looked into the possibility of building a submarine base out in the North Sea somewhere. It was the stuff of madness. Something about a long tunnel on the seabed running out to a patch of deep water. They planned to protect the subs in some underwater base. Kind of a forward position to attack the Germans.'

'Fascinating. Go on.'

Duncan held up his hands. 'That's it. And it's just rumour. I'm not sure my interest in marine mythology would expose me to the right sources, but I've never heard anything about *Leviathan* progressing, let alone completed.' He shook his head vigorously. 'The technological challenges would be incredible. The cost ...'

'Yeah, okay. Thanks anyway.' Gill swept his hand across the table and scooped up the nearest article. 'I'll give these a second read-through if that's okay. Then I need to hit the road.'

When Gill reached the road junction in Invermoriston, he realised he had gone too far. Cassy's details had indicated a loch-side farm, but he'd seen little agricultural land for miles in either direction. Industrial forestry covered nearby hilltops, while a thick swathe of deciduous woodland smothered the banks of the loch and followed a river upstream. He paused his search to take a photo of the Thomas Telford Bridge. Built in the mid-nineteenth century and now bypassed by the main road, the two arches of the old bridge spanned a fast-running river in a daring feat of engineering that managed to be beautiful and practical.

He turned around in the car park of a pretty hotel and headed back slowly towards Fort Augustus. Travelling in this direction for a few hundred metres, he found a gap in the crash barrier that led down to a rickety wooden gate. Confident he'd found the address he was looking for, he turned off the road and followed a short track until he reached a single-storey dwelling surrounded by run-down out-houses. Stepping out of the car, he immediately sensed no one was around. No one answered his knock at the house, nor did he see anyone when he worked his way around the outbuildings. The air was warm, and a wisp of woodsmoke hung in the still air. Having no other lead to follow, he struck into the forest, trying to locate the source of the smell.

A maze of little paths ran through the intensely managed woodland, past rough stacks of logs and branches. He came at last to a clearing around a black hollow, where a thin column of blue smoke escaped to the sky.

'Mind you don't get too close,' said a southern English accent. Gill turned to find a burly youth standing at the edge of the clearing with an armful of dry branches. '200 degrees centigrade in a pit two metres deep. You fall in there, mate; you'll never be seen again.'

'Sorry. Didn't mean to disturb anything,' said Gill.

The lad tossed the branches onto a pile, turned and spat. 'Not that it would bother me. You're trespassing anyway.'

Gill did his best to muster a smile. 'Technically, there is no law of trespass in Scotland. Anyway, I've got an appointment with Claire Sweem.'

'Don't give a shit,' said the lad. 'Far as I'm concerned, this farm ain't Scotland.'

The lad stepped towards him, and for a moment, Gill anticipated conflict. The lad's right arm came up abruptly, and he pointed down another track leading towards the shore. 'Me mum's down that way.' Then he turned and walked back into the forest.

Gill watched him go and gave himself a shake to exorcise the encounter. Then he set off down the track, walking briskly for two minutes until he came to a similar clearing. There he found a black hole in the ground with no smoke. It was about two metres square, with a ladder poking out the top. Gill called out until a small, dirt-stained face, run around with a mane of wild grey hair, bobbed out of the hole.

'Hi. I'm Gill McArdle. I'm looking for Claire.'

The figure sprang out of the hole. 'That's me. Claire, that is.' She peered at him before thrusting out a dirty hand. 'Your office said they was sending a lady. Somebody called Jill?'

Gill gave her thin hand a gentle shake and resolved not to wipe his hands on his trousers. 'Sorry. Common mistake.

I'm Gill, short for Gillan.' He glanced around him for any sign of the boy. 'Sorry I'm late, by the way. My colleague gave me your address as Invermoriston farm.'

'That's right.' The wiry figure stood before him, wringing her hands. 'This here is a charcoal farm. We grows our own trees, turns 'em into charcoal.'

'I met a lad …,' Gill turned and pointed back up the track.

'Andrew,' said Claire, nodding her head vigorously. 'That's my Andrew.'

'I hope I didn't upset him. I think I might have.' Gill was uncertain.

Claire pulled a tight thin smile. 'He's protective of me, see. Doesn't like to meet strangers in our woods.'

'You spoke to Cassy,' said Gill. 'In my office.'

The head started nodding again. 'Yes, yes. You come about the monster?'

'Aye. Cassy said you reported a sighting a couple of weeks back.'

Claire's wide eyes stared frantically at the ground for a few moments. 'Twelve days ago.'

Gill turned and looked around him. He couldn't even see the water through the dense layers of foliage.

'Andrew was fishing. He likes fishing. It was after supper time. I went down to the shore to bring him a sandwich, and we was chatting, like. Suddenly this wave comes.' She thrust her hands up as if mimicking a geyser, 'Just came from nowhere, splashed right up the bank, soaked our feet and washed away Andy's sandwich.'

Gill pulled out a notebook and scribbled a few details. 'Did you see what caused the wave?' he said, glancing at her.

'Must have come right up close to the shore. The spot where Andy does his fishing is deep water. He reckons the creature came in close to take the fish that were at his line.'

'Exciting,' said Gill. 'And quite frightening, I imagine.' He scribbled another note. 'Did you see a creature?'

'Andy reckons he did, but it was pretty dusky. I couldn't see nothin' properly. Ang on. I'll go get Andy. He'll tell you better.'

Claire scuttled back up the path before Gill could stop her. For a few minutes, he walked around the charcoal operation. The pit here was cold. Claire had been filling jute sacks stained black from a previous day's burn. Gill worked out that some of the machinery back at the house must be for bagging the charcoal.

'You a reporter then?' Andy strode into the clearing, to within striking distance of Gill. For now, his hands were in his pockets and his manner more subdued.

'I write for a scientific magazine based in Dundee,' said Gill. 'Never really thought about it like that, but yeah, you could say I'm a reporter.'

'Yes or no, woulda done,' said Andy turning away. 'We saw the creature down this way if you wanna take a look.'

Gill followed behind, and Claire walked beside him, taking two quick, short paces for each one of his. 'You folks lived here long?'

'Ten, eleven years,' Claire replied. 'My husband Bob worked in a car factory in Luton. Always wanted to come live up here. Been up on holiday a few times. We bought the forest and the charcoal business with his redundancy.' She stopped and wiped her nose a few times. 'Poor old Bob. He's been gone a couple of years. Bloody throat cancer.'

'I'm sorry,' said Gill, stopping to look at her properly. 'But you seem to have made a go of things.'

Claire's smile had genuine warmth for the first time. 'Me and Andy love it here. The locals are a bit weird, but we keeps to ourselves.'

'And your business is doing well,' said Gill as they started walking again.

Claire nodded. 'Lots of tourists means lots of barbeques. We get by.'

A couple of minutes later, they caught up with Andy, who was standing staring into the black waters of Loch Ness.

'Don't get too close, darlin', said Claire grasping his sleeve.

Andy tore his arm free of her grasp and turned to face Gill. 'Do you believe in ol' Nessie then?'

Gill took a step nearer the water and stared out over the loch. 'I dunno, Andy. I imagine Nessie's legend has some basis in reality.'

'What like?' Andy demanded.

Gill shrugged and turned to face him. 'Maybe a creature. Maybe a natural phenomenon.'

'That Mr Kerr, he believes in the creature.'

'Is he the archaeologist?' Gill asked.

'Yes,' said Claire. 'Bout three year ago. Martin Kerr he said his name was. He was diggin' holes just along here.' She turned away from them and struck into a wide patch of immature birch. Gill and Andy followed.

'The previous people planted these trees, said Claire. 'Not long before that, this land was just bog to the loch's edge.'

Looking around him, Gill could see they were standing in the base of a hollow disguised by the presence of the trees. He considered the geography and reasoned this area had once been a small bay in the loch. Silt from the nearby river had gradually turned it into a marsh. The extension of the charcoal forest had added roots and fibre, making the ground firmer underfoot. Claire stopped suddenly and turned through degrees, as if puzzled by the forest, before setting off again. A minute later, she halted beside a large rectangular boulder. 'I remember 'im leavin' his stuff on this rock,' she said, clasping a hand on a large stone. 'Then he dug a load of trenches startin' about here and running down to the water.'

'He was working on his own?' said Gill. 'That's unusual.'

'Yep,' said Claire. 'Although Andy helped a few days, didn't you love?'

Andy shrugged but didn't respond.

'Did Mr Kerr mention what organisation he was with?'

'Nope,' Claire replied. 'He didn't say where he was from. He just turned up one day and asked for permission to dig. My Bob wasn't keeping well at the time, so I didn't know whether to say yes or no. But when he offered money, I told him he could.'

'He paid you?'

'Aye. Two hundred pounds in cash. Made me sign a sheet of paper that allowed him access for a month and ownership of anything he found.'

'And did he find anything?' Gill asked.

Claire and Andy turned to face each other. 'Not that he ever told us,' said Claire, nodding furiously again.

Before she could say anymore, Andy cut in. 'He said he wanted to work in private. But it was hard going, like. I offered to help him, and he would give me a tenner to help him lift the topsoil and get him started on a new section. Or some days, he would have me backfill the holes he'd finished.'

'And did you ever see him uncover anything?'

'I come down one night at dusk. Fair creeped me out. There was this one trench with bones at the bottom. Not small bones like a human. Big ones.'

Gill's eyes darted between mother and son. 'And he never mentioned them to you?'

Claire shook her head. 'A few days later, he was gone. We was away for a couple of days, and when we come back, Mr Kerr was gone, and he'd filled in all his holes so neat you could barely see where they was. Didn't leave as much as a note.'

Gill nodded. His hands dropped onto his hips as he kicked at the scrub of blaeberries at his feet. 'Would you be willing to let another dig take place on your land?'

'Price has gone up to four hundred for the month,' said Andy immediately.

Gill nodded. 'I might need to bring in a bigger team, a few vehicles.'

'In that case, six hundred,' said Andy, raising a hand to stop his mother's silent protest.

'I'll talk to my boss,' said Gill. 'But in principle, we might have a deal. Also, the law states that you own a good proportion of anything we might find.'

'That's fair,' said Andy.

'Okay. I'll be back in a few days with some instruments to survey the site. If my boss signs off on this, I'll bring the money then.'

Gill shook hands with Claire. Andy had already turned his back, striding away to where he had been working. Gill shook his head and started back towards his car. On the way, he made two calls. The first was to Fiona. Had she booked any more work after she finished at Montrose? Could she raise a small crew? The second was to Cassy.

'Good call on Invermoriston,' he told her.

'You on to something?'

'Could be. Looks promising. We'll find out in a few days. Meanwhile, I've another name for you to research. A guy called Martin Kerr.'

Gill's heart was beating fast when he arrived back at his car. The exertion of the brisk walk, he told himself.

Chapter 17

It was Thursday morning. Gill ran up the stairs to the office, knowing that he was unlikely to be first at his desk even though he was early. Across the extended pens marking the physical boundaries of each magazine, early risers were already working or returning with coffee from a machine. A hand or two went up in greeting, but no one called out, as silence was the unofficial etiquette at this time of day. Later, when the clock passed nine, the phones would start to ring, and the advertising people would reluctantly appear at their desks, their endless phone calls adding weight to the office din. But for now, it was quiet. If he was honest, this was the only time of day he could work productively in the office.

Craig was already in, well ahead of the time he had agreed with Gill. They planned to sit and talk through the page layouts for the Caithness story. Cassy too was at her desk, which is where Gill gravitated first.

'Morning, Early Bird,' he said, laying his laptop onto his desk before turning to face her.

The banter he expected didn't materialise. Instead, Cassy met his gaze with a serious expression, the morning's post lying half opened in front of her.

'I'm glad to see you. Quickly, grab Tony's office before someone else does.'

'What's up, Cass?' said Gill.

Cassy's only reply was to gather up a few sheets of paper and march the few steps to the publisher's office. She scanned the room booking form on the door, scrawled in her initials and waited for Gill to join her. He sat down apprehensively, anticipating a letter of resignation.

'What's the matter?'

'This,' said Cassy, sliding a typed letter across the desk towards him. 'I mean, we get some weird stuff in here, but this is the first time we've had a death threat.'

Gill took the paper from her and read. It didn't take him long. 'This came in the morning post?'

'Yeah. Postmarked yesterday in Inverness.' She examined the envelope again before passing it back. 'What's this all about?'

'I have no idea.' Gill reread the letter, then spoke it aloud. '*I know who you are. I know where you live. I know where you work. I'm giving you one warning to stay away from her. I've waited 30 years for this, and if you think that you're going to swoop in at the last minute and steal her from me, you'd better think again. Stay away from her and from me. This is my moment. If you try to take her from me, I will, repeat, will kill you.*' The paper was unsigned.

He tossed the letter in its bland bold type onto the table and stared at Cassy. 'That's bizarre.'

'It's really aggressive, Gill. Who's this person talking about? Are you involved with someone?'

Again, Gill shook his head. 'Nobody. I've lived like a monk this past year. I've not had the headspace.' He twisted the letter towards him. 'Are you sure the writer is talking about a woman?'

'Stay away from HER,' said Cassy, with emphasis. 'That's what he says. Besides, no woman would write this kind of crap. Is this about Salina? Does she have a man in her life?'

'Why are you asking about Salina?'

Cassy threw a glance heavenward. 'Oh! Hi, Salina! Great to hear from you, Salina! Talk again soon. SALINA!'

Gill shrugged. 'Okay. She's nice. But engaged, apparently.'

'Apparently?'

'Well, it's not as if you know it. I spent four days with her the week before last. I don't think her fiancé as much as texted her when I was around.'

Cassy clenched her right fist and gave Gill a mock punch. 'She's a professional girl. Probably they talk at night. Honestly, you know nothing about women.'

Gill gently pushed her hand away. 'We've worked together for a few days. It's hardly grounds for a care home magnate to take a hit out on me. Besides,' he said, tapping the envelope, 'Inverness postcode.'

'Maybe Salina is warning you off herself,' said Cassy.

'I think she's well capable of putting me in the picture without resorting to this.' He picked up the letter and thrust it back into Cassy's hands.

Cassy read it again. 'This reference to thirty, is that Salina's age?'

He shrugged. 'She's about that. I haven't asked.'

'Or it could be his age,' Cassy suggested. 'Or maybe it's been that long since he's been with a girl.'

Gill smiled and ran the back of his hand across the stubble on his chin. 'But you have to say that as a death threat, it's utterly useless. I mean, "Come on, moron." Stay away from whom?'

Cassy dipped her head towards him. 'What are you going to do about it?'

'What can I do? It's a non-specific threat. Probably some head-case having a laugh.'

'At least tell Tony about it.'

'Do we need to? I mean, there's no threat to the office.'

Cassy straightened and leaned back from him. 'You think? I can't wait to sit alone on the top deck of The Ferry bus this evening. Maybe I'll get to meet this nut job personally.'

'Okay, Cassy. I'll mention it to Tony. The chart on the door says he's due in at 10 am, so I'll catch him before I hit the road again.'

They finished their meeting without saying another word. Gill took the letter to his desk and searched it for anything of significance until Craig called him over to sit at his Mac. Soon he was immersed in his work and managed to put the letter out of his mind until Cassy whispered to say that Tony was in his office. Together, they grabbed him before he got caught by somebody else.

Gill was taken aback by how dismissive Tony was. He read the letter and laid it back on the desk while he unpacked his briefcase.

'I wouldn't worry, Gill. When you do any kind of work in the public domain, you always get some negative feedback.

I'd advise you to follow the usual precautions and keep on with your life. You'll probably never hear from this guy again.'

'Usual precautions?' quizzed Gill.

'Someone has threatened you, so contact a police station and get them to log it; issue you with a crime reference. Maybe even give them a copy of the letter if they ask for it.' He stared at Gill, measuring his response. 'It's really all you can do.'

Gill nodded, lifting the paper and putting it back in its envelope.

'Do you know any police officers? You could just take it down to the local station, I suppose.'

'Aye,' said Gill. 'I'll work something out.'

'Anyway,' said Tony, looking at Gill directly. 'Talk me through this proposed new excavation of yours.'

'Have I ever let you down on a dig?' Gill was immediately aware he sounded defensive.

'No. But Montrose was a big layout for us. It's my job to ensure the company gets bang from its buck.'

Gill laid his hands flat on the table. 'Okay, these are my thoughts. I've not come across a single credible person who believes, without reservation, there is a creature living in Loch Ness. So, the only player still in the game is the theory that an unknown species migrates into the loch, stays to breed or give birth, then returns to the open sea.'

'Species? I thought we were looking for a monster, singular?' said Tony.

'Not enough food for a high-end predator. I can show you the stats but in the meantime, take my word for it. I'm going with species in the plural because the only reason for animals to undertake a difficult migration is to breed.'

'Interesting,' said Tony. 'But Ness is a long way from the sea. How can that idea hold substance?'

Gill glanced at Cassy. 'We know the lochs in the Great Glen connected to the ocean at the end of the last ice age. One theory is that water channels still link the loch to open sea, most likely at the Inverness end.'

Tony didn't look convinced. 'Can we prove that?'

'We might,' said Gill. 'Many birds, fish and mammals migrate to breed. The one thing they all have in common is a high mortality rate after their breeding cycle,' said Gill.

Tony wasn't nodding, but he didn't seem ready to dismiss the idea. 'Go on.'

'If it exists, our beast is aquatic, be it fish, reptile or mammal. Like any other species, it would lay its eggs or birth its young, then the weak specimens would probably end up in shallow water, near a river mouth where the oxygen levels are highest. And a proportion of them would die there.'

'Gill thinks we might find tangible evidence of this at Invermoriston,' added Cassy. 'Near the river mouth.'

'Wild guess,' said Gill, laying his hands on the table in front of him. 'The angle I want to take on this is the migration theory. It's the last, best hope to find Nessie. We gallantly do the dig. Ninety-nine chances out of a hundred say we find nothing. But we've looked and reasoned, and unlike anybody else, we draw a line under this thing and say conclusively that nothing unusual lives in the loch.'

'That'll be popular with locals,' muttered Cassy.

'What if you do find something?' asked Tony.

Gill suppressed a smile. 'Different opportunity entirely.'

Tony put his hand inside his jacket pocket and pulled out a printed email. 'I've got a first sales estimate from the distributor this morning on issue ten, where we led with Montrose. They're moving copies between outlets to meet demand. Sales efficiency might go as high as eighty-seven per cent.'

Cassy immediately tapped on her phone before letting out a low whistle. 'Sixty-two thousand copies sold. Plus digital! That's more like it.'

'And my reason for mentioning this?' said Tony raising his voice. 'With one cracking issue behind us, we can't afford to follow it up with a dud.' He paused to let Gill see his point of view. 'Your narrative must be compelling. I'm not sure you're "Hey ho, no monster after all" storyline delivers the punch you need.'

Gill spread out his hands. 'I'm limited to the facts of the situation. If we don't make a scientific breakthrough in every dig, then that's the way things are.'

'Talk me through this migration idea. Convince me it's got merit,' said Tony.

Gill gave a long sigh. He wasn't sure how convincing he could be. 'There are two known proponents of the theory. One is Martin Kerr, the guy rumoured to have found bones at Invermoriston, and he hasn't been seen for three years. We know of another man called Lehman. I've heard he's researching in the Ness area, but he's tricky to get hold of.'

'Without an expert witness, this is all circumspect,' said Tony. 'Tell you what. Let me think about it until the end of the week. In the meantime, let's all consider alternative storyboards.'

Tony tapped the table with his knuckles, dismissing Gill and Cassy with a professionally encouraging smile. As they left the room, Gill wrestled with dark thoughts. Turning to Cassy, 'Any luck with finding those guys?'

'Martin Kerr is at least a real person. I picked him up in several archaeological web pages spanning a period of about ten years, although nothing recently. He appears mainly as a footnote because he was a volunteer.'

'Is he associated with any specific areas of interest?' asked Gill.

'Not at first, but in later years, he's associated with the big lochs, crannogs, that sort of thing. Then he just disappears.'

'Okay. Can you contact some of those old digs and see if anyone remembers him?' said Gill. 'What about Lehman?'

Cassy shook her head. 'Can't find anything on him. Not even a mention on an electoral roll.'

'So, it's an assumed name?'

'Looks like it. I did what you said and started to look for blogs and websites, but there's a maze of wee websites with a passing interest in the loch.'

'This guy is more determined than that. Bit of an ego too. He's put serious time into background work and ongoing observation of the loch. I suspect he will have a big shop window on his research.'

Cassy smiled and slid across a post-it note with a web address. 'I searched for all the domain names registered in the last five years that mention the loch. Mainly B&B's, gift shops and the like. But try this one.'

'TheLochNessDiscovery.com,' Gill read aloud. 'What's it about?'

'The domain has been active for three months but doesn't have a public website. Just a login screen.'

Gill flicked the note between his fingertips. 'Curious. Whoever created the website must know that the search engines will pick up the site name. If it's active, he must plan to go live quite soon.' Gill stopped and thought for a second. 'Do we know anyone who could get us a sneak peek behind the login screen?'

Cassy tossed her head back. 'You thinking of hacking this guy's website?'

'Nothing illegal,' Gill countered. 'Just check for security weaknesses we could legitimately exploit.'

'Bit dodgy if you ask me.' Cassy took back the note. 'What do you hope to find out?'

'He probably has a website built behind the login screen. Something that isn't ready yet. But even if I could get a mobile number for this guy. Something to take me forward.'

'Okay,' said Cassy. 'I'll ask Craig. He's a bit techy.' She folded her arms and leaned towards him. 'Tony is going to get twitchy about the timeline towards the next issue. What's your plan from here?'

Gill sighed and twisted in his chair. 'I've got lots of solid background material from my meetings with Duncan and Brightman. Let's get all that briefed to the team so we can start working on some provisional layouts. Then I'll go north again tomorrow. See if I can nail a proper story.'

'Still under pressure?' said Cassy.

Gill closed his eyes. 'People have been looking for "Lucy" for a hundred years without success. Tony seems to think I can do it in a fortnight.'

'You said yourself. There's a story here.'

'Aye, but give me six months, give me a year.'

Cassy jumped up and walked to the whiteboard on the office wall. Starting with the Whaligoe eel, she wrote down a list of the people Gill had met over the past two weeks. 'This list,' she said. 'Have I missed anybody?'

Gill stared at the names, his left hand drawn tightly across his mouth. Sitting up again, he said, 'the package you forwarded to me. The vintage military drawings. Did you manage to trace the sending address?'

'A mailbox in Helensburgh. No identification.'

Gill thought for a moment, then started scribbling on his pad. 'Do me a favour,' he said. 'Type this up and post it to the mailbox. Let's see if anybody bites.'

Cassy scanned the note. 'Project Leviathan. What on earth is that?'

'Probably another red herring. But I'm curious about it because of the timing. Someone sent me that package very deliberately.'

Cassy tapped the board and focused his attention. 'Anybody else?'

Gill ran a hand through his hair. 'The little old lady I met to talk about her amazing shrinking mountain. Nobody else.'

Cassy added Mrs McLean to her list and turned back to him. 'Good. Now, can we cross-fertilise any of these names?'

'How do you mean?'

'Do any of them have insight into some areas where you're stuck?'

'Well, the one that leaps out at me is Salina. She doesn't know anything about my interest in Loch Ness.'

'Hot-looking oceanographic expert. Detailed knowledge of aquatic environments and marine animals.' Cassy held out a hand. 'Might be worth a shot.'

'More likely, she'd conclude I'm an idiot,' Gill retorted.

'Can you see past your schoolboy crush?'

Gill grimaced. He felt called out. 'Okay,' he said eventually. 'I'll think of an angle. She's due back from Orkney later this week. I'll track her down.'

'Ahmed.' The phone had rung only twice. Salina's response was crisp.

'Hi, Salina. Gill here.'

'Hey, Gill.'

'How's Orkney?'

'Good trip. The weather improved after we spoke, so we got finished on schedule. Gave me time for a day's sightseeing.'

'So, you're on your way back?'

'Tomorrow. We'll drop the DSV back to Oban and then head back to St Andrews.'

'Would your schedule allow you a couple of days on Loch Ness? Bed, board and reasonable expenses courtesy of *Mysterious Scotland*.'

Salina's response wasn't immediate. 'Is this business or pleasure?'

'Business.'

'Pity,' she replied. 'If you'd said "pleasure", I could have taken time off in lieu. If it's business, the Uni will charge you.'

'Okay. Pleasure then. How about we take a cruise on the loch together?' He gave her a few seconds to decode his mixed messages before continuing. 'I'm trying to solve a puzzle on the loch, and I've met a fellow scientist. I want to get the three of us together.'

'Are you onto a story?'

'Not sure. But it's make-or-break this week. I need to decide if it's got legs.'

'Can I bring my diving gear?' Salina asked. 'I've never dived Loch Ness, and I've heard it's amazing.'

'That works. I want to survey our dig site from the water so it should be easy to organise a dive for you.'

Salina left a brief pause. 'Okay. Let me double-check my diary. If it's still clear, I'm in. Text me where we're staying, and I'll see you tomorrow evening.'

Gill hung up and immediately called Alexandra Brightman.

'Sandy. Gill McArdle here. I'd like to book a trip out on your boat.'

Chapter 18

'You are kidding,' said Salina. '6 am?' It was Friday evening, and they were sitting together in the bar of a traditional hotel in Drumnadrochit. It was an atmospheric building but in dire need of a refurb.

'That's the only time she could do,' Gill replied. 'And she's got another booking at midday.'

'Okay. But I seem to remember you positioned this as two days R&R. I'd not banked on such an early start.' Salina groaned. 'If I'm diving, I won't be able to eat any breakfast.'

'We can get some afterwards.'

'I've thought of a new condition to this little enterprise,' said Salina, pointing at him from where her hands rested on the table.

He raised his eyebrows and waited for what was coming.

'Safety rules say I can't dive solo. You mentioned that you'd done a bit of diving before. You'll need to come with me.'

'I haven't dived in years,' Gill protested. 'And that was in the Med, not some freezing Scottish loch. Besides, I don't have a dive suit.'

'No worries,' said Salina. 'I've got a van full of St Andrews finest.' She looked him up and down. 'I'm sure I'll have a suit that fits you.'

Gill started to protest, but Salina's hand went up. 'That's my condition. Take it or leave it.'

The following morning at 5.45 am, Gill shivered on a jetty on the northern outskirts of the village. He stood watching Salina selecting gear from her van, standing still while she held various suits against him to check she had the best size. Lithe and athletic, she was already dressed in a black, tight-fitting layer to wear under her drysuit. Feeling his attraction towards her surge, he forced himself to turn away.

The light at this time of year always amazed him. Sunlight rippled the surface of the loch, a silver ribbon that ran as far as the eye could see. At the end of the jetty, the engines of the 'Ness Explorer' were already idling. Brightman was on deck tapping through her phone for the latest weather forecast while the boat's skipper set about some safety checks.

'Hi Sandy,' he called out. 'Grand morning.'

Sandy and skipper John left the boat and came across to help them with their oxygen tanks. They were out on the water a few minutes later and easing across Urquhart Bay.

'Invermoriston you wanted, as well as a dive on the steep ledges?' said Sandy. 'It will take us a while to get down that far. We pass some nice water on the way, so I suggest you suit up.'

Salina was already pulling her dry suit over her thermal layer. Gill was not as well prepared and chided himself for a slight shyness as he stripped to his underwear and started to peel on the suit against his bare skin. Salina was smirking at him, perhaps relishing his discomfort.

'Urquhart Castle,' said Sandy, pointing to a group of substantial ruins on a headland. 'Best place to see the beast. Well, the best place apart from the deck of the *Ness Explorer*.'

'You see Nessie quite regularly, Sandy?' said Salina, moving up into the cockpit beside her.

'Most days. Twice on a Sunday,' Sandy replied, flicking on a bank of monitors.

'Nice kit,' said Salina. 'The sonar and sounders I recognise, but what's this one?'

'Acoustic sensor. We monitor a range of frequencies,' Sandy replied.

Sandy tuned the instruments to the prevailing conditions while John slowed the boat, bringing it within a stone's throw of the shore.'

Salina leant over the sounder screen. 'Bloody hell! Look at the depth. This close to the shore, and it's over thirty metres.'

Gill struggled his arms into his suit and shuffled over to join her. It had been many years since he'd worn this kind of gear, and he'd forgotten how the thick rubber skin pressed against his flesh. He took a moment to digest the information on the screen. Seeing his dismay, Salina interpreted the data for him.

'This kind of sounder doesn't just look straight down. That would only give you a single depth. This device casts out a beam, port, starboard and forward of the boat. What you are looking at is a graphical interpretation of the data. Like a perpetually updating map of the loch's floor.'

'Gill mentioned you're an oceanographer,' said Sandy, smiling at Salina. 'Let's see if you've EVER seen anything like this.' She nodded to John, and the boat steered ninety degrees to port straight out into the loch. The map on the sounder constantly changed, the axis updating to reflect the ever-greater depth. A few hundred metres from the shore, the loch's floor appeared remarkably flat against the steep sides of the canyon walls.

'Two hundred and fifty metres!' marvelled Salina. 'Way deeper than most of the coastal waters I spend my life exploring.'

Sandy nodded to John, and the boat turned back towards the shore. 'When you go into the water, you'll need to keep a close eye on your depth. The thermocline lies at about ten metres this time of year. The temperature will be between twelve and fourteen degrees centigrade at that level. Below that, the water will be five to ten degrees colder.'

Salina turned to look at Gill. 'Do you hear that, dive buddy? Keep a close watch on me. No sneaking off on your own.'

Gill was feeling nervous now. He sat and ran through the series of hand gestures he'd learned at a summer dive school many years before. Salina watched him before forming a silent gesture with her own hands. 'Are you okay?'

Gill formed the response with his right hand. 'I'm okay.'

The boat was slowing now and drew to a halt ten metres from the shore. John cast a diving buoy out into the water to warn other vessels while Sandy made final preparations with Salina and Gill.

'Just twenty minutes on this dive,' said Salina. 'Then we'll regroup.'

'Do you have torches?' asked Sandy. 'In this whisky-coloured water, there's not much light below five metres.'

'Dammit. Didn't think of that,' said Salina.

'Just a second.' Sandy ducked into the forward compartment and returned with two waterproof torches with blue-tinted lenses. 'Take these. I recommend you swim to the shore and then follow the canyon walls down to your elected dive depth.' She tapped the sounder screen. 'We'll monitor your lateral movement on this.'

Gill and Salina entered the water. After carrying out their last buddy checks, they half swam, half flipped across to the shore. They arrived at a long, broken rock face with bracken and heathers anchored in thin soil, hanging just out of reach. Salina signalled Gill, and then together, they turned their bodies and used the weight of their legs to propel them under the water.

The sunlight thinned immediately. They swam over to the rock face, and as he watched the boundary between land and loch plummet like a cliff into the depths below him, Gill sensed how vulnerable he was. Salina signalled with a thumb down, so he nodded and followed her as she swam deeper into the dark water. She paused again at five metres. Gill could barely see her now and was relieved when her torch flicked on. She signalled down again, and he nodded. The canyon walls were changing now. Slime and silt smothered the rock surface, and Gill was careful not to brush against it as it set off cloudy cascades that dimmed even their torchlight. Salina was levelling out their descent, striking an angle similar to walking down a flight of stairs. When she stopped to check their depth, Gill did the same. They were at twelve metres. Gill felt the water cool around his body when they started to descend again. He had heard what it was like, but he had never passed through a thermocline, the layer between a cold body of water and the warmer surface water. Salina shone her light at him, checking his status. He formed the 'okay' with his hand, and they continued down. They had agreed they would stop at twenty metres and then gradually ascend. His heart was pounding, and he was relieved when Salina signalled that the descent was over.

Slowly Salina flipped over to the wall of the canyon. Joining her, Gill found the wall entirely soft to his touch. He pressed his hand into the silt, feeling for the hard rock underneath. Gradually he squeezed his arm into the soft layer as far as his shoulder, and still, he could feel no stone. Salina touched him on the arm, tapped her watch and indicated they should begin the ascent. He moved to pull out his arm but found the silts gripping him tightly. He moved to turn his knees to face the wall, to give some weight to his push but found his knees ebb into the soft mud. With nothing solid to lean against, he was now semi-submerged, and panic threatened to engulf him.

Salina's hand was in his face rotating slightly from side to side. 'Is something wrong?'

Gill pointed at his trapped arm with his free hand and made a tugging motion. Perhaps it was his imagination telling him the pressure on his trapped arm was increasing.

Salina moved quickly. Getting into position beneath his trapped arm, she started to scoop violently with both hands. An explosion of silts and mud enveloped them, but just as suddenly, Gill's arm sprang free. Salina grasped his waist and, with a few strong kicks, lifted them clear of the cloud. They stood treading water for a few moments while Salina steadied him. With the lights shining near their faces so he could see the whites of her eyes; calm, professional, and totally engaged in the moment.

Something in the light above them changed. Gill glanced up to see a huge black shape advancing towards them. Tentacles dashed around them, leaping out to surround their bodies, pressing on them, pushing them deeper. They were back in the dirty water again, the creature sucking them lower. For a moment, Gill saw a cold, loveless eye sweep past his face. Huge and blue above a gaping mouth. He considered surrendering to terror but checked himself with the thought that this would be an interesting way to die. The mouth stretched towards him, the eye almost in his face, then suddenly the scene changed. The eye was Salina's torch, and the mouth was the debris-strewn outline of her dive suit. She was clasping his shoulder and pointing to the surface. Noticing his hands were free, he realised he had dropped Sandy's torch.

Together they began to kick towards the surface. Gill could feel his blood pounding in his head. About halfway to the surface, Salina made him stop and rest. She swung the torch beneath them. The loch appeared to have a false bottom as the mudslide created a dense blanket along the level of the thermocline. Gill could feel the water becoming warmer, and his panic subsided again. Just then, a black shadow passed overhead, a great black shape visible against the thin daylight. He gripped Salina's free arm tightly. She shook herself free from him and made a V shape with her hands. 'It's the boat.'

He nodded and, when he received her instruction, continued the ascent.

Chapter 19

A few minutes later, they were back on board the *Ness Explorer* in brilliant sunlight. Gill was breathing heavily and, for a moment, had nothing to say.

'Looks like you got caught in the silt fall,' said Sandy. 'We watched it happen on the sounder. Sorry if we set that off. I thought we had the boat well enough back from the banks, but maybe not.'

'You didn't cause the fall,' said Salina flashing a glance at Gill. 'We managed that all by ourselves.'

'I got my arm stuck in the silt,' said Gill.

'My fault,' said Sandy. 'Should have warned you about that. The canyon walls are caked with silt. It's sediment that washes off from the mountains. We reckon it's as much as eighty metres thick when you get onto the loch floor.'

'Can I use your forward locker to change?' asked Salina.

'Sure. Won't give you a lot of privacy, but we'll leave you to it,' said John. 'Meanwhile, on to Invermoriston.'

The boat picked up speed slightly, and whether out of habit or easy-going nature, John put some music on speakers while Sandy kept a close watch on the monitors.

Gill slumped in the stern and panted. He wasn't sure what to make of the last few minutes. The one thing he did know was he never wanted to as much as paddle in this great loch ever again. Salina was upset. He could tell from her gestures and her haste to go and change. The forward locker did not have a door, and he could see her legs as she peeled back her thermal underlayer. He couldn't help noticing that she had nice legs. Long, with warmth from her natural colour, even though the cold water left goose pimples across her thighs and down her calves.

He turned away, setting his mind to getting out of his wetsuit but finding himself weak and slightly shaky. No sooner had he disentangled himself from the breathing apparatus than Salina was beside him. 'Here, let me help.' Her voice was clipped, but some warmth crept back into her eyes.

'Sorry,' Gill mumbled. 'I didn't do great down there.'

'You did fine,' said Salina. 'You reacted well under the circumstances.' She freed one of his arms from the heavy suit and forcefully gripped his wrist. 'It was a near thing, though. You could have died. And that responsibility lies with me.'

He gave his head an irritable shake. 'I don't think so.'

'Stand up a second.' Salina tugged his arm. 'I was the dive leader. I got a chance to dive Loch Ness and jumped at it. No planning, next to no safety prep. I didn't adequately check the credentials of my dive partner.'

'So, you're impulsive,' he said, exploiting her tight grip on him by jerking his body to pull her towards him.

Their faces were close enough for him to feel her breath on his face, and for a long moment, she said nothing. Then she started tugging on the sleeve of his other arm. 'I'm engaged, Gill,' she said quietly. 'Let's keep this professional.'

Gill nodded. He stood bare-chested, facing her. Her eyes darted around his impassive face, and then she turned away to join the others in the cockpit.

The boat picked up speed, and for twenty minutes, Gill sat alone with his hurt pride. He'd asked the skipper to swing into Invermoriston Bay so he could survey the potential dig site from the water. The boat slowed as it passed the spot where the river tumbled into the loch, then eased back to idling speed as it approached the forested shoreline.

'It got a bit shallower as we passed the river mouth, but look at the sounder now.' The skipper tapped the screen, and Gill looked as the silted river mouth gave way to the sheer depth of the loch, the floor dropping away steeply.

'Lucy can swim almost to the bankside and still be in thirty metres of water,' observed Sandy.

'With all this deposition, diving must be dangerous just about anywhere in the loch,' said Salina.

'You don't fancy another dip?' asked Sandy.

Salina glanced at Gill. 'We'll pass, thanks.'

'In that case, we just have time for a spin down to Fort Augustus,' said Sandy. 'The bed of the loch breaks up a little at that end.'

'How do you mean?' asked Gill.

'It fragments into channels, probably old river beds or earlier erosion by glaciers.'

The boat accelerated again, and Salina joined Gill at the stern as he enjoyed the strengthening sunshine.

'So, Mystery Man. Have you discovered anything?' she asked, forcing a little reconciliation into her eyes.

Gill shrugged. 'I've got a potential dig at Invermoriston. A guy did some archaeology there a couple of years back. But even though he seemed excited by his preliminary finds, he covered his tracks and disappeared without revealing what he discovered.'

'And why are we out on a boat?'

'Context. I want to get a feel for the place. Understand the geography.'

'You're not actually looking for monsters?' Her smile had deepened a little into amusement.

He squinted at her in the sunlight. 'Ninety-nine per cent of me isn't.'

She laughed.

He continued. 'We have this myth - a monster in a loch. A tale that goes back a hundred years. And we've got a bunch of recent sightings, which are raw data for my investigation. Those people are seeing something. Misinterpreting it perhaps.' Gill stopped and shook his head. 'What is it about this place?'

'And what facts have you gathered?'

Gill could see the scientist in Salina needed a hypothesis to match the data. 'Nothing. Nothing concrete. And in two weeks, I've got to write a long article about it. Then a week after that, I'll be on to the next thing.'

'Nessie just has to stay quiet for a few more days, and then you'll leave her alone.' Salina moved and sat beside him, and for a brief moment, their bare knees touched. He looked at her. 'What are you working on next?'

'I'm back at Oban next week with people from the Scottish Geological Society.'

'To survey your growing sea stack?'

'Yes. They're disputing my initial findings. We have to repeat the survey with the SGS present.'

'Back on the good ship, Harlequinn?'

'No. We've rented a different boat. The SGS are suspicious the equipment on Quinn's boat might be giving erroneous data.'

'Even though your readings on the DSV corroborated the Harlequinn's data?'

'Arthur and I have done a good deal of submersible work around Scotland. We're good at judging things by eye. The sea bed has changed, I'm certain of it.'

Gill regarded her pained expression for a few moments. 'But you have doubts.'

'On paper, I agree with the SGS. It's not likely. In those fast-moving waters, the stack should be eroding. If I reported the thing was ten metres lower, no one would question it.'

'Will you be diving next week?'

'Not in the submersible. We've blown the budget on that. We might free dive down to the peak of the stack. Depends on the conditions.'

'Well, you take care.'

She nodded, and for a moment, she laid a hand on his bare thigh and looked away.

Fort Augustus and the entrance to the Caledonian Canal at the southern end of the loch were visible over the bow. Three yachts bobbed in the open water, taking in their sails as they waited their turn to enter the canal system.

'Gill,' called Sandy. 'Take a look at this.'

Gill and Salina went forward and looked at the sounder. The water was shallower here, and in place of the abyssal plain of the open loch, a series of high ridges rose from the loch floor to mid-water.

'Like drowned canyons,' observed Salina. 'I'm more used to seeing this in coastal waters.'

Sandy nodded. 'There are acres of this, full of nooks and crannies.' She turned to Gill with a professional expression. 'If we do have a beast in this loch, this is where it would hide.' She reached out and highlighted a particular feature. 'Some of these recesses are cave entrances, probably underground rivers.'

The boat came to a halt and sat idling for a few minutes.

'Beautiful spot,' said Gill.

'Aye,' said Sandy. 'We'll run home via the east bank now.'

'Wait a second. What's that?' Salina pointed at an object floating just below the surface beside the boat. Long and white, they all realised together it was a dead fish.

'Och, dammit,' said Sandy. 'John, pass me your net and circle round.'

John repositioned the boat, and Sandy scooped up the fish and laid it on the deck. It was a substantial fish, perhaps 12 lbs, its skin a rich copper colour marked with vivid red spots, even while its eyes were white in death. 'It's a ferox trout,' said Sandy. 'The anglers troll for them at depth. Then after a long fight, they haul in the fish and then throw them back. Quite often see them like this. The fish are too tired to recover.'

'Knackers their swim bladders,' added John.

'And another over there,' said Salina, pointing.

'Sorry, but I can see one too,' said Gill from the other side of the boat.

Sandy asked John to circle a few times, and after fifteen minutes, they had counted more than a dozen dead fish.

'Do you think it's a poisoning incident? Perhaps one of the yachts has discharged something?' said Gill.

Sandy was shaking her head. 'They're all deep water fish. If there was poison, I'd expect to see a lot of small fish on the surface.'

'Gather a few up,' said Salina. 'I'll take them back to St Andrews and put them through the lab. Sandy, do you have a cool box I could borrow?'

The dead fish overshadowed the remainder of the trip. The east shore of the loch was austere; mostly steep mountainside cascading down into the loch, where the steep incline continued to the bottom. The only thing they saw to break the monotony was the Foyers Hydro-Electric power station. Its settling lagoon churned as water poured down from Loch Mhor on the high ground behind the station and through the turbines. Outside the protective walls of the lagoon, the water fizzed and bubbled as the remaining energy dissipated into the loch.

Gill pointed at the ugly blue building. 'That thing looks big enough to empty Loch Mhor in an afternoon.'

Sandy shook her head. 'This station only runs at peak times. During the night, it operates in reverse, drawing surplus power off the national grid to pump water back up the hill.'

'Bit of an eyesore,' Salina commented.

Sandy nodded towards the south. 'Aye. And another newer one just over that ridge at Glendoe. They did a far better job of hiding that one. Huge tunnels, all underground.'

'Wasn't there a problem with that facility?' Gill said.

'It hadn't been open long. Then in 2009, a rockfall blocked the tunnel carrying water from the reservoir to the power station. Took them years to dig a new tunnel around the damaged area.' Sandy glanced at her watch. 'Need to get back, folks. Hold on tight.'

She nodded at John, who eased the boat towards its top speed, the bow pointed towards Urquhart Bay. The engine noise made it difficult to talk, and Gill satisfied himself by taking in the scale of the loch, imagining it empty of all its water, the steep banks of the mountains continuing to the valley floor far below them. Try as he might, he found it difficult to imagine that only a few tens of thousands of years ago, vast glaciers were scraping out these valleys as the ice edged towards the open sea, propelled by gravity. He stole glances at Salina, who seemed lost in thought while she leaned against the wheelhouse. Her eyes closed, and long black hair flowing out behind her as the speeding boat bumped over the ripples on the loch.

The goodbyes with Sandy and John were hasty as their afternoon tour party was already mustering on the dock. Gill helped Salina get the diving equipment to her van. Salina too was getting ready to leave.

'I can't persuade you to stay another afternoon?' said Gill. 'I think my offer was for two nights.'

Salina looked at him and then at her feet. 'I'd better not.' She kicked at the cool box at her feet. 'Besides, I need to get this lot back to my lab before it matures into crab bait.'

'Thank you for the dive today,' said Gill. 'Sorry I put us in danger.'

She leaned forward and gave him a simple kiss on the cheek. 'You're welcome, Mystery Man.'

She picked up the cool box and waved it at him. 'Tell Sandy I'll be in touch. And don't forget you owe her a torch.' Then she climbed into her van and drove away.

Gill watched her join the main road, heading south down the loch, when he felt his phone vibrate. He glanced at the screen and picked up.

'Cassy!'

Cassy's voice sounded clipped. 'Tony agrees to fund the Invermoriston dig.'

'That's great news,' he said. 'But why are you guys in the office over the weekend?'

Cassy took a few seconds to respond. 'It's just Tony and me. Something came up. Any chance you could come down to Dundee?'

Gill glanced at his watch. 'Can it wait until Monday? I can drop in and see the Invermoriston landowner today to tee things up. But I need to spend tomorrow at Dad's.'

Cassy muffled the phone for a few seconds. 'Tony says that's fine. Monday 8 am in his office.' Gill could detect a tremor in Cassy's voice.

He considered pushing her to find out what was wrong but decided against it. 'Right. See you then.'

Chapter 20

Rough hands shake her, and Salina is suddenly awake. Startled, she sits up, banging her head on the bunk above.

'Snap to it,' says the man. 'Captain just sounded all hands.'

He looks at her quizzically, and she realises she has recoiled from him. Despite his urgent shaking, kind eyes peer at her from a mass of facial hair. 'You alright?'

She rubs her head. 'I was. Correction! I am, still in a very deep sleep.'

'Aye,' he says. 'Sorry to disturb you.'

'Where are we now?' she hears herself saying, even though she's thinking, another damn dream. Another damn boat.

'Five hundred miles west of the Minch. Almost home, girl. Now, up you get.'

He gives her a last gentle shake, and then he is gone. She glances down at herself, her mind on modesty, but finds she is fully dressed. Moleskin trousers, Arran sweater. Knitted cap. Seaman's clothes. The faraway rumble of a thudding engine. The smell of salt. A gentle rise and fall. She swings her legs out of the bunk and screws her eyes tight shut to extinguish the dream. The boat lurches for a moment, then eases back to a steady rise and fall. It's no good. She can't shake the dream, so she stands and swears quietly. Resigned to face whatever awaits her.

Her legs carry her out of the bunkroom, along corridors and up ladders and after a few minutes, she hauls open a heavy wooden door and steps into the wheelhouse. "Rough-hands" is facing the sea. He and three others stand with their backs to her, binoculars scouring open sea.

One man stands in the middle of the small room. 'Second mate. Relieve the starboard watch, please.'

'Yes, skipper,' she hears herself saying. And then, after a pause, 'What are we looking for?'

'Desert islands' drawls one of the stationary figures. 'We're gonna drop you off on one.'

'Gentlemen, please.' The skipper scans slowly to port. 'Escorts report U-boat activity on the northwest fringe of the convoy.' He pauses. 'We're a day and a half from home. Let's make it safely.'

The room falls silent, and Salina takes up the binoculars "Rough-Hands" passes to her as he leaves the bridge. She adjusts the focus, and then she is gazing at a grey, slow-moving mass of sea. She catches a glimpse of a column of smoke and follows it down to a pair of funnels. She pulls back her gaze to reveal a small merchantman, about 2000 tonnes, on the same course as her own boat. She scans left and right, making out a second, a third, eventually counting past a dozen other vessels on her side of the watch.

The minutes pass.

Then hours.

Her task is rendering her soporific with its monotony. She wonders if she fell unconscious on the deck, would she wake up at home, safe in her bed?

Her eyes are beginning to strain, so she lowers her glasses to study her own vessel for a few moments. It's relatively small for a freighter, a row of large, covered hatches stretching across the deck up to a low bow that rises and falls, casting water before it. She glances back at an area of wooden panelling at the rear of the cabin. A well-polished but straightforward brass plate declares, *MV Arran Star*.

'Eyes forward, lass,' says the skipper, never taking his eyes off the water.

She refocuses her glasses and begins another slow sweep of her watch. She wonders what she will do if she sees a torpedo or a periscope. Should she shout or scream, or is it better to watch death unfold, surrendering to its advance so she can wake up again and be herself?

The first mate is relieved, and another crew member takes up the glasses, switching sides with Salina so that the freshest eyes scan the water with the most significant threat. A few minutes after the new member takes up the watch, he drops his glasses onto his chest and says quietly, 'Captain.'

Away in the distance, the bland grey sky is painted orange as a plume of flame erupts from one of the far off vessels. Somewhere in the cabin, a radio crackles into life as call signs and orders beat out like a drum.

'So much for the peace and quiet,' says the crewman.

The captain lets out a weary sigh. 'Steady as she goes.'

Salina watches as a second, larger explosion rips through the stricken vessel. Even at this distance, she can see the ship rapidly easing out of sight. She glances at the skipper, standing impassively, his thoughts perhaps with another captain battling to save himself and his crew, even as his boat dies around him.

A few minutes later, a smaller, slimmer vessel races past them on the starboard side. The crewman twists to flash his glasses over the boat. 'HMS Dianthus,' he says matter-of-factly before adding, 'Good hunting, darlin'.'

Another hour passes in weary silence, and they leave the sunken freighter far to their stern. The Dianthus and another escort are laying depth charges, the water behind them erupting in plumes of white spray.

'We're losing speed,' says the captain after a while. The first mate arrives to relieve Salina but leaves the bridge quickly with orders to find out what is going on. An uneasy silence falls over the bridge for six minutes until he returns.

'Engine's overheating again, sir. Chief engineer says we need to drop to impulse.'

'If we drop to impulse, we'll be dead. Tell the Chief to work his usual magic.'

'You might need to see for yourself, sir. Glowing red hot, she is.'

The skipper takes off his binoculars, passing them to the first mate. 'Very well, you have the bridge.'

Salina watches the captain leave, and as she does so, she catches the eye of the first mate. He nods at her uncomfortably. 'Look sharp, number two.'

Salina picks up her binoculars again. Already the *Arran Star* is slipping to the rear of the fleet. The Dianthus has noticed and is moving in their direction, her communication lights blinking irritably.

'We should let them know,' says the crewman, moving towards the radio set.

'Not that way,' says the first mate, blocking his path. 'Don't want to advertise our predicament. Use the old-fashioned method.'

The crewman nods and diverts to a cupboard full of triangular flags.

The ship rocks a little as the Dianthus makes a fast pass of the freighter. 'Can't blame her for not wanting to linger,' observes the first mate.

Tense minutes follow until the captain huffs back into the wheelhouse. The others look at him, and he says nothing, just giving a slight shake of his head. 'What's happening?' he asks.

'We're about two miles astern of the fleet. HMS Dianthus signals she can cover us to nightfall, then she'll have to rejoin the convoy.'

The captain gives a brisk nod. 'That takes us that much closer to home. Germans can't track us at night.'

The atmosphere in the small room bristles with tension. Salina clears her throat. 'Am I the only one here who thinks this is inevitable?'

The first mate glares at her. 'What are you talking about?'

Salina shrugs. 'What would you chaps say? We'll be in the drink before the night is out.'

He steps towards her, 'How dare you …'

But she cuts him off. 'I've got an instinct about it, alright.' It's only in the silence that follows she realises she's been shouting.

'I think,' says the captain, 'That we would be right to take some precautions. First mate, make sure everyone is wearing a life jacket. And essential personnel only below decks.'

The first mate scowls at Salina and leaves the bridge.

'Have you ever drowned,' asks Salina. 'Or come near to drowning?'

"Rough-hands", or George, as he is actually known, is working beside her in the tiny galley while she sprawls half standing, half lying across a narrow wooden work surface, a mug of tea clutched far enough from her body she won't burn herself if it spills.

George shrugs. 'Fell off a puffer one time on the Clyde on the way back from Bute.'

'Were you scared?'

'At first, but they doubled back for me. Buggers circled round a few times before picking me up.'

Salina feels herself smiling a tired smile. 'How cruel!'

George nods. 'That's puffer boat captains.' He pauses and glances at the ceiling. 'Engine revs have dropped again. That's not good.'

Salina eases her exhausted body into an upright position. All sense of forward motion has now ceased. She taps George on the arm. 'I'm going out to see if there's any sight of land.'

George nods, distracted but still working on the stew he has been warming on a little gas stove.

She sees a door out onto the deck. But to get to it, she needs to pass down a corridor intersecting a steep stairway running down to the engine room, and in the other direction, up to the bridge. As she reaches the confined crossroads, she is almost bowled over by a big man emerging from the engine room. She takes a sudden step back as he shouts a hurried apology and continues up the stairs without stopping. In oily blue overalls, the big man powerfully strides away from her. Her heart quickens as she recognises something familiar about him. She considers following, but the call of the water is potent. She needs to escape the ship's stale air. To slip outside and feel some spray on her face.

It's gone midnight, and the sky is black, apart from the misty disc of a new moon rising in the east. The sea was calm earlier but seems unsettled now, a moderate wind starting to irritate the surface into rows of brisk waves. She moves towards the bow, looking for a sheltered spot, stepping carefully over obstacles littering the cluttered deck. As she passes the first cargo hold, she turns back and looks up at the wheelhouse. She can just make out faces moving behind the glass. On impulse, she waves, but no one sees her, or at least, no one waves back.

A yellow flash fills the night sky, and the ship lurches as if struck by a much larger vessel. The movement is so sudden she is thrown sideways onto the deck amid an avalanche of noise. She pulls her hands to her ears as flurries of debris rush over her. Pulling her arms up over her head to protect herself, she feels an intense rush of heat. Immediately she detects singed wool and the unmistakable smell of burning human hair. The explosion passes in just a few seconds, and her hands rush over her head and body, checking for injury, extinguishing small fires.

The explosion hit the stern of the boat at an angle. Its effect has been to expose all three internal decks to the sea at once, and it begins to list immediately. The lights go out as the engine room is submerged, and a deep explosion ripples through the vessel's fabric as cold seawater hits the ship's over-heated turbine. Salina glances up at the wheelhouse, but the faces have gone. They'll have a job, she thinks. The base of the wheelhouse is already underwater and disappearing fast. She's aware now that the angle of the deck is steepening, and if she doesn't move soon, she'll lose her grip and be tossed against the wheelhouse wall. She begins an urgent scramble to get to the bow of the boat. She reaches it just before the hatch covers start to spring off the cargo holds, each ricocheting off the boat's gunnel before disappearing into the sea. Perched on the bow, she considers her options.

A small lifeboat appears from the vessel's stern, its single occupant pulling heavily on the oars to bring it around the boat's bow. His back is to her, but she can make out the man who passed her on the stairs a few moments before. She watches him, all the time adjusting her foothold, knowing that if she is dislodged, her spent limbs will not hold her. The lifeboat stops, some thirty metres forward of her position. The man stows the oars and calls out to her.

'Jump clear.'

Salina processes what he says. 'I can't!'

He shouts again. 'We need to be clear when she goes under.'

She doesn't have the strength left to call him, so she vigorously shakes her head.

'Save yourself. Salina! Jump now! Jump before it's too late.'

The ship lurches deeper as another internal compartment surrenders to the sea, and she knows the boat doesn't have long. She chooses to leap, squeezing her eyes closed and letting her arms flail as she falls towards the sea.

And falls.

Falls.

Salina awakes with a jerk, face down on sheets that have spun away from the edges of the mattress. She is panting, sweating, her hair plastered about her face. She pushes up from the bed on all fours as if keeping her nose above water, then turns and drops exhausted onto her back. She sees the room around her and recognises she is back in her flat. Her left-hand swings to her forehead, and she tries to push away the nightmare. She knows her brain is trying to fool her as the smell of cordite and burnt wool lingers in the room.

Chapter 21

Tony was last to arrive as the clock ticked towards 7.52 am in the Dundee office. Gill and Cassy were sitting in the conference room, flicking through a stack of photos. A single rifle bullet, gleaming in its copper casing, sat upright in the middle of the table.

'What do you think?' said Tony, starting without even a greeting.

'You say these all arrived by email?' said Gill pointing at the photos.

'Yes, from an anonymous email account,' said Cassy.

'While the bullet came by post?'

'Courier delivery last thing on Friday afternoon. I didn't get hold of Tony until Saturday morning.'

'He's thorough,' said Gill. 'This is me leaving Duncan Campbell's. This one is from a car park when I first met Sandy Brightman. And another photo of me on the shore at the Invermoriston site. The last one is just before Cassy and I spoke yesterday. It's Salina and me on Brightman's boat.'

'All from the Loch Ness area,' Tony summarised.

'Yes.'

'Which means the guy making death threats is upping the ante,' said Tony.

'And this is why you've sanctioned the dig?' said Gill.

'Yes, because this guy is worried. Something is happening on the Ness he doesn't want us to see,' Tony reasoned.

'Our sensible response should be to stay clear of the place,' Cassy said.

Gill reached out and fingered the bullet, holding it up to the light. 'Depends how serious he gets.' He tossed the shell to Tony. 'Are you certain it's genuine?'

Tony caught it with both hands and scowled at Gill. 'I showed it to the guys on the gun magazine. It's standard-issue British army circa 1990. And it's a live round, so don't throw it.'

Gill leaned back in his chair and thought for a second. 'Tell me again why I should want to spend the next five days digging in the edge of a forest beside an exposed lake?'

Tony forced a smile. 'So many people think archaeology is dull. Maybe the added danger spices things up for you?'

'Tony, we're talking about people's lives here,' snapped Cassy. A few heads across the wider office turned to stare at the conference room. They couldn't hear, but they'd seen the body language.

'Which is why Gill is going to stay away from the dig,' said Tony. 'Fiona can manage things. Talk Gill through anything they find.'

'Sure!' said Gill, trying to keep exasperation out of his tone. 'Fiona loves the threat of a little sniper fire to keep her team focused on their work.'

'We'll put up a high screen,' said Tony. 'Even if our guy is that serious, and I doubt it, he's hardly likely to start firing wildly. Besides, I've already decided we should involve the police in this. I bet our guy won't go near the place if he sees the boys in blue.'

Cassy frowned at Gill. 'What do you think?'

'We must explain the threat to Fiona and the rest of the team. No one gets exposed to danger if they haven't signed up for it. Secondly, there's no way I'm staying away from the dig.'

'Can someone remind me what we're looking for?' asked Cassy. 'Are we certain this dig is worth the risk?'

Gill drummed his fingers on the table. 'I agree with Tony. Someone is desperate to keep us away from Loch Ness. And Kerr's dig site is our single best lead. We have to push it to get to the story.'

Tony nodded. 'Okay then. Let's get to it.'

Cassy and Gill followed Tony out of the conference room and set about their tasks. Gill spent a few minutes with Craig, looking at potential double-page layouts that would capture the haunting beauty of the loch. Then they sketched out several graphics they might require if the dig story developed. As they were finishing, Gill dropped his voice and asked. 'Did you have any luck with that website we discussed?'

'You mean the barely legal hacking job?' Craig replied loudly.

'Thanks, buddy. Appreciate your discretion.'

Craig glanced around. 'It's tricky. This guy has deeper security than I was expecting.'

'Can you crack it?'

'Maybe. But I might have to play a bit dirty.'

'How so?'

'I can subject the site to what's called a "Brute Force attack." Basically, you hit it with every possible password and hope to get lucky.'

'And is that legal?'

Craig bobbed his head from side to side. 'Kinda depends. But you can buy software that will do it for you, so that's half the battle.'

'Okay, let's press on.'

'Gill. With a million access requests an hour, if their webmaster is any good, he'll know someone's trying to hack him.'

'But he won't know who's doing it?'

'No, but he might just decide to take his content offline completely.'

Gill shrugged. 'He might decide he's onto a good thing and throw it open for the world to see.'

'And the little matter of your death threats?'

'The walls have ears,' said Gill.

'Well, it's Dundee. We all like a juicy murder from time to time. But you've got to ask yourself, what if our webmaster and your wannabe assailant are the same person?'

Gill winked. 'Counting on it. Meanwhile, don't do this from the office. Find a nice coffee shop somewhere with a VPN.'

Craig nodded. 'If this guy kills me, I'll come back and haunt you. You know that, don't you?'

Gill threw a hand in the air as he walked away. 'Sounds perfect. If you can manifest a half-decent apparition before the issue thirteen print deadline, I'll honour your sacrifice with a double-page spread.'

The rest of Monday disappeared while Gill organised the logistics of the dig. He marshalled people and equipment while Cassy arranged accommodation and other practicalities. After the morning's excitement, the day was busy but routine until a call came in from Salina late in the afternoon.

'Got the preliminary lab results on those fish.'

'That was quick.'

'Not really. We found the cause of death on the very first test.'

'Which was?'

'Radiological. For their personal safety, the technicians always first check our specimens with a Geiger counter.'

'Bloody hell.'

'I've sent the fish to a more specialist laboratory for further analysis. I won't know any more until the end of the week.'

Gill and Cassy were back in the office early on Tuesday morning, making final preparations for Gill heading north again later in the day. As a matter of conscience, he had emailed Sandy Brightman to let her know the news. While asking her to keep it quiet for now, Gill wanted to know if she knew of any more fish kills. Sandy's response popped back almost immediately, confirming no more reports. But she wanted Gill to call her as a matter of urgency.

'Sandy. Gill McArdle. How are you?'

'I'm grand, Gill. As far as I know, I don't glow in the dark. But you'll let me know as soon as you get more information?'

'I will, Sandy. But from what Salina can gather, the radiation levels were quite low. I don't think we were exposed to anything harmful.'

'That's good, very good,' Sandy breathed. She spoke quietly, and Gill could detect a gentle tremor in her voice. 'Gill, we had a separate incident up here yesterday,' she continued. 'It's not made the local news yet, but the Ness fraternity is buzzing with it.'

'What's up?'

'Do you remember the power station I pointed out to you on the banks of Ness?'

'I do.'

'And you recall it has a settling pond to prevent debris going up into the system?'

'You pointed out a submerged protective cage where the power station meets the loch.'

'The thing is, Gill. Something hit it last night. Hit it hard enough to take one of the protective grilles off its mountings.'

Gill said nothing.

'They've closed the station for the time being,' Sandy continued. 'There'll probably be some kind of investigation.'

'Any idea what happened?' asked Gill.

Sandy sighed. 'The biggest naturally-occurring creatures in this loch are migrating salmon. Whatever ran into the power station had to be several tonnes to do this kind of damage. No one saw it, and no one has a clue what's going on.'

'Thanks for the tip-off. I'm back up on the Ness tonight. I'll drop in on you first thing tomorrow and update you on a few things on my end.'

The call ended, and Gill made hasty preparations to leave.

'What's up?' Cassy asked, watching him bundle his laptop into a bag.

'Sounds like "Lucy" has started to play hardball,' said Gill.

Sandy and Gill sat in silence in the small visitors' car park outside Foyers power station. It was Wednesday morning. Gill had checked into a local hotel the night before and called Sandy to offer her a lift to their morning appointment. Now Sandy sat beside him, her thin hands clasping her knees. From the corner of his eye, Gill could see she was gently shaking.

'You okay?' Gill asked.

Sandy smiled, forcing herself to relax. 'Just having a moment.' She turned to face his puzzled expression. 'I want to believe, you see. Now and then, I come up against a scrap of evidence that might finally convince me a creature does live in this loch.'

Gill nodded. 'And then you're disappointed.'

'Indeed. Still, we live in hope.' Sandy glanced at her watch. 'Come on. It's time.' She opened the door and stepped out into the blustery morning. A light rain was falling, and further down the loch, a grey curtain made steady progress in their direction.

As they walked down to the security office, a barrel chested man in a thin suit walked towards them. Gill recognised him as one of the journalists he'd seen at the Whaligoe Steps.

The man nodded curtly at Gill. 'Good luck with those bastards,' he said, tilting his head back at the office as he bustled past without stopping.

Sandy glanced at Gill. 'You keep your press card in your pocket. Let me do the talking.'

As they stepped up to the office, a thin glass panel opened slowly to reveal an unsmiling face.

'Alexandra Brightman and colleague to see Phil McLaren,' said Sandy. 'I have an appointment.'

Papers rustled slowly, and eventually, an anonymous hand presented them with security passes.

'Wait in the lobby, please. I'll let Mr McLaren know you're here.'

Phil McLaren was an earnest man in his mid-fifties. He gave Sandy a fleeting hug before turning to Gill.

'Phil, this is Gill McArdle. He's a scientist friend of mine. I hope you don't mind me bringing him along.'

Gill smiled and presented a business card. He had wrestled with his conscience and decided not to mislead Sandy's friend.

Phil flicked the card between his fingers for a few seconds while he thought. 'Okay. But no photographs, and please do not quote either myself or other employees unless it's cleared through the firm's Edinburgh office.'

'Agreed,' said Gill.

Phil nodded at Sandy. 'Okay then. Follow me.' Then he led them down a series of corridors until they reached an outside door, where he indicated a rack of hard hats and fluorescent vests.

'You're the General Manager here?' asked Gill, adjusting the clasp inside the hat to ensure it was well-fitting.

'Aye. Of this facility and another one quite like it down the road.' Phil pointed at a set of double doors behind them. 'That's the main turbine hall. It's very simple. When the national grid calls for us to generate, we open up the valves on Loch Mhor, allowing water to plunge through the pipes and drive the turbine. The water exits the turbine into the settling pools at the edge of Loch Ness. When demand for electricity dips in the evening, the grid permits us to draw power. We use that to pull water out of Ness, back up to Mhor.'

'And you've suffered damage to the settling pond,' said Sandy.

'Aye. I'll show you.'

Phil led them outside and onto the concrete apron of a small harbour. 'The key thing for us is to filter out any debris before it can get into the pipes and damage the turbine. The facility up on Mhor looks just like this one.' He pointed to a row of orange buoys a stone's throw from the wall. 'We have an exterior curtain of dense netting to keep out fish and other small debris.' Then beneath our feet, we have a heavy steel sluice facing the loch-side and an interior one with a narrow mesh, facing the station.'

'And how long does this equipment usually last, given normal wear and tear?' asked Sandy.

'The exterior netting gets damaged by big pieces of debris, so we patch that quite regularly. The sluices normally last for years.' He pointed at a flat-bottomed boat where a small team had gathered part of the exterior curtain onto the deck. 'It has a hole big enough to drive a car through.'

'Is this part the sluice?' Gill had walked ahead a few steps and pointed at a twisted metal grille about the size of a garage door.

Phil nodded. 'Part of it. This is the middle section, which is strange because normally, it's only the top section which gets a bash now and then.'

'Do you get stuff in the water that's big enough to impact the grille?' asked Gill.

'Yes. Tree trunks occasionally. We had an abandoned rowing boat once. Never seen anything hit it mid-water like this.'

The three stood around the metal. It was clear the unit's centre section had come under intense pressure. The fixings connecting it to the rest of the structure had sheared, and across one corner, the grid was buckled and torn.

'Presumably, you create quite a suction when you start pumping back to the upper loch,' said Gill.

'We do at the start of a cycle while pressure builds in the system,' said Phil. 'But the flow rate back up the mountain is much slower than when the water comes back down again. I've never known our suction to pull in anything besides dead leaves.'

Gill knelt and ran his hand over the main impact point. 'To do this level of damage, how big a collision would you need?'

Phil ran a hand around the back of his head. 'Depends on two things. How big it was and how fast it was going.' He glanced at Sandy. 'How fast do you reckon "Lucy" can go?'

Sandy thrust her hands in her jacket pockets and gave the metal grid a vacant kick. 'There's a question. Let's have a guess and say a little faster than walking speed.'

Phil pulled out his phone and punched in a quick calculation. 'Then I'd estimate you are looking at something above three metric tonnes.'

They stood silent for several long seconds, staring at the damaged metal. 'And you didn't detect anything in the loch?' asked Gill.

'To be fair, our instruments just monitor our processes. I mean, we have an automated radar lookout for boats getting too close, but that's about it. Anyway, this damage happened at night. It was only when we noticed a slowdown in the water intake flow we realised we were getting an increase in small-scale debris building up on the interior sluice.'

'Can I take a sample off the damaged piece?' asked Gill, producing a scalpel and a small plastic bag.

'We've had a look and didn't see any discolouration on the grille,' said Phil. 'Something just whacked it and then backed off. But if you want to do some analysis, be my guest.'

Gill stooped down and started to pick at the grille, lifting paint flakes from where the metal had buckled and dropped them into a small clear plastic bag.

'If I may, I'd like this for my museum,' said Sandy, pointing at the twisted metal. 'When you're finished with it.'

Phil shrugged. 'Don't see why not. I'll check with my boss.'

'Have you had much media interest?' asked Gill.

'A few hacks have turned up,' said Phil, hastily adding, 'No offence. But I've just been referring them to head office. But I doubt if they'll even let the BBC in here. Too much bad blood.'

'Why's that?' asked Gill.

Phil shook his head, and Sandy stepped in. 'A few years ago, the company lost a tunnel at Glendoe. The innovation at that site was to take water through deep underground tunnels rather than have pipes on the surface. Anyway, it was a major setback, and the media unfairly portrayed the company as amateurish.'

'I remember that.'

'You don't share information if experience says someone might use it against you,' Phil added.

'Anybody else been asking for information on this incident? Apart from journalists?'

'Not sure. We can check with security on the way out.'

'How do you know that guy?' asked Gill when they were back at the car.

'We met more than ten years ago. These days we play a little bridge together. Phil's quite good. Thoroughly inscrutable.'

'How did you meet?'

'He visited the museum and asked to speak with me.' Sandy looked across at Gill and met his gaze. 'He was new to the area at the time. He'd made a sighting, you see.'

Gill nodded slowly. 'So, he's a believer.'

'He is.' She paused. 'Please don't think any worse of him for it.'

Gill started the car and prepared to drive off. Then he remembered the list of callers Phil had jotted down for him in the security office. He glanced at the note. Six names. Only one was familiar. And it was the only one he needed. He apologised to Sandy, switched off the engine, and then jumped out of the car to make a call.

He had to walk twenty paces to get a clear signal. When he got through, it went straight to voicemail. 'Arthur, it's Gill. I need you to pass a message to our mutual friend, Mr Lehman. I gather he was turned away by security at Foyers. Tell him I've met the people at the power station and seen the impact damage first-hand. We need to meet in person if he wants to know what I learned. Call me. Thanks. That's it.'

Ernie Lehman sank deeper into a good chair and thought. It had been a long few days, but worthwhile. Save for a few details; everything was falling into place. He gazed out over the loch from his vantage point in the dining room and smiled to himself. Letting his head drift back on the soft leather headrest, he almost felt sorry for Gill McArdle. The bullet had been Jim Ritchie's idea. Maybe a little crude but a pretty garnish to the photos Jim had been tasked to send. And Jim had been useful over the years. A simple creature, like a faithful dog, he'd been a forceful presence while Lehman focused on the critical elements of the plan.

McArdle! His message to Arthur had been pathetic. As if this apprentice had any valuable knowledge to trade with the Master! The man was splashing around like a fish in shallow water while he, Lehman, was the angler ready to net the catch. McArdle's tiresome presence on the Ness this past week had been a thing of chance. Inconvenient at first, and a distraction from the migration getting underway around the loch. But the journalist's efforts could bring a beneficial publicity. So, it was simply a matter of keeping the fish on a tight line while the Master finished his work. Lehman's eyes drifted closed, and his smile deepened.

A courteous clearing of the throat beside him roused him from near slumber. 'How was dinner, sir?'

Ernie Lehman didn't even open his eyes. 'Just fine, thank you.'

'Can I get you anything else, sir?'

'A good malt. Speyside.'

'Can I recommend the 18-year-old Macallan, sir?'

Lehman sighed. 'Don't you have anything more challenging?'

'In that case, sir, the Glen Moray 25 Years Old Portwood Finish.'

Lehman's nod was only visible to someone trained to interpret the wants of the wealthy. 'Very good.'

Lehman's eyes remained closed. Just a little longer, and he could announce his discovery to the world.

Chapter 22

Fiona heaved a bag of tools from the back of her ancient Land Rover and dropped them into a wheelbarrow. Behind her, a rental firm unloaded industrial fence panels and the rubber blocks to hold them upright. Gill stood among Fiona's modest workforce, ready to start ferrying the screens down to the edge of the loch. He was aware of smiles and a little excitement around him. Feeling self-conscious, he realised that his reputation had been the driving force in their recruitment. The only dour face was Fiona.

'Where are we going with this lot?' he asked.

'I've picked a spot close to where we'll be digging. There's a break in the tree cover and a flat ground to pitch our HQ.'

'Perfect.'

'Explain to me again why you're so certain no one will shoot us, and yet you still think we need screens for our protection?' Fiona whispered as they carried a panel between them down the narrow track.

'Just taking precautions, Fi. I don't think we'll have any bother.'

'Just hope it's all worth it,' she muttered as she lifted her end of the screen clear of a tree stump.

'You briefed your guys?'

She nodded.

'I might just give them one last chance to duck out before we get started,' said Gill.

'None of them will want to leave. It's me you need to worry about.' She waited for his startled reaction, then stuck her tongue out at him.

As they assembled on that Thursday morning, Gill observed Fiona's crew was an eclectic university mix. A few years ago, it would have been American and Scandinavian accents rising above the flat tones of lowland Scots. Today the most prominent voices were Germans, Koreans and a smattering of Chinese.

'Right, people. Gather round,' Gill called over the babble. 'Let's be clear from the outset; this is Fiona's dig. My role here is to provide technical guidance and represent the dig sponsor. But day to day, you answer to Fiona.'

He took a moment to look around the faces. 'We mentioned there's a non-specific threat against this dig. I want you to know that we have the landowner's full permission and the force of law on our side. However, if anyone decides, at any time, they're taking an unwarranted risk, then you're free to punch your card with Fiona and then bail out. I've got no problem with that.'

'Hope you're good with a shovel then,' observed Fiona from beside him.

'Yeah, right,' said Gill over a ripple of laughter. 'Dig plenty first. Then bail.' He turned and held out a palm to Fiona. 'Right, boss. What's the order of business?'

Fiona stepped up beside him. 'Yesterday afternoon, while you guys were humping gear from the vans, Gill and I did an initial sweep with the magnetometer. Today we'll open up some old trenches originally dug a few years back. So remember, because the ground has already been disturbed, the sediment layers will be a bit mixed up. So, when you're sifting, make sure you don't miss anything. Make up your teams, and let's get to it.'

The meeting broke up, and Fiona tapped Gill on his arm. 'Walk the site with me a second.'

They made their way into the thin forest that grew by the loch-side. Small orange flags dotted the ground, the results of their initial survey.

'He dug a lot of trenches,' said Gill.

'Aye. The ground isn't well compacted, so it's easy to see where he was digging.' Fiona surveyed the neat rows of flags. 'Whoever he was, he made a reasonable fist for a guy working on his own.'

Yesterday, they'd worked the ground, inch by inch. But this was Gill's first chance to see the outline of all Kerr's excavations. He could make out a series of trench outlines running down and across the gradient of the land. 'He did a good job maximising his ground cover. What's your plan?'

Fiona pointed to the furthermost flag. 'We'll start closest to the river. Logically, that's the most promising spot. Then we'll reopen the trenches progressively closer to HQ.'

Gill nodded. 'Makes sense.'

Fiona looked at him. 'Do you think this guy found something?'

He nodded. 'I do.' Then left her to organise her teams while he wandered wordlessly around the site. Like Sandy the previous morning, he was shaking slightly.

They both anticipated making rapid progress, even with a small crew. What they hadn't counted on was the weather. By early afternoon, a low pressure had moved in from the west, drenching them in sheets of fine rain.

'This is killing us,' said Fiona as the rain penetrated the leaf cover over their heads and gradually filled the trenches with water.

Gill nodded. 'Your call, Fi. But I'd suggest an early finish, followed by an early start.'

'Damn right,' grumbled Fiona. 'I hate this work. Makes me wanna get a job in a call centre.'

The following morning brought sunshine back to Invermoriston, and most of the team were on site by 7 am. Working carefully and methodically, the group reopened Martin Kerr's pits. The backfill in Kerr's excavations was so loose the team could work quickly, so by mid-morning, it looked like they had achieved a great deal. Back at the tent, Gill and Fiona caught up.

'Better today,' he asked.

'It's not raining, and no one's shot at us yet, so yeah, okay,' Fiona replied.

'Seen anything of interest?'

'Not a button. You?'

'One or two pieces of human detritus. Nothing to get excited about.'

Work continued through the long afternoon until Fiona called a halt just a little before 6 pm. The length of the day, combined with so little in the way of finds, weighed on the young team. The forecast for the next day was fair, and Fiona called a slightly later start. The crew worked all day Saturday, digging each of the holes deeper than Kerr had gone and attempting a few new trenches in promising looking areas. Gill needed to spend Saturday on his laptop and making calls. The next issue of the magazine was shaping up. But he had resolved that if the dig produced nothing of significance by the end of the weekend, he would build the next issue around the *Caithness Kraken*. This meant he needed more words. In a quick call to Duncan in Fort Augustus, he organised a brainstorming session with his new contributor. Finally, he'd called his father, reminding him that he couldn't be in Stonehaven this weekend.

After meeting with Duncan, Gill was back at the dig site by mid-Sunday afternoon. They were nearing the end of the last of Kerr's trenches.

'Still nothing?' asked Gill.

Fiona shook her head. 'I thought you said the weird kid at the house had seen some bones?'

'I don't know if you can call him "weird." "Socially isolated", I'd say. But you're right. He did claim to have seen something. I'll ask him.'

He turned to walk away, but Fiona gave a little flick of her head that bid him stay. 'When you talk to him,' she began. 'Warn the charming little shit to stop spying on my girls.'

'How so?'

'Cathy caught him trying to watch her while she took a pee in the woods.'

Gill sighed. 'She should have been using the portaloo back at the car park.'

'Agreed. I've reminded them all in no uncertain terms, even though it's a bloody long walk. But if it's any reflection on young Andy, I'd say he's definitely on the weird scale.'

'Okay. Leave it with me. Meanwhile, let's get our own house in order. Tell the girls that none of them should leave the dig site unaccompanied.' He looked at her. 'Including you.'

Fiona nodded and turned away. 'Aye. Like I'm every nutter's dream girlfriend.'

Gill smiled and started to walk up the hill. He recalled the first time he had met Fiona. She'd been playing in a hockey match, staff versus students, and she had been the goalkeeper. She had been formidable with her big-boned frame, armoured under protective layers. He couldn't remember the exact score. Six nil, he thought, in the students' favour. She'd been in his life, in one guise or another ever since.

He found Andy with his mother up at the house. Andy was tipping big jute bags of charcoal into a hopper while his mother weighed off neat paper sacks of the finished product. She ran the top of each bag through a binding machine with a finishing flourish. Mother and son were black from head to foot.

'That looks like hard work,' said Gill, mustering a business-like smile.

'Least favourite part of the job,' said Claire.

'But the last bit we have to do before we get paid,' said Andy, grunting as he lifted four of the finished sacks into the back of an old transit van.

'You're off on a delivery round?' said Gill.

'Aye. We pack to order. This lot is going to a garden centre in Inverness in the morning.' Andy paused in his work and fixed Gill with white eyes glowering from a soot black face. 'You needin' somethin'?'

'Couple of things,' said Gill, glancing around the yard. 'Firstly, I want to make an apology.'

'Oh, dear. What's wrong?' said Claire.

'I found out not all of my people have been using the portaloo we provided.' Gill glanced at Andy. 'I think you encountered one.' He paused just long enough for the boy to catch his meaning and then look away. 'I just wanted to say I've reminded them all, and it won't happen again.'

Andy shrugged defensively. 'Makes no difference to us. Long way back to the house just because you need a slash.'

Gill nodded. 'Agreed, but we have rules for a reason. I'll make sure they use the facilities we provided.'

Andy moved to go back to his work. 'Anythin' else?'

'Yes,' said Gill. 'When we spoke before, you said you had seen some bones in one of Martin Kerr's trenches.'

'Strugglin' to find them are you?' said Andy.

Gill looked confused. 'But we stood down at the loch together. You showed me where he had set up his camp.'

Andy clapped black dust from his hands. 'That's where his camp was alright. Maybe the bones were closer to the river.'

Gill nodded, biting back on his impatience. 'Do you remember where? Could you show me?'

Andy turned away. 'Sorry, mate. Don't remember.'

Fiona and the others were clasping mugs of tea when he arrived back down at the tent. Even though the temperature had dropped slightly, he saw no immediate sign of rain. Gill manoeuvred her out of the team's earshot. 'Andy hinted Kerr may have had another site, a little along from where we are now.'

Fiona dug in her back pocket for a chunky notebook she always carried. 'Maybe we missed it, but we surveyed all through the woods to the mouth of the river. I only found one piece of disturbed ground and we've dug it already.'

'What about going the other way?'

'Can't go that way with the magnetometer. Once you get around that little bend in the shore, the ground changes. It gets much rockier.'

Gill nodded pensively. 'Aye, going that direction takes you outside the deposition arc of the river.'

'Which kinda takes us away from your brief. Working to your theory, these animals would be most likely to die at or near the river mouth, not in some random bay round the corner.'

'Okay. Do me a favour and survey the soft ground down to the river mouth again. Take a few people with you and make sure you mark up anything worth investigating.'

'What are you going to do?'

'I'm going to do a recce the other way. See if I can spot any possible sites.'

Fiona grunted. 'Mind you don't fall in the loch.'

Gill grabbed his rucksack and turned southwest, away from the river mouth, picking his way over the rocky shore. The marshy low-lying land that backed onto woods quickly gave way to shingle banks interspersed with stretches of solid rock. Within a few minutes, he found himself working along a rocky cliff line six metres above the loch's surface. The forest here was unmanaged; a dense thicket of bushes and trees crowding onto the rock edge. Pausing, he looked down into the dark water. From this vantage point, he could just make out the submerged stones that had historically been the loch's shore. During construction of the Caledonian Canal in the early nineteenth century, the water level of the loch had been raised by two metres, drowning the old shoreline so that the rocks below looked like a row of broken teeth.

After half an hour of challenging walking, he dropped into a little sandy bay. Here the shoreline was punctured by a natural cavity in the rock. Picking his way along a little stream, he followed the channel until he emerged into a distinct clearing behind the rocks. He stood in this verdant amphitheatre, a depression in the ground ringed by high trees and looked around. A still, dark pool of unknown depth lay in the middle, fed from above by the trickling stream.

Gill stepped off the rocks and onto the soft grassy surface beside the dark pool, his heart beating a little faster as he realised the possibilities in this place. Looking around, it appeared that this area would have been part of the loch at some point in history, almost like a mini harbour. It owed its existence to the tiny stream that had etched it out over centuries, then gradually filled with silt under changing conditions.

Gill started to work his way around the ground, sweeping aside ferns until he found what he was looking for. He pulled away the loose vegetation to reveal a long rectangular indentation in the soft ground.

'Game on,' he said to himself.

A proper survey of the area revealed the first trench he'd found was one of four dotted around the little bay. Fiona recalled her people from their forays near the river mouth and set about the new site. Sunday afternoon was well gone, so they marked up the new locations and then used the remaining part of good daylight to mark a safer trail through the woods linking Fiona's HQ with the latest excavations. With morale rising, and the light failing, Fiona called a halt for the day.

Gill caught up with the team as they gathered around Fiona's car. 'I sense we're about to have a busy couple of days,' he said. 'Can I buy anyone a pre-emptive beer?'

The following morning was an 8 am start. After an initial burst of order-giving and organising, Fiona settled to work in a trench nearest the water. One of the crew had spotted a bone fragment in the backfill. Commandeering this patch, she elected to work alone.

Everyone stopped for a food break at 11 am. After grabbing a burger, Fiona nodded at Gill and steered him away from the others. She led him to her excavation and pulled back a tarp. Gill stooped beside her to get a better view. A row of substantial bones snaked across the bottom of the open pit.

'Looking like vertebrae,' said Fiona. 'Very soft and quite old.'

Gill smiled as Fiona pounced on him, grabbing his wrists in her hands. 'If this bone is what I think it is …' she paused. 'Then I'm going to retire and write a bloody book.'

The excitement that had built up in him erupted as nervous laughter. 'I can barely believe it,' he said.

'I'll muster my team and get them briefed. Make sure no one blabs about this.'

'Take your time and do it right, Fi,' he said, easing himself away.

It was early afternoon, and Gill was on his way to meet Sandy. He decided he had one courtesy phone call to make first.

'Arthur. It's Gill. Did you get my message from last week?'

'Hi, Gill. Yeah. Spoke to our guy.' Arthur paused. 'Paraphrasing what he said. I don't think he's interested.'

'That's a pity.' Gill thought for a second. 'But hey. No problem.'

'What's going on, Gill?'

'The thing I'm working on gets more interesting by the day. I had hoped for information exchange to speed things along a bit.'

He could hear Arthur pause. 'If you want me to try again. Do you want to give me a few titbits; see if we can bait him into meeting you?'

'No, it's okay. Sorry to have involved you.'

Gill hung up. Lehman was out of the game. From now on, the bones would do the talking.

Chapter 23

Three local grandees sat huddled with Sandy Brightman in the corner of *The Huntsman* bar. Gill couldn't make out their voices, but something in their tone echoed their expressions. The local news had picked up on the power station incident. They all knew this was going to shake things up.

Gill would have preferred to stay at the dig but decided it best to keep his promise to Sandy and brief her cohort of local "Lucy" experts. Grounded and serious, they were all seasoned monster hunters like her. Stuart Mackenzie, a local landowner. Robert Dias, a historian, and John Hunter, a retired solicitor.

Sandy introduced them, and then posed the question on everybody's lips. 'Gentlemen. As usual, we're meeting to consider if we have any new evidence to confirm the existence of our elusive friend.'

The men shuffled their feet for a few moments until Sandy continued. 'Robert, we've had several new sightings over the last few days. Can you review them for us?'

Robert cleared his throat. 'Nearly all are at the Fort Augustus end. What is intriguing to me is it's a new form of sighting. Unfortunately, there are no decent photographs, but all reports indicate a shape about six metres long. Size and colouration resemble a basking shark, moving at about three knots, at a depth just visible to the naked eye.'

'Any observations about this creature rising to take a breath?' Sandy clarified.

Robert shook his head. 'No. It just continued at a steady speed. So, I guess that points to it being a fish then.'

'Not necessarily,' said Sandy. 'The bigger whales can go up to an hour between breaths. Especially if they are moving slowly.'

'None of the creatures you've mentioned can survive in fresh water,' said Stuart.

'What veracity do the sightings have?' asked John.

'None of the usual suspects, if that's what you mean,' Robert replied. 'I've spoken to several of these contacts.' He lowered his voice and dipped his head towards the group. 'We are writing them up at the moment, but these are the most credible sightings we've had in years.'

Sandy glanced at Stuart. 'What's happening up at the Inverness end?'

Stuart looked uncomfortable for a few moments. 'Nothing as tangible. But I feel something odd is going on.'

Sandy pressed him. 'How so?'

'Well, birds, fish and animals are all behaving strangely. Take the sheep, for example. Very skittish at the moment. Their grazing is irregular, and they are tending to clump in defensive groups on high ground.'

John snorted. 'What's that got to do with the loch?'

'It's just different, that's all I'm saying. If you want to talk about the loch, the fishing has completely gone off. The half dozen sports boats I operate in Urquhart Bay have barely caught a thing these past three days.'

'And the birds?' John clearly wasn't impressed.

Stuart nodded at the door of the bar. 'Step outside and try to hear one.' He paused, waiting for a retort from John that didn't come. 'The dawn chorus,' he continued. 'Normally, it would just about wake the dead at this time of year. Try going out yourself tomorrow morning. You'll barely hear a cheep.'

'Actually, that's right,' said Sandy. 'My husband is an early riser and remarked on that just this morning.'

John pointed at Gill. 'You were with Sandy on the power station thing. What did you make of it?'

Gill sighed. 'Just more mystery, I'm afraid. The damage to the exterior of the station is significant.'

'You don't sound terribly excited,' said John.

Gill sighed. 'I'm perplexed by the lack of organics on the damaged grille. Normally, if a living thing collides with a physical barrier with that kind of force, I'd expect scales or skin, something to point to the animal in question.'

'You took some samples, though,' said Sandy.

'Yes. I mailed them to my Dundee office, so they received them yesterday and placed them with a lab. It will be a couple of days before I get anything back.'

'I'm still very concerned by the presence of radiation in the loch,' said Robert. 'Any more news on that?'

Sandy pulled out a paper diary and scanned a few pages. 'I reported it to the environmental people the same day I got the preliminary results. They were out the following day and the day after and didn't find any dead fish. They took some water samples. Everything seems fine.'

'We've no more reports of any fish kills,' Stuart reported.

'I should explain that Gill's friend, Dr Ahmed, took the original fish samples away for testing. Gill, do you have any news for us?'

Gill leant forward. 'Okay, this is all very unofficial; please don't repeat it. Dr Ahmed is waiting for the final tox report and will communicate formally with the relevant authorities. But she did phone me last night to give me the findings. Before I explain, does anyone know if any fracking is going on in this area?'

The other men looked at each other, and then Sandy answered for them all. 'Not aware of any. Why?'

'The chemical detected in the fish was Iodine 131. As long as you're not exposed to a large quantity, it's a relatively benign isotope for humans. It's what's known as a radioactive tracer. It's got a short half-life, with an application in the fracking industry. Companies use it to trace underground watercourses during test drills.'

'Do you think someone has drilled an unofficial well?' asked John.

'That's one possibility,' Gill replied. 'Somehow irradiated water penetrated the loch at a deep enough level to kill ferox.'

'Surely if you dropped a chemical in the loch, it would quickly be diluted,' said John.

Gill shook his head. 'Not until it reached open water. In a confined watercourse, even one far below the water level, you could still have a high concentration.'

'Especially if deployed by someone who isn't an expert,' said Stuart.

'This might be a distraction,' said Sandy. 'I can't see how it has anything to do with "Lucy."'

'Maybe the creature emits the stuff,' said Robert.

Gill was shaking his head. 'This chemical is manufactured in nuclear power stations. You have to expose certain specific elements to limited doses of radiation. This chemical couldn't naturally appear in nature.'

'Well, it sounds like the authorities will have all the information they need to pursue the source of this chemical.' Sandy glanced at Gill. 'I know you need to get back. Can you tell us anything about your excavations at Invermoriston?'

Gill looked around the earnest faces. 'We are testing the theory that the creature is not one animal but an entire species. We are speculating they migrate into the loch by an unknown route, breed and then leave again.'

'What, every year?' John looked dumbfounded.

'Possibly. But some larger animals have an irregular breeding cycle. They might only return to the loch occasionally or under certain conditions.'

'Can you prove any of this?' said John.

'That's the aim of the dig. If the theory has any substance, then migrating animals will suffer a proportion of deaths while in the loch. We are extrapolating from the behaviour of other living creatures to anticipate where the Ness migrants might die. We've chosen a likely spot, and we're taking a look.'

John blinked at him. 'Found anything yet?'

Gill's gaze was unwavering. 'It's too early to tell.' He waited for further questions, aware that Sandy was giving him a sideways look.

His phone buzzed to alert him to a message, so he stood and shook hands with the group. Sandy quickly closed the meeting, promising to reconvene if new information came to light. She touched Gill's arm as he quickly gathered his things to leave. 'If you find anything, you'll include me, yes?'

'Trust me, Sandy. You'll be the first.' She nodded curtly and turned away.

Gill was standing in the middle of the car park before he could get enough reception to make a call. 'Fi. Just saw your message. What's happening?'

Fiona's voice sounded strained. 'Are you far away?'

'Drumnadrochit. Just ten minutes away.' He paused, listening to her breathing. 'Fi, what's up? What have you found?'

'Just come. Alright.'

Gill stood at the edge of the trench and stared at the bones.

'Dammit,' he said at last.

Fiona and the rest of the team were gathered around the hole, making a small arena of grim faces.

'We stopped digging as soon as we realised the remains were contemporary,' said Fiona.

'You're certain?' said Gill. 'I don't see any cloth fragments.' He turned sideways and pointed to the angle of the bones. 'The crouched position is reminiscent of late Pictish burials.'

Fiona scowled. 'If he was Pictish, he had a bloody good dentist.'

Gill leaned into the hole and brushed a few soil grains from the exposed skull. 'See what you mean.'

'Right. Tea break everyone,' Fiona called out. She watched as her crew peeled away from the trench and trudged off towards the tent. When they were out of earshot, she turned to Gill. 'What now?'

'We need to call the police,' said Gill. 'They'll want the site to themselves. Probably best to send everyone home for a few days.'

Fiona sighed. 'Bugger. It'll be a job getting them all back again.'

Gill gesticulated at the body in the hole. 'What else can we do?' He moved back over to the edge of the trench. 'How much further did you get with the vertebrae?'

Fiona nodded at the line of bones. 'Another few segments. Then we came across this guy. Thought he was part of the animal at first.' Fiona shuddered. 'I've dug up human remains before.' She shook her head. 'Never like this.'

'What alerted you?'

Fiona looked up into his face. 'The smell. The stronger it got, the more I realised things weren't right.'

Gill leaned forward, grasped her shoulders, and embraced her. 'I'm sorry, Fi. Tough one.'

Detective Sergeant Lundy and half a dozen constables arrived in under thirty minutes, stamping their authority on the situation with methodical efficiency. Aware their day's work was over, Fiona's crew were preparing to leave until the DS made it clear that no vehicles or persons were allowed to leave the site without his superior's permission.

By the time the senior officer arrived, they had all been sitting outside the Sweems' homestead with their arms folded for over an hour. The officer locked his car and strode up to Gill without speaking, scowling at him while he paused to light a cigarette.

'Hello, Detective Inspector. How was the drive up from Fort William?' said Gill.

The officer scowled at him. 'What. The hell. Are you doing here, McArdle?'

'Same as usual. Digging holes.'

'Before we start ...' George Wiley made a theatrical show of glancing into the woods in several directions. 'Anything mysterious we need to watch out for?'

Gill smiled and looked at his feet. For once, he was short of a suitable repost.

'Okay, Lundy,' said Wiley. 'Show me the body.'

'My archaeologists,' said Gill. 'Can we let them get on with their day?'

'No one leaves without my say so,' said Wiley.

'The body is a skeleton. You can't think we're suspects?'

'Not going to repeat myself,' said Wiley as he trailed into the woods on the heels of his DS.

An hour and a half later, Wiley radioed up from the loch shore to inform them that Fiona's crew could go but that Gill was still needed. Fiona wanted to stay on-site, but realising her discovery had left her shaken, Gill encouraged her to go. He chased her off to her lodgings, then walked down the winding trail to the shore. Arriving at the dig, he found the police had thrown a wide cordon around the body. Wiley had taken up residence in Fiona's tent and sat drinking tea as Gill arrived. All around him, officers were probing the ground with sticks and other improvised tools.

Gill suppressed a surge of anger. 'DI Wiley, your people can't treat my site like this. They are tramping over ongoing excavations without any regard.'

Wiley took a long sip before replying. 'It's a crime scene, McArdle. That takes precedence.' He laid his mug down on the table. 'But I'll tell my men to tape around the other holes. That should keep them safe.'

Gill nodded curtly. 'Thank you.'

'What brings you to Loch Ness?' Wiley waved vaguely in the direction of the dig.

'I was about to ask you the same question.'

Wiley smiled. 'That's the beauty of a national police force. More opportunities across the region.'

'I notice you weren't promoted. That's a pity after your hard work on the McKellar murder.'

Wiley clenched his mug and leaned towards Gill. 'We both know that case had its red herrings. I should have charged you with wasting police time.'

'You seemed to have plenty to waste. It took you a year to solve that murder.'

Wiley gave a thin smile. 'It's so pleasant to have another chance to work together. So again, please. Why are you digging holes on the banks of Loch Ness?'

Sheepishly, Gill told him.

'So, this Kerr chap who disappeared, you reckon he's the guy in the hole?'

'You're the detective. But in your shoes, that's where I'd start.'

'If you are so certain about the victim's identity, do you have any idea who murdered him?'

Gill thought for a second, then slowly and deliberately shook his head.

Wiley wiped his mouth with his hand, then stood and walked towards him. 'I think you might have a tiny suspicion.'

'How can you know that?'

'As you said, I'm the detective.' Wiley smiled, a thin row of yellow teeth suddenly emerging from underneath his untidy moustache. 'Come on.'

'It's just that, since I started working on this story, I've had two death threats mailed to my office. They're in my car.'

'And did you report them?

'My office did. To the local police in Dundee. I can get you the crime reference numbers if you want.'

Wiley waved a hand dismissively. 'Who wants you dead?'

'If I knew for certain, I'd have shared that information already.'

'But you suspect someone?'

Gill nodded. 'There's a guy around here somewhere called Ernie Lehman. I haven't met him, but apparently, he doesn't think highly of me.'

'Why not?'

'I can't be sure, but he seems to think he is on the verge of solving the myth around the Loch Ness Monster. He sees me as competition and resents my presence on the loch.'

'Hardly likely to try to kill you over a myth,' retorted Wiley.

'Well, he's the only person who springs to mind,' said Gill. 'And if he feels that strongly about me, he might have held similar opinions against Martin Kerr.'

'We'll check out both names. What else can you tell me about them?'

'I'll phone my office in a minute and get them to email you everything we have on Kerr. We've been trying to track him down. If that's not him in the hole, we might still achieve that.'

'And Lehman?'

'Slippery character. I've been trying to reach out to him without success. I don't know what he looks like, although I've got a rough idea of where he lives. Some of the folk around here have met him. I can give you their names.'

'Okay.' Wiley glanced at the long path back up through the woods. 'Pop up to your car and fetch me those death threats.'

Chapter 24

The evening light dappled the waters of the loch as the sun dipped behind the forest. DI Wiley let out a sharp whistle, drawing his DS in from the woods like an obedient collie. 'Time to call it a night, Lundy. Make sure we have a marked car up at the house tonight. I don't want anyone tramping through here until we've picked it clean.'

Gill wasn't sure he believed what he had heard. 'Wait a minute. Aren't you going to leave someone down on the site?'

Wiley looked around at the darkening forest. 'I don't fancy it myself. Do you?'

'If it's what it takes.' Gill was fighting to keep the indignation out of his voice. 'I've got a dig to protect.'

'Be my guest,' said Wiley. 'Just keep behind the tape. We've got a forensics team coming in the morning.'

Gill nodded. 'I'll use Fiona's tent. I've got some camping kit in my car.'

Gill moved to start back up the hill but paused as Wiley grasped his arm. 'Your lead on Martin Kerr might be a dead end. No mention of anyone of that name on the missing person's register.'

'Hardly confirms the body isn't Kerr's.'

'Granted,' said Wiley. 'But generally, when a person goes missing, someone notices.'

'Well, I'll leave it with you, Detective. I've given you all the information I have to hand.' Gill turned to leave.

'Wait a second, McArdle.' Wiley moved towards him and pulled out a cigarette. He didn't light it straight away but stood tapping the tip against the surface of the pack. 'What do you make of the young lad, Andrew Sweem?'

'You hardly suspect him do you?'

Wiley snorted. 'I suspect everybody. You've met the lad. Antisocial, bordering on aggressive. And he was one of the few people who knew where Kerr was working. Put that together with his knowledge of the forest, and it starts to look promising.'

'Well, I doubt he had anything to do with it,' said Gill as the pair started to make their way up to the cars, trailed obediently by Wiley's DS.

'Let me know if you spot him creeping around,' said Wiley, glancing at him. 'You sure you'll be alright down here?'

'Don't worry about me, Inspector. I'm a sound sleeper.'

As it turned out, Gill did not sleep well on Monday night. With only eleven days until the next magazine went to press, his mind spun with contrasting storylines. And although he tried, he could not put the thought out of his head that barely half a mile from his tent, the body of a man, the body of another archaeologist, lay partially uncovered in rich, damp soil. When he did finally sleep, Cassy's cheerful voice rang in his dreams, challenging him to impractical daring while his father wandered through the dig site, vacant and vulnerable.

He awoke suddenly to soft daylight, jolted alert by a sound close to the tent. A twig breaking and leaves being disturbed. And as he listened, he could discern breathing, heavy like someone had been running. He glanced around, looking for something to defend himself with, and suddenly regretted his lack of preparation. After a minute, he could detect no more movement outside the tent, just the steady pulse of breathing. He eased himself out of his sleeping bag, his heart banging in his chest. He had no means of defence, so fight or flight were his best options. The inner shell of the tent lay unzipped. The outer shell was loosely sealed will Velcro strips. He gathered himself into a standing position, then dashed forward, exploding into the small clearing in front of the tent.

The deer had been grazing close to the flysheet. A mature roe female, she recoiled from his appearance and danced around the treelined hollow, looking for an exit. With higher ground and dense undergrowth to her back, she elected to cut across the grassy hollow, forcing Gill to jump out of her path, springing over him and out of sight among the trees. She left Gill lying sprawled in front of the tent. He was shaking. For a moment or two, he thought he would be sick.

When the feeling passed, he got to his feet and started to boil water for some tea. It was 5.15 am, and any further thought of sleep was gone. He glanced around the clearing, then went inside to get dressed.

The draw of the bones became irresistible. Drinking the remains of his tea, he zipped up the tent and made his way to the dig site. The crime scene tape wove through the trees like a prop from a game. He ducked under it and stepped carefully to avoid leaving clues to his presence. The trench had been covered with one of Fiona's tarpaulins and weighed down with branches. Gill removed these and gently pulled back the cover.

The skull wasn't quite face down. Instead, it appeared turned away, with the chin dropped close to the ribs, as if embarrassed being found like this. One arm lay exposed in the loose soil, the phalanges of the fingers pulled close to the neck in a foetal impression. Loose soil still covered the lower half of the body. Without ceremony or ritual, it looked like someone had folded the body into a corner of the trench. The skull's shattered temple suggested this death was no accident.

He sat for a moment, paying a personal silent homage.

Now to the other bones. The question that grasped Gill was whether the killer had been aware of the animal remains when he had buried the man they presumed was Kerr in his own pit. They had become partially covered again as Fiona, or possibly Wiley, had brushed dirt aside to see the human remains better. But the unidentified backbone was visible, snaking across the bottom of the pit. Whoever had disposed of the body could not have missed Kerr's discovery. Glancing around him, Gill lay on the ground so that he could brush aside as much dirt as possible to see the bones. A short row of lumbar segments gave way to a compressed section of thoracic vertebrae, their dorsal spines rising from the bottom of the pit. This meant the animal was positioned belly down. The size of the remains suggested a substantial mammal, but they would have to do a lot more digging before identifying it. He considered for a moment if he should break off a sample for analysis. But the purist in him kicked against damaging the bones. Feeling a prick in his conscience, he put away the thought and restored the tarp to the way he had found it.

He was tiding away his breakfast things around 7.30 when he heard the forensics team approach noisily through the woods. Guided by DS Lundy, they trooped passed Gill with barely a nod. Evidently, Inspector Wiley wouldn't be down to the site for a couple of hours yet. That suited him. Cassy had arranged a conference call between Gill, herself and Tony for 9 am. So, he worked for an hour, then found a quiet spot by the loch and dialled in.

'Morning, Cassy,' said Gill, leaping into the vacuum as an automated voice opened the call.

'Hey, Gill.' Cassy sounded strained. 'Tony, are you on yet?'

'Morning, guys.' Tony's voice was crisp and clear.

'Tony's at a board meeting in London,' Cassy explained.

'Talk quickly, Gill,' said Tony. 'The session starts at 9.30.'

'The dig is at a standstill while the forensics team do their thing.'

'How long might that last?'

'At least a couple of days. If they find anything, it will complicate things, and they might throw a cordon around the whole wood and shut us down for several weeks.'

'Okay.' Tony allowed himself a few moments to think. 'What about the other leads you were pursuing? What's his name ... Lehman?'

'Nothing concrete,' replied Gill. 'He still refuses to meet me, and although he seems to have some good material, he's not likely to give it to us. Especially as our dig might implicate him in a murder.'

Cassy broke in. 'We are still doing some desk research on him that might give us an idea of what he's working on, but that's not getting very far either.'

'What's happening on the loch?' said Tony. 'Anything going on that we can pin a story on?'

'We're still getting over a dozen sightings reported to our office each week,' said Cassy. 'Gill, you're closer.'

'Aye. The jungle drums are booming around here. We had the damage to the power station, plus several very credible sightings earlier in the week. Something's up.'

'We're less than two weeks from going to press,' said Tony. 'If you've nothing concrete, I assume you'll park Loch Ness as the lead story?'

'I've had time to think about this.' Gill surprised himself at how reassuring he sounded. 'I want to approach this as a two-part story. We'll use the first issue to set the context. We'll review all our evidence to date, then link it all to the mystery of the missing archaeologist.'

'Won't we shoot ourselves in the foot by attracting the attention of the big dailies?' asked Cassy.

'As things stand right now, they could catch us up pretty quickly. If we get a quiet week for news, they could throw resources at this and eat our lunch. I think it's best to publish what we've got and own the story. Five weeks from now, the dig will be complete, and we have the exclusive rights to how the story ends.'

'I like that,' said Tony. 'Got human interest and a big draw for readers to buy the next issue.'

'Aren't we in trouble if this is an ongoing police investigation?' The others were silent for a moment as Cassy had a point.

'We're still a news outlet,' said Tony.

Gill came back in. 'And I checked with Fiona. She records everything she does, so we have photos of the Kerr grave with the unidentified animal bones.'

'Can we use those?' said Cassy.

'Let me check with legal,' said Tony. 'They'll know either way.' He paused. 'But it's a good angle, Gill. Given the timelines, it's maybe the best route open to us.'

'Are you coming back to the office, Gill?' asked Cassy. 'The next issue still needs a tonne of work.'

'No, I want to stay here and see how things develop with the police investigation. Besides, now we've agreed on the way ahead, I can write it up from here.'

'You're sure?' asked Tony.

'I'm going to draft the editorial and the lead article today. I'll be in touch tomorrow afternoon to tell you how it's shaping up.'

Shortly after 11 am, Wiley and another senior officer from Fort William descended on the tent to shelter from a rain shower. Gill took the opportunity to visit his lodgings for a wash and recharge his laptop. After a bite of lunch, he began writing up his work and found that the words flowed effortlessly. By mid-morning, Gill had sketched out not only the current issue but a couple of scenarios for the next, depending on how the facts played out. By 6 pm, he had emailed his drafts to the office and got ready to head back to the woods.

As he parked beside the farm cottage, Inspector Wiley emerged accompanied by a female officer, followed by Claire, her face twisted by anxiety. Andy Sweem sat scowling in a police car, accompanied by a male officer.

'Well, I am sorry, Mrs Sweem. But as I explained, the law grants me twenty-four hours to question your son.'

'But my Andy ain't done nothin' wrong. He's a good lad. Just misses his father's guiding hand.'

Wiley stopped and turned. 'And for that, you have my sympathy. But Andy didn't help his situation by taking a swing at one of my officers and trying to flee the scene.'

Claire held her thin hands out in front of her like inverted claws. 'But them's just small things. Ardly enough to jail 'im.'

'Assaulting an officer conducting a murder investigation isn't exactly child's play, Mrs Sweem. Now, if you'll excuse me.'

He strode towards his car, and Gill had to move quickly to intercept him. 'Busy day, Inspector?'

'Doing my job.' Wiley jumped into the passenger seat and waited for his female colleague to start the car. As she did so, Wiley ran down the window. 'You staying on-site again tonight?'

'That's the plan.'

'You'll have company. The uniform guys will be here overnight with a switch-over around midnight.'

Gill frowned. 'Why the fuss?'

'Forensics are still working, so it will be tomorrow pm earliest before they move the body.'

'Can you fill me in?'

'No.' Wiley started to rewind the window but paused mid-way. 'And Gill …'

Gill tilted his head to show he was listening.

'Somebody paid an out-of-hours visit to the graveside of your erstwhile colleague. If I find out it was you, I'll charge you. Clear?'

Gill nodded, and Wiley drove off without another word.

The run-in with Wiley dampened his spirits a little. Gill foraged in the tent for provisions to cook alongside the ingredients he had been able to buy locally. Dipping into Fiona's boxes, he found an unopened bottle of cheap red wine. He held the dark green bottle in his hands for a few moments, reasoning that he wouldn't be exercising the following morning. Cracking open the seal, he decided tonight's cuisine would be army ration lamb curry, washed down with a dusty merlot. He took a swig from the bottle and hoped the curry would taste better than the beverage.

The noise woke him gradually, rousing his mind free from the grasp of too much red. The gentlest sound of running water, and a sound that seemed familiar; the deep breaths of the deer. As he became more fully awake, he smiled at the irony. The deer was urinating against the side of the tent. As Gill listened, the sound continued, moving steadily around the tent perimeter. Then a sudden smell of petrol blasted his senses. He ripped the sleeping bag from his body and stood upright just at the moment as a sheet of flame shot up in the door opening. The flame danced for a few moments, consuming the tent awning, then began to sprint left and right in a dash to encircle the entire tent. Gill glanced around him. Seeing the wine bottle, he grabbed it by the neck and smashed it against the table. Armed with the jagged stump, he attacked the rear flank of the tent with a single long blow. Propelling himself out of the gashed tent, he somersaulted onto the forest floor. Gill spun onto his back, shielding his face as the rest of the tent, and the tree branches above it, burst into flames.

His heart pounding, he eased himself further away from the inferno. Off to his left, he detected the firelight reflecting off a metal surface. Turning to face the shiny object, he saw a figure standing at the edge of the clearing. As Gill watched, the figure started to advance. Tall and athletic, the man carried a long blade, glinting in the firelight. Faced with fight or flight, Gill reasoned he was no match for the figure stepping towards him. Tugging a branch to pull himself upright, Gill chose to escape and sped into the dark. Immediately the going was slow and painful. Without footwear, the ground was full of traps and hazards. Behind him, he could hear his assailant thrashing at the trees blocking his progress. Gill had only one goal. Tacking to the right, he hit the trail to the dig site. The clearer path meant he could run faster here, but his pursuer had also found the track and was gaining on him.

The police constable who came running the other way almost cleared Gill off his feet.

'What the hell is going on?' the young officer demanded, gesturing at the glow through the trees.

Gill pointed behind him. 'There's a guy with a machete. He's trying to kill me.'

Immediately the officer unholstered a revolver and took a defensive posture against anyone coming at them along the path. The oncoming figure stopped, his breath visible in the moonlight that lit him from behind.

'Drop your weapon and put your hands behind your head,' called the officer.

The figure ducked from view and disappeared into the trees. The young officer took a few steps to follow him, but Gill reached out and grabbed his arm. 'Don't, man. If you go after him, the other guy has all the advantages.'

The officer thought for a second, then nodded. He grasped his radio set. 'Officer Dunns to control.'

Gill did his best to keep watch around them while Dunns called in the attack. Then in a few moments, they were moving again. 'Come on,' said Dunns. 'Back to the police tape. We'll wait for back-up.'

Chapter 25

At 8 am the following morning, Inspector Wiley was back in the woods and seemed less than excited by the early start. He lit a cigarette and stood looking at Gill for a full minute before speaking. Gill sat on the tailgate of his car with a blanket around his shoulders and a borrowed jacket laid over that. A soft rain fell, and he could feel his hair smeared against his forehead.

'You look awful,' said Wiley casually.

'Thanks. It's hard to keep a decent dress code when you're camping.'

'Did you get a good look at your guy?'

'As I told PC Dunns. I never saw his face. He was big. Six foot plus change. Bulky too.'

'Any ideas?'

Gill shrugged. 'Maybe Lehman, but I don't know what he looks like.'

Wiley drew on his cigarette. 'Tell me exactly what happened last night.'

Gill accepted a cup of tea from Dunns and repeated his story. Wiley listened impassively, occasionally flicking ash away from his body. Dunns took up the story from his perspective, and Wiley, with cigarette in mouth, jotted down a few notes.

'Lucky for you, McArdle; I left one of my officers last night.'

Gill nodded sheepishly. 'Aye.' He glanced at Dunns. 'Since when have you guys been armed?'

'Chief Super's discretion,' said Wiley. 'Given we had an officer in an exposed position and two death threats against yourself.'

'Did you find any evidence up at the car park?' Gill wanted to hear good news.

Wiley shook his head. 'Mrs Sweem remembers hearing a car drive away about 3 am. But she didn't see it and the whole yard is a mess of faint tyre tracks. Nothing that helps us.'

'No CCTV?'

Wiley snorted. 'In like, a hundred miles?'

Gill shivered and got to his feet. 'If there's nothing else I can help you with, I'll go and get changed.'

'I take it your camping days are over.'

Gill nodded.

'Go back to Dundee for a few days,' said Wiley. 'You should be able to get your excavations back sometime next week.'

'When are you going to move Kerr's body?'

'Won't be today.' Wiley's face creased into a scowl. 'And anyway, it's not Kerr.'

'What do you mean?'

'The Sweems described Kerr as a tall, athletic man in his early thirties. According to forensics, the body in the forest is of a male aged sixty to sixty-five.'

Gill nodded soberly. 'I see.'

'And I got one of my people to check with the Scottish records office. Martin Kerr, the archaeologist, died six years ago.'

Gill looked puzzled. 'But that would have been two or three years before these excavations.'

'So, whoever was working here was using Kerr's name as a cover,' said Wiley, looking pleased with himself.

'Lehman?' said Gill.

'Maybe. Right now, I'm concerned with identifying human remains and resolving any culpability in the death.'

'Still, whoever was pretending he was Kerr must have had a hand in this killing?'

Wiley had run out of patience. 'Go home. I promise someone will call you when we're finished here.'

It was late afternoon when Gill got back to Dundee. He didn't go into the office. Instead, he dropped Cassy a quick text, and then after locking the front door of his flat, he crashed out in his bed for a long night of much-needed sleep. On Thursday morning, he awoke refreshed and went for a long run along the riverside.

Cassy was always in the office ahead of him, no matter how early he was. She waved at him and then joined him a few minutes later at his desk, armed with a coffee for him, and a bulky package clutched to her chest. He updated her on Martin Kerr.

'Explains why he just disappears,' said Cassy. 'I wish I'd checked with the National Records office.'

Gill gave her an encouraging smile. 'Your job description says "Office Manager", not "Private Detective." We're all on a learning curve here.'

'And the police came and took away your bullet,' she added matter-of-factly.

He glanced up at her. 'Oh, aye?'

'Part of their investigation into your attempted murder,' she continued in her best everyday voice.

'I'm still breathing, Cass.'

'You're the editor of a magazine, not a special forces commando,' she said with force. 'You could have died in that tent.'

'Aye, but I didn't.'

'But is it worth it, Gill? Could you do your job without risking death half the weeks of the year?'

Gill knew she was right. Someone was trying to kill him, and he wasn't close to knowing who or why. And he'd never been enthusiastic about the Nessie material. He couldn't see any glory in it, and his few remaining pals at the Uni would laugh at him if they knew. What was in it for him if he decided to continue? What did he lose by stopping?

'Thing is, Cassy. Since Callanish last year, I feel this job is more than just an occupation. It's hard to explain, but at some level, I feel called to this.'

Cassy rolled her eyes. 'Next thing, you'll be coming to work in a cape and a mask.'

The heavy package she was carrying was becoming a burden to her. For effect, she held it high above his desk before dropping it heavily onto the nearest empty surface, making him lash out a hand to rescue his coffee. 'And here's another bunch of whacky diagrams for you to look at. Have a wee keek for your calling in that little bundle.'

'Project Leviathan?' he said, glaring at her while shaking drips of hot coffee off his fingers.

'This morning's post. I haven't been through it for razor blades or scanned it for chemical or radiological contaminants, so go carefully. Oh, and they're marked *Ministry of Defence*, so if you read them, you're probably going to go to jail.'

He studied her face for a few moments. 'You okay? You seem a bit stressed.'

'I work in an office, Gill. What's stressful about that?' She glanced up at a wall clock. 'You've got three-quarters of an hour before the phones start ringing.' She tapped the package. 'I'll leave you to it.'

Gill slid the contents of the pack onto his desk. Like before, the smell of old papers assailed him. Most of the documents were large sheets the size of ordnance survey maps, so he scooped them up and bundled them into the conference room. Laying them out across the wide desk, he soon found technical drawings resembling the first package but of more recent provenance. Depths and elevations ran across nearly all the papers, typed this time rather than hand-drawn. This time he saw geographical locations he recognised, and after a few minutes, he managed to lay them in order, left to right. Next came a series of more detailed drawings, sections blowing up detail of the larger map, and then other sketches and cross-sections. These he laid on the floor, relative to their connection to the bigger picture. Finally, at the bottom of the pile came a single A3 sheet that was the key to it all. Gill gripped the paper and sank into one of the chairs, absorbing the information. He was still staring at it a few minutes later when he heard a tap on the glass. It was Tony.

'Sorry to disturb you, but I've got an editorial meeting with *Game and Gun* starting five minutes ago,' said Tony. He stared at Gill for a few seconds, then turned to catch the eye of the other editor. 'Give us five, Jake.' Then he came in and closed the door.

Gill stood up and laid the A3 sheet of paper face down on his chair. Through the glass, he gesticulated until he caught Cassy's attention, bidding her to join them.

'What's up?' asked Tony as Cassy slammed the door behind her.

'Lucy,' said Gill. 'I think we've nailed her.'

'Okay, tell me.'

Gill spread his hands out to encompass the connected drawings, left and right. 'This is a topographical layout of the Caledonian Canal, running from Fort William, up through Loch Ness, all the way to Inverness. These smaller diagrams are detailed sections through the locks and rivers.'

'Okay. I know it. I sailed it once with my family when I was a kid.'

'What would you say if I asked you to imagine a second canal, built thirty metres below the first?'

Tony blinked. 'I'm not sure I understand.'

'Well, look at this.' Gill grasped a piece of paper. These lines represent the path of the current canal and its river sections, with all the locks marked and numbered.' He stopped and pointed at another set of lines, weaving back and forward across the existing canal. 'But look here. These lines represent a separate watercourse, deep below ground, running to a gentle gradient with its sections linked by locks.'

'I don't get it,' said Tony. 'Why would anyone build a canal below ground?'

'Okay. Look at this one.'

Tony crouched over one of the maps. 'I recognise Loch Ness, but I can't interpret the detail.'

Gill tapped the map. 'This section covers a depth from fifteen down to one hundred metres. It relates to this cross-section.'

Tony shook his head. 'All I can see is what looks like massive pipes connected to some kind of factory.' He twisted the sheet around to better grasp the context. 'It's all built below ground, so I'd say it looks like a pumping station.' He scratched his head. 'Is it a hydroelectric scheme?'

Gill shook his head. He picked up the A3 sheet and passed it to Tony.

Tony stared at it open-mouthed for a few seconds before laying the sheet on the table and sliding into a seat. 'Submarines!'

Cassy snatched a random sheet of paper towards her. 'Sorry, Gill, I don't get it.'

Gill drew his finger across the top edge of the paper. 'The water surface would be about here. The rest illustrates a submarine base built eighty metres below the surface.'

'So, what are these big circles?' said Cassy, pointing at four disks in the centre of the drawing.

'They're submarine docks. Another sketch shows their longitudinal layout. They're massive.'

Cassy scowled at the papers. 'All these years of monster sightings, and that's what it was? Submarines in the loch?'

'And it might explain the dead fish we found,' said Gill.

'Like a leak or some other accident,' said Cassy.

'Possibly.'

Tony let out a sigh. 'It could explain the damage to the hydroelectric plant. A sub ran into it.'

'The results from the lab are due back this morning,' said Cassy. 'I'll chase it as soon as we finish here.'

'But how could all this be built in secret?' said Tony, spreading his hands across the maps.

'At this stage, we can't know for certain it was built. I don't think we can use this material until we know the facts on the ground. To do that, I need to speak to the source.' Gill looked at Cassy. 'Can you send another letter to the Helensburgh mailbox and tell our man that we really need to meet? Send it by courier. I want him to get it today.'

Cassy glanced at her watch. 'I can do that.'

Tony stood up again and walked around the table. 'Show me our dig site on these maps.'

Gill searched for Invermoriston and then tapped the map south of the village.

'It's a couple of miles from the submarine base,' observed Tony. 'Do you see any link between the two?'

'Not at the moment,' said Gill.

'What about Lehman?'

Gill drew out a chair and sat down. 'He's been chasing this story longer than us, so we have to assume that he knows about the submarines. Maybe that's the big reveal he's planning for his website. And the whole thing fits with one of the few facts we know about Lehman.'

'Remind me,' said Tony.

'That he believes "Lucy" is a species rather than a single animal. That they migrate to sea rather than live in the loch.' He stared at Tony for a long moment. 'Makes me think Lehman already knows what's going on here.'

Tony nodded. 'So, you think all this migration nonsense is just a cover story for submarine movements?'

'Perhaps,' said Gill. He looked at Cassy. 'I need Craig to finish his desk research. Is he in the office today?'

'He's offsite,' said Cassy stiffly. 'Working on an article. I'll phone him and ask for an update.'

Tony was staring at the maps again. He looked troubled. 'I wonder if we should consider national security?'

'In what way?' asked Gill.

Tony gesticulated at the structure under the rock. 'Well, let's say your source is a whistle-blower tipping us off about some secret government base. Are we making a mistake if we reveal it?'

'We're a democracy, Tony. Our government isn't meant to have secrets.'

Cassy leant across the table towards them. 'You know how the Scots feel about the naval base at Faslane,' she whispered. 'Imagine the fuss when this story gets out.' She let her hands erupt upwards in a mock explosion. 'Secret government submarines polluting the loch. And the death of the Loch Ness Monster. All in one headline.'

The three of them looked at each other, glancing back and forth until finally, Tony spoke. 'As yet, I'm not convinced. But if that's going to be the headline, let's make sure it appears in our media first.'

Tony stepped away from the desk and reached for the door. He stopped and waved a finger at Gill. 'Facts. I need facts. I'll have another quiet chat with my friend in legal. We'll think through how this might play out.' He was halfway out the door when he paused again. 'Great work, by the way. *Mys.Scot* feels like a slog sometimes, but you seem to have a knack for turning over the right damp stones.'

Cassy watched Tony scooping up the *Game & Gun* team and redirect them to his office. She started to gather up the maps into their decades-old folders. 'When are you heading back north?' she said quietly.

Gill shrugged. 'Until we can get back on site, I'm not in any rush.'

'Don't you think you should try to prove or disprove this whole submarine theory? I mean, your source seems pretty cagey. What if he never gets back to you?'

Gill picked up the A3 sheet showing the layout of the submarine base. 'It's eighty metres below the surface, Cassy. I can't exactly grab my snorkel and flippers.'

Cassy sighed and let her chin drop onto her chest for a few seconds. Then with a swift movement, she placed her left hand on his breastbone and grasped his shirt lapel with her right. 'Pity you don't know anybody with a DSV,' she hissed. 'Then they could have gone down for you and taken a bloody look!'

Sheepishly, Gill gripped his phone a few minutes later. 'Hey, Salina. It's Gill. How's it going?'

'Good. Busy.' Her voice was mellow and warm.

'You in St Andrews or Oban?'

'Still in St Andrews. We're upgrading the Corryvreckan dive from ASV to a DSV, so it pushed us back a few days until I can get all the gear organised.'

'Interesting. What sparked the change?'

Salina sighed. 'The good people from Scottish Geological Society did an initial sweep of the area in a trawler with decent kit. Their work confirmed the data we pulled off the Harlequinn. No one has a clue what's going on, so it's been decided that we'll need to go down and take a closer look.'

'The SGS guys must be intrigued.'

'Utterly perplexed,' said Salina with a gentle laugh. 'Anyway, how are you getting on with your "Lucy" hunt?'

Gill twisted his body to turn his back on some nearby colleagues. 'Very well. We've just had a massive lead drop into our laps.'

'Awesome. Tell me.'

'Are you sitting somewhere private? It's too early for this to get out into the public domain.'

'Hang on a second.' He heard the sound of rustling, then a door closing. 'All clear.'

'You recall the sample I took off the damaged portion of the power station?'

'Yes,' said Salina.

'The results just hit my desk. It's a high spec antifoul.'

'Like on ships?'

'And other vessels. Like submarines.'

Salina gasped. 'You're kidding! Are you certain the grille wasn't painted with the stuff in the first place?'

'I've checked. The grille is galvanised. We found flakes of zinc in the sample as well. The evidence points to a collision.'

'Still, it's pretty circumstantial.'

'Salina, it's only part of the story.' Over the next few minutes, Gill brought her up to speed on the *Project Leviathan* drawings. Salina listened quietly, occasionally murmuring to let him know she was keeping up.

'So, the thing is,' said Gill. 'I need to get deep under the surface of Loch Ness to find out if they ever built the base.'

Salina left a pause. 'Aah. And I had the misconception this was a social call.'

'Look, no pressure. Even if you can point me in the right direction, I just need some way of getting down there to take a peek. What about the Autonomous Submersible Vehicle you planned to use next week? Could I get hold of it?'

'We were renting it from the Marine Laboratory in Oban. But that's complicated, Gill. They staff it with their own crew. You'd have to bring them up to speed. And if you're right, we might find ourselves in the deep stuff with the military.'

'Aye. It's complicated,' said Gill. 'We don't know if the base was ever built, or if it was, whether it's still operational.'

'Let me think about it.' She paused. 'My schedules are all over the place, but I'll do what I can.'

'What about Arthur? Do you think he'd be available to lend a hand?'

Salina grunted. 'He's off sick. Mental trauma he suffered while retrieving the creel boat bodies. Apparently.'

'Working on his book, you mean.'

'Probably. He wasn't shortlisted for my job, which shouldn't have surprised him as he's a technical guy rather than a career biologist. But since then, his attitude has been a little less than professional.'

'Sorry to hear that.' Gill paused, uncertain how to proceed. 'When do you finish, by the way?'

'Three weeks. The wedding is just over a month away.'

'You must be excited.'

Salina switched the phone from one hand to another, and he imagined her twisting her left hand to stare at her engagement ring. 'I'm sure it will be a lovely day,' she said.

Silence hung between them for a few moments.

'Have a think about the DSV and get back to me,' Gill said and signed off the call.

Gill had planned to leave the office early and work from home. But the day tumbled on, and he snatched writing time as best he could. He had to treat all the submarine information as subjective until he had more facts. Sitting at his desk, he sketched out two articles, one for the scenario where submarines were confirmed and a second where their existence was just a theory. Tomorrow was the regular Publisher's Meeting. For once, Gill was looking forward to it. A brief conversation with Tony confirmed they would reveal the facts in their possession to the other editors. Their collective insight would influence how he eventually wrote up the story. After that, he would be heading back to Stonehaven. It was almost two weeks since he'd seen Gordon. Their brief phone calls suggested no change.

'Got a second?' Craig appeared beside Gill's desk just as he was packing his laptop.

'Sure,' said Gill, glancing around. 'Conference room?'

Craig nodded and made his way to the empty room. Gill went via Cassy's desk, tapping it with his knuckles in a conspiratorial manner. She gathered up a folder and followed without a word.

'Just wanted to give you an update,' said Craig as Cassy closed the door.

'Any progress?' she asked.

'Was I able to find the password?' said Craig, 'No, I wasn't.' He glanced at them. 'As I suspected, the weight of enquiries crashed the website.'

'So, we're no further forward,' said Gill.

'I wouldn't say that,' Craig answered. 'After the website crashed, it automatically reset itself. As it came back up, its security protocols were briefly disabled. In short, I was able to download the entire site.'

'Awesome,' said Cassy. 'Let's have a look then.'

Craig laid his laptop down on the table and started to tap. 'Before you get excited, we're not home and dry just yet.'

The others watched as a screen loaded. To the naked eye, there was no discernible pattern. Visually it just appeared to be random letters, numbers and symbols.

'It's gobbledygook,' said Cassy indignantly.

Gill hunched over the screen. 'No. It's in base programming code. We'll need to parse it through some kind of translation tool.'

'Exactly,' said Craig. 'I've already tried several apps covering the main programming languages. But I still have some work to do.'

'You mean you can read this stuff,' said Cassy, waving her index finger at the screen.

Craig nodded. 'I've done some checking around. I know of websites where I can take a small piece of the code and see what happens. The app will try to crack the encryption by rotating certain variables.'

'Any idea how long?' Gill was doing his best not to sound impatient.

Craig shrugged. 'I might get lucky in an hour. Or, I might still be looking at garbage for another week.'

Gill clapped him on the shoulder. 'Well, good work so far. Stay on it for another couple of days.'

'The program runs in the background,' said Craig. 'In the meantime, I'll keep working on the layouts for the next issue. If we get lucky, we get lucky.'

Chapter 26

George Wiley drew on a cigarette while he stared at the sea. DS Lundy stood silently beside him, watching a rain shower moving slowly down the length of Loch Linnhe towards Fort William. Wiley was making a grand show of thinking, and DS Lundy knew better than to attempt casual conversation. Instead, he leaned at an awkward angle, with his foot just keeping the fire escape door ajar while Wiley took a last long drag and tossed his fag end into the bushes.

'Right,' said Wiley. 'Just like we talked about.'

Lundy opened the door for his boss and reluctantly followed him inside. The interrogation suite was a silent minute's walk away at the end of a long corridor near the cell block, and he did his best to dodge Wiley's smoky wake. As they walked in, Andy Sweem sat sullenly at a table where he was enduring a second uncomfortable morning. The constable guarding him nodded at Wiley, then glowered at Andy. The lad had lost his cool twice already this morning and was on final notice. If he had another violent outburst, Wiley would charge him with Assault.

Wiley glanced at the officer while he and Lundy drew up their seats and stepped through some formalities.

'Now, Andy. Let's go over this again.' Wiley's tone displayed a practised boredom designed to convince his suspect he held all the cards.

Andy dropped his arms across the desk and allowed his forehead to fall onto the crook of his right arm. 'Sodding hell,' he muttered. 'How many times?'

'As often as it takes to get this straight,' said Wiley. 'I've talked to the Fiscal, and he's happy for us to keep you for a day or two. Longer if you have another poke at one of our constables.'

'Don't like talking to cops,' said Andy, his face still hidden from view.

'You don't like talking to solicitors either,' said Wiley. 'Are you still refusing to have a legal representative at these meetings?'

'Don't want one. Don't need one.'

DS Lundy opened his case file. 'You're in trouble, Andy, because you ran from us. This is a murder investigation, and we only wanted to ask you a few questions.'

'I didn't do nothin' wrong,' Andy said in a muffled voice.

'Raise your head, son. We can barely hear you,' Wiley snapped. He waited for Andy to raise red eyes over the edge of his sleeve before he continued. 'You mentioned before you suffered some abuse you got from your dad. Was it physical, or was it, you know ...' Wiley gave a jerky little shrug. 'The other kind?'

Andy's head flew up. 'He beat me! That's all. Any excuse. An' the sicker he got, the worse the beatings got, alright?'

'Is that why you killed him?' said Lundy, taking a sheet from the case file and laying it in front of his boss.

'I told you before, I didn't kill 'im,' Andy shouted, specks of spittle flying out in front of him.

'Was it self-defence, Andy?' If Wiley's thin smile was an attempt at empathy, it was a poor one. 'Three years ago, you were just a lad. But you probably didn't know your own strength. Did he come for you one night, and for once, you fought back? Tell us, Andy. A jury might have some sympathy.'

Lundy leaned back in his chair and looked away. Wiley was leading the witness, and any confession would be inadmissible.

Andy's face fell back onto his outstretched sleeve. 'Don't want no jury.'

'Tell you what I'm trying to do here,' said Wiley, tapping the sheet in front of him with a cheap biro. 'I'm looking at things I can prove.' He paused to scribble a footnote on one of the sheets. 'I have to warn you unless you speak to us, the facts as we understand them will do the talking.' Wiley paused. 'Even when we let you go, you'll remain a person of interest in this inquiry.'

Andy made no response, his eyes hidden from sight.

Wiley slowly unpacked a pair of reading glasses and shuffled the papers in front of him. 'So, your father is last seen by the hospital treating his cancer in November 2019. Shortly after that, the Inverness hospital got a letter from your father stating he's returning to Luton to link up with his old GP. He says he's trying to get faster treatment from NHS England. The Inverness hospital waits for the English hospital to make contact requesting your father's medical notes, but no letter arrives.' Wiley looked up and peered at Andy over the thick rim of his reading glasses. 'Then Covid happens. Everything goes mental for a few months, and no one has time to track down your poor old dad.'

Andy said nothing, so Wiley continued. 'At this point, your father has effectively disappeared off the system. He's never been a great filler out of forms, tax returns and the like, so when his communication with the authorities becomes even more erratic than usual, no one flies a red flag.'

Wiley left the facts hanging in the air for a few moments, and then Lundy picked up the story. 'Here we are, three and a half years later. Your father's body is discovered on your land.' He opened his palm towards the boy. 'If it wasn't you, Andy, who was it? Your mum? This mysterious Mr Kerr?'

'Told you before,' said Andy sullenly. 'It was Kerr. That's why he disappeared.'

'And Mr Kerr's motive was what?' said Wiley.

'Whatja mean?'

Wiley cleared his throat. 'Why would this man, a paying guest on your parents' land, want to kill your father?'

Andy made no response, so Wiley continued. 'Had they argued? Had Kerr witnessed your father beating you?'

Andy's face dropped down again onto his sleeve. All they could see was his brown hair, long and unwashed. Wiley seemed fed up looking at it. He glanced at Lundy, then leaned down to speak into the recording device. 'Interview paused at 11.23 so the senior officer can take a comfort break.' He stood and stretched before moving towards the door. He grasped the handle but then turned, almost as an afterthought. 'Off the record, Andy, you don't need to worry.' He gave the lad a forced smile. Andy blinked at him, his face perplexed. 'Your mum is in the interview suite two doors down,' Wiley continued. 'She's told us pretty much everything. All I'm trying to do here is match up a few details.'

After a moment, Andy's head rose slowly from his arm. 'What you sayin'?'

Wiley moved away from the door and leaned over the table, close to Andy's head. 'She's confessed, you see,' Wiley said quietly, his voice just audible to Lundy. 'She says she killed your father in self-defence, and you tried to protect her. You helped her bury the body, that's all.'

Andy was face to face with him now, eyes blinking. Wiley eased back, most likely to push away from the boy's stale breath. 'In a few hours, I'll likely be able to let you go.' He shrugged. 'Your mum, well, she's going to go to prison for a very long time. How old is she now?' He let the question hang for a moment before waving a hand dismissively. 'Ach, never mind.'

Andy clenched his jaw, restraining his anger. 'I told you it was Kerr,' he hissed.

Wiley stared back at him. 'Why would he do that, Andy?' He made a show of gathering up his folder. 'Fair play to you. You've stuck to your story. Means I'm starting to believe you. And now your mum has confessed, I think we're pretty much done here.'

Wiley started to turn away, but Andy leapt up and grabbed his wrist. Immediately Lundy and the duty constable moved to restrain him. But Andy's gesture was not a violent one. 'My dad saw the bones,' he said.

'What bones?' snapped Wiley, his wrist still in the boy's grip.

'Them bones by the loch.'

'You mean Gill McArdle's dig site?'

'Yeah.'

Wiley shook off the grip and settled in his chair to face the boy again. 'Why on earth would Kerr kill your father over some old bones?'

Andy's eyes dropped again, focusing on his hands. 'Mr Kerr said they was important, but they had to stay where they was for a while longer until he finished some other work.'

'What happened?' asked Lundy.

Andy gripped his head with his hands, his pointed elbows trying to plough furrows in the tabletop. 'Mr Kerr gave me money to fill in all his holes. When dad heard Mr Kerr was leavin', he wanted to know what he'd found out.'

Wiley gave a flick of his head. 'What did you tell him?'

'Me dad made me show him where Mr Kerr was diggin'. He said he knew what the bones were. He got real excited and said the newspapers and TV people would come. Earn us a stack of cash. Mr Kerr said all that would happen later. He didn't want no one looking at them yet. Dad said he would call the TV his-self. That's when they argued.'

'Kerr and your father?' said Wiley.

Andy lifted his head and nodded. 'Down near the bones. Kerr picked up a shovel and threatened him. Dad called me to help him.' His voice dropped to a whisper. 'But I stopped him from escapin' from the hollow near the loch. It was my chance to teach him a lesson, you see.' Andy glanced at the officers, searching for sympathy. 'He tried to escape, but Mr Kerr hit him once from behind,' he continued. 'That was all it took.'

The room fell silent for a few moments while the officers absorbed this new narrative.

'Something I don't understand,' said Lundy. 'If Kerr planned to return to the animal bones another day, why did he bury your father in the bone pit?'

Andy bowed his head again. 'Mr Kerr took all my father's clothes. Said he'd burn 'em. Destroy the evidence, he said.' Andy started to look uncomfortable. 'Told me to bury the body in one of the old charcoal pits on the hill. Then he cleared off. Left me alone with him, lyin' there, all naked and muddy, his piss running out of 'im.' He shuddered. 'Me dad was only a little man, but him being dead, he weighed a tonne. It was gettin' late, and my mum would be lookin' for us. My arms were shakin' an I was alone cause Mr Kerr had left.'

'What did you do?' asked Wiley.

Andy paused while he remembered. 'I put him in the bone pit. Tucked up tight in a corner so that if Mr Kerr came back, maybe he'd dig right down to the monster bones and not notice me dad.'

'And you told your mother everything?' asked Wiley.

Andy shook his head. 'I told her, me and dad argued. That it was a bad one. I told her dad hated us, and he wasn't coming back.'

Wiley left a long pause. 'But she must have known?'

Andy's shrug was immediate. 'We never talked about it again. When we ever spoke about my dad, we just talked like he'd died of cancer.'

'Did you write to the hospital, or was it your mother?'

'That was me,' said Andy.

'You're sure? You know we'll be able to verify that.'

'Yeah,' said Andy. 'I wrote the letter.'

'Did you ever see Kerr again?' Wiley asked.

Andy shook his head. 'Never.'

Wiley glanced at Lundy, then back at the boy. 'Andy, why did you let Gill McArdle dig on your land if you knew your dad's body was there?'

Andy lifted his closed eyes to the ceiling, then dropped his gaze again. 'Never meant 'im to dig where he did. Sent 'im the other way. And the cash were too good to miss.' He shook his head. 'Folk payin' good money to dig a lot of old holes.'

Lundy cleared his throat. 'Andy. In a little while, I'm going to charge you for the things you've done wrong. That will mean more questions, I'm afraid. And from now on, you definitely need a solicitor present.'

'But I didn't kill 'im,' Andy protested.

Wiley got to his feet. 'No, but by your admission, you colluded in his murder and then concealed his body.' He tapped the table. 'Sit tight, son. We'll be back in a sec.'

Once outside in the corridor, Lundy was the first to speak. 'Reckon he's telling the truth?'

Wiley gave a curt nod. 'I think we're getting somewhere.'

'Do you think he'll get a stretch?'

Wiley scoffed. 'Some minger will probably bag him diminished responsibility.' He jerked a thumb at the closed door. 'I'll go back in and get all that on tape. You go out to Invermoriston and fetch the mother. Let's see if she's as innocent as the kid thinks.'

Chapter 27

Throughout the slow drive up to Stonehaven on Friday evening, Gill had a lot to think about. For the first time, he envied the other editors in the company. During the weekly Publisher's Meeting, they'd talked about their upcoming editions and outlined the ones coming after that. The other titles had as many as half a dozen issues in some degree of preparation, so it gave Gill the appearance of a row of passenger jets coming in to land at a busy airport. The furthest ones were just lights in the sky, while the nearest were gliding down, about to land safely. However, *Mys.Scot* was the closest thing the company had to an actual newspaper. It hadn't been planned this way but had evolved to become news-driven, subject to last-minute changes, chaotically approaching the airstrip with smoke pouring from its engines. Tony was signalling an eventual crash seemed inevitable, and Gill was beginning to realise it wasn't just the magazine that was the problem. It was the way he was leading it.

As for his immediate task of completing the next issue, he'd not found the meeting helpful. While Gill tugged at the leash to push ahead with the Ness revelations, the other editors had retreated behind the safety of the few known facts. Tony had come down firmly on the fence. He thought

Gill should keep pursuing the news story but develop a fistful of other great articles in case the Ness adventure didn't reach a point where they had something worth printing.

Of course, Tony was still helpful as a mentor. But it was a long time since he'd worked on fast-moving news media, and he seemed more comfortable with the steady plod of the monthly periodicals. One thing was clear. For Gill to keep this job, he'd need to get organised. In a long queue of cars approaching roadworks near Perth, he paused to think what his life would be like without *Mys.Scot*. He smiled, remembering a beautiful but maddening girl called Alice he'd dated as an undergrad. Was his working life comparable to a turbulent love affair? Passionate and unpredictable, full of unexpected pleasures and unanticipated dangers. Or was he just struggling with change as he drifted into middle age; sparks flying from his engines – landing gear locked in the up position?

The weekend at Stonehaven was like any other he had recently experienced. The groundhog day routine of listening to Gordon's stories while they worked on the *Icthus* together, sanding down the boards in preparation for painting. And when his father went inside to make tea, Gill had to fend off a neighbour's concerns about the increasing disturbances of Gordon's night-time noises and ramblings.

That evening Gill lay awake wondering how long he could keep Gordon at home and struggled with the knowledge that moving him into a care home would feel like a betrayal.

During late Sunday afternoon, they lingered too long over their chess game, waiting for a spell of rain to blow over. They were both eager for some air, and at the first glimpse of sunshine, they were soon pottering together down at Gordon's weather station. Someone from the manufacturer had been up to check the installation, but Gordon still wasn't happy with some of the readings.

'According to this thing, sea level is down another 3 mm this month,' Gordon muttered. 'If this data is accurate, I'll be able to walk to Denmark in a few years.'

'And the guy was sure that the pontoon isn't messing things up?' Gill could hear the frustration in his own voice.

'No. The GPS works independently of wherever the equipment is situated.'

'What about interference of some kind?'

Gordon shook his head.

The ring of Gill's mobile offered a distraction. He listened for a few seconds before thanking the caller and hanging up.

'Girlfriend?' asked Gordon.

Gill smiled. 'No. It was a police officer. He was phoning to tell me they've finished with my dig site at Invermoriston. It means I can get back to work.'

'Sounds important. The university will be very proud of you.'

Gill gently closed the door on the apparatus. 'I don't work at the university anymore, Dad. I went to work at a magazine. Remember?'

'Oh,' said Gordon. 'Let's go in and have some tea. Then you can tell me all about it.'

Monday morning and Gill arrived at Invermoriston at 10 am, followed by Fiona and three others a few minutes later.

'Sorry, Gill. These are all I could manage at short notice. I'll have a few more later in the week if we still need them.'

'No problem, Fi.' Gill glanced at the eager faces. 'The appeal of digging up mythical creatures just isn't what it used to be.' He leaned towards them and shook their hands. 'At least this time, we know where to start.'

Fiona addressed her team. 'Guys, can you start unloading the tools?' She flicked her chin at Gill. 'I've got another tent. It's borrowed, so look after it.'

'Do they know about the fire?' said Gill under his breath.

'Aye,' said Fiona. 'That's why there's only four of us.'

'Wiley's DS said they would pop by every few hours. Hopefully, the presence of a police car will deter any trouble.'

'What about night-time?'

'Let's see if there is anything worth protecting,' said Gill.

Fiona nodded at the farmhouse. 'No sign of the Sweems?'

Gill paused and stared at the buildings for a few moments. 'I haven't seen anyone, and I couldn't reach anyone at the house last night.'

'Is Andy still in custody? Surely they would have to charge him or release him by now?'

'Don't know. DS Lundy was keeping his cards close to his chest. All he said on the phone was, enquiries are continuing.'

Fiona picked up a wheelbarrow and started down towards the shore. 'Just so we're clear. Me and my guys are outta here before dark.'

'Agreed.'

For the next fifteen minutes, they made their way in silence down to the dig site. The sun was shining, its light diffused by the gently swaying branches above their heads. It was the first time Gill had been back here since the night of the fire, and as he walked, the woods whispered gentle threats.

A well-worn and muddied path now weaved through the trees to where crime scene tape still fluttered from the branches. A tarp covered the dig site, and Gill was dismayed to see several other holes dug indiscriminately across the tiny glen.

'Somebody's been out with a metal detector,' said Fiona with barely disguised disgust.

'Looking for clues, murder weapons, whatever,' Gill said.

Fiona moved the logs weighing down the tarpaulin and lay down on the mattress of blaeberry bushes so she could reach into the hole.

'How are you, my beauty?' she whispered to the bones. The pit had expanded to allow extraction of the human remains. Fiona reached to brush aside some earth that had fallen over the vertebrae. 'I still don't understand why Kerr never finished his dig. Why get this close to something and cover it up again?'

Gill squatted beside her. 'I guess he was like us. He saw the animal's position in the ground and realised he had a lot more work to do to excavate it entirely.'

'Do you think he was called away and never got back to finish the dig?'

'No. The fact that he paid Andy to fill in the trenches suggests he made a deliberate choice.' Gill carefully stepped into the hole and ran his fingers along the vertebrae. 'Perhaps he got this far and had seen enough.'

Fiona turned to where the others stood chatting, tools at the ready. 'Well, let's get this thing out and see for ourselves.'

She started by marking one metre on either side of the original hole. Then she and her team began to take away the earth, layer by layer. By lunchtime, they would be down to the level of the bones. By the end of the day, if everything worked well, the rest of the animal would be exposed. Gill worked with the others at the back of the chain, where he methodically sifted the earth. He was absorbed examining a small bone fragment when his phone rang. It was Salina.

'Gill. Can you help me out?'

'What's up?'

'I have a DSV sitting in Oban, and due to the bad weather, we can't get out to sea.'

Gill glanced up at the clear blue sky. 'Bad weather?'

'Yes. A big swell is coming in from the Atlantic. The skipper of the service vessel I'll be operating from can't guarantee the safety of the DSV until conditions ease down a bit.'

'How can I help?' asked Gill.

'I've a new team member coming in as Assistant Pilot for the DSV. I need to do her orientation training over the next two days, and I wondered if you might be able to suggest a freshwater location where we could launch our boat?'

Gill smiled. 'I guess you'll need something that challenges her without being explicitly dangerous?'

'That would be perfect.'

'I think I might have just the thing. Can you meet me in Urquhart Bay in about two hours, and we can scope out a dive.'

'Sure. We'll drive up just now, then bring the DSV up early tomorrow morning.'

'Salina,' said Gill.

'Yes?'

'Thank you.'

'You're welcome,' she said, her voice glowing. 'Can you help me with one practical thing?'

'Shoot.'

'We could do with some accommodation locally. We'll be tired after the dive, and I don't want to drive back and forward to Oban for the next three days.'

'Leave it with me,' Gill replied. 'See you this afternoon.'

Chapter 28

As Duncan Campbell drove into Invermoriston Farm, two officers got into a police car and got ready to leave. Gill watched Duncan's car pause inside the farm entrance. But when the police patrol left, he drove in and parked up. Gill strolled over to greet him.

'Trouble?' asked Duncan, flicking his thumb at the tail lights of the disappearing car.

'Let's just say that nothing seems to happen in my job without unforeseen complications,' said Gill, reaching out to shake his hand. 'Walk with me. I'll fill you in.'

'So, how can I help?' said Duncan as they approached the dig site.

'I have a lot of editorial to write over the next couple of days. I'd like to push some of that your way.' Gill pointed to the area where Fiona and the others were working. 'And any minute now, we'll have some bones to identify. If their provenance isn't immediately obvious, I think I'd benefit from your opinion.'

Duncan nodded, his eyes widening at the prospect of what lay ahead of him. Gill, meanwhile, had seen Fiona's body language, standing erect at a vantage point over the excavations, her hands on her hips.

'What's up?' he called.

Fiona glanced in his direction. 'Another animal. Smaller this time. It's lying at an angle to the original bones.'

Gill leapt up beside her. Frustratingly, they still hadn't reached the skull or underside of the original animal. 'That's going to take a bit of a rethink,' he said.

'Aye. We're going to need a bigger hole.' She turned to face him. 'I'm going to mark up the extended excavation area and remove the top cover. Then it's time to call it a day.'

Gill was disappointed. 'I'm in Urquhart Bay most of tomorrow.'

Fiona gave a wicked laugh. 'Looks like you won't be here for the grand unveiling.' She tapped him on the shoulder. 'Don't worry. I'll keep you informed.'

'This is Duncan, by the way,' said Gill. 'He's a contributor to *Mys.Scot*, come to lend a hand.' Gill beckoned to Duncan to join them, offering to pull him up onto their vantage point. 'What do you think?'

Duncan stared down at the partially exposed bones. 'Can I take a closer look?'

'Sure. But mind where you put your feet,' said Fiona.

Duncan stepped down and ran his hand along the backbone of the larger animal. 'The vertebrae are quite heavy,' he said at last. 'If this animal were waterborne, I'd expect to see a bigger cartilage gap between the caudal vertebrae.'

Gill nodded. He'd made the same observation and pushed it to the back of his mind.

'Bovine perhaps,' said Duncan. 'Pity we can't see the scapula or skull yet. That would nail it.'

'I'll reveal all tomorrow,' said Fiona gesticulating to a colleague to toss her some marking string. 'What are we going to do about security tonight?' she asked, looking at Gill.

'Loosely cover the bones. We're not going to put anyone at risk down here. Besides, I've seen three police cars at the farm already today. I think we'll be alright.' He glanced at his watch before nodding to Duncan. 'Can you join me at Urquhart Bay? I'll show you our other line of enquiry.'

When Gill and Duncan arrived at the little harbour on Urquhart Bay, midway through Monday afternoon, Salina and her colleague were already there.

'This is Ellie Adams,' said Salina as they all shook hands. 'Ellie recently left the Navy and is retraining to run DSVs and ASVs for the university.'

'And this is Duncan,' said Gill. 'He's a Padre in these parts, and he's also a writer. He's working with me on the next issue.'

Duncan stood blinking at Ellie. Tall and slim, she cut a far fitter figure than Arthur Deveron. 'Well, it looks like we're the newbies,' he said, leaning forward to shake her hand again in what seemed like a redundant gesture.

Gill stepped in. 'Have you given Ellie the background for this proposed dive?'

'If you mean, is she aware of our objective over and above the training exercise? Yes, she is,' said Salina.

'It's almost impossible to believe,' said Duncan, gesturing at the loch. 'There might be a submarine base right under our noses.'

'The military is good at keeping secrets,' said Ellie.

'Yes, they are,' said Gill. 'Did your navy time include work on big submarines?'

'I visited one for a job interview. Decided to stay with small boats.'

Gill nodded, feeling a little nervous that in Ellie and Arthur, they had two ex-Navy people on their team. 'So, what's the plan?'

Salina scanned the docks. 'We need to identify a launch site and get any necessary clearances. Do you know who runs these jetties?'

'No, but I know a woman who does.'

'Tomorrow is explicitly a training day,' Salina continued. 'Ellie has never manned one of our boats. We need to get her properly oriented. It will be the second day before we do a run past this secret base of yours.'

Gill nodded. The week was slipping away. If the editorial team worked late on Thursday & Friday, he calculated they could still make the 8 am print run in five days time. That didn't change the fact he had a very tight window to finish his research and get it written up. Tony would be blowing a gasket and phoning more frequently as the week rolled on.

'Were you able to find us accommodation?' asked Salina.

Gill let his hand fly to his forehead. Several times he had meant to ask Cassy, but he'd completely forgotten. Salina looked at him; her face pulled into a strained smile.

'You guys can stay at mine,' said Duncan. 'I'm in a big empty rectory in Fort Augustus, just down the road.'

'Are you sure?' said Salina, smiling at him. 'It's not just us. We have Tom and James who run our surface rib.'

'Certain,' said Duncan. 'It can be our base of operations. And there's a tonne of parking.'

'Thanks, Duncan. I'll organise the food side of things,' said Gill.

Salina glanced sideways at Ellie. 'Gill's in charge of food. We'll probably starve.'

The four chatted for a few minutes over the practicalities of the next few days. When Salina and Ellie produced a detailed map of the loch to plan their training day, Gill excused himself and took Duncan for a short stroll into Drumnadrochit to catch Sandy Brightman. As it happened, they were just in time. As Gill strode across the car park, Sandy and a staff member were locking up the exterior door of the visitor centre.

'Evening, Gill,' said Sandy, opening the door again before telling the girl that she would lock up. She was about to let the door close but paused when Duncan trailed behind Gill.

'This is Duncan. He's a writer helping me with this issue,' said Gill breathlessly.

Gill was surprised when Sandy didn't move to pull the door open. Instead, she let it go, and Duncan had to catch it before he could slide into the porch beside them.

Sandy blinked at Duncan and, without changing her expression, said, 'I'm aware of Mr Campbell. I didn't know he was a writer.'

'Have we met?' asked Duncan, extending a hand in greeting.

Sandy didn't answer the question and managed to ignore the outstretched hand. 'To be honest, Mr Campbell, I didn't know you were still in the area.'

Duncan shrugged. 'Still here. Still doing what I can.'

Sandy retreated into the foyer, allowing the others to follow her. Gill thought she looked strained. He could imagine why.

'This submarine thing is going to anger a lot of people if it's true,' Sandy said quietly.

'Sorry,' said Gill. 'I know it's not good news.'

'When you phoned the other evening, I didn't believe it at first.' She paused to throw a cool glance in Duncan's direction. 'But when you think through the evidence of the last few years, it does seem plausible.'

'What makes you say that?' said Duncan.

Sandy shrugged. 'The frequency and variety of sightings. The fact that thorough sweeps of the loch never produced any firm results. Suddenly it all makes sense.'

'I wanted to ask you about that,' said Gill. 'If the submarine base exists, wouldn't it have been picked up during umpteen sonar sweeps of the loch?'

'Only if it had distinct external features,' said Sandy. 'If it's just a sheer wall, it would look like any other steep drops in the loch. No, the bit I find hard to understand is how to build something like that without it becoming common knowledge.'

'Duncan and I were chatting about that in the car,' said Gill. 'We have a theory.'

'Which is?'

'The Foyers hydroelectric facility linking Loch Mhor to Loch Ness. I bet there was heavy equipment going in and out for years in the 60s and 70s, and no one ever blinked.'

Sandy thought for a moment. 'Followed by the Glendoe facility a few years later.' She paused and suddenly shook her head. 'No. A project like that would require so many people. And my friend at the plant has always been a believer.'

'Could all be part of the delusion, I suppose,' said Duncan.

Sandy's next glance at Duncan was positively icy before turning back to Gill. 'Can you prove any of this?'

'You remember Salina? This week, her St Andrews crew is up in the west doing survey work with a submersible. Bad weather means they can't get out to sea for the next two days. They've offered to come and help me do a little survey in Loch Ness.'

A flicker of a smile crossed Sandy's face. 'That's fortuitous. But you can't just drop equipment in this loch without contacting the relevant authorities.'

'That's why I came to see you. Can you help me make the necessary calls?'

Sandy nodded. 'Most definitely.' She glanced at her watch. 'Come back inside. We might still catch the relevant people at their desks.'

'How was your night?' asked Gill the following morning as they stood watching a 4x4 reverse a trailer towards the jetty.

'Fine,' said Salina, gesturing to the driver that he should tilt right a little. 'It's a lovely house. Very big.' She smiled at him quickly before turning back to her task. 'Incredibly tidy for a bloke living on his own.'

Before excusing himself the night before, Gill had stayed long enough to share a takeaway meal with them all. Everything in him had wanted to stay and continue his conversation with Salina. But the pressure of work, plus the conviction that getting to know her better wouldn't do either of them any good, sent him scurrying back to his hotel to scope out yet another version of his lead article.

'How did you sleep, Ellie?' he asked.

Ellie gave a brief shrug. 'Okay. Always struggle a bit when I'm away from home.'

'You fit for today?' asked Salina.

'Yeah,' Ellie replied. 'Woke up a few times, that's all. Another coffee, and I'll be fine.'

'Old houses,' said Salina. 'They do creak and groan at night.'

'It's like someone was prowling around,' said Ellie. 'You could never tell where the sounds were coming from.'

'Maybe it's haunted,' said Salina dryly. 'Ask Gill. He'll investigate it for you.'

'But you know what I mean,' Ellie protested. 'And those bolts on the inside of the doors, what was all that about?'

Salina smiled. 'Girl, I'd worry if the bolts were on the outside.'

Ellie shivered. 'I think Duncan is a bit strange.'

'He's harmless,' said Salina. 'Just a bit intense.'

Unloading and commissioning the DSV took two hours, during which time small knots of people wandered past them, wondering what was going on. When they were finally ready to get out on the water, Gill was itching to go back to the dig. He'd had a text from Fiona. She'd exposed most of the bones, and they awaited his inspection. He watched the DSV motor out of port with its support rib, then called Duncan to join him at Invermoriston in half an hour. Before that, he had a house call to make.

'Sandy about?' he asked in the reception area of the Ness Explorer Visitor Centre. He followed the directions and found Sandy in a small, cramped office, piled high with books and academic papers.

'Everything okay?' she asked.

'Salina and Ellie are out on a test run, and I'm heading back to my dig site.'

'It's all go.'

'Yes. And in my rush yesterday evening, I didn't get a chance to ask you about Duncan.'

'What about him?'

'You seemed unsettled to see him. I wondered if you two might have history?'

Sandy dropped her gaze and thought. 'Not personally. Mr Campbell does have something of a reputation.'

'Which is what?'

'I'd rather not talk about it, Gill. It's just rumours, really.'

'Come on, Sandy. Is there anything I should know that's relevant to my team's welfare?'

Sandy leaned back in her chair and bit her lip. 'You know he used to run his rectory as a respite centre for young teens?'

'Yes.'

'Well, certain accusations were made. Inappropriate behaviour. Nothing proven, you understand, but enough drip, drip, drip to cause his funding to dry up.'

'Okay.'

'And I gather some of your team are staying with him?'

'Yes. Ellie, Salina and two guys from St Andrews.'

Sandy held her hands in front of her. 'That'll be okay, then. They're all grown adults who can look out for each other. I'm sure there won't be a problem.'

Gill sighed. Nothing on this job was easy. 'Thanks for mentioning it. I'll keep an eye on things.'

Fiona was on a tea break when Duncan and Gill arrived at the dig site. While this wasn't necessarily a bad sign, Gill observed the weary expressions on the faces of her small workforce. Taken together, their body language didn't scream "ground-breaking discovery."

Fiona spotted him before he could call out to her, pulling herself out of an old camp chair and motioning to one of the lads to put the kettle back on the stove.

'Follow me,' she said, walking over to the dig. The excavations had expanded since Gill had last been down, and the heaps of spoil obscured a clear view of the hole until Gill stood right above it. He stared at the bones in the pit and, for a few long moments, said nothing.

'What do you reckon?' asked Fiona.

'Highland cattle,' said Gill twisting his neck at an angle. 'Aurochs if we're lucky. But I'd be surprised if they're that old, given how damp it is here.'

Fiona pointed to the smaller animal. 'Looks like the calf went in first. Its forelegs were deepest. The mother followed it in.'

Gill squatted and rubbed a smooth rock surface exposed by Fiona's digging. 'They must have been following the watercourse down to the loch to drink.'

'Before getting irreversibly stuck,' Fiona continued, watching Gill as he stood up and dusted off his palms. 'Sorry, boss. No monster this time.'

'Yeah,' he said. 'Pity.' He caught Duncan's expression. Thin-lipped and tense. 'Sorry, I built your hopes up.'

Duncan said nothing for a moment. Instead, he moved forward and looked down at the bones. 'There's an old drovers track along the banks of the loch. Maybe someone stopped to water their animals and lost a few on the way.'

'Very careless of him,' said Fiona. 'These animals probably starved to death.'

'Cattle have always been very precious,' said Gill. 'A drover wouldn't just abandon them.'

'Does it matter?' said Duncan.

Gill shrugged. 'It's my nature. I'm always curious.' He caught Fiona's eye. 'What's your plan from here?'

Fiona looked at her watch. 'I'd like to take another day and a half to finish up. I'll recover the bones, and once we've cleaned them up and properly identified them, maybe a local museum will want them?'

'I'm sure Sandy Brightman would be delighted. Another exhibit for her visitor centre.'

'What will I do with them in the meantime?'

'Leave that with me. There's a firm I've used in Falkirk called Lossuary. They can dry the bones and store them for us. When do you think you'll have the remains boxed up?'

'Photos are all done, so I'll have them packed and ready to ship by tomorrow lunchtime.'

'Great. I'll call them in a minute and arrange collection.'

One of the crew offered Gill a mug of tea which he accepted. Then he picked his way carefully down to the loch-side and stared out over the water. While he navigated this anti-climax, he stood watching the gently rippled surface stretching into the far distance. He'd known the likelihood that the bones would be mundane, so this didn't explain his disappointment. But his "tell" had convinced him there was something here, and for once, this instinct had let him down.

Chapter 29

Gill was waiting for Salina and Ellie while they parked the DSV in a secure compound for the night. The women looked tired but were chatting happily as they approached him.

'How was your day?' he asked. 'Find any monsters?'

Salina pulled her hair free of the jersey she had just tugged over her head. 'Loads. Monster soup out there. How about you?'

Gill looked down at his feet and shook his head. 'No. Our dig didn't find anything significant.' He looked at Ellie and back to Salina. 'Everything okay for tomorrow?'

Salina smiled at Ellie. 'When we weren't getting our lefts and rights mixed up, everything was perfect.'

Ellie giggled as Gill arched his eyebrows in mock terror. 'Everything is on the wrong side to what I'm used to. Turn left to go right! It's okay. I've got it now.'

The women laughed again, whispering reminiscences of the day at each other while Gill helped them with their kit bags.

'Well,' said Ellie. 'Time for a shower, then we're off to see the bright lights of Fort Augustus.'

Salina's eyes flitted between them. 'Actually, I think I might have a sad archaeologist to look after. Are you okay going back with Tom and James?'

'Sure,' said Ellie. 'As long as I'm not home alone, Chez Duncan, I don't mind.'

Salina turned to Gill. 'You wanna grab a bite, and then you can drop me back later?'

Gill smiled. 'Aye. That'd be great.'

It took several minutes to double-check the boats, stow their stuff in the van and agree on a start time for the following morning. Then Tom and James drove off, with Ellie squeezed precariously in the front seat between them. Ellie waved wildly while Salina and Gill responded as enthusiastically as they dared.

Salina let out a sigh.

'Tiring day?' said Gill.

Salina nodded deeply. 'Ellie's lovely, but we barely know each other, so it was quite intense spending a full day locked inside a tin can with her.'

'You seemed to be getting on okay as you came off the boat.'

'Yeah, we're good. We'll be even better once I've knocked her into shape.' She turned abruptly to Gill. 'To the pub, I think.'

'But you don't drink?'

Salina's threw him a wicked smile. 'I dunno. Try me on a double tomato juice over ice, with a dash of Worcester sauce, then stand back and watch me part-tee.' She paused to take a brief sniff of her armpits. 'I normally get a shower after a dive. You sure I don't smell?'

Gill shrugged. 'Maybe just a tiny bit.'

'Lemme think. I could …'

Gill cut across her. 'Salina, you're fine. A couple of hours chatting to you will be a big improvement on the rest of my day whether you smell or not.'

She held out her hands to him, trying her best to draw him out of his disappointment. She must have found his response half-hearted because she thrust her right arm around his waist and used it to slowly steer him up the path towards the village. 'Come on, Grumpy. Tell me your troubles.'

Walking along together, the setting sun lighting up the cottages around them, Gill was at ease with this gentle intimacy. He spoke about his misplaced instinct that he'd find significant remains at Invermoriston. Then voiced his struggle with the monthly grind of work deadlines. He confessed he should have called Tony today but had dodged it, feigning he couldn't get a decent signal. For the most part, Salina just listened, tugging gently on his arm when she thought he was too hard on himself. Now and again, she would flash a perfect smile. He knew she was trying to encourage him, and it pained him, knowing their fledging friendship would soon be over. They walked on past the pub, enjoying the light and air too much to go inside straight away.

'Tomorrow will be a big day,' said Salina as they eventually turned, resolving that it was time to eat.

Gill lifted his jaw as if checking out the sky. 'Maybe we will find something significant. Maybe I will finish the day dashing out an article about how we thought we'd solved the "Lucy" mystery but didn't.'

'Twice,' finished Salina.

'Twice,' agreed Gill. 'Total washout.' He glanced at her. 'But great fun nevertheless.'

When Salina smiled but said nothing, anxiety crept up on him again. 'Ellie,' he said. 'Will she be alright tomorrow?'

Salina's arm slipped from his, her hand brushing against his fingertips. 'She's fine. We had a great day. But you remember what it's like down there. Once you get to ten metres, it's as black as night. Ellie had to navigate by instruments, pushing the DSV forward by relying on the boat's sensors.'

'She didn't freak out?'

'No. Even when I ran a series of drills, she kept her cool the whole time.'

'What kinds of drills?'

Salina took a deep breath. 'I'd blindfold Ellie and then take control of the boat. Then I'd alter its position, speed and orientation before dropping Ellie back in control. See how long it took her to get her bearings again and get the boat back on its original course.'

'Left and right?'

Salina smiled. 'Our DSV is different from the ones she's used to. Ours is the old-fashioned type; you push the rudder left if you want to go right. She was so embarrassed!'

The air was cooling now, and the hum of happy voices drifted out of the pub's open windows. Gill held an arm towards the door. 'Shall we?'

'How did you meet your fiancé?' said Gill as they settled at a table.

'It was a family introduction. Nareef owns a chain of care homes in the south and is in the process of buying a bigger chain in the Midlands. My folks think he's a good catch.'

'Do you?'

'He's a nice guy. He took me sailing the first time we met.'

'Excellent! So, he's handy with a boat?'

'He can sail a forty-foot yacht pretty much on his own, so yeah, he's handy.'

'Well, the south coast is the place for those boats, so I hope you'll have a lot of fun.'

'How is your father doing these days?' said Salina, changing the subject. 'Last time we spoke, he wasn't keeping so well.'

Gill rotated the remains of the single glass he had savoured since arriving, trying to drive some life back into the remains of the beer. 'He's doing okay. Getting to the point where it's hard for him to stay independent.'

'That's tough for you.'

Gill shrugged. 'We lost my mother and brother, suddenly and quite close together. We had no time to prepare.' He paused and lifted his gaze to her dark brown eyes. 'I'm losing dad one little piece at a time. I'm not sure which is worse.'

She reached out and touched his hands and seemed uncertain what to say.

'Have you ever lost anybody close?' he asked.

Salina gave a gentle shake of her head. 'My mum and dad are still in their late-fifties. I have three younger stay-at-home sisters. So, the leading candidate in the family for violent or premature death is me. And so far, I'm doing okay.'

'The rest of the family aren't risk-takers then.'

'No, my dad is a gynaecologist, and the closest he gets to danger is Saturday morning golf.'

'And your mum?'

'Ah!' said Salina. 'By day, she is the frumpy, fussy hostess that marshals the social life of the Pakistani community in south Glasgow.' She made a show of splaying her hands out in front of her. 'While by night … she's much the same.'

Gill smiled. 'Not even golf?'

Salina laid a single clenched fist down on the table in mock surprise. 'My mother has just two ambitions in all the world. The first is to see me married by age thirty, and second, to see me push a pram by age thirty-one.'

Gill arched his eyebrows. 'She missed the first one, didn't she.'

Salina dropped her gaze. 'Maybe second time lucky.'

Gill was mindful of melancholy rolling up on her like a mist at the end of a sunny afternoon. He wanted to distract her. 'How did your family end up in Glasgow?'

Salina's body relaxed, her eyes glancing up and right as she recalled old history. 'My father is from a Christian family. Many years ago, he was finishing his medical degree when he discovered that his parents had pledged him into an arranged marriage with a girl he'd never met.'

'Your mother?'

Salina shook her head with a furtive smile. 'Unknown to his family, my father was head-over-heels in love with a girl he'd met in the city. That lady was to become my mother.'

'Why the secrecy?'

'My mother is from the Muslim community. Her family would never have tolerated that union, so they fled Pakistan together.'

'I didn't realise any Christians lived in Pakistan.'

'Always a small number. Becoming even rarer these days; just a few per cent of the population.'

'What did your folks do?'

'They managed to get into India, and then from there, my father could reach the UK and find a job. That took him to Glasgow, where I was born.'

'I have to say; you don't sound very Weegie.'

'I'm from the south side. The better part of town, apparently.'

'What about matters of faith? Do you consider yourself Muslim, or Christian, or nothing?'

Salina's head dropped forward, and she peered at him from behind a flow of long dark hair. 'You're big on personal questions tonight.'

Gill shrugged. 'I don't mean to pry. No matter. Just leave it.'

Silence hung between them for a few moments. Then Salina pushed back her hair. 'My dad really believes, so I guess that made an impression on me over the years. Why does it matter to you?'

Gill puffed up his cheeks, then blew air out slowly. 'I met a girl last year …'

'Oh yes?' Salina's eyes were sparkling again.

'Not like that. A Christian girl. Never met anybody like her before.'

'What made her special?'

Gill thought for a moment. 'I guess it's because she really believed. Not like she was raised to it or brainwashed or anything. She had fire in her belly and had seen things that convinced her, you know, God, Jesus, all that. Like it's all real.'

Salina nodded. 'Do you believe it's real?'

Gill bobbed his head from side to side. 'I've always wanted to believe in something. I think it is intellectual laziness to assume that the world, the universe, is just a cosmic accident. Believing in God, any god, doesn't come naturally to me. Feels like an intellectual shortcut. But I can't get over the conviction the universe exists for a purpose. So it's logical to conclude it exists as an act of will. Whose will; I'm not sure.'

Salina laughed. 'That's the best non-answer I've ever heard.'

'Do you have faith?'

Salina sat back in her chair. 'Yes. Of sorts. Although I'm not used to people asking me about it.'

'Of sorts? Who is handing out the non-answers now?'

'You know. Instinctively I believe. But I don't have a context to explore that thought. So it just sits in a "think about it tomorrow" box.'

'This girl,' Gill continued. 'She has a remarkable gift. She can see things in the future.'

'You're saying she's a prophet?'

Gill fiddled with his glass again. 'No stone tablets or locust snacks, but yeah, that describes her.'

Salina glanced to her right, distracted by a burst of activity near the bar. 'I've never met a prophet, but I understand the principle.'

'And you believe it's possible?'

Salina thought for a second, then nodded. 'How did your encounter with her affect you?'

Gill realised he must look awkward. He glanced down at his glass, then up at her face. 'I'm not sure to this day what was going on.' He shook his head. 'I really should take more time to think about it. I'm a scientist. Somewhere along the line, I'll need some proof before I can move forward.'

She leaned closer to him and whispered. 'I've got proof.'

She was hesitating, self-conscious. So, he pressed her. 'Go on.'

She shook her head, embarrassed she had spoken. 'No. I'm sorry I mentioned it.'

'Go on, Salina. Proof. One scientist to another.'

She lifted her eyes to meet his. 'It's because I have a guardian angel.' She dropped her gaze again. 'I see him in my dreams.'

Gill laughed, catching himself when he realised she was serious. He coughed, then asked, 'Sorry. I mean, do they have guardian angels in the Bible? I thought it was all just folklore.'

She nodded. 'I've looked into it, and I'll give you an example. Joseph, the earthly father of Baby Jesus, sees an angel in a dream who warns him to take his family and flee immediate danger.' She glanced up and smiled at the young waitress who laid down cutlery and napkins for them. 'There are lots of other examples like that.'

Gill laid his cutlery out slowly and deliberately. 'Can't believe we're talking about dreams and angels. It's all a bit surreal.'

Her voice was crisp but not unfriendly. 'You started the conversation.'

He nodded profoundly and lifted his hands. 'I know. A piece of me is fascinated by this stuff. Just can't reconcile it with my scientific side.' He paused to check her expression. 'Do you go to church?'

'Not these days,' she replied. 'I'd like to, as a way to explore faith, but my dad goes to a rather traditional church. I appreciate it helps him, but I find it rather dry.'

'You ever thought about going to something more modern?'

'Yes, but I've never done anything about it. I have an inner terror about going to a meeting where everyone is being happy-clappy, and I don't have a clue what's going on.'

'Your angel. Can you tell me about your dreams?'

She looked away for a moment, noticing the waitress approaching them again, this time with food. 'It's all quite personal, Gill.' She shrugged. 'Let's just sum it up by saying I have the sense someone is watching over me.'

The conversation paused as the waitress laid a fish supper in front of Gill and a paella for Salina. 'You make a living by debunking myths,' said Salina. 'Be it waterhorses or monsters living in lochs. You brush aside the mystery and find scientifically grounded explanations.' She smiled. 'I guess my point is, I like my angel just the way he is. I don't want you to rationalise him away.'

Gill nodded, even though he wasn't sure he agreed with her. He chased chips around his plate, encouraging them to cool. 'Scientific or supernatural, I'm at a stage in life where I just want to find out what's real.'

She glanced around then said quietly, 'Which is a valid objective. And it's only a short segue from there to ask what you're going to do if we actually find submarines in Loch Ness?'

'Write a story about it very, very quickly and put it in my magazine.'

'You might be arrested.'

'I doubt it. "Local magazine researching the mysteries of the loch finds secret military base." If it does exist, someone was bound to run across it eventually.'

'Diving in the loch - I might be arrested!'

'I'll visit you in prison and bring you a cake with bolt cutters inside it.'

She gave him a mock kick under the table. 'You're so kind.'

'I'm more worried about what I'm going to write about if we don't find anything.'

Chapter 30

Gill stood on the pontoon, watching Salina & Ellie warm up the craft and run through some checks. The new day had come in colder than expected, and a steady breeze lifted the loch's surface into a gentle chop. Tom and James were happy enough to proceed with the dive, but the team looked to Salina to make the final decision. She put in a call to Oban to confirm that the crew would be moving back to their original plan the following morning, so with the knowledge that today would be their only chance, Salina decided the dive was on.

'Don't take any risks,' he called to her as they prepared to close the hatch.

'No weather at one hundred metres,' she called back. 'See you later.'

Gill had toyed with the idea of joining the crew on the rib. However, the thought of spending a full day on the water became less appealing as the first of several showers started to beat its way down the glen. Besides, a text had come in from Fiona. She and her team were wrapping up the dig site by lunchtime, and she had something she wanted to show him.

He watched the DSV and the rib ease out of the little harbour, following a line of buoys into deeper water. When the DSV finally disappeared, he turned and walked briskly back to his car.

Apart from three vehicles belonging to Fiona's team, the Invermoriston farmhouse still showed no signs of life. He stepped past the lightless cottage and down into the woods. The absence of even the faintest smell of wood smoke made the forest seem even more empty, and he found himself regretting the unintended trouble he'd brought on the family. He had to remind himself they were the ones implicated in a murder. That killing, plus the attempt on his own life, made this a dark place. He was confident that after today, he would never come back here again.

On the way down, he passed some of the crew carrying tools, stopping to chat for a few minutes and thanking them for their hard work. Down at the dig site, the team had packed away their tent, and the remaining tools lay in barrows, ready to return to the van. Fiona was still dressed in muddy overalls while she worked to fill one of the remaining trenches. He waved to her as he stepped down into the hollow.

'Gill. You're just in time. Another half-hour and I would have nothing to show you, apart from a few photos on my phone.'

'Morning to you too,' he said. 'Did we overlook a thorny tusk? Did you decide that the row of crocodile teeth warranted another look?'

Fiona pulled a face and glanced at her watch. 'Meter's empty. It's time to go.'

'What have you got?' he said, stuffing his hands in his pockets as the cool draught of the next shower rolled towards them down the loch.

Fiona beckoned to him, and together they squatted in the remaining trench. 'What do you make of this?' she said, pointing to a line of pale-coloured soil running horizontally across the trench wall.

Gill shrugged. 'It's a line in the dirt.'

Fiona pulled a face. 'You're meant to be the ruddy expert! Don't go slack on me now.'

Gill scowled at her before leaning closer to the exposed layers. He rubbed some of the pale soil onto his fingers and examined it. 'Looks like clay. It's very fine.'

'Where did it come from?' Fiona was looking at him intently. 'Or put it another way, does it remind you of anything?'

Gill stood back and stared at the layer, forcing himself to see it in context. Squatting into the trench floor, Fiona pointed at the lowest substrate. He started to grasp what she was suggesting. 'Grits and sands, probably from the little burn that flows through here, the layers enhanced by all the organic matter deposited here each autumn. And above the line, the same thing.' He drew his hand to his forehead. 'Have you tried dating the layer?'

Fiona grinned. 'That's better, ya big numpty.' She paused to draw her forefinger up the gradient. 'Based on the deposition rate, I'd say it was about 1200 years old.'

'The same as the aurochs?' said Gill.

'The same as the aurochs,' said Fiona. 'They didn't get stuck in the mud, Gill. They were caught in a mini tsunami.' She turned and pointed around the little bay. 'They were down at the water's edge, probably enjoying a safe watering hole, when suddenly, wham! A wall of water engulfs them.'

Gill nodded quickly. 'I see it now.'

'What I can't figure out,' said Fiona. 'Is where the clay came from.'

'Post-glacial debris,' said Gill. 'The detritus of rivers that flowed into the loch for a millennia after the ice had gone. It's a fine powder. The walls of the loch are covered with the stuff.'

Fiona peered through the gap in the rocky foreshore to stare across the opposite bank over a mile away. 'So, a silt fall on the loch walls beneath the opposite shore was enough to toss up a wave, five to eight metres high?'

Gill nodded. 'It's shallower here than the rest of the loch, which will have emphasised the height of the wave. But a surge big enough to spill this silt across the loch must have been quite a deluge.'

'Find a local historian,' said Fiona wiping her hands and climbing out of the trench. 'A wave that big would have created quite a mess. I know it was long ago, but someone might have recorded it.'

She reached the top of the bank and turned to offer Gill her hand. 'What are you so happy about?'

Gill tugged against her weight and pulled himself up onto level ground. Impulsively he hugged her. 'You clever girl. You always give me something to write about.'

They laughed together for a few minutes, and Gill reviewed Fiona's photos before jumping back in the hole and taking a few of his own. He was emerging again when his phone rang.

'Hi Cassy,' he breathed. 'You catch us at a fortuitous moment.'

'Save it, Gill. Where are you?'

'Invermoriston,' said Gill. 'What's up?'

'Our friend with the submarine plans. He took our bait.'

'Project Leviathan?'

'It's all yours. But there's a catch,' said Cassy.

'Which is?'

'Our man will be in the Kingshouse Hotel in Glencoe until midday. He says this is his first and last contact. If you don't make it by twelve, you'll miss him.'

Gill glanced at his watch. 'Better get moving. Thanks, Cassy. Anything else?'

'That's it. Phone me later, yeah?'

Gill hung up and paused to give Fiona another hug. 'Gotta dash.' He pointed back to the trench as he started to walk away. 'Excellent work.'

The drive up to the edge of Rannoch Moor felt longer than the sixty-six miles on the satnav. Fort William was choked with cars as all the major roads moved at the slow pace of relaxed people on holiday. It was 11.55 am when he drew up at the hotel. As the only significant building for miles in either direction, it was a landmark he knew well. He burst into the hotel reception, but given the time of day, it took a few minutes to track down a member of staff. A pretty blonde with a tenuous grasp of English struggled to understand his question. In her opinion, no one was waiting for him.

Back out in the car park, he scanned the vehicles to see if he could see anyone sitting in a car. This was fruitless too. Then he spotted a sign for a walker's bar at the back of the building and set off to find it. The bar was not busy. An older man to his left sat, intently reading a magazine, but did not look up as Gill walked in. Two older ladies sat drinking coffee at a heavy pine table while another old couple, perhaps husband and wife, sat silently side by side in an alcove near the bar. Gill focused his attention on a middle-aged man sitting at the bar in walking clothes. He was deep in conversation with the barmaid, a black-haired version of the girl he had met in reception. Gill went to the bar and leaned in, making sure he was in the man's line of sight. Instead of a flash of recognition, the man gazed coolly in his direction, and then carried on talking to the girl.

'Can I get you something?' said the girl, breaking away from the man mid-sentence.

'No, well, maybe. I'm meeting someone,' said Gill. He gave the girl a strained smile and walked back across the bar. He had just resolved to leave the room and try somewhere else when the older man by the entrance spoke.

'If you're ordering a drink, Mr McArdle, I'd have another coffee.'

Gill turned to stare at the man. He still hadn't yet looked up at Gill. But the magazine he recognised. "Coywolves on Speyside", *Mys.Scot*, issue four.

Gill sighed and took several deep breaths as he regained his composure. 'Are you enjoying my article?'

The man removed his glasses and tucked them away in a worn leather pouch, then closed his magazine and laid it on the table. Only then did he lift his gaze to face Gill with dispassionate pale blue eyes. 'Remarkable creatures. Once they got into the Cairngorm forests, it made it just about impossible ever to eradicate them. I hope the person who released them knew what he was doing.'

'You disapprove?'

'Whether I approve or not isn't the point.' He tapped the magazine gently with the palm of his right hand. 'I'm simply remarking that public safety often gets a low priority.'

'Milk and sugar?' asked Gill.

The man gave a single nod. Gill walked to the bar and ordered a cafetiere and shortbread. Consciously he did not look at the man. Instead, he monitored him out of his peripheral vision. He paid for the drinks and returned to the table, where he sat without being asked. Estimating the man was in his mid-seventies, Gill sat looking at him, although neither spoke for a long moment.

'Gill McArdle,' said Gill, thrusting out a hand towards the man with such suddenness, he almost alarmed himself.

The other man didn't flinch, his eyes steady and unwavering. After a few seconds, he reciprocated Gill's gesture and shook his hand, firm and brief. 'Steven Ackerson.'

Gill nodded. 'Okay, Steven.' He paused, then added, 'Thank you for meeting me.'

Steven gave a barely perceptible tilt of his head. 'A wee bird tells me you've been doing a little fishing in Loch Ness.'

Gill nodded.

'You know you're not going to find anything.' The pale eyes weren't defiant, but they didn't give anything away.

'We haven't found a submarine base yet, but we suspect they're operating in the loch.'

Steven's eyebrows arched, and a faint smile beckoned for more detail.

'We had suspected sightings of a small sub about two weeks ago,' Gill continued. 'They coincided with a small collision at the power station. Paint samples I took from the site points are consistent with the anti-foul paints used on submersibles.'

Steven nodded slowly and turned a little to scan the room. 'I'm aware of the incident. The Navy put in a DSV to sweep the southern end of the loch. Someone reported fish with radiation poisoning.' He turned to face Gill again. 'You don't know anything about that, do you?'

'We reported the incident, but I can't explain it,' said Gill brushing away the question. He stared at Steven, trying to get the measure of him before pressing on. 'But it begs the question. How did the Navy happen to have a DSV in Loch Ness? They didn't bring it in on a truck; somebody would have noticed that. So the evidence still points to some kind of base.'

'There's no base. Instead, picture a large military rib out of Faslane on a training exercise. If you don't believe me, you could check with the lock keepers on the Caledonian Canal. It passed up on 24th April with a dozen personnel and dropped back down through the locks three days later.'

'But that's a rib, not a DSV.'

'The smallest of the Navy's DSVs can submerge in a metre of water. That one made its way up the canal attached to the bottom of the rib. Once in the loch, it was free to go about its business.'

Gill sat impassively, weighing the merit of this new suggestion. 'Why the secrecy?'

Steven shrugged. 'Radiation. If someone detects an unusual spill, the government prefers to study it without the glare of the media.'

'And the collision?'

'What can I say? It was a long mission, and the pilots couldn't be relieved until well after dark. Even if you put an experienced navigator in a thirty-million-pound-boat, they get tired and bump into things.'

Gill smiled at the dark-haired girl as she laid down their drinks, waiting until she was gone before he continued. 'Let's wind back a bit. If you are the person who has been sending me secret documents about submarine bases …?' He waited until he got a slow nod of acknowledgement. 'Why then are you going through all this cloak and dagger just to tell me no such base exists?'

Steven sipped his coffee and laid down his cup without causing a ripple on the surface. 'Because the existence of any base isn't the point I'm trying to make.'

'What is the point? Surely you've taken a risk in sending me these papers? You seem to think you're taking a risk in meeting me now.'

The older man didn't start speaking right away. Instead, he sat glaring at Gill, uncertain perhaps if talking to him was worth the risk.

'About one hundred miles east of Dundee, there are a series of deep depressions called the Devil's holes,' he said at last.

'I've heard of them,' said Gill. 'Someone floated the idea that they might have been the home of the large eel that washed up at Caithness recently.'

Steven shrugged, slowly casting his gaze around the people in the bar. 'The holes are a drowned valley landscape. It's very silted now. Not rocky the way congers like it.'

'Unless you're a very large conger.'

Steven picked up his cup and took a slow sip. 'Another distraction.'

'Okay. Sorry, please carry on.'

'During the first world war, a British K Class submarine developed a specialised form of ambush. She would lie on the soft mud in one of the Devil's holes, listening to ships passing overhead. Her commander had a register of any British ships scheduled in the area. So, when a promising target passed overhead that wasn't on her manifest, she would pop and take a look at it.'

'And blast it if it was German,' said Gill.

'Exactly. Quite successfully. So successfully that the Admiralty started a steering group called *Project Leviathan*. This team drew up plans to build a secret submarine base in the Devil's Hole, accessed by an undersea railway in a tunnel, running below the sea bed.'

Gill stared at Steven, looking for any sign that he was the victim of a strange joke. 'You're not about to tell me they ever built something like that?'

'Ah! The Brits built a lot of long tunnels back then. We were very good at it, so it's not as mad as it sounds. But a hundred miles under the sea! Absolutely not,' said Steven. 'The military parked the idea without digging as much as a yard. Total nonsense, right from the start. But strategically ...,' he took his forefinger and drew an imaginary line across the table. 'The idea had taken root. Any submarine base invisible to an enemy would have incredible strategic value.' He paused for effect. 'Then came the second world war.'

Gill inclined his head towards Steven.

'The Navy started looking for a new site. Somewhere with immediate access to deep water, located among mountains to make it more defensible. Aspects of the Devil's Hole plan went back on the drawing board. This time they were looking for a land-based site with more than one route to the sea.'

Gill nodded but said nothing.

Steven looked away and waved a hand. 'Anyway, that war proceeded at a pace, and the submarine project went back into the deep freeze. Until the Cold War.'

'The Navy ended up at Faslane on the Clyde,' said Gill.

Steven nodded. 'There has been a submarine presence on the Clyde since the second world war. Eventually, it became the home port for Britain's nuclear subs. But when I joined the project in 1974 as an apprentice engineer, it was slated to go in a very different place.' Gill remained mute until Steven prompted him. 'The second set of drawings I sent you.'

'Loch Ness?'

'Aye.'

'But it's miles from the sea.'

'Compared to the Devil's hole plan, it was a dawdle. Think about it. The surface of the Ness is barely twenty metres above sea level. All we had to do was build a series of tunnels below sea level linking the lochs along the Great Glen Fault. Pressure doors would act like locks on a canal.' He glanced at Gill to make sure he was following. 'The Submarines would be housed in deep bunkers along the loch-side and could slip out to sea using the easterly or westerly exits.' Steven glanced around him. 'As part of a complex deal with the Americans to buy the Polaris missile system, they agreed to part-fund the project. So, by 1969, the project looked like it would go ahead.'

'What happened?'

'When I joined the service, we dug a series of deep wells along the line of the Great Glen fault. The public story was something about investigating local geology on behalf of the hydroelectric industry. Things were looking good for a while. We even found water courses deep underground that suggested that nature had done some of our work for us. You know, soft areas of rock that drilling machines could easily work through.'

'I'm guessing you hit some kind of problem.'

'We did. Something we hadn't foreseen. Something quite frightening.' Steven stopped and stared at a spot far above Gill's head for a moment. 'How much do you know about the Great Glen fault?' he asked.

Gill thought for a moment. After his research these past couple of weeks, he knew quite a lot. 'That it is an ancient fault line between two supercontinents that came together two hundred million years ago to form Pangea. Later this landmass split up again, and the Atlantic Ocean formed as the continental plates slid apart. Now landlocked and away from the main action, geologically speaking, the Great Glen Fault became inactive.'

'Then came the ice ages,' said Steven. 'Huge glaciers found the rocks along the old fault line were weaker than the surrounding rock. They did their work for hundreds of thousands of years until they had bulldozed the Great Glen and created some of the deepest Lochs in Europe.'

'Then, as the ice melted and the sea rose, the lochs were connected to the sea for a few thousand years,' Gill continued.

Steven shrugged. 'Maybe, but the land was rising, bouncing back after the weight of the ice had lifted. Eventually, these huge bodies of water ended where they are today, just a little above sea level.'

'So, what was the problem?' Gill was doing his best to remain patient.

'Quite simply, the Great Glen fault isn't as dormant as we thought. Geologists inspecting our test wells found an unstable environment.'

'What do you mean?'

Ackerson deliberated over another slow sip of coffee. 'Put quite simply, the earth's crust is relatively thin where the fault is deepest. The possibility the fault might become active again made it too risky. Putting nuclear subs in a potential earthquake zone was a nonstarter.'

Gill experienced a sudden chill. 'The Great Glen is a potential earthquake zone?'

'That's what I said.'

'And you're saying nothing was ever built?'

'No. The project was abandoned. We developed the Faslane base on the Clyde instead, and *Project Leviathan* went on ice forever. The team working on it had all signed the official secrets act, so everyone scattered to do other jobs when they finally cancelled the project.' Steven paused. 'With one exception.'

'I'm guessing. You?'

'The wells we had dug were fitted with instrumentation in the early days to help us measure the instability we encountered. Much of the equipment has ceased to function over the years, but the higher-ups decided that I should keep monitoring data from the surviving wells. I had other duties, of course. It became routine. Boring. Eventually, I retired, and as far as I knew at the time, no one picked up that particular duty.'

'So why reveal all this now?'

'One of the test wells sits near the site of a new hotel near the Beauly Firth.' He pulled out a scrap of paper, wrote down a postcode, and passed it to Gill. 'Here. You can check this for yourself.'

'What's important about this particular well?'

Steven cupped his chin with his left hand and leaned on the table, dipping his teaspoon in the dregs of his coffee. 'A defence contractor went to recover the old MoD equipment and ensure the well was safe. The equipment is pretty old now but still active. Not that there was anyone left who could interpret the data. That's why they pulled me back to Faslane for a few weeks.'

'What's the deal?'

'For two decades, my ageing machines have logged a significant increase in stresses along the fault.'

'Couldn't the machines be faulty? You say yourself they're old.'

Steven lifted the cafetiere and refilled his cup. 'We've checked some. The machines work fine.'

'And?'

'Tectonic pressures are higher now than when we abandoned *Leviathan*.'

Gill said nothing for a few moments. Instead, he swept his hand across the table, catching a few loose sugar grains and pushing them off the table. 'Steven, I'm sure you mean well. But I've visited the Scottish Geological Society as part of my Loch Ness enquiries. I specifically asked them about seismic activity in the region, and they assured me all is quiet.'

'It might be quiet, but their tools sit at ground level and detect movement. They don't measure pressure. Despite their greater sophistication, they're not measuring what my machines are measuring.'

Steven stared intently at Gill, looking for any sign that the younger man wasn't following him. Then he held his hands in front of him, holding them a few centimetres apart as if he were about to clap. 'Imagine you have two rock surfaces. One side represents the southern part of a vast continent of rock. The northern side is another plate of the earth's crust.'

Gill nodded. He was following.

'Then take a big metal bar with a spring inside,' continued Steven. 'The tension on the spring measures the degree to which the two rocks are pushing closer together or pulling apart.'

Gill nodded again.

Steven swept his left hand away with a flourish. 'Well, it's a hell of a lot more complicated than that, but basically, the pressure in the rocks has increased beyond anything we ever measured before.'

'Okay,' said Gill. 'Let's say that's true. And I don't know; I don't have the expertise. Why haven't we seen reports in the news? Why hasn't the MoD got scientists crawling all over this?'

Steven looked away and gave a half-hearted shrug. 'What do you think? It's like the Coywolves. We set a low priority on public safety.'

'Considering how the Scots feel about Faslane, admitting to your seismic thingeys would mean admitting to the Loch Ness plan,' said Gill.

'Exactly. Fuel for the Nationalists and embarrassment for the military.' Ackerson shook his head irritably. 'A small but significant earthquake risk across the highlands is an inconvenient fact no one wants to face up to.'

'Don't they agree with your interpretation of the data?' said Gill.

'They agree. It's just getting the people at the top to realise the recent spike in activity points to immediate danger. They'd rather sit on it than take the tough decisions.'

Gill sat back in his chair, trying to understand what was happening. 'Why bring this to me?' he said. 'Why not take it to mainstream media?'

Steven laid down his cup and was silent for a few moments. 'I did. Two of the big newspapers. They weren't interested.'

Gill nodded. 'I'm a little bit further down the news food chain.'

Steven's head tipped a little. 'I've read your magazine. You do some deep investigative pieces. I thought it might be more up your street.' He stopped and looked directly at Gill. 'Maybe I made a mistake. I'm not sure you believe me.'

Gill sucked in a breath and turned away. 'It's a wild story. I can see why the majors didn't take you on.' He thought for a second, then asked. 'Did you insist on anonymity by any chance?'

Steven nodded. 'I've signed things, you see. I'll end my days in prison if this gets out and my name is closely attached to it.'

Gill leaned forward and gently tapped the table in front of Steven. 'That's your problem. From an editor's perspective, you can't run a story like this and not quote a source. No source means zero credibility.'

Steven stared at him impassively for a few seconds. Then he got up and moved around the side of the table so he could stoop and whisper close to Gill's ear. 'Sorry to have troubled you, Mr McArdle.'

Gill held up a hand. 'Wait, I'm not saying I don't believe you.'

Steven glanced around the room, checking again they weren't being overheard, his face devoid of expression. 'People need to know. I thought you might be the man to tell them.'

Gill steadied his voice before speaking. 'If what you say is true, what will be the outcome?'

Steven lifted his gaze and looked out of the window. 'An earthquake, probably. Tremors. The northern landmass is sinking and wants to move eastwards. The south is rising and wants to move west. Whether it does that violently or gradually, I can't say for sure. I expect people will need to die before the experts start looking at the problem.' He looked down again at Gill, and for the first time, he appeared uncomfortable. 'I have a conscience, Mr McArdle. I needed to tell someone about this.'

'And what do you expect me to do?'

'Write about it in your magazine. Warn people,' he whispered. He stooped to pick up a hat from his seat. As he did so, he passed Gill a small plain card with a handwritten number. 'If you have any questions in the next seven days, call me on this mobile. It's a "burner." I think that's what you call it. No one can trace it back to me. That said, I'll only use it once. One week from now, I'm being stood down. Then I'll go back to my fishing and my anonymity, and that phone goes in the sea.'

He didn't wait to see if Gill had any questions. 'Thank you for the coffee,' he said. Then he turned and was gone.

Gill sat on for a few minutes. The rain had started again, and he was in no immediate hurry. He recorded the main points of Steven's story on his notepad, substituting his source's name with a pseudonym. He could check out the new hotel Ackerson mentioned, as that was the only data he could corroborate. Could he get a longer-term perspective on the Great Glen from another source that might add veracity to Ackerson's story? On impulse, he grabbed his phone and dialled Brightman.

'Sandy, Gill McArdle here.'

'Gill, thank goodness you called. Where are you?'

'I'm in Glencoe. I've just had an interesting meeting, and I wanted to pick your brains about some geological questions.'

'Gill, never mind about that. My skipper radioed in. He's just heard about an accident out on the loch.'

Gill experienced a sudden rush of dread. 'What kind of accident?'

Chapter 31

It was a long and fretful drive back up to Loch Ness. As Gill drove into the car park beside the pontoons, an ambulance was just leaving, its blue lights flashing. He slammed his door closed and ran onto the dock. Feeling a rush of relief to see the DSV and the rib moored in the harbour, he steered towards a knot of people clustered at the back of the team van. Salina sat on the tailgate, her hair and face wet, and a blanket drawn tightly around her shoulders. He pushed in between Tom and James and looked in her face. She immediately stood, and for a moment, they held each other in a strained embrace.

'What happened?' he asked. 'Are you alright?'

Salina nodded, mouthing a "thank you" as Sandy Brightman passed her a steaming mug. 'We hit a silt fall at about one hundred metres. We must have dislodged something. A big lump of debris hit the DSV and drove us down another fifty metres.' She waved her free hand in front of her face to chase away tears, then gulped her drink. 'The motors choked out, and the instrument panel lit up like a Christmas tree. I honestly thought we were going to die.'

Gill glanced around. 'Where's Ellie?'

Tom leaned in. 'She's okay. A bit smacked about. They've taken her to Inverness for X rays and to treat some cuts.'

'She freaked out,' said Salina. 'As soon as the DSV started to plunge, she just lost control. She tried to break open the hatch. I had to subdue her, Gill. I mean, physically restrain her.' Salina pulled a hand to her mouth, and Gill moved to embrace her again, feeling the press of her head against his shoulder.

Tom nudged James and pointed to the lorry crane reversing into the yard. 'Let's get her out of the water and check for damage.' As they walked away, Sandy and the others went with them, leaving Gill and Salina alone.

'I'm so sorry I put you through this,' whispered Gill.

She sniffed and wiped her nose with the back of her hand. 'It's not your fault. You were doing your job. I was doing mine.' She pulled back from him a little, dabbing her face with the heel of her thumb. He could see her knuckles, already purple with bruising from where she'd struck Ellie.

'Salina, we need to get you some help. You've had quite a shock.'

'No. I'm alright. I just need to know Ellie is okay. Can you take me to her hospital?'

'Of course. Let's get you changed, and we'll go up there straight away.'

Gill beckoned to Sandy, and after Salina had dug out her kit bag, he drove them both the short distance to the museum. There, Sandy guided Salina into the ladies cloakroom. The building felt warm, and Gill noticed for the first time how unpleasant the weather had become. He stood with Sandy in the foyer, watching low clouds scud over the loch.

'That was a close one,' said Sandy.

'Unbelievable,' said Gill.

'You were going to ask me something when we spoke earlier.'

Gill nodded. 'It's linked to the silt fall that almost did for Salina and Ellie. I need to find out if they're common.'

Sandy drew her hands to her hips and thought for a moment. 'I've been around here for forty years. Never encountered one.'

'What about the longer term? I wonder if any crop up in historical records. Even in local mythology or clan histories?'

Again, Sandy thought, then shook her head. 'Nothing I can think of.' She jerked her thumb into the depths of the museum. 'One of my volunteers is a bit more familiar with local history. She's not in this afternoon, but I'll ask her to check first thing in the morning.'

Gill nodded, 'Thanks.'

Sandy's expression became troubled. 'You were thinking about silt falls, just as one was happening out on the loch?'

Gill leaned back against the nearest wall. 'My dig down at Invermoriston. At the last moment, we found evidence of a small tsunami. We think it's what killed the aurochs.'

Sandy's left hand drifted up to tug her long tail of hair. 'The amount of silt carried down into this loch by a thousand wee rivers. And, of course, the loch has no current to take it away. It all just settles. I suppose things like this can happen from time to time. But I doubt it was a coincidence it happened today.'

'What do you mean?'

Sandy glanced at the cloakroom door to check it was still closed. 'Salina and Ellie must have caused the silt fall. Probably the wash from their engine set it off while they were up against the canyon walls looking for your sub base.' She paused while Gill nodded to concede the likely trigger for the accident, then continued. 'She probably hasn't had a chance to tell you yet, but they didn't find anything.' She paused again to emphasise her next statement. 'We've confirmed that no submarine base exists in Loch Ness.'

'I guessed,' said Gill. 'I'm only sorry the girls had to take a risk to prove it.'

The door beside them swung open, and Salina appeared. Dressed in jeans, calf-high boots and bottle-green cashmere jumper over a fresh shirt. She looked much better.

'Thanks, Sandy,' she said, passing her kit bag to Gill and turning to give Sandy a gentle hug.

'Right,' said Sandy. 'Are you two off to Inverness right now, or do you want something to eat?'

Salina looked at Gill. 'I'd like to go straight away,' she said.

It was after 6 pm when they arrived at Inverness Raigmore Hospital. It was a bustling, busy place, and it took twenty minutes to track Ellie down. She was being assessed in A&E when they arrived, and it was an hour before she was admitted to a small private room. Salina waited anxiously for an additional hour to speak to a doctor. While they murmured together in a corridor, Gill watched from a distance, studying the doctor's expression. He watched Salina smile and nod her thanks as the conversation ended.

'How is she?' said Gill as Salina walked briskly towards him.

'Not bad,' said Salina. 'Mainly cuts and bruises. Her wrist is fractured but not broken. They're mainly treating her for shock, so they've sedated her for now.' Her gaze lowered to the floor. 'She's got a nasty bump where she hit her head against the side of the boat.'

'When this is all behind you, she'll thank you for taking control.'

'Maybe.' Salina stopped and stared at the open door of her friend's room. 'I doubt she'll ever want to go in a DSV with me again.' She mustered a bitter smile. 'I'm not sure I'll ever want to go in a DSV with me.'

Gill reached out and gave her upper arm a gentle squeeze. 'You'll be okay.'

She nodded, her eyes down. 'I need to check with Tom. See if the boat is seaworthy for tomorrow.'

'You're not going to man the DSV on your own?'

She shook her head. 'I need a few days out of the water. James doesn't like it, but he's qualified to co-pilot the boat, so he and I might swap places. I'll call Arthur again to see if we can tempt him back.'

The conversation paused as a nurse walked up to Salina. 'The doctor says you're welcome to stay at Ellie's bedside tonight. When she wakes up, it'll be a help to have a familiar face.'

'Thank you,' said Salina. She turned to Gill. 'Sorry. After visiting time, it's ladies only, apparently.'

Gill held up a hand to signal his understanding. 'Absolutely. You should be here. Give me a minute. I'll go grab your bag from the car.'

She gave him a fleeting hug and turned to walk slowly towards Ellie's room.

Gill made his way through the hospital and out to the car park when he glanced at this phone. It was 8.30 pm, and his phone had been on silent during the journey up, and he had consciously avoided it while sitting with Salina. Now, to his dismay, he had six missed calls from the office. He dialled immediately, praying Cassy hadn't already done what any reasonable person would and gone home. After three rings, the phone picked up.

'Cassy. It's Gill.'

'Where have you been? We've been desperate to reach you all afternoon.'

Gill sighed. 'The dive in Loch Ness went pear-shaped. One of the crew was injured. I've been up at the hospital.'

'Oh, man. That's terrible. Was it Salina?'

'No, the new girl, Ellie. Only cuts and bruises, but she got quite a fright.' He paused, anxious not to receive more bad news. 'What's up?'

'Craig cracked the website, Gill. He's got screenshots of the whole thing.'

Gill punched the air. 'Awesome. Mail it to me, will you.'

'Already done.' Cassy paused. 'You were right, by the way. It's Ernie Lehman's site. It has pictures of him and everything. He's a right egotistical little shit with a drum to beat.'

'How so?'

Cassy sounded flustered. 'I'm sorry. It's something I should have seen earlier.'

'It's not a problem. Tell me now.'

She sighed. 'The surname Lehman cropped up in some of the desk research we did two weeks ago when we first started looking for Ness connections. In 1932 a man called Henry Lehman raised a stir by producing a series of photographs purporting to be the Loch Ness Monster entering the loch from the Fort Augustus end.'

'Never heard of him,' said Gill.

'The photos were quickly dismissed as fakes. Lehman was American, married into a well to do family of local landowners. The scandal ruined his reputation. He drowned a year later after a night on the whisky.'

'And this links to the present-day Lehman, how?'

'Our Lehman is the dead man's grandson. The website admits while the photos were forged, they were reconstructions of events Henry had seen with his naked eyes.'

'So, Lehman is trying to redeem his grandfather's reputation,' said Gill.

'Exactly.'

'That's brilliant, Cassy. I'll find a corner to download it all and then speak to you in the morning.'

'Gill. There's something else,' said Cassy with an edge to her voice.

'Go on.'

'We had a phone call from a lady neighbour of your dad's. She didn't know how to reach you, so she called the magazine.'

'Oh. What's up?'

'Your dad was out wandering at all hours last night. At some point, he got lost within a few hundred metres of his house. A police car brought him back.'

Gill's free hand ran across his forehead and through his hair. 'Okay. Text me her number, would you? I'll give her a shout.'

'I'll do it right now. And Tony wants to speak to you. I asked him if that was an ASAP, and he said "no." It was more urgent than that. Can you call him at home?'

'Thanks, Cassy. I'm on it. Thanks for working so hard to catch me.'

A few minutes later, Salina found Gill standing self-consciously at the entrance to the ward. She had slipped out and, with a smile of thanks, took the bag he'd brought her.

'You look stressed,' she said, brushing his arm. 'Everything okay?'

'I'm fine,' he said. 'Just picked up a bunch of messages when I stepped outside.' He was aware his smile must look forced. 'Lots to do.'

'Can I help?'

'You stay here. But if you don't mind, I'm going to shoot off. I'll text you in the morning, and when you're ready, I'll come and pick you up.'

She nodded. 'Thank you.'

'Do you know if you'll be heading back to Duncan's or St Andrews?'

'Hopefully, one more night at Duncan's, then back to Oban the following day. I've texted Arthur, but he hasn't responded.'

'Holiday mode,' said Gill.

She nodded. 'Good news is that the boat is okay. Tom said he had to give her a serious hose down, but other than that, she's good to go.'

'That's positive,' said Gill. 'Well, I'll see you tomorrow. Call if you need me.'

He felt strange saying that as he walked away. Surely the man who should be at Salina's side right now was her fiancé.

Gill had to make a decision. He could spend time hunting for somewhere to download his emails or jump in the car and get to his father's side. He also knew they needed him in Dundee. It was less than three days until the magazine was due to go to press. But with Salina safe, he knew where he was needed right now. He would get his dad settled for the night and then make a plan for the morning. He had three hours in the car. Plenty of time to talk to Tony and work out what on earth he was going to write in his magazine.

'Gill, where's your mother? She should be back by now.'

Exhausted by his long day, Gill fought against a lump in his throat as he took his father gently by the hand. 'I know she should, Dad. I know.'

'Well, I'm going to go and look for her. I can't settle until I know she's home.' Gordon started to swing his legs out of bed, again.

'Dad, I'll go and look for her in a minute. I know she'd want me to look after you first.'

'Have you spoken to her? She's probably stuck in traffic.'
'I haven't spoken to her, Dad.'
'Is it still raining?'
'It's stopped now.'
'That's good. She'll be home soon then.'
'Of course, she will.'
'I'm so desperately tired. I need to close my eyes for an hour.' Gordon sank back into the bed, but no sooner had he seemed to settle when he sat up again and gripped Gill's hand. 'Wake me the minute she gets in. I want to hear all about her day.'
'I will. Rest now.'
Gill crouched by the bed and leaned over his father, gently stroking his silver hair for what seemed like an age. When he was certain Gordon was finally asleep, he drew back his aching arm and breathed deeply. The poor light of the bedside lamp made his father's features look even more sunken. He could see the old man hadn't slept properly for days, making him look older than his years. Gill glanced beyond the bed to the dressing table that had been his mother's. Her brush set and a modest array of perfume bottles were all that remained of her. A photo of the four of them hung on the wall just above his father's head, and he stared at it for several minutes until his neck started to ache. A wave of emotion had stalked him these past few years. He had eluded it, run away from it, even as it hunted him. But now it had Gill cornered, and its net descended like a cold mist. He gave up his resistance, and with his forehead dipping against Gordon's arm, he wept. Gently. For a long, long time.

Chapter 32

Salina jolts awake as she senses movement. She's been asleep in a semi-sitting position, and her neck feels stiff and sore. Again, a definite sideways lurch. Fully awake now, she finds herself sitting on a horseshoe-shaped bench made with some vivid orange material over a thin layer of padding. She sits alone, but around her, a dozen similar booths cluster around a drinks bar. The occupants, thirty or so men and women of various ages, sit in groups. The women wear old-fashioned dresses, and the men wear raincoats or heavy jackets and waistcoats. Strangely, almost all have hats.

'Not again,' says Salina standing up and clapping her hands fiercely against her cheeks. 'Not-a-bloody-gain!'

'Are you alright, madam?' A young man in black trousers and waistcoat appears beside her on his way back to the bar.

'Not sure,' she finds herself saying. 'Probably not.'

The man smiles encouragingly. 'Sorry, madam. Been a bit of a night of it. Got tossed all over the place on the way over. Probably won't be much better on the way back.'

Her senses are aflame now. She picks up snatches of weary conversation, set against the almost soothing sound of a big band playing a swing number oozing from a nearby speaker. She notices a logo on the man's breast pocket, a picture of a golden lion leaping over a red spoked wheel. The words *British Railways* are emblazoned underneath. She glances around the wide room. 'Are we on a train?'

The man smiles politely. 'No. You left the train behind in Stranraer.' As if to underline the man's pronouncement, she feels the floor moving again and realises she's on a ferry.

'I can't do this again,' she says quietly.

The man seems taken aback. He reaches out to grasp her arm and gently but firmly presses her back into her seat. 'Now, don't you worry about a thing. Happens all the time. Folk travel all day, and it starts to catch up with them. I recommend a stiff Haig over ice. Pep you up for the last bit of your journey.'

Salina looks at him, puzzling, then shakes her head. 'Remind me. Which sailing is this, please?'

The man's smile is straining. 'It's the twenty-two hundred hours,' then glancing at his watch, 'although truth be told, it's almost morning.'

'What about the date and the year?' Salina asks.

The man straightens and lets his smile fade into a dour expression. 'I know we're running late, miss, but there's no need to be rude.' He glances at his bar, where a small knot of customers is gathering. 'Excuse me.'

'I'm just not doing this again,' Salina calls to his back. But he pays her no heed, and she slumps back against the uncomfortable seat, wondering what to do. An elderly lady nearby briefly catches her eye, and then looks away.

Salina gets to her feet again and follows the carpet slightly downhill to the back of the bar. She opens a glass door marked with *First Class lounge* and steps into a carpeted foyer. Left and right, a corridor spans the ship's width, where at each end, a door leads out onto the decks. She strides up to one but finds the glass black and uninviting. Another wide corridor runs down the ship's length with signs announcing *Second class passengers* and *Commercial vehicle drivers*. Her eyes find a brass plaque carrying the same railway logo and the vessel's name. "MV Princess Victoria - built 1947 by William Denny and Brothers, Dumbarton." Salina thinks for a few seconds, but no ship of that name springs to mind. She turns around and walks over to a mahogany counter. A man in an officer's uniform fills out entries on a paper form.

'Can you point me to the ladies?' Salina asks.

The man regards her for a few moments, then gesticulates round to his right. 'Certainly, madam. Just down the corridor, second door. You can't miss it.'

She thanks him and makes her way down, steadying herself as the ship rocks a little. As she pushes the heavy door aside, she sees a pair of generous porcelain sinks. She sets a cold tap running and starts to scoop handfuls of ice-cold water into her face. 'Wake up, Salina. Wake up,' she whispers. She stares at her face, her eyes glaring out at her from under the brim of a large hat decorated with artificial flowers. She tosses it off in frustration and unwinds her hair from where it has been vigorously pinned. She stares at herself, but nothing changes. But she feels better, seeing her long black hair falling back around her shoulders, the way she usually wears it.

Another idea springs to mind. Her tightly tailored jacket is becoming an encumbrance, so she strips it off and uses it to wipe her face before discarding it. Then, folding the sleeves of her white blouse up to her elbows, she steps back into the corridor and returns to the purser's office. At her changed appearance, the officer behind the counter takes a slight intake of breath.

'Can you help me? I was due to meet a friend on this sailing, and I'm not sure if he made it on board, or if he's travelling first or second class.'

'Certainly. What is his name?'

Salina thinks for a second. 'Raphael.'

The purser takes up a clipboard. 'Mr Raphael. I'll just check the passenger manifest …'

'No, that's his first name.'

'And can you tell me his surname, please?'

Salina opens her mouth, then shuts it again. 'I'm not sure. I only know his first name.'

The purser lays down his pen and gently pushes the passenger manifest towards her. 'I have initials and surnames, miss. And I have vehicle details for those who didn't come by train. I'm not sure I'm able to help you.'

Salina spins around. 'No problem. I'll probably be able to track him down.' She leaves the man staring after her and steps back through the door into the first-class lounge. She makes her way around the orange horseshoes, scanning the faces. From his vantage point, the steward she'd met earlier watches her impassively while he dries glasses and suspends them from hooks above the bar. She can detect no sign of her rescuer, so she turns on her heel and leaves the lounge again. Down the corridor, she comes to the second-class accommodation. Here the seating is long benches with even less padding. She finds another bar, emphasising beer rather than spirits, although a small choice of whiskies tinkle together in a brass fixture as the vessel eases into forward motion. A steward is making sandwiches out of thick white bread at the bar. On chance, she decides to approach him. 'Have you seen Raphael?' she asks.

The man continues cutting while glancing up at her. 'Sorry, miss. Who ye after?'

'Never mind.' Salina is already turning, and she jogs back out into the corridor. She judges from the vessel's layout the Commercial Driver's bar must be on the opposite side of the passage. But no door is evident, so she moves further down the ship until the corridor splits left and right. The door on the left is locked, so she turns and pushes on the right. Stepping into a dimly lit room hung heavily with smoke, she finds a crowd of men, all speaking at once. She hesitates only briefly, ignoring the stares of the nearest man who notices her, and digs an elbow into his mate's ribs until he too turns and gawks.

Her strategy is the same. She approaches the bar. A lean young man with a moustache stands and his sleeves rolled up, pulls beer into a glass. He stops as soon as he sees her. 'Sorry, love, this is the driver's bar. Are you lost?'

She has to raise her voice above the background noise. 'No. I'm looking for Raphael.'

The ship lurches as it builds forward momentum into a rising sea, and Salina has to grip the bar to keep her balance. The barman just sways on the spot as if his shoes are nailed to the floor. 'Sorry, love. Don't know any, Raphael.'

'Never mind, I'll ask around.' She turns around and approaches the first table. Quickly she works her way around the bar. Gaping, incredulous faces, politely tell her they don't know anyone by that name.

Frustrated, she makes for the door, glad to leave the quietened room with its many watching eyes. As she grips the door handle, the man who first made eye contact with her stands up and gives his cap a gentle tug. 'Excuse me, miss. We had a bloke in here earlier. Might be the chap you are looking for.'

'Raphael?' asked Salina.

The man tips his head and looks away. 'Well, we know him as "Daft Raphy." Seen him occasionally on this run. Takes a big Luton van to the continent twice a month. Coloured chap,' he said quietly. 'Like yourself.'

Salina scans the man's eyes for malice and finds none. 'Thanks. Where is he?'

The man turns and points to a table in a corner. It is unoccupied, but an empty pint glass stands in a small pool of condensation. 'He was here a minute ago. Might have gone to check his rig.'

'Naw,' says his friend. 'Took his jacket, so guess he was going out on deck.'

'Then he's crazy,' says the first man before turning to Salina and dipping his eyes apologetically. 'Just that it's a wild night. We'll be out of Loch Ryan soon, and it'll be getting bumpy.' He gesticulates at the empty seat and smiles mischievously. 'Why not wait for him here. He'll be back in a moment.'

Salina glances around the expectant faces. 'I need a bit of air myself. But thanks for your help.'

She backs away from them and exits the bar out into the corridor. Her stomach pitches as the ship mounts a wave and shudders to a halt for a moment. She just has time to grab the handrail when the boat lurches through the wave, tipping forward so that her body catches up with itself again. The shudder passes, and the vessel settles back into a normal motion of rising and falling.

Salina senses danger is near. She speeds past the purser's office and tries to open the door out onto the deck. At first, it appears jammed closed. A voice rises in protest behind her, but she ignores it and leans her weight against the glass and steel. She has to push hard until the door cracks open, allowing cold air to rush past her carrying little darting bullets of water. Once she has forced it open far enough, she sidesteps through the gap and out onto the deck. Behind her, the door slams shut again, driven by the fierce winds. Within moments she is soaked to the skin, her thin blouse hopelessly inadequate against the driven rain. She finds a safety rail fixed to the ship's side and stays as far from the sea as she can manage. Looking up and down the deck, she can't see a soul. Towards the bow, the way forward is a stairway going up to the ship's bridge. It is chained off to deter regular passengers, so she heads for the stern.

Step by careful step, she makes her way down the length of the ship as the twin hazards of wind and water conspire with the lurching vessel to throw her off balance. Towards the stern, the handrail abruptly stops, and she has to cling to the exterior cabin wall as she works her way around the bulkhead towards the stern. Water is being whipped up from the bow, being flung the length of the ship, and drenching her again before she finally staggers into the cover of the rear shelter deck. She finds a few rows of seats nestling under a metal covering, and she drags herself towards the nearest one. In the dim light, a bulky figure rises and extends an arm to guide her into the deepest part of the shelter.

Salina breathes deeply, seeing for the first time the stern of the vessel and the ephemeral stain it is leaving on the mountainous sea. Fractured moonlight illuminates Loch Ryan, and she can see the ship has just completed a southerly turn out into the Irish Sea. The wind seems much faster than the ship, almost propelling the vessel along as great waves plunge behind her, tear at her stern, then overtake her. The boat falls into another momentary suspension as another impatient wave bullies past.

Salina lets her right arm rest on the man's thigh while she wipes strands of wet hair out of her eyes. 'What are we doing here, Raphael?'

His smiling eyes rest on a distant object, but he says nothing.

Suddenly she feels anger rising inside her, and she slaps him hard on the shoulder. 'Why are we doing this again?'

She waits. But he just stares ahead without answering.

'I love the sea. It is my life. Why do you keep using it to kill me?'

His nod is slow and barely perceptible, but he does not look at her, and still, he does not speak.

She moves close to the right side of his face and shouts in his ear. 'Why are you in my dreams? Why are you torturing me?'

Slowly the man turns to face her, sweeping her hand off his thigh and grasping it in his own. 'Truly, you are loved, Salina Ahmed.'

She can just make out his eyes. They seem dark and kind, and she searches them for meaning. Finding none, she steadies herself and hits his shoulder again. 'If I am loved. This,' she pauses to hit him a third time, 'is a strange way of showing it.' She sits breathing heavily before raising her fist and hitting him again. Far beneath them, she part hears, part feels, a deep bass sound. The contortions of the ship have dislodged something large as it tries to cross the angry sea at an angle to the waves.

'Hush now, child,' Raphael says. 'It's beginning.'

Salina bites back. 'If it's all the same to you, I'd like to cut past the misery and wake up tired and sweating.'

He looks at her, nodding as if to indicate he hears, even though he continues to sit. She can see his body tensing up, and as a frown gathers on his face, something dawns on her. 'You're not enjoying this any more than I am!'

He sighs. 'One hundred and thirty-three people will die.' He pauses and nods. 'Precious lives.'

'But this is just a dream, right? You can snap your fingers, and it'll all be over.'

He turns slowly and looks down at her, his shoulders sagging as he considers how to answer her. 'Whether your experience tonight is a dream or if it is reality, on a day in January 1953, the ship still sinks, and people still die.'

'This is real?'

Raphael nods. 'Maid Margaret. The Arran Star. The girl on a herring boat. It was all real. Once upon a time.'

Another almighty crash erupts far beneath them, and the ship starts to visibly list to starboard. Salina is distracted. 'What's happening?'

Raphael looks out behind the ship as another mighty wave overtakes the boat and bears down on the vessel. 'A lorry has slipped off its mooring on the vehicle deck. It's causing a domino effect. Lots of extra weight is slipping to the stern.'

'Will she capsize?'

Raphael shakes his head. 'No, she's too well built for that. But she is being submerged from the rear. The following sea will breach the vehicle doors in a minute or two. And then the sea will take her.'

Salina looks at him, hot tears blowing off her face as the gale strengthens again. 'Do something.'

He hangs his head in a sudden admission of frustration. Then he lifts one hand and gesticulates back and forward between them. 'I don't get to change the past, and this calamity is already written. But you and your future, Salina Ahmed? I have permission to offer you an escape.'

Salina slumps back away from him. 'What do you mean?'

He sits looking at her for a moment, then calls out to her in the wind. 'When the time comes, will you trust me, Salina Ahmed?'

'Why? Why rescue me and not all these other people?'

'Because you have a destiny. And the courage to walk into it. But first, you must survive tomorrow.'

'Tomorrow?'

He doesn't wait to give her an answer. Somewhere down below, they can hear men shouting at each other. He says, 'We've done enough here.' He offers Salina his right hand, and she takes it. Together they get to their feet. The unnatural movement of the ship conspires with the wind to throw her off balance, but Raphael's stance is solid, and she steadies herself against him. He leads her out of their shelter, and inch by inch, they edge towards the sea rail. They pause and look at each other just as the ship's tannoy starts to sound a series of loud blasts.

'You love the sea,' he yells over the wind. 'Do you know the sea will never love you back?'

Her grip on his hand is ferocious as the terror of her imminent death rises up within her.

He leans to speak to her again. 'Instead, will you learn to trust the one who made the sea?'

Before she can respond, a massive wave crashes over the ship's stern. She is torn from him and flung through the air.

Flying.

Spinning.

Drenched in sweat and gripping the rail at the end of Ellie's bed, Salina awakes. Ellie is conscious but confused, struggling with the various wires attached to her body. The machine beside her bed bleeps an urgent alarm call as Ellie starts to panic. Salina throws off her slumber and moves to gently embrace her colleague. 'Hush, Ellie. We're okay. We're okay. We're both gonna be okay.'

Chapter 33

The short hours Gill slept were precious. Avoiding his laptop, he set to work in the kitchen sorting some of Gordon's debris from the last few days. Gill was frying eggs and bacon when his father came down shortly after 8 am.

'Gill! When did you arrive?'

'Last night, Dad. We spoke briefly, but you were pretty tired. Not surprised you don't remember.'

Gordon rubbed his hands together. 'Breakfast! A guest who cooks is welcome indeed. Will you be staying long? I wanted to take another look at the weather station. I've got a new theory.'

'Didn't the company come out to fix it?'

Gordon thought for a second. 'Yes, they did. A chap was here for almost two hours. Said there's nothing wrong with it. That got me thinking about it from a fresh angle.'

Gill sucked on his teeth. 'Got a manic couple of days coming up, Dad. But I'll be up again next week. Can we talk about it then?'

'No problem. You're always busy. And how are things at the university?'

Gill had a fleeting guilty moment before ignoring the question. 'Listen, I've arranged for you to have some company over the next couple of days.'

Gordon waved a hand at him. 'No need. I've plenty to do.'

Just then, Gill heard a tap at the front door and the sound of it opening and closing. Fiona appeared in the kitchen and gave Gill a brief hug. 'Morning, Gill. Morning, Dad. How are we both today?' She'd bought Gordons's favourite newspaper and laid it in front of him as she stooped to kiss his forehead.

Confusion spilt across Gordon's face as Gill and Fiona exchanged news on the DSV accident the day before. Gill poured tea for them all and checked what everybody wanted to eat. While Fiona excused herself to hang up her coat, Gordon tugged on his sleeve. 'Who is that girl?' he asked.

'That's Fiona, Dad. You know her.' Patiently Gill stood up and steered Gordon to the small living room. He pointed to a picture over the fireplace of his brother Davey and Fiona on their wedding day. 'She was Davey's wife. You remember, don't you?'

Gordon's head stuttered. 'Yes, yes! Fiona. Of course.'

'Fiona is going to stay with you for a couple of days. She's just finished a job for me on Loch Ness, and she'll tell you all about it.'

'Over and over,' said Fiona quietly. She was standing at the door behind them.

Gordon suddenly brightened. 'I'll need to show you the new boat. The launch is this weekend. Come and see.'

'Breakfast first,' said Fiona. 'Smells too good to miss.'

The three settled into a gentle conversation while Gill served the fried breakfast, and Fiona made a fuss making the filtered coffee that she knew Gordon loved. For a brief moment, they were a family again, the gaps in their ranks less obvious, less painful. Gordon settled to his newspaper at the end of the meal, and Fiona volunteered to do the washing up.

'How's it going with the next issue?' she asked as she ran water into the sink.

'Not great,' said Gill. 'I'm all over the place and don't have a central thread to pull everything together.'

'I take it the submarine thing came to nothing?'

'A big fat zero. And caused a shed load of trouble for the people trying to help me.' He suddenly remembered Cassy's email. Fetching his laptop from the kitchen counter, he opened the lid. Mercifully, his dad's broadband was working okay. A stream of emails with large attachments started to download.

'Sorry,' said Gill. 'I've just remembered that someone in the office found a website belonging to the mysterious Ernie Lehman. They've sent me some screenshots.'

'Is this the guy who thinks the creature migrates into the loch?'

'Aye. I mean, look at this stuff. He has a graph plotting the peaks and troughs of sightings. He says here the creature has a reproductive cycle of twenty-six years duration.'

Fiona grunted. 'Does he speculate what kind of animal it is?'

'He doesn't speculate. He announces it. He's one hundred per cent certain it's a dwarf basilosaurus. "It is up to seven metres long. A serpent-like cetacean with the same head to body ratio as modern-day whales,"' read Gill.

'Evidence?' said Fiona, scrubbing the frying pan ferociously.

'Let's see. We have some dubious photographs. There are pictures of solitary ripples that are the animal's bow wave, apparently.' He paused. 'Oh, look, have you seen that anywhere before?'

Fiona leaned back from the sink so her soapy hands stayed over the bowl. 'Bloody hell, Gill. That's my Auroch!'

'Not an Auroch, Fiona. The backbone of said basilosaurus. At least, that's what Mr Lehman thinks.'

'Hang on. Does that mean Lehman and Kerr are the same person?'

Gill shrugged. 'Maybe. Lehman clearly has access to Kerr's work.'

'Is there a picture of him?'

'Haven't seen one. Wait a sec. I'll open up a few more files.'

Fiona dried her hands and came and stood behind him. 'So much text. This guy could blog for Scotland. Back a bit, you just passed one.'

Gill stopped scrolling down and hovered over the image. They saw a well-dressed, rather serious man with black, obviously coloured hair, gelled straight back over his head. He was standing with binoculars around his neck, the long ribbon of Loch Ness in the background.

'Damn it,' said Gill slapping the tabletop.

'You know this guy?'

'Oh yes,' he said, slamming down his laptop lid. 'I know him.'

Gill grabbed his mobile and dialled. The phone rang five times, and he suspected it would go to voice mail. 'Arthur Deveron.' The answering voice sounded clipped. Clearly, the call was an interruption.

Gill exhaled slowly before speaking. 'Oh, I apologise, Arthur. I thought this was Ernie Lehman's number.'

'Who is this?'

'How's the basilosaurus hunt? Spotted any big ones today?'

'Gill? Is that you?'

'You've been threatening me, Arthur. Do you remember?'

Arthur didn't respond. Gill could hear him breathing, and he glanced up at Fiona before continuing. 'That wasn't you the night of the fire. Do you have some goon to do your dirty work?'

'I've no idea what you are talking about.'

'Well, let's talk science then. You and I like science, don't we, Arthur? I'd like you to hear directly from me that your migration theory is garbage. I wanted to tell you that personally before I pick up the phone to the police.'

Arthur let out a long sigh. 'So, you've finally stumbled across my nom de guerre. Tried to warn you, Gill. If the game's too rough for you, you can skulk off back to Dundee.'

'Never mind about me. It's where you're going you should worry about.'

'Yeah? Tell me where I'm going.'

'You've pictures on your website of the Invermoriston bone pit …'

Arthur interrupted, 'How can you see my website, Gill? What have you done?'

'… and in the bone pit, we found human remains.'

'Nothing to do with me,' said Arthur after a moment.

'Given you're the kind of person who issues bullets for calling cards, I think it could have everything to do with you.'

'And your evidence for that is what?' said Arthur forcefully.

'It's a real pity, though. If you'd just been a little more open, we could've worked together on this.'

'Listen to you,' Arthur retorted. 'You're nothing but a smash and grab hack. Pull a few half-baked facts out of the air and spin a story from them. This project took years of observations, decades. You think you can come in here and sort it all in a fortnight?'

'The only half-facts are on your website, Arthur. The Invermoriston skeleton, for example. If only you'd dug down another few centimetres.'

An exasperated cough erupts on Arthur's side of the call. 'And what's your theory, Gill? That all the Loch Ness sightings are just submarines patrolling the loch? Give me a break.'

'I've got other sources; other ideas,' Gill retorted.

'You mean that old nutter Ackerson? I reached him through an old navy contact just last week. What a fruit cake!'

It was Gill's turn to feel surprised. Arthur pressed his advantage. 'If you're so clever, explain why the Great Glen fault would suddenly spring to life? After millennia, it just suddenly becomes active again?' He paused. Gill said nothing, so he continued. 'I'm aware of the silt falls. They are part of the natural life cycle of the loch. But you've only been studying it for a fortnight. So, what would you know?'

'The science is still up for grabs. I don't think either of us can fully explain what is happening in Loch Ness. What I do know is that I have evidence linking you to the Invermoriston murder.'

'Not my dig,' snorted Arthur. 'I sub-contracted that piece of work.'

'You won't mind if I share that with the police. Just so they can eliminate you from their enquiries.'

'Give them this number. I'll sort it out.'

'And should they ask for Arthur Deveron or Ernie Lehman?'

'My grandfather's name will be held in high esteem very soon. I'm proud to have the honour of completing his work.'

Abruptly the line went dead. Gill sat staring at the phone for a full minute without saying anything. Beside him, Gordon turned a page of his newspaper, absorbed in his reading.

Fiona spoke first. 'Sounds like that went well?'

'He's a sod,' said Gill, flicking through his contact book for George Wiley's number. 'But if I'm honest, he did make one good point.'

Fiona shrugged at him to continue. 'I'm no closer to explaining all this than Arthur. I mean, honestly, why would the Great Glen fault suddenly spring to life?'

Fiona nodded. 'As a student, I did fieldwork in that area. Geologically, it's pretty dead.'

'Aye. That's what the folk said at Scottish Geological Society.'

Gordon cleared his throat loudly and abruptly laid down his newspaper. 'Six trillion cubic metres,' he said.

Gill blinked. 'I'm sorry, Dad.'

'That's how much oil and gas we've taken out of the North Sea to date.' Gordon's tone was matter-of-fact, like he was relaying the weather forecast. 'We've taken six trillion cubic metres of light petroleum products out of the seafloor north of Scotland and replaced it with much heavier water.' He waved a hand impatiently. 'It's all physics, but the pressure changes in the upper parts of the North Sea continental shelf must be immense.'

Fiona carefully took her seat at the table again. 'You know me, Gordon, I'm not very good at physics. Can you explain that a bit?'

Gordon looked briefly impatient, but then his face became animated again. 'This is my new theory about my weather station. The sea level appears to be falling because it really is.'

Gill ran a hand through his hair as Gordon continued. 'But it's not that the sea is getting lower. It's because the land is rising.'

'Geostatic bounce,' said Fiona. 'I studied that at uni. It's because the land rises as it springs back after the weight of ice-age deposits disappeared.'

'But that would be millimetres every few decades,' said Gill.

'Exactly,' said Gordon. 'And I measured another two millimetres this week alone. Something exceptional is happening. That's when I remembered an old research paper we had back in the office. Something dull, "Theoretical distortions in the earth's crust as a result of long-term oil extraction." Something like that.'

Gill stared at his father; eyes wide, uncertain.

'Well, don't you see? It means my weather station is tickety-boo. The readings are entirely accurate. So we don't need to worry about it anymore.'

Gill tapped his father's hand gently. 'That's great, Dad' He smiled. 'Something we can take off our lists, eh?' He thought for a second. 'Dad, the geological forces you are talking about. Would they be enough to reactivate the Great Glen Boundary fault?'

Gordon shook his head. 'No way of knowing. It depends on how the stresses run in the rocks. The Great Glen is so very long. It mightn't suffer any impact.' He laughed suddenly. 'Then again, in geological terms, a boundary fault means the earth's crust is very thin, so the whole thing could shear apart. What a firework display that would be!'

Fiona glanced back and forward between Gordon and Gill, trying to decide what she made of it all. Gill met her gaze, making sure he had her attention. 'Are you okay looking after the fort here? I need to be away for a few days.'

She nodded, saying nothing.

'I've got a couple of calls to make. Then I need to get back to Inverness. Somewhere in the next forty-eight hours, I've got to pull a magazine together.'

Gordon had settled back to his paper. Gill kissed the top of his head and went upstairs to gather his things.

Gill tried calling George Wiley. The inspector wasn't in yet, so he left a message with a desk sergeant. He was still throwing clothes in a bag when Cassy's face appeared on his laptop. He dropped what he was doing and moved closer to the screen. 'Morning, stranger,' he said, trying to mollify her concerned expression.

Cassy glanced around her before speaking. 'Gill, all hell is breaking loose here. It's Thursday, and Tony is doing his nut. It's all I have been able to do to stop him stepping in as emergency editor.'

'I'll speak to him in a minute, Cass. I promise. Before I go back on the road.'

'Don't expect him to sound happy.'

'Thanks for holding the fort. I owe you. Are the rest of the guys available? I want to brief you on the lead stories. Some of it's for the mag. The rest needs to go on our website today.'

Cassy put her microphone on mute and disappeared off-screen before returning with Larry and Craig. Gill watched their heads bob until everyone found a seat and squeezed close to the camera.

'Right, guys. We lead issue eleven with the geology of Loch Ness and the Great Glen Boundary Fault. Larry, I've jotted down some bullet points for the lead article, which I'll mail you in a sec. Can you work up a rough draft by late morning and mail it to me?'

Larry nodded. 'Aye, I see your notes. Nae problem.'

Craig pushed towards the screen. 'What about the other theories; migrations, submarine bases, and all that?'

'Those theories are the also-rans. Let's use the drafts we have but drop them further back in the issue. Treat them as worthy but discounted theories.'

'After the success of last month's issue, we've got high demand for ads, Gill,' said Cassy. 'If we are struggling for copy, the girls won't have any trouble selling another two double-page spreads.'

'Fine. Do it.'

'Wha' aboot the *Caithness Kraken*?' asked Larry.

'I can't conclusively link it to The Great Glen, so run it as a separate story. You should have Duncan's redrafts by now?'

'Aye,' said Larry. 'An' plenty of associated background. It'll be a job tae work out whit tae use.'

Gill nodded. 'Send it to me, and I'll comment if I can. If I don't get back to you by close of play today, make the decisions yourself.'

'Fair enough. Same wi' the west coast creel boat?'

'No. The sinking of the *Bounty* ties to the Glen. As does the "Incredible Shrinking Mountain." Leave me to write those.'

The team knocked decisions back and forth for a few minutes, and Gill started to feel a rising sense of optimism, pride even, that they would get the job done. He had one last big question. 'Cassy, can you talk us through the deadlines.'

She sighed theatrically. 'Well, the weekend is buggered if that's what you mean.'

Gill put on his best pleading face. 'Assuming everyone can give up part of their weekend in return for suitable compensation …'

'We'll need roughs completed today,' said Cassy. 'With everyone back in tomorrow to edit Craig's layout. Then, Gill. It's you and me in the office on Saturday morning looking at colour proofs. The printing machine starts running at 4 pm on Saturday afternoon.'

'That's early,' muttered Craig.

Cassy twisted round to face him. 'After the last issue, Tony upped the print order to 200,000. The printer has to start early to meet the distributor's deadlines.'

Craig whistled. 'Bet he's regretting that.'

'Speak of the devil,' said Cassy quietly.

'Thanks, Cassy. Tell Tony I'll phone his office line as soon as we finish our call.'

Gill elected to get in the car and drive while speaking to Tony. He judged that Tony would do most of the talking. He was right. Tony didn't actually use the words "disciplinary meeting", but he figured the personnel manager joining them for a chat on Monday morning wasn't being invited for her charming personality. By the time he joined the Aberdeen bypass, Tony had finished his rant and moved on to the matter at hand. The next issue of the magazine. Gill filled him in, aware of a long silence at the other end of the phone.

'I'm going to talk to the printer and see if I can knock the order back by fifty thousand copies,' Tony concluded.

'You don't like it then?'

'Well, it seemed so promising a few weeks ago. Where we have ended up, frankly, takes an exciting story and makes it glacial.'

'Is that a pun?'

'Gill, I don't feel much like laughing.'

'Before you phone the printer, ask Craig to show you the draft front cover. It's a play on the poster for the original Jaws movie.'

Tony sighed. 'I'll take a look. Just promise me one thing. After this issue, no more hand-to-mouth. Honestly, I can't cope with the stress.'

Chapter 34

It was just before 4 pm as Gill completed the three-hour drive from Stonehaven to Inverness. A quick text exchange with Salina confirmed she was still at the hospital. Ellie was much better and would move onto a ward for 24 hours. Salina had barely slept, and Ellie was chasing her to go and get some rest. Gill reckoned he could take her to Duncan's, and with a bit of charity, he could finish the rest of the draft from the rectory's kitchen table.

As he pulled into a petrol station, he was trying to feel optimistic about the rest of the day. Gordon was safe at home with Fiona, and Salina would soon be getting some much-needed rest. Meanwhile, Duncan could help him put the finishing touches to various articles. Somewhere, "Ernie Lehman" would be assisting the police with their enquiries. Yeah! Things were looking up. Watching the numbers on the fuel pump skipping ever higher, he tuned out for a few seconds, enthralled by their rhythmic ascent.

A jolt under his feet snapped him back to full attention as a loud bang filled the air. He spun around, imagining there'd been a collision. Instantly, the power went out, the fuel flow cutting off before the noise had finished echoing off distant buildings. Turning through three hundred and sixty degrees, he looked for an explanation. But besides the power cut, the only unusual thing was that everyone else on the forecourt was doing exactly the same thing. Even the traffic on the road was stopping, with people climbing out of their vehicles, checking for collision damage. He watched as everyone milled around for about thirty seconds, then gradually, got back in their cars and filtered back into the traffic. A few moments later, the power came back on.

He checked the fuel pump as the gauge lit up again and went inside to pay. The tills were still resetting, and a group of frustrated customers queued while they waited to pay by card. When the cashier nodded at Gill to come forward, he just managed to pay in cash. Getting back into his car, he tried to continue his journey. But the power cut had knocked out the traffic lights, and vehicles were beginning to snarl around the city. He pulled over and put on the radio to catch the midday bulletin. The headlines rolled by, the latest chapters in overly familiar stories. Then he caught what he wanted.

'... And as we go on air, we are getting reports of a small earthquake in the North Sea. We have no reports of any injuries at this stage, although some localised power cuts are in progress. We'll bring you more on this story later in the bulletin.'

Gill dropped the volume to where it was barely audible, keeping track of the programme while he fished in his glove compartment for a business card. Finding what he wanted, he dialled John Houston at SGS. The number was engaged. Popping it on redial, Gill waited. After it timed out for the sixth time, Gill tried a different approach. His text read. 'Hi John. Gill McArdle here. I'm in Inverness RIGHT NOW. Do you need any info from the ground?' He laid down his phone and waited.

John Houston's number called back ten minutes later. 'Gill, you're up north.'

'I am. I was standing in a petrol station when I heard an almighty bang.'

'Goodness. Any damage where you are?'

'The power went out. Nothing too bad. Can you tell me what happened?'

John sighed. 'The event you experienced was a 3.8 concentrated about 100 miles north and east of the Black Isle. Barely enough to rattle windows.'

'Okay, can you tell me why you sound so worried then?'

John didn't respond straight away. 'I'm not sure what I should be telling you, Gill. We're still analysing data.'

'John, I've got friends in this area. If there's anything we should be aware of…'

'We had a 1.9 between Claymore and Piper late last night,' John sputtered. 'Then another one, 2.2 east of Beatrice oilfield in the early hours. In and of themselves, they are tiny quakes, but enough to put the oil industry into a spin. It hasn't made the news yet, but all the oil platforms in the northern part of the basin are capping off as we speak. Just as a precaution.'

'Precaution for what, John?'

John's voice was shaky and uncertain. 'We only get tiny quakes up north, Gill. And they are normally separated by months, not hours.'

'You're saying this could be part of a bigger event?'

The retort was robust. 'I'm saying nothing of the sort. We need to look at the data we are gathering and see what comes out of our forecast models.'

Their conversation stalled to allow a muffled conversation Gill couldn't make out, and then John came back on. 'Look, I've got to go. I'm glad to hear you're safe, and thanks for the report.' With that, the call ended.

He was just thinking about what to do when his phone rang again.

'Hey, Gill, it's Salina. Your number was engaged for ages. Just checking where you are?'

'Stuck in traffic not far off the A9. The lights are out, and it's gridlocked.'

'I heard about the quake. Very exciting. Did you hear it?'

Gill quickly shared his story, then added, 'How's Ellie?'

'Much better, thanks. It was good I was here. She woke up in the early hours quite distressed. It was a blessing, really. She yanked me out of a bad dream I was having.'

'And how are things between you?'

'We've talked a lot about what happened yesterday. Cried a bit. Laughed a bit. Very girly.'

'It sounds healing.' The conversation paused, so Gill continued, 'What now?'

'She's zonked,' said Salina. 'The doctor wants her to sleep and has given her a pill.'

'And what about you?'

'I just need to sleep, and I won't need any pill.'

Gill gave a tiny groan of exasperation. The traffic around him was barely moving. 'I'll be with you as soon as possible, but the town centre traffic is solid.'

'It's no problem,' said Salina. 'You've plenty to do. Why don't you hole up somewhere until the traffic clears and get some work done? I'll jump in a taxi. I'm close to the A82 here, so I won't need to go through the town.'

'You're sure? I don't want to let you down.'

'It's no problem. I'll see you at Duncan's later.'

'I don't know. I don't want to leave you on your own.'

'I'm a big girl, Gill McArdle. I can look after myself! Besides, all I want to do for the next 24 hours is sleep.'

As they rang off, Gill could feel his aspirations for the day going up in smoke. He needed somewhere to work in peace for a few hours. He could see a supermarket close to where he was sitting, so he edged out of the traffic and found a parking space. A few minutes later, he settled into a second-floor café. Popping open his laptop, words began to flow.

Gill returned to his improvised workstation with a sandwich and a large pot of tea. Time to take stock. The last hour had gone well, and half of the magazine was complete aside from a couple of final edits. The remainder of the articles lay strewn across his laptop in various states of readiness. He needed a moment's diversion, so he poured himself a cup of tea and opened a news app to watch the early evening news. The North Sea quake was now the lead story, with the media reporting the shutdown affecting oil and gas platforms. A small fire had broken out at a refinery on the Black Isle but was under control by the time the news bulletin went on air. The radio host interviewed an expert from the SGS, and it took him a few minutes to recognise her as Agnes Fairbank, John Houston's boss.

'Well, it was a remarkable event. We just aren't used to quakes of that magnitude in this country.'

'And has the danger passed?' the interviewer asked. 'Or should we expect further shocks?'

'Our data indicate small aftershocks, but these are diminishing. They won't be visible to the naked eye.' She smiled reassuringly at the presenter. 'I doubt we will feel a seismic event like that for many, many years.'

Gill muted the App and opened up another file from Craig. This layout had the first two pages of the lead article, and it was essential to get them right. He read for a few moments, marking up corrections as he went.

At that moment, Gill wasn't sure he felt a movement. If someone had slammed the nearby kitchen door, he wouldn't even have looked up. But something had interrupted his conscious thoughts. He felt it again. The barest shiver in the fabric of the building, visible only in short-lived rings that danced across the surface of his drink. Distracted from his work, he stood up and walked to the window. Human life was going on as usual. The traffic had cleared on the nearby carriageway, and in the car park, a couple walked towards the store, laughing at a shared joke. His eyes detected movement, and he raised his gaze. Across in the Moray Firth, a great skein of geese had taken to the air, seagulls flapping in their wake.

The vibration came again. Gentle, soundless, like a faraway giant rolling over in his sleep. Ackerson had said this would happen. The Great Glen Fault would awaken from a long slumber. It wouldn't tear the ground; Ackerson seemed sure of that. But his conclusion was valid. Loch Ness wasn't a safe place to hide boats full of complex weapons systems.

Aftershocks. The lady on TV had said they'd come. Entirely natural. Quite harmless. Why was his pulse racing then? Why did he have this sense the danger had not passed? He'd followed this instinct before, and it demanded action again. Out in the car park, a large motorbike gave three throaty roars. Gill got to the window just in time to see the big black bike exit the car park and slide out into traffic. Remembering the mysterious black clad Biker-guy Gill had encountered in Harris the year before, this was the last nudge he needed. Certain that danger was near to hand, he snapped his laptop shut and gathered his things. He needed to go to Loch Ness.

Chapter 35

It was late afternoon as Gill re-joined the A9. The traffic lights were working again, and Inverness was returning to normal. Gill drove through the city and swept up the A82 towards the loch. His anxiety hadn't lifted, and he wasn't sure what he was looking for. The one thing he was certain of, he didn't have enough working hours left to squander them on a fruitless chase. He sped through the open countryside until the loch came into view.

The traffic slowed, the vehicles in front of him picking past a layby choked with cars. His senses were alert to anything out of the ordinary, so he mounted the grass verge and parked in the shadow of a big white tourist bus. Knots of people stood on a viewing platform strewn with tired-looking picnic tables. Everyone was staring at the loch. Gill joined them, his hands on his hips under the tails of his old tweed waistcoat. The shimmer came again, the tiniest vibration just perceptible under the soles of his feet, setting off shrieks from a group of tourists. They were Korean, mainly young and female, their arms and phones pointing at the water. Gill moved closer to the verge and peered down at the water, some twenty metres below him. Two separate waves ran across the surface. One ran parallel to where he stood and crossed the loch, diminishing as it went. A second had emerged from the opposite bank, leaving the shore at an angle. He watched its progress as it crossed the narrowest part of the loch, crashing into the opposite bank with enough force to rustle the low-lying branches of a thicket that tumbled down to the water's edge.

Beside him, shrill girls talked excitedly into mobile phones. He wondered what was Korean for "monster." He felt his phone vibrate and retrieved it from his pocket. It was a text from Arthur.

'Migration is now in full swing with multiple sightings up and down the loch. But you won't read about that in any trad rag. Check out the facts at *TheLochNessDiscovery.com*. Now watch and learn, part-timer.'

He started to compose his response but decided against it and shoved his phone back in his pocket. He stood and looked at the loch, doing his best to wipe a sneer from his face. That Arthur thought the loch was full of migrating beasties was so beyond reason to anyone who knew what was causing these ripples. Because he knew now. Silt falls were causing the waves as little ledges of soft clay collapsed in the shallowest part of the loch. He shook his head, suppressing his contempt for Arthur Deveron. Then, at that moment, Gill was filled with a sudden dread. Like a physical punch in his back, he suddenly understood what was happening and foresaw the possibility of catastrophe.

Gill thought desperately for a moment, needing to reach out to someone in authority. He grabbed his phone and tabbed quickly through pages of contacts.

The phone rang twice. 'George Wiley.'

'Inspector. Gill McArdle.'

Wiley sighed. 'You just caught me. I got your message, thanks. We're still in the process of tracking him down.'

'I'm not calling about that.' Gill paused, thinking about what to say. 'You're aware of the seismic activity in the North Ness area and the Black Isle?'

'Yes, Mr McArdle, Fort William does have contact with the outside world.'

'Right. You know I've been working in the Ness area these past two weeks?'

'Yes.'

'I've discovered an urgent issue affecting public safety around the loch.'

'Do you mean the guys setting fire to tents?'

'No, no, more fundamental. I think this seismic activity could trigger severe flooding.'

'Not my department,' Wiley grumbled. 'If you have concerns, I think you should speak to environmental health people. Yeah, give them a shout tomorrow. See what they make of it.'

'This is urgent. I can't leave it to the morning.'

'County council then,' said Wiley sounding bored. 'Holyrood even.'

Gill was exasperated. 'No time for that. I'm almost certain...'

Wiley cut him off. 'Gonna have to go. Thanks again for the tip on Deveron.'

The phone went dead, and Gill stared in frustration at the blank screen. Another ripple passed under his feet. More substantial this time, a distant boom accompanied it like faraway thunder. Gill grabbed his phone again and started to type furiously. *'John Houston, SGS. I'm at Loch Ness right now.*

Continuing seismic activity is an immediate threat to public safety. Need urgent evacuation of loch-side homes. G.McA.'

The reply took a few minutes. 'Relax, Gill. Things are calming down. We've a big meeting on Monday to review all the data. Hopefully, enhance our forecast models. Thanks for all your help. I'll be in touch next week. John.'

Gill immediately texted back. 'No, stuff is happening NOW.'

He waited several minutes. This time a reply didn't come. Thinking desperately, he had only one other number he could ring. Ackerson's mobile number. He punched in the digits and waited.

The phone rang a dozen times. He was considering hanging up when the line connected.

'One time call, Mr McArdle. Just so you understand.'

Gill stood staring at the loch as a solitary two-metre-high wave made stately progress towards his position from an origin far away across the loch. 'It's happening. Just like you said. The fault has gone active again.'

'Yes, I'm here at Faslane watching the data coming in with some colleagues. Or at least, I was until you called me away.'

'Are you picking up all these small tremors?'

'Yes, we've rigged the half dozen active units to feed live data.' He paused briefly. 'Nice to be proven right once in a while.'

The wave he had been watching crashed into the bank below him, tearing branches from the low-lying trees. The Korean girls shrieked and moved back from the edge.

'What's going on?' said Ackerson.

'The tremors are setting off waves in the loch.' Gill waited for Ackerson to respond. 'Hello. Did you hear what I said?'

'Yes, I'm just puzzled, that's all. The seismic shifts are at the lower end of expectations. Even when they peak a couple of hours from now, it's not going to amount to much. I'd be surprised if it were enough to create water disturbance.'

'Did you factor in the silt?' said Gill.

Another pause. 'What do you mean?'

'You must know the walls of the loch are coated in silt. Goodness knows how many tens of metres thick. Some of the ledges in shallower water have already collapsed, throwing up significant waves. What if a big one goes?'

'I'm not sure that's likely.'

Gill spun around and started to walk back to his car. 'You're the self-declared expert, Ackerson. Imagine a wall of silt, averaging twenty metres thick and two hundred and fifty metres high. Then imagine a wall like that, collapsing along a front, twenty miles long. My question to you is this. If it goes, should we be worried?'

Gil heard the sound of a door opening. 'Hang on a second. I'm going back to my desk.' Gill endured another long pause as another door opened and closed, then a third. Then a thud as the phone was laid down on a table. He could hear Ackerson typing furiously. The typing stopped, and then another pause.

Ackerson's distant voice was faint, but Gill heard an expletive before Ackerson scrambled to pick up the phone. 'The potential displacement is over three hundred million tonnes of water. In that kind of confined space ...,' he tapped on his computer again, 'Gill, you're right. This kind of compression in a gorge as narrow as Loch Ness ... you need to warn people.'

'I've been trying! The police, SGS. I even tried a couple of radio stations, but they thought I was a prank caller. I can't get anyone to take this seriously. You need to do something.'

'I can push it up the chain of command,' said Ackerson. 'But it might take hours before this thing reaches the right desk.'

'No, you need to do something faster than that. Before this thing peaks.'

'I'm just one man, Gill. For pity's sake, that's why I've been speaking to people like you. To make the public aware of the danger.'

'And I'll do my bit. Information will be on our website this evening, and my magazine will be in the shops on Monday. To the extent we're able, we'll be all over this. But given the level of risk, that might not be fast enough.'

'Somebody could activate the emergency mobile alert system,' said Ackerson.

'What's that?'

'Where've you been, Gill? The government gave it a test run three weeks ago. It's a system for broadcasting an emergency message across the entire mobile network.'

'Do it.'

'Have you any idea how many rules I'd need to break to hack that system from this chair?' Ackerson protested. 'And even if I manage, the thing might not function properly.'

'You need to do it, Ackerson.'

'No, it's too risky. Aside from the likelihood I'd spend the rest of my life in prison, I have to make a rational decision. People panic during evacuations. They panic, and then some people die. Not sure I want that on my conscience.'

'Ackerson, make the call, or put me in touch with someone who will.'

'I'm going to run some numbers on this. See if I can work out how much of a shake we'll get, and whether it's likely to crash the silt columns.'

'Ackerson …'

'Goodbye, Gill. We'll likely not speak again.' Then the line went dead.

Chapter 36

Arthur Deveron trudged defiantly through the woods, following on the heels of Jim Ritchie. He wasn't in the mood for mindless chat, shooting down Jim's attempts at conversation until they both walked in silence. Tall and athletic, Jim carried a shovel over each shoulder as he led them down towards the water's edge. The loch was coming into view when Jim suddenly halted.

'Why are you stopping?' demanded Arthur.

Jim lifted one of the shovels and gesticulated towards a small clearing. 'That's where I torched the guy's tent.'

'Pity you didn't finish him,' hissed Arthur.

Jim grunted and started walking again. 'You didn't say there'd be a cop with a gun.'

'Let's just get this done.'

Jim paused to check his direction, then started walking again. 'It's down here.'

The two men continued in silence for several minutes, Arthur panting as they negotiated various obstacles in their path. Finally, Jim jumped into a verdant hollow Arthur recognised from the photographs. 'Just in here,' said Jim.

Arthur sat on the bank and slithered down into the hollow. From here, it was easy to see how this had once been a little bay, now silted up by the burn running through it. Around the confined basin, the tell-tale signs of disturbed earth showed where McArdle's people had been digging. Jim had moved to stand beside one, dropping the shovel blades onto the ground.

'This the one with the bones?' said Arthur.

Jim nodded.

'Get started then. I'll be with you in a minute.'

Jim's expression hardened for a moment as he realised he would be doing most of the work himself. Then he tossed one shovel aside and started to dig in the soft earth.

Arthur moved beyond him, picking his way through the soft ground, following the stream bed through the gap in the rocks until he emerged on the loch shore. He stood watching the water for a few minutes as he had done before on so many occasions. To his far left, a wave became distinct from the other ripples on the loch, its energy running counter to the prevailing wind direction. He watched it impassively, his camera hanging by his side. What was one more wave if you never got to see what was underneath it? Midges boiled in a cloud around his head, and as he stood panting, he inhaled one. He spat, wiping his mouth on his sleeve as the little wave rolled past. Today had been full of waves like this. Not once had he seen evidence of an animal below the surface. But they must be here because that's where the trail of clues had led him. He shook his head in disgust, cursing the uncertainty starting to crush him. That was why he needed the bones. It was time to play his trump card. No one would be able to dismiss him because no one could ignore the bones of the Loch Ness Monster.

He regretted having waited so long before coming back for them. He would have pressed on if the idiot Ritchie hadn't let the landowner see the bones. They could have worked something out if Ritchie hadn't panicked and struck the man. Money would have talked. Instead, the fool had covered the bones again and escaped to protect himself. The only relief for Arthur in this situation was at least Ritchie had obscured his identity by adopting the name of an old archaeology buddy who'd died a few years back. And he was fit and strong; key attributes for a wannabe archaeologist. Just a bit lacking in the strategy department.

Arthur shook his head and turned his back on the loch. He'd tried to believe that keeping bones safe hadn't been a disaster. Back when Ritchie discovered them, Arthur still needed to prove the existence of the underground watercourse. That had taken longer than he'd hoped. Using the fracking chemicals had been a risky bet but worth it in the end. And for all those years, any time he could slip back to Loch Ness, he'd spent countless hours observing the water. Unproductive hours when he should have gone back for the bones. Gone public there and then.

He walked back across the dell, pleased to see Jim was making good progress. He picked up the spare shovel and joined him, tossing the earth aside. After six urgent strokes, he was interrupted by a text coming in. Arthur fumbled for his phone and read aloud.

'National Emergency. For the attention of all citizens. Immediate evacuation of the Great Glen area – Fort William to Inverness. By order of Ministry of Defence, Emergency Powers Act.'

Arthur reread the message and laughed. The text obscured the sender's identity, but he could see the handiwork of an adversary.

Jim had also stopped digging and was staring at his phone. He held up the same message for Arthur to view with a puzzled expression. Arthur waved his hand dismissively. 'Pay no attention. That's just Gill McArdle trying to flush me out.'

'How'd he get my number?'

'Who knows,' said Arthur. 'Just dig, alright.'

Gill was on the phone with Cassy when the evacuation text came through. 'Hang on a second, Cassy. Are you seeing this?'

'Seeing what?'

'Ackerson has done it. He's issued the alert. Oh, thank goodness.'

'Not seeing that here,' said Cassy. 'Mind you, it might be local to your area.'

'Keep an eye on the news for me. If it's a public broadcast, most media outlets should get it too.'

He could hear Cassy tapping on her PC. 'Nothing on Reuters, nothing on the BBC,' she said. The line crackled as she pulled her phone closer to her mouth. 'Yup, it's happening. Twitter is going crazy. Fort William to Inverness. Will that cover it?'

'To be honest, Cassy, I have no idea. It's certainly the main danger area.'

Cassy paused. 'Gill. Where are you?'

'Urquhart Bay.'

'So, you're right in the middle of it?'

'Aye, but it's fairly high ground here.' Gill thought for a second. 'Cass, I'm going to have to call you back. I've got a couple of people I need to check on.'

The increase in road traffic was not instantaneous, but the roads were noticeably busier by the time Gill reached the Ness Museum. He tossed his car into the nearest available space and ran into reception. The visitor centre manager was closing the till, and in the background, a tannoy advised visitors to leave the building.

'Mr McArdle. What's going on?' she asked.

'It's the loch. These tremors could set off some big waves. Where's Sandy?'

'She took an extra party out on the water this afternoon. They're not due back for over an hour.'

'Have you tried reaching them?'

'Aye, but I cannae get through.'

Gill pulled out a phone and tapped Sandy's number. The network was busy. He leaned on the desk, uncertain what to do. 'Which way did they go?'

'South. She's with a group of Americans who wanted to see the power station "Lucy" bumped into.'

'Okay. Clear this place and get to higher ground. Keep trying to reach her. Then tell her to get ashore and away from the loch as quickly as possible.'

Gill backed away from the desk, the germ of an idea seeding in his mind. Back on the road, he would have liked to have put his foot down, but instead, he joined a long column of slow-moving traffic heading south. Bizarrely, the traffic going the other way was just as busy. 'What part of "Get out of the Glen" do these people not understand?' he muttered.

As he passed through Invermoriston, the force of habit made him glance at the farmhouse through the trees. Beside the barn, almost hidden from sight, sat a gleaming black 4x4, which reminded him of Arthur's car. If he'd had more time, he was tempted to investigate, but just now, his priorities lay elsewhere.

Reaching Fort Augustus, he paused, considering if he had time to collect Salina. He dialled her number and found he had service. After four rings, the call diverted to voicemail. At this stage, he had to assume that she and Duncan were already evacuating. Nosing out of the traffic, he turned onto the narrow road on the east shore that would take him to the power station. The road was empty, allowing him to accelerate. Glimpsing Foyers power station in the distance, he swung round a bend, narrowly missing a vehicle speeding the other way. Feeling shaken, he proceeded with care.

A knot of workers stood in the car park, hands in pockets, no great urgency on their faces. Gill pulled up and spoke to one. 'I'm looking for Phil. Do you know where he is?'

The man tilted his hard hat down at the building. 'He's still closing up, pal.'

Gill thanked him and drove down as close as possible to the gate. He flung open his boot and grabbed the new diving light he had bought for Sandy. Ripping open the box, he paused to check the lamp was charged. He clipped off the filter cover and tested the strength of the beam. It would do. Taking the heavy torch, he dashed inside. The security hut was closed, but Phil stood outside, locking the main door. He heard Gill approaching and turned to face him.

'Sorry, Gill. Can't talk just now. There's some kind of alert going on.'

'Sandy Brightman is still on the water,' Gill panted. 'We need to contact her.'

Phil thought for a second. 'I noticed them pass along the west bank about half an hour ago. They came past us heading for Fort Augustus.'

Gill showed Phil the powerful torch. 'If we can see her, we can make her see us.'

Phil stared at him, wordlessly assessing Gill's plan. 'Okay. I think I can help.' He flung open the door again, and Gill followed him inside the power station. They made their way down through the building and out to a shed housing the maintenance rib. Phil opened an equipment locker and produced a pack of flares. 'Do you have any idea what's going on?' he asked as they half ran, half walked outside onto the jetty.

'The seismic activity is making the silt columns in the loch unstable,' said Gill. 'If they fall, the displaced water could pose a local tsunami risk.'

Phil took the safety wraps off a flare. 'Says who?' he said, holding the tube aloft until the flare ignited and shot into the sky with a "whoosh."

'MoD,' Gill replied, watching the luminous pink light settle in the sky and begin its drift back towards earth.

'Good enough for me,' said Phil, cupping his hands over his eyes to better see the *Ness Explorer*. The boat was motoring along the far shore, heading northeast up the loch. He shook his head. 'She's not changed course.' He broke the seal off another flare, launching the vivid pink firework high into the air. He tossed the container aside and looked across the loch. 'Right, she's paused. You're up.'

Gill lifted the torch and focused the beam on the boat's position as closely as possible. His grasp of Morse code was tenuous, but he remembered one essential phrase from his hillwalking days. Flicking the light on and off, he tapped out the letters SOS. He paused for a few seconds and then repeated the sequence. *Ness Explorer* still wasn't moving, so Phil fired off the last flare in his pack. As the glowing ember of this last marker dipped towards the water, Gill saw turbulence surge at the stern of the boat as she fired up her engines. She was coming towards them.

It would take them several minutes to cross the loch at full speed, so Gill tried Salina again. On the first two attempts, the network was busy. On the third, she didn't pick up. Gill left a voicemail. 'Salina. I'm hoping you've seen the alert and already evacuated. When you get this, can you let me know you're safe?' He hesitated, then instinctively added. 'Take care.'

Phil stood with his hands on his hips, his head jutting forward as if mentally urging the boat to make faster progress. He glanced at Gill just once. They both understood that the jetty was hopelessly exposed to any danger on the loch.

After a gruelling five-minute wait, Gill watched the skipper throttle back as the boat finally came alongside. Sandy was on the bow, ready to toss a rope to Phil. Gill reached out a hand and pulled his friend ashore. With the skipper's help, Sandy guided the tour party onto solid ground. 'Is this to do with the alert?' asked a burly American.

The skipper stepped in to reassure his party and steer them towards the power station building. Sandy placed a hand on Gill's arm, restraining him until the others were out of earshot. 'I've got a lot of friends along this glen. How much danger are we in?'

Gill shook his head. 'No way of knowing. The tremors might pass without incident, or they might not. I spoke to someone earlier who seemed to know what he was talking about. He believes it should calm down in a few hours. Then we can take stock.'

'What should I do with my party?' asked Sandy. 'Unless Phil can produce something, we don't have vehicles to move them to safety.'

'I'd stay here for now,' said Gill, nodding towards the power station. 'This building is pretty solid. You should be safe.'

Sandy nodded as they started walking again. 'I'm always happiest when I can see the loch.'

It took several minutes to reach the control centre above the main turbine hall. Gill stood in the middle of the room, checking his phone, while the others milled around, staring at the water.

'What's wrong?' asked Sandy.

'It's Salina,' said Gill. 'She still hasn't replied to my messages.'

'Maybe she can't get through. You said yourself the lines are pretty busy.'

Gill shook his head. 'I've had intermittent coverage. If she's heard from me, she would have replied by now.'

Sandy's gaze dropped soberly. 'I hope she's not in a place without any signal.'

Gill slipped his phone away. 'She's at Duncan's. It's a big old stone house.' He thought for a second. 'Given your concerns about Duncan, I'm going to go and find her.'

Sandy held up her hands as Gill started to move. 'Is that a good idea? Fort Augustus lies lower than the loch. If anything happens, you'll be exposed.'

Gill pointed to the vast expanse of still water. 'Keep a close watch. If anything happens, text me. I'll find her and bring her back here.'

Chapter 37

Duncan stood in his kitchen, his chest rising and falling with each deep breath. He glanced at the kitchen clock. Almost 7 pm and he was overwhelmed by the sudden opportunity presenting itself. Tom and James had returned at lunchtime to collect their stuff; decamping back to their accommodation in Oban. Then a few hours later, Salina came back alone in a taxi. It had been two hours since she had drunk tea with him in his kitchen.

He had wished her a good sleep, then listened as she climbed the stairs, the weight of her exhausting night hanging on her, making her feet fall heavily on each wooden tread. He'd lingered in the kitchen, listening to the floor above him creak a few times, then fall silent as she collapsed into bed. Then he waited. After an hour, he rose to close the ground floor curtains and lock all the doors. Listening, listening, making sure, then sure again, he was alone in the house. Apart from her.

He exhaled and detected a tremor in his breath.

The sound of traffic outside was easing. Although many summer days were busy, cars had flowed past his door this afternoon until he thought they might never cease. Probably an accident on the Fort William Road, throwing up a long tailback. He'd seen that before, though it was gone now. And his phone, with its endless calls from Dundee, tossed away where he couldn't hear it. He wanted no distractions.

He revised what he would say to her tomorrow when she awoke. How unwell she'd looked when she went to bed. How the shock of the accident had left her weak and seeking comfort from him. He would plead the pressures of work, excusing himself to avoid her. Then he'd encourage her to go home, to get some proper rest. To call in if she ever passed this way again.

The throaty sound of a heavy motorcycle bit into his consciousness. An unfamiliar vehicle had pulled into the entrance to his driveway. Some stranger was abusing Duncan's private property, pulling over to check directions or take a rest. The engine idled for a full minute, crowding into Duncan's senses until it so unnerved him he thought he would need to chase the stranger away. Then he heard the throttle roar, the ruck of gravel underneath a rapidly accelerating wheel. The sound moderated, gradually easing off into the distance, taking its distraction with it.

Duncan thought about the girl upstairs. It had been Ellie he wanted, but this other girl would do. And he was confident that when he presented himself to her, she would desire him too. He looked at the clock again. He had planned to wait until dusk, but now a desperate urge rose up in him, and he couldn't bear the thought of her any longer. Noiselessly he opened the kitchen door and eased out into the hall. He stood silently, listening to the empty building. He stepped onto the first stair, where she had trod heavily a few hours before. His movement was feline, silent and deliberate. He knew any change of mind would happen to him before he reached the final step. And he knew what he was about to do was wrong. His life spent in service to the church left him in no doubt about that. But he also believed his years of sacrifice entitled him to take a few crumbs from the altar. A little pleasure along the way to ease the burden of his work. And he'd be gentle with her. A loving act. There would be no consequences.

He stepped onto the top landing, his pulse racing with anticipation.

A sound woke Salina, and she found herself in an unfamiliar room. She groaned inwardly at the prospect of another dream. But then it dawned on her. This was Duncan's house. She'd come here from Ellie's bedside in the hospital. She was lying in the clothes she came back in and desperately needed a shower.

The noise came again. More insistent this time. Someone was trying to open her bedroom door.

'Who's there?' she called.

No one answered, so she struggled to her feet and moved to the door. The metal bolt she'd run on the inside of the door was still in place, so she eased her head against the wood. Behind the door, she heard someone breathing.

'Who's there, I said?'

The door sagged towards her as someone leaned their weight against it. 'Let me in,' said a male voice.

'Duncan. Is that you?'

The door creaked, and part of the frame groaned as the man shouldered against it. 'Come on, Salina. My house. My rules. I promise I won't hurt you.'

Horrified, Salina backed away from the door. And bumped into an unseen figure standing behind her. She spun around and found the burly olive-skinned man from her dreams in the centre of the room. She recoiled to scream, but Raphael pulled the forefinger of his left hand to his mouth and hushed her. 'Don't be afraid,' he whispered.

'How did you get in here?' she demanded.

He pointed at the curtains fluttering at the open window.

'You're real!'

Raphael made a performance of patting his arms and shoulders, then gave a little nod.

'Why are you here?'

He pointed at the door, now shaking on its hinges. 'Rescue mission.'

She gulped. 'Am I going to drown?'

'Only if you linger.'

She thrust a hand towards the door. 'What about him?'

'Leave this to me.'

'How will I escape?'

Raphael turned and pointed at the window. 'Will you be surprised if I ask you to jump?'

Salina dashed over to the window and stared down. A drainpipe passed within reach, and Duncan's car was parked below the window. 'I see,' she said. Taking a deep breath, she jumped up onto the window sill, turned round and started to reverse out into the void.

Back in the room, her attacker lunged at the door, almost throwing it off its frame.

Salina gripped the drainpipe and started to descend. In a few seconds, she'd be able to drop safely onto the roof of

Duncan's car. But before she completed her exit, Raphael leaned out and called down to her.

'Can we talk about Southampton?' he said.

She screwed her face up at him. 'What? Now?'

'You need to know. Nareef's yacht has been for sale for eighteen months. And he plans to move you to Birmingham.'

'But my job? How will I do it from there?'

'From Birmingham? I've no idea. Maybe it's time to jump, Salina.'

Behind Raphael, there was a crash as the door finally yielded to its attacker. Raphael smiled at Salina. 'Excuse me.'

His head disappeared, and Salina dropped onto the car roof with a grunt, then slid off the windscreen and bonnet before landing in an undignified heap on the driveway. She sat upright and dusted herself off. At that moment, a strong vibration shook Fort Augustus, the windows frames of the rectory rattling violently for a few seconds before falling still again. Cries from disturbed birds rose into the air, and somewhere inside the house, a piece of crockery slipped from its resting place and smashed on a hard floor. Moments later, a sound like a tower block being demolished erupted all around them, thunderous at first, echoing away into some faraway chamber.

As she looked about her, Gill McArdle's car screeched off the main road and hurtled to a stop beside her. He threw open his door and called. 'We need to go.'

The thunderous crack still echoed between the mountains when Sandy Brightman dashed onto the observation deck in front of the power station. The loch below her sprang alive with multiple small waves zig-zagging across the surface. She stood watching, her ears acute to the sound ebbing away into the distance until the loch fell calm again. But now, a different force started to pull at the water's surface. Sandy watched as the water ebbed from vast swathes of loch-side, cavernous gullies opening up along miles of shoreline in just a matter of moments. She watched as the *Ness Explorer* was plucked from her mooring and sucked from view.

One of the American tour party stood beside her. 'What the hell?'

'Inside, everybody,' Sandy shouted. 'Right now.' She chased everyone back into the control room before stealing a glance back at the loch. The collapsing silt walls were compressing the water column across long stretches of the deep loch, creating an unusual pressure reminiscent of loading giant springs. But as they fell, the silt walls were disintegrating, the compressed energy springing back again in upward eruptions that tore the mud-streaked surface of the loch into an ocean storm. Sandy stood transfixed as multiple huge waves coalesced into fast-moving walls of water thirty metres high. Strong arms grabbed her from behind, pulling her back inside, tossing her to the floor before the outer door slammed closed. Immediately she heard the sound of crashing glass and roaring water as the first wave tore across the lower parts of the building. The lights went out, and some of the men started shouting. Sandy rolled over, groping for her phone, shaky fingers trying to punch some meaning into a simple message. Her text to Gill was a single word. 'Waves!'

Gill was slamming the passenger door when Sandy's text came in. He read it as he ran round to the driver's side. Salina was fumbling with her seat belt, so he reached across to help her. Their eyes met just as the belt clasp found its mark. 'What's that noise?' whispered Salina, her face close to his. They both stopped and listened, aware of a faraway roar. Gill didn't reply, tossing the car into reverse and swinging onto the Fort William Road. Tyres squealed as he accelerated forward, the car's speed creeping up to fifty, then sixty, then seventy miles an hour as they sped through the village. Coming to a junction, Gill dropped down a gear, struggling to keep control. The car shuddered for a second, clipping a wheelie bin and sending it spiralling into a garden. They were on a straight road now, and Gill pushed the accelerator to the floor. As they rounded a slow bend, they found themselves rapidly gaining ground on a single slow-moving motorcycle. The driver casually made a spiralling motion with his right hand, beckoning Gill to overtake. Gill moved the car across the lane, faintly aware of the courteous wave the cyclist gave them as they flashed by.

'I know that guy,' said Salina, twisting round to get another look at the fast disappearing figure. With a gasp, she turned to face forward again.

'What's wrong?' Gill glanced up at the rear-view mirror to glimpse what Salina had seen. Crushing the last few houses in the village, a great wall of water spread across the valley behind them. Gill accelerated again, pushing the car to its maximum as it weaved and dipped along the tree-lined road towards Loch Oich. As the valley narrowed at the mouth of the loch, the deluge of water in the confined space made the wave grow taller.

'Gill!' Salina was screaming at him now, the rear view full of the obliterating wave that bore down on them.

As if from nowhere, the motorbike reappeared, shooting past them in a throaty roar, its power propelling it far ahead of them on the empty road. Salina stopped looking at the wave and shrank into her seat to better grip the fast-moving car. The water was gaining on them, and they had no way to escape.

Gill rounded a bend to find the motorbike obscuring the road ahead, with its driver standing in front of it, gesticulating wildly for Gill to turn left.

'Watch out!' screamed Salina.

Gill moved over to the right side of the road to overtake the stationary figure. 'No!' Salina shouted. 'Do what he says. Turn left!'

'Go where? It's just a hedge,' Gill yelled.

Salina leaned across him. 'We need to jump!'

Wrenching the steering wheel from his grip, she forced the car to swerve left of the waving figure.

At that instant, Gill saw the entrance to a narrow tarmac track. The speeding car lost contact with the road for a moment as it mounted a slight rise, crashing back into the middle of the lane and tearing up the hill. For several terrifying seconds, Gill fought to keep the car from slithering off into a deep ditch on one side or into tall rhododendrons on the other. He drove until he ran out of road. Pumping the brakes, he slithered to a halt outside a small hotel.

Gill leapt out of the car just in time to see the water tear into the middle section of a pretty garden. The hotel was in an elevated position, and it was possible to see how the water had filled the valley; the normally flat surface of Loch Oich exaggerated into a torrent of muddy water. Salina sprang out of the car to watch as the surging water passed ten metres below them, its flanks tearing at the trees on the hillside.

His chest heaving, Gill watched the pulse of water recede, puzzled why the sound was not diminishing, only to see a second pulse filling the valley below them, its waters streaked with debris.

Gill's phone rang, and he fumbled to answer it. 'Hello.'

'Gill. It's Sandy. I'm checking you found Salina?'

'I did. We're together. How are you?'

'The power station took a thumping. But we're all okay. How are things looking?'

Gill paused. 'The whole glen south of Loch Ness looks devastated.'

They spoke for a minute longer then Sandy rang off.

He felt a touch as Salina gripped his wrist. She was shaking. They were both shaking.

'The biker-guy. Raphael,' said Gill. 'I've seen him before.'

Salina's attention focused on the catastrophe unfolding below them. 'What?'

'I met him on Harris. He offered me one of his swords.'

Salina half turned, puzzled. 'That man is my guardian angel,' she said.

Gill fell silent, realising the same enigmatic figure he'd met on Harris a year ago had today saved their lives. And that somehow, he was known to Salina. In the blaze of the moment, it was too much for him to unravel. 'Did you see if he made it?'

Salina shook her head. 'The water took him.'

'He saved us both.'

Salina dropped her hand into his as the roar of a third great water surge rumbled down the valley below them. 'Yes. Yes, he did.'

Chapter 38

After the interview, Gill decided he was getting the hang of this. They'd been the last guests on a Wednesday morning news programme broadcast from Dundee. And all things considered, it had gone very well. Gill suppressed a wry smile as he watched the producer's assistant disentangle Salina from a hidden microphone. After several days of good sleep, Salina looked vibrant again, laughing happily with the girl as they traced a wire back through her clothing. When finally she was free, Salina thanked her rescuer and walked over to where he was sitting. Gill himself felt exhausted. Having survived the deluge and its aftermath, he'd pushed through the remainder of the issue to achieve a delayed Sunday morning print deadline. After that came all the interviews.

The first one happened by chance. When the fifth and final surge had passed their position, he and Salina had waited long enough to ensure their safety before making their way down onto the wreckage-strewn A82. The road was severely damaged, but piece by piece, they picked along the banks of Loch Lochy until they arrived in what remained of Fort William. What had hit the town was no longer a wave but rather a slow, relentless surge of water that had bulldozed everything before it. Cars, trees, and rubble lay strewn where the water had pushed them. Finding the road blocked, they abandoned Gill's car and continued on foot. They stopped to help a group trying to reach survivors trapped in a partially collapsed office building. As night fell, a Scottish news team saw their efforts and stopped to talk to them. Hoping to record survivors' stories, the TV crew couldn't believe their luck when Gill gave them a ninety-second soundbite describing the origins of the disaster. The major networks around the world had picked up that short camera piece and run it relentlessly. Numerous interviews followed. Between that and finishing the magazine, he'd barely slept.

The first print run of issue eleven went to press and was in the shops on Monday morning. It sold out within twenty-four hours, so Tony called the printer and ordered another quarter of a million copies. Signs were, it would be their highest-selling issue.

'You looked great out there,' Gill said, nodding to a faraway sofa where the presenters were wrapping up that morning's edition.

'Yeah, not bad yourself.' She stopped and looked around her. 'Makes you think, though.'

'What do you mean?'

'You get a whole month to prepare a magazine. These guys have to do this five times a week.'

He tried to suppress a smile. 'Thanks. With twenty-five days until I get to do it all again, I feel positively chilled.'

The assistant producer held the door for them, so they thanked her and walked out into the lobby. 'Would you like to see my office?' he said. 'The team would love to meet you.'

'Sure. It's quite close, isn't it?'

'Just along the waterfront, so we could walk. Or take a taxi if you like.'

She settled the matter, linking arms with him and walking along the river towards Dundee's V&A museum. Although she was smiling, her gaze was downward, some part of her wrestling with something else.

Gill cleared his throat, determined his next question shouldn't spoil the moment. 'I noticed this morning you're not wearing your engagement ring.'

She glanced at him, then back at the water. 'I've talked to Nareef about his long-term plans. It turns out he hasn't been completely honest with me. So, I've decided to call it off.' She waited to see if he would respond, but he filled the gap by just nodding soberly. 'I've not told my parents yet,' she added.

'What will they say?'

'Mum will be furious. Dad …' she paused, 'I think he'll be alright with it.'

He did his best to give her an encouraging smile. 'How so?'

Salina pursed her lips as if struggling to form the words. 'I'm going to remind him we can't let traditions stand in the way of true love.'

Gill looked away, studying the red stonework on a refurbished hotel. 'And how will you know if you ever find true love?'

Salina's laugh startled him. 'I really don't know.' She tugged on his arm. 'Come on. I'm sure we'll be able to explain it with biology. You're a scientist. How will I know when I am in love?'

He stopped walking and half turned to face her. 'I know you love the sea. You love its beauty; you respect its danger, and you want to explore it. It's clear to me you'll never be happy unless you spend the rest of your life immersed in the stuff. So, when you find yourself feeling like that about a human being, then you'll know you're in love.'

She nodded thoughtfully, briefly meeting his gaze then looking away. 'Hmm, I'll need to think about that.'

Gill gave her arm a gentle tug, and they started walking again. 'In the meantime, if you need a handsome stranger to keep up appearances with your family, I'd be happy to oblige.'

She arched her eyebrows in feigned disbelief. 'Thank you, that's a really kind offer.'

'Just while you get yourself sorted out,' he added. 'I mean, just as an arrangement between friends.'

'Of course.'

Her arm slipped gently from his, and she gathered his hand into her own. Their fingers locked together, and they walked the rest of the way to the office in happy silence.

Arriving at the *Mys.Scot* office, they avoided the cramped lift and stepped briskly up the stairs. Reaching the second level, Gill stood back and opened the door for her. Salina, however, lingered, distracted by something down in the street. Hearing the sound of a throaty motorbike revving on the road below, Gill let the door swing closed and joined her at the window.

'You look rattled all of a sudden,' he said.

Salina turned to face him. 'The motorcyclist by the loch who saved our lives. We both agreed we'd seen him before.'

Gill stopped and thought, sobered by the memory of the man who had died trying to save them. 'Raphael. I saw him a few times on Harris. What about you?'

'Just that once in a real-life, but I've seen him many times in my dreams. Every time I sensed I was in mortal danger, but that he was protecting me.' She pointed at the street below. 'Recognise that guy?'

'Can't be,' said Gill, staring. 'The water took him.'

The engine revved again, and Raphael looked up at them, the hilts of his twin swords visible over his left shoulder. When he had their attention, he held his right hand aloft and clenched his fist. He sustained the salute for several long seconds, then flexed the bike's throttle and drove away.

'How did he survive?' Gill whispered.

'He always survives,' said Salina. 'In my dreams.'

Gill stared at her, and she returned his gaze. 'We need to figure out who he really is,' he said.

'The swords. Did you see?'

Gill nodded. 'He always has them when I see him.'

'He protected us,' said Salina. 'Why would he do that?'

Gill shook his head. 'No idea, but I'm going to find out.'

They stared down at the empty street for a long moment before Gill grasped her hand again. 'That's a mystery for another day. Come on in and meet the team.'

Chapter 39

Editor's comment – Mysterious Scotland, issue 11

As I begin this issue, I feel the highest priority is to add my voice to the thousands expressing their condolences to the people of Fort Augustus, and Fort William caught up in last weekend's catastrophe. Their fortitude as they rally to rebuild their towns should be a call to arms for the rest of Scotland. And let's lay our tribalism aside, for today, in our shared grief, we are one United Kingdom.

Some of you will be aware from our web content that 'Mysterious Scotland' was working in the Ness area last week. Our staff and collaborators were caught in the disaster. I am sorry to report that Duncan Campbell, contributing journalist and Arthur Deveron, assistant engineer, are both missing, presumed drowned.

We often make the mistake of thinking we live in a safe world. The turbulence of environment and geography so rarely seem to touch us. And yet, Ben Nevis is yesterday's Mount Everest. The geological forces that created Scotland's highlands were as tumultuous as those at work in the Andes or Himalayas today. Scotland's 'Great Glen,' running from Fort William to Inverness, is a long-dormant scar left by violent forces that once shaped our land; a starkly visible reminder of what nature can do.

Mys.Scot has been investigating several stories in recent weeks, all of which have their origin in the reactivation of the Great Glen fault. Surveys of the sea bed on the west coast demonstrated massive forces at play. Submerged sea stacks have risen upwards, and sea caves crushed. These changes have been conclusively linked to the loss of the creel boat 'Bounty' out of Oban early last month. The same pressures almost certainly caused a rare animal to fall victim to the first ripples of change. The eel dubbed the 'Caithness Kraken' abandoned her lair when the rocks around her buckled, as the area south of the Great Glen rose and the northern area began to fall.

But it was the loch itself that beckoned us in recent weeks. Sightings of an old and elusive friend, the Loch Ness Monster, stood at an all-time high and we were determined to shed new light on an old mystery. And what a killer we discovered. Thousands of years of deposited silt piled hundreds of metres high against the steep walls of the loch, just waiting for nature to give it a nudge and send it all tumbling.

I can find some mercy in all of this. Our consulting archaeologist, Fiona Hamilton, was excavating at Invermoriston when she detected the tell-tale signs of smaller inundations in the recent past. Her expert knowledge, coupled with real-time data from a decommissioned MOD research project, was enough to alert the authorities to a real and present danger. The Scottish Geological Society was the first official body to stand up and express concern. But it takes extreme courage to stand alone on the rampart and shout an urgent warning. In Fort William last weekend, one anonymous individual took that risk by triggering the UK's automatic alert system. Without his courage, many more would have died. Please join me in saluting him.

In the following pages, we explain how thousands of years of accumulating silts sowed the seeds of this disaster. We explore what triggered the event and whether it could ever happen again.

Can I urge you, the next time you explore the wild places of our beautiful land, to take a moment to appreciate the natural forces that have shaped what it is today? Perhaps like me, you will feel a little smaller, less sure of yourself and your place in history. Above all, remember, this ancient, injured land is, Mysterious Scotland, and she's not done surprising us yet.

The End

If you have enjoyed 'The Ness Deception,' I would be so grateful if you could leave a review on the site where you bought the book. And please stay in touch. This story is going to get a whole lot bigger in the months to come.

Tormod Cockburn

The next adventure is ...

The Stone Cypher

Magazine editor and part-time archaeologist, Gill McArdle is getting it together. Or at least, he thinks he is, until the death of a friend throws his life into turmoil. He's on Orkney, researching an etched stone carrying an ancient religious motif. But he's perplexed as the carving long predates any previous incidence of the symbol's first use. Either someone is tampering with Orcadian archaeology, or Gill is facing a puzzle that can't be resolved. During his research, a secretive teenager passes Gill a notebook, packed full of numbers. Unexplained and impenetrable, the analysis points to a mystery among the stars. As Gill battles to unlock the truth he realises he's on the cusp of his most startling discovery yet.

Mysterious Scotland Reader's Syndicate

Join our Readers Syndicate at TormodCockburn.com for new publication alerts and for free material. There are three character-based stories, plus a novella explaining the origins of the waterhorse bones Gill found on Harris. All are free and exclusively available to members of the Syndicate.

Acknowledgements

My thanks to Anne Brownlow and the many other readers who helped shape the early draft. Thanks too to James for catching my aspiration for the cover and finding just the right photo. To Audrey, for so many things, not least the final proofread of the text.

To Freddie Roberts, Kenny Dempster and Steve Coates whose fireside tales inspired aspects of 'The Ness Deception.'

While no character in this book is based on anyone, living or dead, it would be remiss of me not to acknowledge the inspiring work of marine biologist, Dr Adrian Shine. While my book is a work of fiction, Dr Shine has devoted a lifetime to the study and preservation of Loch Ness. Along with presenting a clear-eyed assessment of evidence for and against the existence of the Loch Ness Monster, he developed methods for studying deep water lochs. He advanced his science around the world, and, I suspect, had a great deal of fun along the way.

Mys.Scot

Printed in Dunstable, United Kingdom